DUST
TO
DUST

BOOKS BY JAMES M. THOMPSON

The Elijah Pike Vampire Chronicles

Night Blood

Dark Blood

Immortal Blood

Tainted Blood

Thrillers

Dark Moon Rising

The Anthrax Protocol

Dust to Dust

DUST
TO
DUST

JAMES M.
THOMPSON

PINNACLE BOOKS
Kensington Publishing Corp.
www.kensingtonbooks.com

PINNACLE BOOKS are published by

Kensington Publishing Corp.
119 West 40th Street
New York, NY 10018

All Kensington titles, imprints, and distributed lines are available at special quantity discounts for bulk purchases for sales promotions, premiums, fund-raising, educational, or institutional use. Special book excerpts or customized printings can also be created to fit specific needs. For details, write or phone the office of the Kensington sales manager: Kensington Publishing Corp., 119 West 40th Street, New York, NY 10018, attn: Sales Department; phone 1-800-221-2647.

This book is a work of fiction. Names, characters, businesses, organizations, places, events, and incidents either are the product of the author's imagination or are used fictitiously. Any resemblance to actual persons, living or dead, events, or locales is entirely coincidental.

PINNACLE BOOKS and the Pinnacle logo are Reg. U.S. Pat. & TM Off.

ISBN-13: 978-0-7860-3732-2
ISBN-10: 0-7860-3732-6

First printing: May 2017

10 9 8 7 6 5 4 3 2 1

Printed in the United States of America

First electronic edition: May 2017

ISBN-13: 978-0-7860-3733-9
ISBN-10: 0-7860-3733-4

*This book is dedicated first and foremost
to Terri A. Thompson, my rock.*

*Others who give me daily inspiration are Brent Williams,
Travis Thompson, Darren Thompson,
Hunter Thompson, and Donovan Thompson.*

CHAPTER 1

Dr. Kaitlyn Williams, known to almost everyone as Kat, stared at her computer screen through bleary, bloodshot eyes. As she studied the chemical formulae that crawled across the screen like mating worms, she unconsciously rubbed at the back of her neck, which was beginning to go into spasms from her long hours in front of the computer. She had been working without a break for the past thirty-six hours and was finding it hard to concentrate, but she was determined to finish collating the serum formulae before she quit.

Finally, after another hour of manipulating the formulae on the computer, she had the relative concentrations of chemicals correct and was ready to proceed. Almost unconsciously, she muttered a brief prayer, "Let this be the one!"

She punched the PRINT button on the machine, and the computer printed out the amounts of each chemical to be added to the serum.

Kat took the printout and mixed the serum according to the specifications she had worked out. Holding the bottle of clear liquid up to the light, she whispered, "I need some magic here." She thought for a moment, and then she wrote the name she had decided on for the serum on the bottle.

With a sigh of fatigue, she went over to the stack of wire cages and took the one labeled BLUE GROUP down and carried it to a table in the middle of the lab. There were twenty-four rats in the cage. Twelve of them had daubs of blue dye on their backs while the other twelve were unmarked.

One by one, she took the twelve blue-dyed rats out of the cage and injected them with five milliliters of clear liquid from the vial she had labeled NEURACTIVASE. When she was finished, she put the cage back on the shelf and stumbled wearily to her desk.

She sat there for a moment, elbows on the desk with her head in her hands. She was bone tired and desperately needed some sleep. With a supreme effort, she raised her head and looked at the clock on the wall. Eleven thirty-five. She glanced out the window to see if it was night or day, so exhausted she couldn't remember if she'd been at work for twelve hours or twenty-four—darkness, unrelieved by stars or moon.

She realized she'd been working steadily for almost a day and a night. She frowned, thinking this was stupid. She was too tired to think straight and was bound to make a fatal mistake in her calculations at this rate.

She glanced to the side of her desk, where her Scottish terrier, Angus, was softly snoring in his bed. Trying to remember when she'd last taken him outside to do his business on the small patches of grass on the edge of the laboratory parking lot, she reached down and gently scratched his ears. His muzzle hair was almost totally white with advancing age, and she felt a momentary pang of guilt that lately she hadn't been giving him much quality time, being so involved in her research.

He stirred and cut his dark brown eyes up at her, then moaned softly in pleasure at her touch. "Damn, big fellow," she cooed. "I'll try to do better . . . okay?"

He rolled over onto his back with his feet in the air, asking for a tummy rub, one of his favorite things to experience.

She complied and after a few moments spent rubbing his stomach, she reached into her left-hand desk drawer and took out a Greenie. "Here you go, Angus. This'll make your teeth feel better."

It almost broke her heart to see him try to stand up, weaving and struggling until he could get his feet under him, moaning softly with pain from his arthritic hips.

Once he got to his feet, he took the Greenie from her hand, being very careful to fold his lips over his teeth lest he accidentally bite her.

With the Greenie sticking out of the side of his mouth like a big green cigar, he circled three times and flopped back down on the pillow in his bed, chewing contentedly.

"Well," Kat said, "I guess you don't have to potty right now, big fellow."

She took another moment trying to decide whether she had the energy to drive home, before she thought, *What the hell? There's nothing waiting for me there*. She glanced at Angus, patted his head once again, and whispered, "Everything I love is here with me." She laid her head on her crossed arms and was almost instantly asleep.

Kat started awake, the smell of coffee making her mouth water. She almost cried out loud at the pain in her neck and back as she tried to straighten from her position slumped over her desk.

"Hey, Doc, you okay?"

Kat slowly turned her head at the question and winced as the movement brought fresh pain. Kevin Paxton, her lab assistant, was watching her with a worried look on his face. He was tall, a shade over six feet, with a lean body and straw-blond hair in a crew cut. Even though he was only in his third year as a grad student at the University of Houston studying organic chemistry, he was thirty years old, due to spending some time in the military. Kat loved to tease him, telling him he looked about twenty years old.

Kat ran her hands over her face before answering, "Yeah, Kevin, I'm okay. What day is it, anyway?"

Kevin shook his head, frowning. "It's Monday, Dr. Williams. Did you spend the whole weekend here, again?"

Kat motioned toward the Keurig coffeemaker on the bench in the corner. "Uh-huh. I guess the time just got away from me."

Kevin walked to the coffeemaker and said over his shoulder, "You know that's not good for your health, Dr. Williams." He twirled the carousel containing the K-Cups of coffee and asked, "You want the regular Breakfast Blend or something more potent?"

She shook her head, still trying to come fully awake. "I think I'd better have the high-octane stuff, Kevin."

He pulled out a K-Cup and said, "Folgers Lively Colombian it is, then," and he proceeded to fill her custom cup with the dark, aromatic blend. When the coffeemaker hissed, signaling it was done, he took the coffee and moved to hand it to her with a handful of sugar packets.

Kat emptied four packets into her coffee and stirred it with her ballpoint pen. She took a deep drink. "Ah, breakfast." She tried to smile but her lips stuck to her teeth, reminding her she needed to brush her teeth and wash her face.

Kevin pointed at the words printed on the cup:

STRESS. The body's reaction when the mind overrules its natural inclination to smash the living shit out of some asshole who really needs it.

"You need to heed those words, Doc, or the stress you're putting on yourself is gonna kill you."

Kat grinned and reread the slogan, smacking her lips at the heavenly taste of Kevin's coffee. "Come on, Kev, quit being a mother hen and set the new batch of rats up to run the maze while I freshen up, then we'll run 'em to get some control times recorded, right after I take Angus out for his morning call to duty."

He held up both hands, palms out. "Don't worry, I've already taken him and he was a very good boy, doing both one and two for me without any trouble at all."

"Well, I'll just get his breakfast."

"Been there, done that. Look at him . . . he's all set."

She glanced over at his bed and saw Angus fast asleep and snoring peacefully, his full tummy pooching out. She turned and grinned at Kevin. "You're too good to me, Kevin."

Kevin shook his head and mumbled as he turned and walked off, "And you're gonna be the death of me, Kat," using her first name when he talked to himself, though he'd never quite dared to call her Kat to her face. In fact, he had a terrible crush on Kat and sometimes wished she'd look at him as less of an assistant and more as a man, a man who loved and adored her.

He went to the rats' cages, hoping he'd managed to keep his adoration of her out of his expression. It wouldn't do for her to realize what a crush he had on her . . . it might taint their working relationship. Hell, it might even get him fired, and then he wouldn't be able to see her every day.

As he pulled the rats from their cages, his face burned as he pictured them together in a romantic setting. After all, she wasn't *that* much older than him, he reasoned. He glanced over at her as she drank her coffee. Though she was in her early forties, she looked much younger. She was attractive, with a pretty, unlined face, long auburn hair usually worn in a twist while at work, and had hazel-green eyes and rosy cheeks . . . at least she did when she hadn't been working for forty hours straight, Kevin thought.

Half an hour later, freshly scrubbed and feeling much more human after showering and brushing her teeth in the women's locker room, Kat prepared to run both the rats she had injected with the NeurActivase and the uninjected, or control, rats through a maze. She needed to make sure that the formula had not impaired the performance of the injected rats, but she fully expected there to be no difference in the two groups' maze times. After all, none of the chemicals she'd combined into her formula were in and of themselves dangerous or toxic to rats, so there should be no danger of the formula inhibiting the rats' performance.

In fact, if anything, the formula should improve the rats' ability to run the maze, if only slightly.

She sat at her desk and stared out the window at the early morning sunshine, drinking another cup of coffee and thinking while Kevin set up the experiment.

Almost three years had passed since she had begun working at the BioTech research facility. Her initial interest had been in the field of traumatic spinal injuries, damage to the central nervous system of such an extent that it left the patient completely paralyzed. The repair and regeneration of that tissue was not a new field of research, but little progress had been made in it.

The National Institutes of Health was funding her research with a series of grants, administered through BioTech. The enormous number of spinal and central nervous system injuries that occurred in the Vietnam and Middle East wars had finally convinced the government more needed to be done to find some way to rehabilitate these veterans. The government's interest was not merely humanitarian. Disability payments and medical expenses on these permanently disabled vets were costing the treasury hundreds of millions of dollars annually.

Kat became interested in the problem when, during her naval residency in neurosurgery, she had operated on several Iraqi War casualties and was unable to do more than just patch their wounds, unable to significantly alter their paralysis or significantly improve their rehabilitation from traumatic brain injuries. Her daily interaction with the young men—boys, really—and their families so affected her that she eventually became depressed and discouraged with the practice of neurosurgery. When her negative attitude began to affect her confidence and the quality of her surgical skills, she decided to quit neurosurgery when her tour of duty was up, in favor of the less-rewarding but also less emotionally traumatic field of research.

She knew that helping these young men and others like them would only come with advances in neurochemistry and not from more useless surgery.

BioTech was a seven-story building a few blocks from Baylor College of Medicine in Houston, Texas. Within its huge, horseshoe-shaped building, there were literally hundreds of laboratories and animal compounds, where everything from super-secret germ and chemical warfare experiments to testing of the latest experimental medical formulations were carried out.

The building was under the joint control of a syndicate of wealthy investors and Baylor professors who oversaw the research grants from the government. But the scientists working there were, for the most part, non-university employees hired specifically for the various and sundry experiments they worked on. It was not unusual for one scientist not to know, or even care, what was going on in the lab next to his.

With her usual thoroughness and eye for detail, Kat systematically pulled together every scintilla of information on the subject of traumatic spinal injuries and their treatment, both nationally and internationally. She found that very little cooperation existed in the field and there was work being duplicated in one area while being done at cross-purposes in others. She slowly collected her material and categorized it into the useless, the promising, and the highly experimental. With that as a foundation, she began to build an ambitious project using her own research as her stones and mortar.

For over a year she struggled along, attempting to find some sort of neuron "glue" that would cause the damaged nerve tissue to reconnect. The problem was that central nervous system cells, those of the brain and spinal cord, do not multiply after birth, and they do not regenerate or heal themselves after injury. She experimented with dozens of substances and enzymes and organic and inorganic chemicals in her serum, concentrating on those that had had some history of success.

She tried using the GM-1 Gangliosides to enhance the functional recovery of damaged or aging neurons and added Imuran to suppress the body's formation of the antibodies that caused the destruction of injured neurons and thus inhibited the healing process.

She added calcium channel–blocking compounds to prevent the influx of calcium into the injured neurons, and she eventually added a thyrotropin-releasing hormone to enhance the body's natural ability to heal and replace injured tissue. But her efforts to develop a serum that would act as a bonding agent for the damaged neurons were short-lived and ineffective. Then, in the past month, she ran across some little-known research suggesting the brain contained a reservoir of undeveloped mystery neuron cells, the cause of their existence and their purpose being unknown and unexplained.

Working from that thesis, she decided to experiment with adding fetal nervous system tissue of unborn rats to her serum. The undifferentiated fetal neural tissue would, she hoped, be forced to change into the host animal's own neural tissue, replacing and repairing its own damaged nerves and brain cells and, hopefully, stimulating the undeveloped mystery neurons.

The shipment of fetal rat brains had arrived the previous week, and she had spent the last three days in a marathon work session to separate out the pure brain proteins from the fetal tissue in hopes that the tissue would contain some stimulatory protein or substance that would cause the dormant tissue in the adult rat brains to begin to grow and divide, or at least heal itself when injured.

If the new serum did not impair the rats' performance, her next step was to cut the spinal cords of the test animals, leaving them paralyzed. She would then see if the serum caused the spinal cord injuries to heal and cure the paralysis.

Kat put on a heavy, bite-proof glove she used when handling rats and took one out of its cage. She placed it in the beginning chamber of the maze and let it smell a small square of Hershey's chocolate. The rat's whiskers twitched and it began to search for the source of the smell. It rose up on its hind legs and stretched to its full height, even tried to climb the walls of the chamber to get at the chocolate.

Once she had the rat's full attention, Kat took the chocolate and put it in a small room at the end of the maze. She took out her stopwatch, glanced at Kevin to see if he was ready to record the time, and then simultaneously clicked the watch and opened the door to the rat's chamber. The rat's whiskers twitched again, and it headed out the door in search of the elusive chocolate. As quickly as it encountered a blind alley, the rat would backtrack and try another avenue and another until it found one that would bring it closer to the smell. Finally, at exactly nine minutes and fifty-four seconds, it ran into the room with the chocolate.

Kat decided to run all the control animals first, and at the conclusion, found the average times for the uninjected rats to be in the neighborhood of ten minutes, give or take twenty or thirty seconds.

Expecting the same results, since all the experimental rats were genetically identical, she placed the first of the injected rats in the maze. At first, the injected rat acted no different from the others that had gone before it. Then Kat noted something strange. The rat seemed to pause for just a second before choosing which alley to take, then it would invariably take the correct one. It was almost as if it was thinking about which alley went in the direction the chocolate smell was coming from, she thought, instead of just blindly trying each one it came to. Kevin clicked the stopwatch as the rat grabbed the chocolate. Kat frowned, sure she was mistaken about what she had seen, and thinking her fatigued eyes and hopeful mind were playing tricks on her.

"Hey, Dr. Williams. This one's time was seven minutes and fifty seconds," Kevin called, an excited look on his face.

Kat stared at him, eyebrows raised. "But that's over twenty percent faster than the others." She reached in and picked up the rat by its tail and held it up. "Look, Kevin, we have a rat Einstein."

She took the rat by the scruff of its neck and examined it more closely. It certainly looked no different from the control rats, save for the blue mark on its back. Probably just a lucky run, she thought.

Kevin laughed as he wrote down the time. Neither he nor Kat laughed, however, when the next injected rat ran the maze only seconds slower than the first. Kevin and Kat stared at the clipboard, then at the watch, and Kat felt the first faint stirrings of excitement. Her heart rate accelerated, and suddenly her mouth was dry.

"Hurry, Kevin, get the next one." She looked at her watch and noted it had been barely ten hours since the injection of the NeurActivase into the rats. "Jesus," she whispered, "nothing could work that fast to produce such profound differences in intelligence."

She tamped down her growing enthusiasm and warned herself to remain objective as she turned and took the third experimental rat from Kevin. With a mental crossing of her fingers, she placed it in the maze. After all the rats had run and the times had been averaged, Kat and Kevin sat in the lab, stunned.

Every injected rat ran the maze 20 percent faster than the noninjected control rats.

"Holy smoke, Doc, what do you think's going on?"

Kat took a deep breath. "I don't know, Kevin, I just don't know." Her mind was racing, questing for answers. At that second she had none. But, instinctively, she realized that the fewer people who knew about this, the better. And that included Kevin. For the time being, she had better keep whatever she'd discovered to herself.

CHAPTER 2

Burton Ramsey, PhD, looked nervously over his shoulder as he handed the ticket agent at Aeromexico cash for his flight to Monterrey, Mexico. He knew ticket agents occasionally notified the DEA when customers paid for international flights with cash, but he didn't want a record of the ticket to show up on his credit card.

He breathed a sigh of relief when he boarded the plane without a visit from any governmental agents. As soon as the flight was airborne, he ordered a double Chivas Regal from the stewardess and reflexively felt in his coat pocket for his cigarettes. As he began to pull one out of the pack, his eyes focused on the NO SMOKING sign above his seat. *Shit*, he thought. *Even the foreign carriers are getting as prudish as the damn American airline companies are.*

Frowning, he stuffed the cigarette pack back into his pocket and accepted his drink from the stewardess without even a thank-you. As he sipped, he began to make notes about what he needed to accomplish in Monterrey.

Dr. Humberto Garza and his lawyer, Felix Navarro, met Ramsey at the airport and took him directly to an empty building near the Monterrey General Hospital. The building had evidently once housed a laboratory, for there were long bar-topped cabinets, each with its own sink, arranged throughout a large central room. This room was flanked on either side with smaller, office-type rooms that still had a few scarred desks and wooden chairs that had been left by the previous occupants.

Ramsey thought he had never seen so many teeth in one face as Garza grinned. "Do you think this will be satisfactory, Señor Ramsey?"

Yeah, maybe for a high school biology project, thought Ramsey, but he forced a smile. "Certainly, Dr. Garza. As I told you over the phone, if you can supply me with the chemicals I'll need, I feel I can finish my research project quite nicely in this building."

The lawyer, Navarro, frowned slightly, and then he shrugged. "My client, Dr. Garza, hesitates to ask this, out of politeness, but I feel I would not be doing my duty to him if I did not ask a few questions about the research you plan to do here."

Ramsey glanced from Garza to Navarro, his lips slowly curving up in a smile that didn't quite reach his eyes. His voice became low and hard, his manner brusque. "I thought I made it clear in our negotiations that my research is completely secret—that is why I'm moving my lab from the States to here."

Navarro felt a frisson of fear turn his bowels to water as he stared into Ramsey's slowly reddening face. This *americano* was huge. Though he looked to be in his mid-forties, he stood ramrod-straight at six feet, two inches, was broad in the neck and shoulders, and had a rugged face that looked as if he could chew up and spit out anyone who angered him. Navarro quickly spread his hands in a placating manner, "Oh no, you misunderstand me, señor." He looked at Garza, who suddenly wasn't showing so many teeth. "We just need some . . . ah, assurance that whatever you are working on is . . . ah, within the law."

Ramsey folded his arms and relaxed a little. "Oh, you mean you need to make sure I'm not making LSD or amphetamines, or something like that?"

Now both Garza and Navarro were smiling again, relieved that the rich *americano* hadn't taken offense at the question. "*Sí, señor*. That is all that the law requires of us."

Ramsey pulled a legal-size sheet of paper out of his coat and handed it to Garza. "Here, Dr. Garza, is a list of the chemicals and equipment that I'll need. You're welcome to show it to a competent chemist of your choice and have him tell you that none of those chemicals are used in the manufacture of any illicit drugs, or for anything even remotely considered illegal."

While Garza was reading the list of chemicals, Ramsey took ten one-hundred-dollar bills out of his wallet and handed them to Navarro, counting them out slowly while he stared at the lawyer. "I am a generous man, Navarro, but I won't tolerate meddling in my affairs. Is that understood?" he growled, all friendliness gone from his tone.

Their eyes widened, and Ramsey thought the two men were going to dislocate their necks with their vigorous nodding as they spread the bills like a deck of cards, their eyes on the cash instead of Ramsey. "*Sí, señor*. There will be no questions asked, either about your research or your work permit, which will be available whenever you need it."

Now Ramsey allowed himself a genuine smile as he stuck out his hand, "Gentlemen, it's a pleasure doing business with you."

On the flight back to Houston and BioTech, Ramsey sipped another Chivas as he once again went over the elaborate precautions he had taken to avoid leaving a paper trail the BioTech Oversight Committee could follow.

Finally, satisfied he had done all he could to avoid detection, he put out his reading light and leaned back to dream about the millions of dollars that would soon be his.

He arrived in Houston at eleven thirty at night. By the

time he retrieved his car from the overnight parking garage and traversed the maze of intersecting freeways around the city to his apartment, it was well after one in the morning. He was exhausted by his one-day trip, but he figured it was worth it if it kept the bloodhounds off his trail.

If BioTech found out what he was about to do, it would not only cost him the millions of dollars he expected to make off his discovery, but it would also earn him fifteen to twenty years in prison.

Burton Ramsey, Ph.D. in biochemistry and paid researcher at BioTech, had begun working on a "blood scrubber" formula to hopefully reduce dependence on dialysis machines for patients with kidney failure. He'd succeeded beyond his wildest dreams. Without knowing quite how he did it, Ramsey perfected a formula that cleansed the blood so completely it took out all of the free radicals and waste products that had caused much of the body's aging. In short, he had a formula that stopped physical aging from progressing, and in some cases would even cause a mild rejuvenation of damaged or aged cells and body organs.

The fly in Ramsey's ointment was that the serum did nothing to stop the aging of the central nervous system and brain, so that even though the body stayed youthful, the mind continued to age and ultimately decay. However, Ramsey was ever the pragmatist and figured half a loaf was better than none, and he knew that many aging millionaires would, too, and would pay practically any price to remain looking youthful well into their eighties.

Reality finally set in when he studied the contract he had signed with BioTech and realized he would get a measly 2 percent of the royalties for his serum—that is, if the government ever approved it for public use.

Ramsey, after much consideration, finally decided the government would probably mark the serum as top secret and keep it for the exclusive use of aging generals and influential politicians, a process that would put nothing in Ramsey's pockets and do nothing for the very people he had vowed to help with his research.

Therefore, he had hit upon the simple expedient of faking his progress notes, destroying his records, and claiming failure of his project. He intended to move to Mexico and spend a year seeing if he could somehow make his serum work on nerves and brain tissue while he waited for BioTech to forget about him and his "failed" research. After that, whether he'd succeeded in improving his serum or not, he would announce to the world his discovery under his own name, and to hell with BioTech and the government that had paid for his work.

Of course, BioTech would be plenty suspicious, so he had to cover his ass—that explained all of the James Bond–style traveling and maneuvering. He thought to himself on the long ride back to Houston, it would all be worth it if he could show BioTech, and especially the medical doctors on the Progress Committee, he was a man to be reckoned with. In addition, if they really tried to push it, he could show the authorities his lab and his chemical requisitions and claim to have made his discovery after moving to Mexico and dare them and their platoons of hired guns and doctors to disprove it.

Burton Ramsey claimed to despise MDs for the plain and simple reason he had lusted to be one for as far back as his memory went. He had not been able to get that MD behind his name for one reason. And it had not been for lack of brains or intelligence or grades or skill or dedication. It had been because of money, or the lack thereof.

When he finished undergraduate school at a small state university in Texas with a dual degree in chemistry and biology, he took his Medical College Admissions Test, scoring well above the needed score, did his interviews, and was accepted at three prestigious medical schools. Unfortunately, he came along at a time when there was a glut of doctors, and scholarships and grants simply weren't as available as in years past. What money there was seemed to be sucked up by minorities under affirmative-action guidelines, which caused him to be forever afterward suspicious of all ethnicities other than his own.

He tried every avenue he could think of to raise money. He had none, his family had none, and he had no friends or patrons who could advance him the enormous sums it would have taken to get through four years of medical school. He had worked his way through undergraduate school, but he knew he could never do that in medical school even though one dean of admissions had said he knew of students who did. But Burton knew his wasn't the kind of brain that could do such a thing.

He was highly intelligent with an IQ just a little short of genius, but he wasn't quick. He made straight As in college, but he did it by hard, unrelenting work. He was a plodder and he knew it. He knew students who didn't have to study, didn't have to take notes in class, and he admired them for their quick minds. But that was before he'd been denied the chance to become a physician.

What made the situation even more ironic was that Ramsey himself wasn't motivated by money. He wasn't seeking the MD degree because of the huge salaries or the lavish lifestyles that physicians enjoyed, but because he felt a true calling to help people and to do good things with his life. The seeds of his bitterness were sown by the cold eyes of the medical school interviewers who failed to recognize his idealism, and by the medical school accountants who awarded the few scholarships available to those less altruistically motivated than him.

In the end he simply continued his studies, getting first his master's degree, then his Ph.D. in biochemistry while continuing to work at night to pay for his schooling. Because he had to work almost full-time, he had to take a light academic load and he was thirty-one years old before he finally received his Ph.D. and could go looking for the kind of job that would finally reward him for all his hard work.

He was never exactly certain when it happened, but at some point, he had begun to display a hatred and contempt for all physicians. It might have occurred in his first research job when he discovered that a man with an MD, doing no more important work than he was doing, was paid a higher salary even though he most certainly wasn't as good a scientist or researcher as Burton Ramsey. Whatever the reason, by the time he was forty, his dislike and contempt for all things *materia medica* was in full flower.

He liked nothing better than to say, loudly if there were doctors present, a good mortician knew his way around a body better than a surgeon any day and for whatever ailed him give him a good chiropractor every time. He was also fond of saying nature healed and physicians took the fees and the credit.

And then, inexplicably, he met and married an MD: Sheila Goodman. She was in her last year of residency in endocrinology and geriatrics, and he was working in a hematology lab in Dallas, beginning his interest in blood and the arterial and venous systems.

At first, he treated her with the same scorn and derision he reserved for all MDs, calling her "the little rich girl who went to medical school on Daddy's money." One day, Sheila stopped him in the hall by placing her hand against his chest. She fixed him with her large brown eyes. "I don't know where you're getting your information, Dr. Ramsey, but my daddy didn't pay for my education. He died when I was nine years old, and my mother worked two jobs to get me through college." He watched her with new interest as she turned to walk away. "I helped pay for medical school by working as a waitress until midnight, four nights a week."

Although Sheila wasn't a beautiful woman by most standards, all who knew her thought her to be quite attractive, mostly because of the goodness and compassion for all things that was mirrored on her face. She was of medium height, with sunflower-blue eyes, a peaches-and-cream complexion, and a body that was slightly boxy but made her look more maternal than frumpy. Ramsey finally got up the courage to ask her to lunch, to apologize for his earlier remarks. Halfway through the meal, he fell in love with her, in spite of her degree.

They stayed in Dallas for four years, until she got a prestigious offer from the Baylor College of Medicine in Houston. He followed her, working first at a lab independent of the medical complex. One day he announced to her he was damned if he was going to follow her around, especially since she wouldn't take his last name and went around calling herself "Dr. Goodman."

He moved out and went to work for first one, then another private laboratory in the Houston Medical Center area. Eventually, his bitterness and constant carping drove them apart and they officially separated. Somehow, in spite of this, they managed to remain good friends. In fact, Sheila was practically Ramsey's only friend.

Now he was forty-four years old and had been at BioTech for four years and was about to finish his research project, and he hoped, in the process get rich. Once all the details of that little business was accomplished, he was confident that he could force Sheila to give up this silly business of fooling around with people's hormones and be his full-time wife.

CHAPTER 3

Kat Williams gave Kevin the day off and spent the rest of the morning encrypting her notes on the new serum in the computer. She wanted no one to be able to discover the changes she had made in the serum that had led to such spectacular results. She admitted to herself that she didn't really know why she was being so cautious, but instinctively she felt it was the right thing to do.

Just before lunch, Captain Sohenshine stopped by Kat's lab unannounced. Kat looked up from her computer, at first annoyed at the interruption, and then terrified when she saw who it was striding through the door as if the lab belonged to him.

Captain "Sunshine," as the researchers called him, was in charge of coordinating the government grants that paid for the scientists' work, and the man was a martinet who took his self-proclaimed role of protector of the taxpayers' money very seriously indeed. Though he was no longer in the military, he insisted on being addressed as "Captain." He was short and squatty, had a pronounced beer belly, halitosis, and washed-out-looking dingy brown hair with a serious case of dandruff.

"Ah, Dr. Williams. We missed you at the monthly conference yesterday."

Kat could feel herself start to blush, and sweat began to trickle from her armpits. She had never been good at lying, always feeling that people could immediately tell when she was speaking anything less than the full truth.

"Uh, hello, Captain Sun . . . er, Sohenshine."

Angus, sensing Kat's discomfort, growled softly from his bed next to her desk, baring his teeth at the intruder.

The captain started at the warning and edged sideways past Angus's bed, watching the dog carefully. Once safely past the dog, he eased up to Kat's desk and leaned over and began to read the computer screen over Kat's shoulder, unconcerned about the rudeness of the gesture. Kat grimaced as she breathed through her mouth to try to avoid the rancid smell of Sohenshine's breath wafting into her face. Kat mustered her courage and stood, putting herself between the captain and the screen. "Just what is it you needed, Captain?"

Sohenshine turned and began to walk around the lab, absentmindedly picking up various pieces of equipment and looking at them for a moment before putting them down and picking something else up. "Well, some of the other scientists on the progress committee were wondering how you were coming along on your 'neuron glue' experiments, and since you weren't there at the meeting to tell us, I thought I'd drop by and see for myself."

Kat blushed again at the implied insult, but restrained her anger, telling herself that now was not the time to fly off the handle. She had to be calm and think through everything she said if she was going to keep her results secret. "Well, ah . . . I've had some small successes and a few disappointments, but on the whole I think I'm making good progress."

Sohenshine frowned, his usual expression when dealing with the scientists. He felt most of them were charlatans trying to waste taxpayers' money on unproven experiments of dubious value. "Well," he said as he puffed out his chest in self-importance, "see if you can't spare the time to come to the next meeting and let the committee in on some of your successes. It is, after all, our job to monitor the use of government funds."

It took all of Kat's self-control not to laugh in the pompous ass's face. Instead, she placed her hand on the captain's back and gently led him toward the door. "Yes, sir, I'll certainly be there."

"See that you are," Sohenshine barked as he marched out the door, dusting his hands together as if to brush off any contamination from her lab as he waddled off down the hall.

Kat took a deep breath as she leaned back against the closed laboratory door, mentally calculating that she had less than a month to show some significant results before the committee would judge whether or not to shut her down.

The next day, Kevin again ran the rats through the maze, and the injected rats' average time came down to six minutes, with some as low and five and a half. Kat could barely contain herself. The rats seemed to be getting smarter. They weren't making the same wrong turns in the maze. It was almost as if they remembered which paths were the blind alleys and which led to the chocolate, something she had never encountered in all her years of research with rats.

When Kevin began to get really excited about the results, Kat cautioned him against undue optimism. "Hold on, Kev. Don't blow your circuits just yet. Let's wait and see if the times remain this good over time."

On the morning of the third day, the injected rats negotiated the maze in three and a half minutes and ran the route with the assurance of previous knowledge. Kat was astounded, and more than a little baffled. She'd never seen anything like this before. It was as if the rats were getting more and more intelligent every day.

"Kevin, I can't wait any longer. I've got to sacrifice one of the rats and see what's going on in its brain."

Kevin took one of the injected rats and put it in a small jar. He saturated a cotton ball with ether and dropped it into the jar and put the lid on. After a few moments, the rat staggered a couple of steps and fell over, fast asleep.

Kat took the unconscious rat and quickly, knowing the rat would feel no pain, cut its head off. She opened the skull and removed the brain and used a microtome to slice the tissue into ultrathin slices.

Kevin used tiny tweezers to pick up the slices and place them on slides. After arranging the slides on the countertop in the order of her slices, he took the first one and put it on the microscope.

Kat bent over her microscope and twirled the knob to bring the slide into focus. She gasped and looked up blinking, as if she couldn't believe her eyes. Looking again, she found to her profound amazement that new nerve cells were actually being produced, and not only being produced and dividing, but binding with the old cells.

She sat back dumbfounded. She was looking at brain cells, central nervous tissue, actually being created by artificial methods. To the best of her knowledge, it was the first time in the history of science that such had happened with a mature organism. She looked again and saw a lens full of healthy, tightly packed nerve cells with the cell bodies sharply defined and the neurons intertwined and interacting with the older cells.

At that moment her heart almost exploded. Gone was the thought of curing traumatic spinal injuries—that was now child's play. Suddenly she could see cures for Alzheimer's disease, Parkinson's disease, strokes, brain damage, brain tumors—the list was endless. She had never been a person who, either by nature or training, had tended to overexcitement; however, in that moment, her heart raced and her head whirled as it never had before. Diseases that had previously been untouchable could now be treated!

It took a while for her brain to quiet itself, for her emotions to come back under the rigid control she had been trained to maintain.

Then she set seriously to work to explore and define the extent of her discovery. The first breathtaking result of the NeurActivase appeared to be in the intelligence impact produced by the superloading of the brain cells. The maze results implied that the NeurActivase made the injected rats two or three times as smart as the control group, which had received nothing. The lowering of the times in which they completed in the maze meant that not only did the serum produce an effect, but that it was progressive and additive over time.

That afternoon she sacrificed both a test rat and a control rat. Both animals were genetically identical, the only difference being the injection of the serum.

She again prepared microscope slides from microtome sections of the brain tissue from both rats. She was amazed and awed to see how densely packed the brain cells were in the tissue section of her test rat versus that of the control animal. She could even see and identify the new neural cells by their more clearly defined myelin sheaths and nuclei. The older brain cells in the test rat, what she thought of as the original cells, appeared less distinct, almost fuzzy, as if they were not as healthy.

To her it was a magnificent sight because it meant that her serum was a catalyst that started the fissioning process of the neural cells and that new cells would be produced as fast as the older ones decayed and died. It was a miraculous breakthrough, because in every living organism that had a central nervous system, the aging process was accompanied by the death of brain cells that were unable to be replaced.

Kat straightened and glanced at Kevin, who was watching her with wide eyes. "Well, Kev, it looks like now we'll be able to teach old dogs new tricks."

It turned out to be her last joke and her last great thrill of excitement.

CHAPTER 4

The next day, the fourth day after their initial injections, Kat put her blue group through their paces again, expecting them to exceed their previous best times through the maze. Instead, the times showed a marked decline. The average time rose a full forty-five seconds. It did not unduly alarm her at that point. A researcher was always prepared for early reverses. After all, she was treading absolutely virgin territory, and every deviation was an important footnote to be logged in to her encrypted computer files under NeurActivase, her code name for both the serum and the experiment.

But some concern entered her mind when, on the fifth day, the test rats' performance continued to decline. The sixth day was worse, with the test rats now taking better than seven minutes to run the maze. With trembling nerves and fingers she sacrificed another test rat and took a specimen for examination. Under the microscope, the brain tissue was still as full of neural cells as ever, but to her dismay, there was clear indication of decay and deterioration in the cells.

The most noticeable destruction was in the myelin sheath component of the nerve cells, the protective outer husk. Instead of being sharply defined and distinct, the edges of the sheathes were fuzzy and ragged—a clear indication of dying cells. There were still some new cells being formed and dividing, but the clear majority of the cells appeared to be decaying and dying.

She was dumbstruck and frantic. She tried to think through what could have gone wrong. Healthy nerve cells didn't just die in a matter of a few days for no reason. It wasn't possible. They acted as if they were being slowly poisoned somehow.

In the end Kat decided to reinject her remaining test animals, hoping that adding more of the NeurActivase would solve the problem, or at least slow the decline in the rats' intelligence.

After she finished with the injections, Kat sat staring at the rats as if she could see the NeurActivase chemicals coursing through their bloodstreams:

NeurActivase entered the rats' bloodstream as a mixture of five distinct chemical entities. Almost immediately, the compounds separated and began to work their magic: The thyrotropin-releasing hormone sped straight to the pineal gland in the base of the brain. As the pineal gland absorbed the compound, the gland's cells were kicked into high gear and began to manufacture thyrotropin in large amounts. The thyrotropin, in turn, sped to the thyroid gland and induced it to increase its production of thyroid hormone, which immediately sped up the rats' metabolism and enhanced their abilities to heal and replace injured tissues.

The second ingredient, GM-1 Ganglioside, entered the rats' brains, where it searched out and coated and entered damaged or aging neurons and began to repair them before they died. It was assisted in this by the third ingredient, calcium channel–blocking enzyme, which prevented the influx of calcium ions into the damaged neurons, one of the mechanisms by which neurons aged and by which injured neurons died.

The fourth ingredient, Imuran, went directly to the bone marrow, where it paralyzed the marrow's production of antibodies to injured neurons and thereby prevented their destruction by the body's own defense mechanisms.

The final and most important ingredient in the serum was a slurry made up of fetal rat brain tissue. The fetal rat brains were ground up and the proteins separated. This protein mixture entered the rats' brains and activated a small nucleus of undeveloped, dormant neural cells. The protein interspersed among the cells in this small area, and, within minutes the cells began to pulsate and change. Their nuclei rippled and stretched, then began to divide. One cell became two, then the two cells became four, and soon these new cells were coursing throughout the rats' brains, bonding and joining with the older cells, forming new, fresh networks of functioning brain cells.

Finally, Kat came out of her reverie and realized it would be hours before the rats showed any changes due to the injections, so she decided to go home and give Angus some quality time and perhaps even grab a few hours of shut-eye for herself.

"Come on, big boy," she crooned as she hooked Angus's leash onto his collar. "Let's go home and get some cookies."

Angus struggled to his feet and gave a hearty bark at the word *cookies*, one of his favorite treats.

Kat could barely contain herself to wait the twenty-four hours she deemed necessary. She rushed to her lab that morning having gotten precious little sleep the night before. For the sake of secrecy, she asked Kevin to take Angus for a walk in a nearby park, saying she hadn't had time to exercise him this morning. Kevin, who loved Angus almost as much as Kat did, readily agreed.

After Kevin left, Kat put the first animal through the maze. The animal made the journey in a little less than six minutes, better than the seven minutes previously. The result was not as good as she had hoped for, but she could at least call it progress. Her remaining animals did just about as well, causing her to briefly hope the extra dose of Neur-Activase had solved the problem.

She put the rats back in their cages, and when Kevin and Angus returned, they spent the rest of the day giving the lab a much-needed cleaning while Angus snored nearby.

And then it all began to go downhill very rapidly. The next day all of her test animals were noticeably less intelligent, fumbling through parts of the maze they had once raced through, and seeming completely baffled by other, more difficult parts.

When he saw the increased maze times and the rats' confused behavior, Kevin shook his head. "What's going on, Dr. Williams?"

She just shrugged, not able to meet his eyes.

Within two days all of the remaining blue group had reached the baseline times of the control group and were threatening to go even lower. The serum was no longer making them smarter; in fact, it seemed to be retarding what brain function they had started with.

Continuing examination of brain specimens just confirmed the maze results; the animals' heads were full of dead and dying brain cells.

Kat was devastated, her disappointment crushing in its intensity. She almost wished she were a drinker so she could drown her sorrows in a bottle of bourbon.

She forced herself to approach the cage containing her test rats, hoping somehow what she had observed earlier would be different this time. She leaned over, anticipation causing a slight tremor in her fingers. Still the same, she thought. Her animals were dying, crawling in sawdust, some already gripped by death throes, all struggling to stay alive.

What had gone wrong? She wondered bitterly. Things had all seemed so positive yesterday. The rats she had injected with her serum, NeurActivase, had shown remarkable increases in intelligence and vitality, running her maze in record times.

Her initial enthusiasm was gone now, replaced by an overwhelming sense of defeat. After four days of stunning accomplishments, during which she had visions of showing the scientific community her discovery, doubtlessly receiving accolades for conquering some of the most devastating diseases known to man, such as Lou Gehrig's disease, Alzheimer's disease, and senile dementia, she was back at square one.

She walked to her microscope and peered once again at the initial brain sections from her injected rats. The changes in their tissue mocked her with what might have been. The brain cells all showed amazing new growth, rejuvenation of aged neurons and nerve sheaths, indications her serum was actually growing *new* brain matter, a feat once thought impossible. How had it all changed so quickly, so drastically, that now her serum had made the rats smarter and more vigorous, and then killed them in a matter of days?

In a fit of rage, she swept the slides and tissue sections to the floor. She'd be damned if she'd let this setback stop her work, she thought. She took a deep breath. There was nothing left to do but to go back to the computer and start over with her calculations to try to discover where in the vast, complicated chemical formulae, the fault lay.

After two hours staring at chemical formulae crawling across her monitor screen like some weird hieroglyphics, Kat could find nothing in her serum that could possibly cause her rats to die, as they all were now, four days after receiving NeurActivase.

She glanced to the side of her desk at a recent study she pulled off the Internet. It reported a compound, dihydroepiandosterone, or DHEA as it was known, that had shown promise as an antiaging chemical. The drug was a precursor in the body to the male hormone, testosterone, which many reputable scientists were taking themselves, claiming renewed energy and vitality.

What the hell? she thought. *I'll give it a try and add it to NeurActivase. After all, what have I got to lose?*

A quick trip to the supply room got her a vial of DHEA. Another few moments in front of her computer calculating an approximate dose for rats, and she was ready. She added two milliliters of DHEA to the NeurActivase and shook the vial vigorously to mix the solutions together.

She went to the stack of wire cages lining a rear wall of her lab and took down the cage that contained her last supply of rats that had not been yet injected. She checked the tag affixed to the wire, making certain the rats were of the GR-4 strain, and then she readied them for injection.

After Kat injected her new, modified NeurActivase compound in each of the twelve rats, she glanced at her watch. It was already four thirty in the afternoon. She knew the Friday-afternoon Houston traffic would be fierce. She decided the hell with it, she'd just go to a nearby restaurant and have a leisurely dinner, and then come back and see how the newly injected rats were doing.

Afterward, she'd spend the night in the lab and get an early start the next morning.

She put the cage back on the stack of other cages, making a mental note to tell Kevin what she had done on Monday morning as soon as he arrived for work so he could mark the tag on the cage with the date and time of injection.

She made sure Angus was comfortable in his bed and that he had plenty of water nearby, grabbed her purse, and ran for the parking lot, hoping she could beat the rush-hour traffic jam and get to the restaurant before the early evening crowds gathered.

As before, the liquid NeurActivase entered a dozen rats' bloodstreams, but it was now a mixture of six distinct chemical entities. Once again, the compounds separated and began their work: Thyrotropin-releasing hormone, GM-1 Ganglio-

side, Imuran, and the fetal rat brain slurry all worked exactly
as before.

Then, the DHEA began converting cholesterol in fat cells
into massive amounts of testosterone, an anabolic steroid
that caused tissue cells to divide and grow and replace injured or dying cells more rapidly than before.

At first there was no visible change in the rats, but soon,
literally within an hour, elderly rats began to stand straighter,
move more rapidly, eat voraciously, and mate with adolescent abandon.

Kat returned from her supper and was exhilarated when
she saw the rats she'd injected just a couple of hours before
acting much more vigorous and youthful than the control
rats. They were running around their cage, mating and playing like very young rats instead of the middle-aged ones
they were.

She decided to go to the women's dressing room, take a
quick shower, change into the sweats she kept there, and set-
tle down on the couch in her lab. Maybe now she could finally get some sleep, after she took Angus for his evening
stroll, of course.

While Kat was in the dressing room showering and taking off her makeup, a slow but steady change began in her
test rats. First they stopped mating and eating, and then, as
suddenly as it had appeared, their vigorous movements began
to slow and they began to twitch and move spastically around
the cage. It was like they had suddenly aged fifty rat years in
the space of an hour.

When Kat arrived back in the lab, she took one look at the
injected rats, and it felt as if she'd been punched in the gut.

The new injection with DHEA added had all been in
vain. The test rats were already deteriorating past the base-

line of the control rats and showed every sign of continued decline. With a sickening despair, she watched another dream slowly disappear. There seemed to be nothing more she could do.

Kat watched helplessly as first their mental, and then their motor skills continued to fail. Soon, one by one, they all died with symptoms very like those of amyotrophic lateral sclerosis, or Lou Gehrig's disease.

Her only consolation, albeit a small one, was that she had been secretive about her early success. She had even underplayed the importance of the rats' new growth of brain cells and their ever-increasing facility in the maze from Kevin, though to be honest, she knew he suspected what a great achievement this had been.

And Kat had certainly made no mention of it to the progress committee, who, so far as she'd told them, still thought she was working on her "neuron glue" without much success.

That evening, as her last test animal died, lying in its own waste products, she cried in frustration. She stumbled to her car and put Angus in his bed in the backseat. Her mind was numb with the enormity of her defeat as she drove to the freeway and headed south, toward Memorial Park. Once there, she drove along the small stream that ran through the park in the gathering darkness, her thoughts a chaotic mixture of rage and self-pity.

Finally, she stopped at a small pullout in the deserted park, took off her shoes, and walked along the water's edge, thinking melodramatically about wading out and disappearing beneath the moonlit surface. This made her chuckle at herself and improved her mood, as the stream was probably less than two feet deep. Instead, she lay back on the cool grass, hands behind her head, and looked up at the stars.

She thought how most men, and in her case women, truly did lead lives of quiet desperation, never rising to the full potential of their dreams or aspirations. She thought how ironic it was that she, Kaitlyn Williams, had been given not one, but two chances at the golden ring—and how she had fumbled both of them. She lay there on the grass, her eyes full of starlight, and her mind on her past.

After a while, Kat noticed the stars were blurred by the tears in her eyes. She sat up and angrily rubbed her eyes until they burned. *Damn it, girl, you're not going to lie here feeling sorry for yourself,* she thought. She stood and made her way back to her car.

She opened the rear door and watched Angus dozing in his bed on the backseat. With a deep sigh, she reached over and took his face in her hands. She leaned into the car and nuzzled him, face-to-face. "We're gonna get through this, big boy," she whispered. "We just have to work harder, that's all."

Angus moaned in pleasure at her touch, as if agreeing with her.

On the drive back to her apartment, she resolved to work her way through her own maze and get the prize at the end. *You discovered a miracle serum,* she thought with determination. *Now you just have to iron out a few bugs and make it work like it should.*

With this new goal in mind, she finally slept like a baby for the first time since she'd discovered the rats' new abilities.

Just after midnight, a key was inserted in the door to Kat's lab. A shadowy figure moved silently over to the rats' cages and began to examine the animals one by one. Finally, seeing that there were only unmarked control rats in the cages, the figure moved over to the medical waste bin.

The lid to the bin was removed, revealing a pile of dead rats, all with blue marks on their backs.

The figure sighed and slumped, replacing the top to the bin, and then left the room as silently as it had entered.

CHAPTER 5

Kat and Angus got to the lab early the next morning, having left her apartment at six o'clock to beat the morning Houston traffic, which was bad even on a Saturday. She took Angus for his morning walk, gave him a Greenie, and got him situated in his bed next to her desk.

After fixing her coffee, she sat at her desk, opened her computer to her NeurActivase files, and went doggedly back to work. She reread the files, going back to the very beginning of her research, and began to make notes on a legal pad on her desk: She could make neural cells appear and she could make them bond and she could make them divide . . . She just couldn't keep them alive very long.

The thought of her failure made her sweat at the thought of what her position might be if she'd gone public with her seeming discovery. This second great failure in her life, as bad as it was, would have been even more intolerable if it had been public knowledge.

She began to work on fixing the formula, plugging away in a sort of haze, praying for another miracle, but not having much hope that one was going to present itself.

Since it was Saturday, the whole building was quiet except for the distant whir of a janitor waxing the halls. None of the other researchers worked on Saturdays or Sundays. Not unless they had something cooking that had to be constantly tended. No one whom she knew of, outside of herself, deliberately worked on the weekends.

She did so because she had nowhere else to go, not because she thought by working every moment of every day that she'd find the magic solution. She'd given up on that long before. It was just that she was more at home in the lab than she was in the Spartan apartment she slept in and sometimes ate in. She had no real friends and only a few acquaintances.

Sometimes, when the loneliness was upon her, she would try out one of the many nightclubs in the downtown area, hoping that being in the presence of so many other people might ease the pain of having no one of her own. This invariably ended badly, the ritualized mating dance of the males who approached her trying to pick her up causing her to be more amused than flattered at their adolescent behavior.

What few overtures she'd had from the other researchers at the lab she'd rebuffed in as pleasant a manner as possible, but still letting them know she wasn't interested in socializing at work.

At one time, while still a resident, she had been somewhat serious about a young man who had worked with her in the navy. He'd been a general surgeon, so they had their work in common, and for a while she thought the relationship might lead somewhere serious. But after her decision to quit neurosurgery, he'd simply disappeared from her life. They'd had no contact since her discharge from the navy.

Her parents were both retired doctors, living in Boston. They were still close, and she visited them at least twice a year, but they were active in the arts and theater community of Boston and tried their best not to interfere in her life, such as it was. Since her discharge from the navy, she'd discouraged contact with friends from her past life, and she intended to keep it that way. She did not inherently dislike people. She simply did not like to see her own failure reflected in their faces. She knew in her heart, of course, that was non-sense, but she didn't care. She wanted to be alone, and her reasons were her own.

At least that was what she would have said if anyone had asked her. The real reason she wanted minimal human contact was that she was embarrassed and ashamed of herself. People meant questions, and questions meant answers. And she didn't have any answers, much less the desire to re-create her pain in conversation.

Kat sat thinking, for some time. Finally, she got up and walked over to the rat cages. She walked delicately, shyly, almost as if she was afraid someone would hear her. She was a slim, auburn-haired woman of little better than average height. Her face was fine-boned and even-featured, with a light dusting of freckles across her nose and cheeks. She was not quite beautiful, though she should have been. There was a sadness about her face that wasn't physical. It came from the bitterness and disappointment deep in her eyes and the thin set of her lips, almost as if she was drawing them in at the beginning of a snarl. You looked at her face, and there was no light shining from within.

Kat had set out to do great things in medicine and it was not going to happen, even when all signs had said she must. Some people were born with the equipment to be concert pianists, some home-run hitters, some great surgeons. Now she was like the home-run hitter whom the pitchers had discovered couldn't hit an outside curveball. She had a flaw, and she just could not grow to accept that fact. In her world, perfection did not allow for a flaw.

She stood in front of the cages, staring at her rats. Some of the cages were empty, all of the rats having died. She had come to inject a new batch of rats and to try once again to find the flaw in her formula. It was a hopeless gesture, and she knew it. It was basically the same old serum that would produce the same old results, but she couldn't give up the dream. Perhaps if she adjusted the dosage of DHEA . . .

She looked down the line of cages, looking for the new rats she'd told Kevin to order. There were no virgin specimens. There were still a few control animals, but they were of varying genetic strains, leftovers from her brief period of trying anything just so long as it might lead to a neuron glue to heal spinal or central nervous system injuries.

She felt oddly irritated, as if she were being held up in some great experiment due to a lack of working material. She said, aloud, "Damn that Kevin!" The rats she'd told him to order were not in place, and she was thoroughly irritated. Come Monday, she told herself, she intended to give the young man a thorough dressing-down . . . though she knew she wouldn't really do it. A word or even a hint of displeasure from her would crush him, and she was much too kind to do that.

Still, she thought, a place of science was no theater for the blind or the forgetful or the haphazard, and damn it, she wanted to inject those rats right now, this very day. She had prepared a new batch of serum before leaving the lab the night before, and she wanted to use it, if for no other reason than to draw another carping memo from Captain "Sunshine" about her rat carnage.

She had little hope of finding any of the other labs open on a Saturday, but she wandered out into the hall and went along, trying knobs or knocking on doors. No one was there, and she was about to give up when she noticed a door ajar just a few yards farther down the hall. She stopped short when she got to it and saw that the lab belonged to Burton Ramsey, Ph.D.

She didn't know Ramsey very well. Having heard he was a man who despised MDs, she'd tried to keep her distance. She didn't know what kind of research Ramsey was doing, but she knew most of the projects at BioTech used experimental animals of one sort or another. With luck, he'd have a few cages of extra rats in his lab and she could "borrow" some so that her day wouldn't be completely wasted.

From her few sightings of him in the halls or cafeteria, Kat thought Ramsey looked nothing like she thought a scientist should. He was a big man, over six feet, with heavy shoulders and large hands. Where Kat's fingers were long and tapering and her nails still perfectly kept, Ramsey's fingers looked as if they'd be more at home curled into a fist.

Kat, even in defeat, kept herself well-groomed. Her hair was always combed and sprayed, or fixed into a French braid to keep it out of her way in the lab, and she always applied a light touch of makeup to cover her freckles, which reminded her of a young schoolgirl.

Ramsey, on the other hand, just didn't seem to care. His clothes usually looked like they'd been trampled underfoot first and then put on, and his hair was unruly and he had a balding spot just at the crown of his head. He had a thick sandy mustache that drooped around his mouth, and Kat had never seen him in a tie, and sometimes not even in socks.

Kat did not know how old the man was, but she guessed somewhere in his mid-forties. They had met only once, some months back when Kat had gone through the line in the cafeteria and found the only chair available was across a table from Ramsey. She'd politely asked him if she could join him. Instead of nodding his approval, he'd huffed and puffed and mumbled something about a body not being able to eat in peace, then he'd taken his tray and stomped out the door toward his lab. With a face burning with embarrassment, Kat had sat and eaten her lunch alone.

Kat eased the door open enough to peek inside Ramsey's laboratory. The lab, like all of them on the sixth floor, was basically one long room some twenty feet by forty feet, with an office cubicle walled off in one corner, another area for the laboratory functions, and another for the computer modules. It was easy, in one glance, to see that the place was empty.

She assumed the cleaning crew had finished in the room and simply not shut the door, which, she thought, was a hell of a way to run a medical laboratory where highly prized work was being done. An industrial spy could have a field day with such security measures. She stepped quickly into the laboratory, leaving the door at exactly the same angle of openness as she had found it.

Kat knew she was technically in violation of both ethics and laboratory security, but she didn't think Ramsey would mind. The man gave no indication that he took his work that seriously, and, in fact, she rarely saw him at work at all. She'd certainly never seen him around on a weekend.

Once inside she glanced around quickly. At the end of the room was a workbench with several microscopes on it and a microtome and other normal lab paraphernalia. She wondered briefly what Ramsey was working on and was almost tempted to go over to the worktable and have a look. But caution overcame her. There was a limit to the liberties she was willing to take, even with a man she barely knew.

The cages were against a side wall. There were twelve of them, triple-stacked. She walked over and slowly looked down the line, glancing at the laboratory rats inside. To her surprise, none of the rats was marked. Each cage of twelve rats bore a label giving the strain and age of the rats. To each was also attached a small tag with some handwritten figures on it.

Kat went to the last cage to her right, the top cage. She looked at the label and saw that the rats were a GR-4 strain, the same ones she used in her lab. That meant they were very high on the genetic purity scale, having been bred and rebred to collect one set of genetic characteristics; in effect, the rats were like multiple identical twins.

She also saw by the tag that they were mixed males and females, which made no difference to her. She grunted, thinking wryly that her serum was indiscriminate: It killed regardless of gender. But she was surprised to see that the rats were five years old. That was a very old age for experimental animals, since white rats only lived about seven years. But then, she supposed Ramsey might be working in geriatrics, though she had a hard time envisioning a man as active and vital as Ramsey being interested in the welfare of delicate little old ladies.

There was a small tag on the cage. She took it in her hand and looked at it. It appeared to be a date, two days past. She assumed it was a notation of when the rats had been received, since lab data concerning treatment certainly wouldn't be handled in such a haphazard manner. If that was the case, and the date was the arrival of the rats, it was almost a certainty that they had not been used in any other experiment and were, therefore, uncontaminated.

Kat actually wanted twenty-four rats, but she didn't think she dare take more than the twelve in the cage. She had noted that the cages were numbered from one through twelve, with the one in her hand being number twelve. She attached no significance to that fact. She put her hand on the handle of the wire cage and hefted it for weight. It wasn't that heavy, and she thought she could probably carry another, giving her the twenty-four rats she needed: twelve for injection and twelve for control. But it was best not to risk too much. These first twelve would serve her purposes for the time being, and she could still use the few rats she had left over as controls if she had to.

She looked around, and summoning up her courage, she lifted the cage off the one below and turned and went quickly across the room and out the door. As she turned to start back toward her own lab, she saw a young woman in a white lab coat hurrying toward her.

She instantly felt guilty, caught. She would have put the cage behind her, but it was about three feet square and almost two feet high. As the girl neared Kat could see that she was a rather dumpy article, in her mid-twenties. She was wearing glasses that gave her face an anxious, pinched look.

She hurried up to Kat, looking first at the cage. "Are those Dr. Ramsey's rats?"

Kat tried to put the best face on it she could. She had no intention of being intimidated by someone so young she still had traces of acne. "Well, yes. I ran short, you see, and I was in the midst of a very important test. Dr. Ramsey's was the only door open, so I thought I'd just borrow a few of his extra rats."

"I don't think Dr. Ramsey would want you to do that. Do you have his permission?"

Kat didn't want to lie to the girl, but she also hated to admit that she had carelessly let her own supply of rats run short. "I'm Dr. Kaitlyn . . ." she trailed off, unwilling to say her last name. She made a vague gesture down the hall. "My lab is just around the corner. Believe me, it will be all right. I simply didn't expect to be working today, and we didn't get my consignment of lab animals yesterday."

"I don't know . . . Dr. Ramsey . . . Dr. Ramsey can get awfully angry sometimes."

She was aware that the young lab assistant's eyes had strayed from her face to the name tag on the front of her lab coat. Her hand started up instinctively to cover it, and then she dropped it defiantly. She thought, *The hell with it. I'm not afraid of Burton Ramsey.* She said, "Look, miss, what's your name? You're Dr. Ramsey's lab assistant?"

"Yes, ma'am. I'm Dottie."

I'll just bet you are, Kat thought, *by the look of you.* "Look, Dottie, there is nothing to worry about. Dr. Ramsey will never even know the rats have been taken. I'll get a consignment Monday morning and my lab assistant will return his cage with new rats of the same strain first thing." She lowered her voice and said, "I'll bet Dr. Ramsey is not the kind who's the first one in, is he?"

Dottie softened a little, shaking her head. "Well, no. In fact, he won't even be in on Monday. But you understand,

Doctor, it'll be my tail if he finds out about this without you telling him."

Kat smiled. "Well, we wouldn't want anything like that to happen, now, would we?"

The girl made a tittering sound, but she said, as if on a sudden thought, "You didn't get any test animals, did you?"

"Of course not!" Kat exclaimed with conviction. "I know old Burton's work like my own." She lifted the cage as if to demonstrate. "This is brand-new stock. Untouched."

Dottie sighed. "Well, I hope you can tell. He never tells me, and he doesn't mark them. He's got his own system, which he hasn't shared with me."

"I know it like my own. Have no fear, Dottie. I wouldn't get you in any trouble with my old friend."

"Oh . . ." Dottie peered at her through her myopic lenses. "I don't recall seeing you around the lab."

"I'm in and out . . . In and out. But Burton and I usually talk away from here." She put her finger to her lips. "Can't be too careful."

She walked away from the girl with absolutely no feelings of shame whatsoever about her lies. She did, however, feel a slight pride in her acting ability. Who knew she could wing it like that?

Old Ramsey would never miss his rats, and, of course, hers was the greater need. She was working on a miracle serum. She doubted if Ramsey was working on anything nearly as important as her NeurActivase.

As she entered her lab with the cage of purloined rats, she said, aloud, "After all, I'm the one person in the world who can make the smartest rats who ever lived . . . even if they only live a few days!"

Before what she thought of as her crash, she had been known as a woman of an exquisitely dry sense of humor and a fairly cheerful person overall.

But all that was in the past. That was before, when she

had had brilliance and talent and confidence. You couldn't be witty and dryly humorous when you were so damn depressed you thought of every day as a mountain that had to be climbed without knowing why.

She put on a lab glove, opened the door of an empty cage, and methodically transferred six of the rats she'd gotten from Ramsey inside to comprise a control group. Then she shut the door and carried the cage with the remaining half-dozen rats over to her lab workbench. Without looking, she reached out and selected a bottle of color and began daubing the fur of her test rats. It was a blue dye, but she really didn't care. Failure came in all colors.

After that, Kat opened the refrigerator door and took out the bottle of fresh serum she'd concocted Friday night. It was basically the same as all the others and would undoubtedly give the same unsuccessful results, so she decided to double the amount of DHEA, using four milliliters instead of two. While she laid out six thirty-two-gauge disposable syringes, she put the vial of serum into a vibrator to make sure it was thoroughly mixed. Then, quickly and deftly, she inoculated the rats one after another.

When the last was done, she shut the cage door and began making notations in her code of just what she'd done. It would go on the cage and then later be transferred to her computer. For all that it mattered, she thought sadly. She wondered when the progress committee was going to demand that she show some results or move on. That would be a fine rejection—being let out of a penny-ante researcher's job in disgrace just like when she'd been discharged from the navy for not being able to do her job as a neurosurgeon.

The rebirth of her hope began Sunday evening, when Kat wandered back to the lab for lack of something better to do. Just out of curiosity, she decided to run the Ramsey group of test rats through the maze. She was surprised to see that they averaged test times almost 10 percent better than the control animals, which was excellent for five-year-old rats. But she knew that they'd just been inoculated with NeurActivase for something like thirty hours and that very soon the cellular decay would begin and the rats would grow less and less intelligent.

On Monday, she ignored the rats and just sat and reread her notes, trying once again to see where she had gone wrong. The next day, sometime Tuesday afternoon, she ran three of the rats through the maze and found that their times had been reduced by almost a minute. That surprised her, since the interval since the injection was now over seventy-two hours, a time frame that should have allowed the deterioration of the neural cells to begin to affect the rats' times.

She forced herself to remain calm, not to get her hopes too high as she had once before, only to have them dashed. She even refused herself the pleasure of making notes and keeping data on the rats' progress. She just kept telling himself, over and over, that this was nothing new. Most likely the expected neural degeneration simply was delayed because of the age of the rats, although that didn't make much sense. The older rats should have been affected earlier, not later, by the neural degeneration.

She was at the lab by dawn on Wednesday morning. In spite of the warnings she kept giving herself to remain calm, she was so nervous that she could barely handle the rats without dropping them. Finally, with a wildly beating heart, she tested one of "Ramsey's rats," as she had begun to call them to herself. The rat sped through the maze in three minutes and fifty-eight seconds, almost 50 percent faster than the control animals.

She slowly picked up the rat, returned it to the cage, and selected another for a trial run. The results of that one and the remaining four were all similar.

Trying to keep her mind from racing, she went into her office and sat down. Little by little she began to analyze what she knew. A little better than four days had passed since the rats had been injected. They were not getting less intelligent; they were getting smarter, if time through the maze was a product of intelligence. In all of her other experiments, intelligence deterioration had been well advanced by the fourth day. Something was different this time. She tried to quell her excitement, to think in patterned squares of analytical calmness.

There were only two variables from her previous experiments. One, the rats were two years older than any other test animals she'd used, and two, she'd dramatically increased the amount of DHEA she'd used because the hormone precursor was known to markedly increase the amount of testosterone in the bloodstream.

She couldn't believe the advanced age of the rats would have had a favorable effect. In fact, the opposite should have been true. And she was hard-pressed to believe that increased DHEA could have brought about such a miraculous change, since it hadn't worked with her previous injected rats, which had all died. But in the light of all the evidence, she had to believe it was the higher dose of the DHEA that had made the difference. She could think of nothing else that had changed.

Suddenly, she got up from her desk and walked over to the rat cage. She studied the rats inside for a moment. She shook her head. They certainly didn't look like five-year-old rats . . . in fact, they looked like much younger rats, at least as young as her own rats were. And they not only looked younger, they were acting younger, too—playfully running around the cage and mating as if they had all the energy in the world.

CHAPTER 6

A pounding, driving headache pulled Burton Ramsey from the depths of slumber. He came reluctantly awake and ran a dry tongue over gritty teeth. As he smacked his lips, he thought, *Jesus, my mouth tastes like something crawled in it and died.* He brought his arm up before his face and squinted, trying to read the dial of his Timex. Wednesday, 9:45 a.m.

He placed his fingertips to his temple and rubbed, trying to ease the knife-like pain in his skull, and rolled over, falling heavily to the floor off the sofa in his living room. Confused, he wondered briefly what he was doing fully dressed and sleeping on his sofa instead of in his bed in the next room.

Memory came slowly, in bits and pieces. Tuesday night he had gone to Bennigan's restaurant on the Southwest Freeway for supper. After eating a chili burger and fries, he had retired to the bar. A group of secretaries, taking advantage of the happy hour special—two-for-one drinks—had invited him to join them. Once he'd concluded that none of them had much more than a high school education, he joined them and drank until well past midnight, bored by hours of meaningless conversation. He despised yuppie, professional women, believing them to be uppity, ball-busting harridans.

Being drunk, but not stupid, he had driven very carefully to his apartment, navigating the evening Houston traffic with as much care as his besotted brain would allow. One more DWI and his license would be history.

He shook his head, figuring his sofa was as far as he'd been able to make it before he passed out with all of his clothes still on.

With trembling hands, he put a K-Cup of French Roast Bold coffee into his Keurig coffee machine, thanking God he'd splurged and bought the damn thing, 'cause he knew in his present state he'd never have been able to make a drinkable brew in his old Mr. Coffee machine. He prayed caffeine would clear his mind and stop the damn pounding in his head.

When the contraption finally hissed and spurted, signaling it was finished filling his cup, he picked up his coffee and downed a handful of Excedrin with his first swallow, hoping they would stay down until the coffee dissolved them.

Three K-Cups later, he thought he might survive his night of frivolity. He threw off all of his clothes into a pile and stumbled into his bathroom to take a shower and brush the vile tastes out of his mouth, feeling almost, but not quite, human again.

It was almost noon on Wednesday before Ramsey pulled into his parking space in the lot behind the Institute. He was hungover and in a foul mood, which was his usual demeanor until his first drink in the afternoon.

He had no more than turned off his ignition key, when one glance at the white sign that designated the space as his parking slot sent him off into a fusillade of cursing. The sign said simply, DR. BURTON RAMSEY. But the sight of it caused him to cry out loud, "That dumb son of a bitch! How many times do I have to tell the cretinous bastard that I am a Ph.D.

and not some M-fucking-D doctor! I'm a scientist, not some overpaid prescription peddler!" He was referring to the assistant director who was in charge of housekeeping.

On several occasions, Burton Ramsey had made it quite clear to the man that he wanted any written material that was either directed to him or about him to bear the legend, BURTON RAMSEY, PH.D., and he was not under any circumstances to be referred to either vocally or in writing as "Doctor" or "Dr."

The assistant director had promised him faithfully that he would have the sign changed. But he had been promising that for the better than four years Ramsey had been at BioTech. Ramsey would have torn the sign down long ago, but it was set in concrete. Besides, he intended on seeing the little worm of an administrator do it himself.

It was well known to anyone who knew Burton Ramsey that he did not like MDs, and that included that part of his estranged wife from whom he was technically separated. He would never tell anyone why he felt that way or how he proposed to support the hypothesis that MDs were a hindrance rather than a help to medicine. His standard answer to any such question was, "It's none of your business. Understand?"

Most people seldom bothered to ask, and those who actually knew him hoped the subject never came up in their presence.

He got out of the car and slammed the door. It was late May, and the air was warm and muggy, typical spring weather in Houston. Ramsey liked to say that Houston had only two seasons: summer and almost summer. Today, Ramsey had on a light-colored linen sports coat that was rumpled and slightly stained. His dark slacks were neat and pressed, because the last time he'd visited his wife she'd done his laundry for him, insisting on ironing his pants and several of his dress shirts.

Today he was wearing the slacks and one of the clean

shirts, though, of course, he wouldn't wear a tie. He also refused to put on any socks, claiming his scuffed loafers felt more comfortable to his bare feet. He also secretly enjoyed the looks of dismay his attire engendered in the scrubbed, polished, and pressed yuppies he passed in the halls of the lab.

He gave the sign a malicious look as he passed it, but he didn't aim a kick at it. That was a losing proposition, even when he didn't have a hangover—and on this morning, he had one of epic proportions. He'd tried to show the secretaries at Bennigan's he could outdrink them, an obviously losing proposition as he'd gotten drunker than a skunk.

After his shower this morning, he'd gone to his tried-and-true hangover remedy of three fingers of vodka, four more Excedrin, half a glass of orange juice, and one raw egg, blended well and drunk straight down. After that, he had found a steak in his freezer, defrosted it in the microwave—a dehumanizing piece of technology that he would ordinarily never use to cook food for himself—and then broiled it in the oven along with some onion and tomato slices. He ate the lot, along with four more eggs and a glass of eggnog sweetened with twelve-year-old scotch.

While he was eating, his thoughts strayed. He reflected that his estranged wife, Sheila, was a good woman even if she was an MD, and an endocrinologist at that. She wasn't perfect, but then God had not chosen to create such a thing as a perfect woman. If Sheila had been perfect, she'd have renounced the prescription pad and been content to work the rest of her life as his lab assistant.

She was one of the few who knew why he hated MDs. And though she found his reasoning a trifle excessive, she'd accepted it, just as she'd accepted many of his ways because she loved him. She'd once told him that, even though they were separated, she had no fear of losing him. "Any other woman except me would very quickly cut your throat after you fell asleep. God knows I've been tempted plenty of times."

He went through the staff entrance to the lab and strolled down the hall, making it a point to nod or speak to only the service employees of the laboratory, then he pushed open the door to his own space. As he walked in, he could see that his assistant, Dottie, was busy at the sink washing something. It was a good sight. He had little enough to keep the girl busy; he never entrusted her with any of the more secretive details of his work, even though she was working on her master's in biology at the University of Houston.

He actually didn't need an assistant, but she was handy in her own way. Basically, he delighted in forcing through raises for her every six months or so. By the hour, she was probably making more money than he was. It gave him a perverse sort of pleasure to screw the medical establishment and run the lab in any way he could.

He suddenly sensed that something was amiss. He looked straight toward the cages of rats and saw that one was missing. "Dottie, where in the hell is cage twelve?" he growled.

She was slow in turning her head. "Sir?"

His voice rose. "*Sir*, my fat ass! Where in the hell is that lot twelve, you ninny? That lot I finished with before I left."

Dottie's eyes rolled wildly in their sockets, looking anywhere but at Ramsey.

"Damn it, look at me! Where is cage twelve?"

"Uh . . . a friend of yours borrowed it, sir."

Ramsey's eyes narrowed. He knew that was a damn lie. He didn't have any friends.

He took a deep breath when he saw tears start to form in Dottie's eyes. Best to go easy on the lass, he thought, or she'll have a stroke.

"That's okay, Dottie," he said, forcing his features into the semblance of a smile.

He took a seat at his desk and opened the drawer to pull

out a bottle of Chivas Regal, figuring he was going to need it before he got to the bottom of this.

He poured two fingers into his coffee cup, took a deep draught, and then he asked, in as reasonable of a voice as he could manage, "Now, why don't you tell me all about what happened to my rats?"

CHAPTER 7

Burton Ramsey only knew two things about Dr. Kaitlyn Williams. The first was that she'd done her residency in neurosurgery, and then, for some inexplicable reason, had opted to give it all up and slog away in laboratory research. He knew not the whys or wherefores, only having picked up as much as he had from overheard conversations in the cafeteria and the administration offices. The second thing he knew was that Williams was a moderately attractive female, even if she was an MD. The net result of his knowledge was enough to cause Ramsey to feel a mild contempt for Williams's supposed choice of research over doing good as a doctor—and a monumental sense of jealousy that the woman had attained the station of not only an MD but became a neurosurgeon.

As he walked down the hall toward Williams's office, he was doing his best to work up a good sense of anger, but it just wouldn't come. He was too pleased. He had an MD, albeit a fairly innocuous MD as MDs went, in his sights. She was caught dead to rights, and he intended to enjoy every moment of it. Williams only thought she had been kidded before!

He opened the door to Williams's laboratory, not bothering with the formality of knocking. As he entered, he immediately saw that Williams was at the far end of the lab, at a workbench bending over a microscope. A young man in a lab coat was at the rat cages. He turned immediately as Ramsey entered, his eyes moving up and down and focusing for a moment on Ramsey's sockless shoes.

The young assistant's eyebrows knit together in an unconscious frown. "Can I help you, sir?"

Ramsey ignored him and kept walking toward Williams. "Hey, Doc!" Ramsey said loudly.

Kat turned her head slowly, looking annoyed about being interrupted, as if she couldn't imagine anyone coming into her laboratory uninvited. Then she saw that it was Ramsey and her heart sank. She stood up and turned to face the scientist, her face burning.

Kat wanted to flinch back, but she forced herself to look past Ramsey. "Kevin, would you be so kind as to take Angus for a walk in the park?"

Kevin looked from her to Ramsey, his eyebrows raised. "Are you sure, Dr. Williams?" he asked, a frown on his face. He didn't trust this guy to be alone with Kat, especially not with the wild look the man had in his eyes. In fact, Kevin thought he ought to just kick his ass.

"Yes, please, Kevin. Dr. Ramsey and I have something to discuss that is better left just between us."

Kevin just shook his head as he went to pick up Angus and carry him out the door of the lab. He'd be damned if he'd ever understand women.

Ramsey couldn't believe the doctor was being so pleasant to her assistant. You'd never catch him saying "please" to anyone who worked for him.

"Doc," he said in an avuncular tone, "down in Texas, where I come from, we call it 'rustling' when some other cowpoke makes off with our livestock." He put his hands on his hips. "Now, I don't know what y'all call it up there in

Yankee-land where you trained, but I'll bet Captain Sunshine won't take kindly to the rats BioTech paid for being shuffled all over the goddamn building."

Kat's face flamed red again and she had just the slightest quiver in her voice. "I didn't 'steal' your rats. I merely 'borrowed' them. For some reason, my consignment was held up last week, and I didn't discover it until the weekend, when it was too late to order any more. I've been intending to send my assistant down to your lab with a dozen rats for the last couple of days. It's just that I've been so—"

Ramsey grinned at Williams's obvious discomfort, then interrupted. "Listen, *Doctor,* I don't want your rats. I want the rats you took from *my* laboratory." He looked over his shoulder to see whether anyone else was listening. "Truth of the matter is that those were my test animals, and I'm close to the end of my project. I wouldn't want anything to happen to those particular rats."

Kat licked her lips with a quick flick of her tongue. She was starting to sweat, to feel faint, and to feel real fear for the first time in her life. The implications of what Ramsey had just said hadn't quite sunk in yet, but she knew she could not give six of the rats back to Ramsey, the six that she'd injected with her serum. They had become the most precious possessions in her life.

Now she cursed herself for being so forgetful and excited and involved in her project that she'd forgotten to have Kevin get twelve other rats and put them in Ramsey's cage and have them returned to Ramsey's lab. If she had, then perhaps none of this would be happening. But one thing was for sure, she was not going to give those rats back to Ramsey or anyone else. Not for anything.

She thought furiously and suddenly the lie came easily. "I can't give you your rats back. They . . . they died."

"What?" Ramsey said incredulously. "What do you mean, they died?"

Kat blinked rapidly. "My lab assistant made a mistake.

He got a step out of phase in an experiment I've been working on. That's why I sent him away just now. . . . I didn't want him to be embarrassed."

Ramsey looked at her in amazement. "Well, I always said MDs were lousy researchers, but I had no idea you couldn't even keep your rats alive." He shook his head, "Of course, on the other hand, better you should kill rats than people."

He looked over at Williams with eyebrows arched and lips curled into a sneer. "That have anything to do with why you gave up neurosurgery?"

Kat had backed up against her workbench. Her mind was racing, and she barely heard what Ramsey was saying as she tried to figure some way out of the mess she had gotten herself into. She straightened up and started to move away from the workbench. "Look, Ramsey, I was wrong to take your rats. I'm sorry. I apologize . . ." Suddenly she remembered what Ramsey had said about the rats being test animals. Her head began whirling with this news from Ramsey—that the rats she'd used had been injected with Ramsey's formula. Kat held up her hand. "Wait! Dr. Ramsey, wait a minute!"

Startled by Williams's sudden transformation, Ramsey stared back at her. "Wait for what, *Doctor*?"

"What were they injected with? Please!" She took two steps toward Ramsey, who was already moving toward the door.

Ramsey frowned at the question, then turned and pulled the door open as he started to leave. He looked back over his shoulder. "What were they injected with? Doc, stealing my rats is one thing, but don't even think about stealing my discovery. What were they injected with, indeed!" Then he passed out into the hall and shut the door behind him.

In the lab, Kat was staring after him, her mind racing, trying to comprehend all of the possibilities of what she had just learned. Though she had consistently displayed a lack of interest in anything to do with her colleagues at the lab, she couldn't help but know that Burton Ramsey, in spite of his personality, his lackadaisical ways, and his too-casual attire, was one of the most respected researchers in the field of blood chemistry in the country.

In fact, it was only because of that very talent and brilliance that Burton Ramsey was able to keep on working at leading laboratories in spite of the fact that the administrators, especially the medical administrators, hated the image he portrayed.

The knowledge made Dr. Kaitlyn Williams almost insane to know what Ramsey had injected the rats with. Because, whatever it was, it was most certainly going to change Kat's life, and it might just change the lives of a great many other people, as well. She was going to have to somehow discover what Ramsey was working on, though she had no doubt that it might be so difficult as to be almost impossible. Researchers were more likely to give away their firstborn children than to give up the secrets of their research.

For his part, Dr. Burton Ramsey was well pleased with his morning's work. He was still whistling cheerfully as he turned into his lab. Dottie looked up from cleaning out a cage. There was a touch of fear in her eyes. Dr. Ramsey might seem happy, but that could change with just one wrong word. "Is everything all right, Dr. Ramsey?"

Burton Ramsey went to his workbench and perched on a stool. "Couldn't be better, Dottie, my girl. Been enjoying my favorite recreation, stomping a worm."

"Dr. Williams?"

"Seen any other worms around here, girl?"

"Is she going to return your rats?"

Ramsey picked up a piece of paper and looked at it. "Woman says they died. In her care, I wouldn't be surprised. She could kill an acre of green onions just with her delicate perfume." He suddenly laughed. "Dottie, I was very mean to Dr. Williams. Of course, Dr. Williams most assuredly deserved it."

"I take it those were new animals and that it didn't matter that she took them."

He looked at her and shook his head. "No, they were test animals. A late experiment."

She had a little hurt in her voice. "Well, Dr. Ramsey, if you'd ever tell me your system, I would know control from test animals and I could have stopped her."

Ramsey yawned. "Doesn't matter anymore, Dottie. Go down and get yourself a cup of coffee and bring me back a glass of ice water." He shook his head and grinned at himself when he had to stop himself from adding "please." Too much time around that damn Dr. Williams, he guessed.

He reached down, opened the drawer, and took out his bottle of Chivas Regal. "I think I've earned a little drink. I tell you, Dottie, this business of bearding rich females in their own dens is dangerous. Frightening. Scary. What that woman has could be infectious, and don't you forget it. Don't ever let her cough on you, Dottie. God knows what you'd catch."

She blushed. "Do you want anything else from the cafeteria, Dr. Ramsey?" She eyed the bottle of scotch, "Something to eat, maybe?"

He shook his head. "No, just something to dilute this vile whiskey with. Wouldn't want it to get around that I was a hard drinker. Soon as you do that, Dottie, you can take the rest of the day off."

She looked disappointed. When Dr. Ramsey was in a good mood, he could be a great deal of fun to be around, though she didn't understand half of his brand of humor. "Don't you have some notes you want programmed into the computer?"

"No, not today. I've got a hangover that is demanding most of my attention, so you won't be allowed to play with your electronic brain today." He said the last dryly, because he not only did not know how to operate a computer, he resolutely refused to have anything to do with what he called "man's last friend."

As a result, Dottie did all his computer work, which, basically, was about all the work he had for her to do. She programmed from notes that he gave her, about three-fourths of which were either bogus or misleading.

Burton Ramsey had always been known as a daring and innovative researcher, but he had surprised even himself with the breakthroughs he had made in his own private research. He already held several minor patents in blood chemistry procedures and formulations, and his present work would neatly dovetail into that, allowing him to claim that his discovery of the antiaging serum was simply the result of old work completed before his arrival at BioTech and, therefore, belonged to him alone.

So he let Dottie feed her "electronic toy" useless information so the progress committee could access it and act like they knew what they were seeing. His data sounded good and looked good, and it might even improve dialysis machines and allow patients to go longer between treatments, but he intended to put dialysis machines out of business. The only question in his mind was who was going to pay him a hell of a lot of money for what he knew.

His contract with the lab was up in one month, and he'd already notified the directors that he had no intentions of renewing. He'd talked mysteriously of doing some humanitarian work in Mexico or maybe taking off a few years and sailing around the world. He said he was tired of seeing his genius go unrewarded by an ungrateful populace. He tried not to smile when he said such things.

Dottie brought him his ice water, and he drank off half and then refilled the glass with the twelve-year-old scotch.

"Well, if those rats were test animals, aren't you very upset with Dr. Williams?"

He took a sip of his scotch and looked gravely at the girl.

"Dottie, I'll let you be the judge. Should I call her out on the matter? Call her out and shoot her down like the dirty dog she is?"

Dottie was never quite sure when he was kidding and when he wasn't. She thought that Dr. Burton Ramsey was easily the strangest man she'd ever met. She'd been astounded to find out he didn't like computers. She couldn't imagine anyone in this day and age who not only didn't appreciate computers, but who thought them absolutely unnecessary.

When she'd asked him why he hated computers, he'd said, "Because they have no soul, Dottie, no soul. They are not man's servant; they are his crutch for the real computer that God gave him." He'd tapped his head. "Think about that . . . in fact, think about anything—just think. You'll be amazed at the results."

He wasn't really upset about the test animals Williams had taken, because their injection had been redundant. His final breakthrough, a way to bind his formula to the blood's normal proteins so that it worked indefinitely and never needed to be reinjected, had come some months previously.

Since then, he'd merely been marking time while waiting for his contract to run out. He'd used the time to establish ties with Dr. Garza in Monterrey, where he planned to claim a great deal of his earlier work had been done, under the protection of the less-stringent Mexican patent laws.

As any tenth-grade science student knew, the blood system was the garbage collector of the body. All of the body's cells gave off waste products as natural by-products of their functioning. These by-products were toxins, and most scientists believed that it was a buildup of these toxins over time that caused the body to age. It had been theorized that if these toxins could be eliminated, it would drastically slow down the aging process. But, as it happened, the bloodstream was a great garbage collector, but it was less adept at destroying the toxins it had collected. That was the function of the kidneys, which were not 100 percent efficient at their best and they tended to get less efficient with age.

Over time, the small percentage of toxins not destroyed by the kidneys were deposited in other areas of the body, causing the debilitating effects known as aging. Basically that was the purpose of a dialysis machine, to assist or replace the kidneys by filtering out the toxins and waste from the bloodstream. Unfortunately, the effect was only temporary and the toxins built back up almost as quickly as they were removed.

That was what made Dr. Burton Ramsey's discovery so valuable. It went to work instantly and kept on working. Furthermore, it worked directly in the bloodstream and was independent of the functioning of the kidneys. His research had astounded even him, and he was a hard man to astound. He was certain that he was seeing signs in some of his research animals that his serum was not only stopping but actually reversing the aging process.

He wished he had the time and the inclination to pursue the matter through the years of research it would entail to try to get the serum to work on the brain, but he knew he couldn't hide the basic discovery that long. What he had right in his own private packet of notes was going to make him rich, and that was good enough for him.

The progress committee could look at his computer data all they wanted to. The real stuff was in a blue spiral notebook that was starting to get a little frayed and dog-eared from constant use. Well, someday he'd have it bound in gold.

Dottie didn't want to go, but he finally insisted she leave. He'd told her to go out and get laid, that watching rats all day was a poor way for an attractive girl to spend her days.

She'd said, with a sigh, "I guess I could go home and study. I can always study."

"Hell of an attitude. I used to have that very same attitude."

"What happened to it?"

He drained the last of the scotch out of his glass. "I left school and entered the real world. In the real world, you don't dare duck your head long enough to study. Some son of a bitch will stab you in the back." He got up off the stool and ran a little water over the ice remaining in his glass before sweetening it with more scotch.

Dottie hung up her smock. "Well, if there's nothing else?"

He shook his head. "Take off."

An hour later, he was still sitting on the workbench stool drinking scotch. It was always a source of amazement to him that Dottie had never figured out his system for separating his test animals from his control rats. And she'd seen him at work thousands of times and never made the connection. The control animals went in the odd-numbered cages, the test rats in the even ones. That, he thought, was what came of depending on computers. You quit observing; you quit thinking.

He heard the crowd in the hall hurrying to the cafeteria for lunch. He decided he wasn't hungry, but if he thought there was a chance to blow some more smoke in Dr. Williams's face, he could be induced to put in an appearance.

He had another drink of scotch and was just thinking of leaving when there came a knock on his door. "Come in." He was proud that he slurred his words only a little.

Most likely it was some flitter tit from administration down to take his pulse. He knew it wasn't a friend because he didn't have any, and Sheila never knocked so it wasn't her. The door didn't move, so he called louder, "Come in, goddamnit, if you're going to."

The door opened and Kaitlyn Williams stood there, wringing her hands.

Ramsey just stared, dumbfounded. He cocked his head

and shook it as if to clear his vision, then looked into his glass as if the answer might lie there.

Kat cleared her throat. "I want to see you, Dr. Ramsey."

Ramsey was almost genial. "Have you come to apologize for murdering my rats, *Doctor*?" He took another drink of his scotch. "If you have, you're wasting your time. I really wasn't emotionally attached to the little bastards—it just pissed me off that you took them without bothering to ask my permission first."

Kat held up her hand. "Look, Burton, I honestly meant to replace the rats, and I had no way of knowing they were experimental rats. Dottie and I thought they were control animals."

Ramsey leaned forward and stared. "Surely you jest. The point is, you took them without permission, not that they were experimental animals. Why didn't you just ask me if you needed them so bad?"

Kat entered the room as if she were walking on eggshells. "Because it was the weekend and you were out of town. I didn't want to have to put off my experiment for two days until you got back."

Ramsey looked at his freshly empty glass, and mumbled, "Yeah, I was out of town, all right." Then he looked up at Williams with a sly look in his eye. "But what was so all-fired important about your experiment that it couldn't wait a couple of days? You on to something big, Williams?"

"How about you call me Kat and I'll call you Burton, since we're neighbors?"

Ramsey snarled. "Fine, Kat, but you didn't answer my question. You on to something so big it couldn't wait a couple of days to continue?"

Kat didn't move, and, in fact, she looked something like a deer caught in the headlights. "No, nothing . . . nothing particularly important. I was just . . . just impatient to get started on a new formula and didn't want to waste the weekend." She began to pace around the lab, running her hands through her hair, thinking about how to proceed. Finally, "But I have to talk to you. It's imperative. Both for me and for you. We have to talk."

"Talk!" Ramsey did a burlesque of a shocked double take. "Talk? You and me? Well, Doctor Kat, I think you are under some delusion." He looked up at Williams from under hooded eyes. "I asked you a simple question about your work, and you gave me some bullshit about 'being impatient' to get to work. I don't believe you for a minute. I think you think you're on to something big and you're afraid I might find out about it and steal your stuff."

Ramsey got clumsily off his stool and rummaged in his desk drawer, looking for another bottle of Chivas. "Ha," he whispered, more to himself than to Williams. "I've got something worth more than you ever dreamed about, and I don't need your piddly little discovery, no matter what it is."

Kat was desperate. "Dr. Ramsey, please listen to me. We have to talk as one scientist to ano—"

"Who's the other one?"

"What?"

"The other scientist? You said we had to talk as one scientist to another. I'm one, who's the other? All I see in here is a misplaced doctor trying to do research and screwing it up royally."

Kat ignored his hostile tone and tried to reason with him. "Would you please listen to me? Somehow, some way, there is a chance that your . . . your work may have . . . have coincided with and caused a synergistic effect with mine. It's extremely unlikely, but there is a chance that our separate experiments may be dually enhancing . . . synergistic."

"I know what the word *synergistic* means, *Doctor*," Ramsey growled, and then he smiled happily, still feeling the scotch. "You want to know what I'm working on, is that it?"

"Yes. Yes, very much. Please, it could mean so much to both of us."

"Then why am *I* not down at *your* laboratory door, begging to know what *you* are working on?"

"Because the effects are showing up in the animals I borrowed from you. I have to know how much effect your experiment could be having on mine."

"I'm not experimenting anymore. I'm through, done, *finis*. That's why I'm sitting here drinking. I'm bored. I always drink when I'm bored. Which is probably the only reason I'm putting up with your presence."

Ramsey smiled, a smile devoid of any semblance of humor or friendliness. "It seems that at some point during my consumption of alcohol, I'd mark it right about the third or fourth drink, I experience a sensation that can only be described as nearly sufferable. I wouldn't call it genial, and certainly not friendly, but it's a window of a great deal more tolerance than I ordinarily display. However, I must warn you, Dr. Williams, it's a fairly small window, an envelope of very limited duration. It usually lasts only about a half an hour, an hour at the most. After that, no matter whether I keep on drinking or stop entirely, I revert to type. I can't tell you how near the edge of the envelope I am, but I would urge you, as one contract researcher for BioTech to another, that being the only common ground I can find between us, to hasten your say and hasten your departure even more."

Kaitlyn Williams was almost trembling in her desperation. She'd never met anyone like Ramsey before, and she didn't have the slightest idea how to appeal to someone who seemed motivated by concerns Kat had never encountered. She was further encumbered by her inexperience in being the supplicant in a situation. In fact, she couldn't recall the last time she'd been put in the position of having to ask something of another human being, colleague or not. "Oh, this is impossible! I don't even know whether you're drunk or not. How can I make you understand how important this is? Can't you put aside your childish prejudice against me for five minutes?"

"Sounds to me, Doc, like this is only important to you."

"To both of us. If you'll only give me some indication of what you're working on. I'm not asking for full details."

Ramsey grinned foolishly. "Sounds like a little boy and a little girl. You show me yours, and I'll show you mine." He suddenly yawned and relaxed back against his workbench. "Clock's running, Doc. I can almost feel the shade being drawn across the window, the envelope being sealed. The monster wants out."

Kat raised both fists in the air in frustration. Her voice strangled in her effort to get the words out. "You cannot possibly understand the importance of this conversation! Just tell me plainly and simply what it will take to compel you to give me some indication, some scientific indication, of what you injected those test animals with."

"You mean the ones you stole from my lab?"

"Yes, yes, yes. Whatever you say, man. Just give me a clue!"

Ramsey lifted his glass thoughtfully and sucked out an ice cube to chew on. He sat for a minute, considering. "Well, maybe it wouldn't hurt to tell you this. As you know, I'm a biochemist, but my specialty has always been the blood. I injected those rats with something that had to do with blood." He smiled broadly. "There! Now are you happy?"

"Oh, goddamn." Kat was almost ready to weep, but she refused to give this bastard the satisfaction. "How did you get to be a research scientist? You're a madman, a lunatic!"

Ramsey whistled. "Boy, I don't know a lot about these matters, but my guess is that's a mighty poor way to ask me for something."

"Then, what? What?"

Ramsey thought for a moment. Actually he was beginning to tire of the game—and of Kaitlyn Williams. What Williams didn't seem to be able to grasp was that he, Ramsey, was finished with the actual research aspect of his project. All that was standing between him and a million dollars was some shady work with mirrors and smoke. Williams was making the mistake of thinking that he could possibly be interested in anything Williams had to say or to propose. He was already looking forward to the evening and night with Sheila, and he'd have been out of the laboratory and gone if this intruder had not thrust herself forward. But a thought came to him. Maybe there was a little more fun to be had from the game. "Maybe there is something you can offer, Williams. Maybe I'll cooperate if you'll do it."

Kat was almost pathetic in her eagerness. "Name it!"

Ramsey opened another drawer and finally found a bottle with about two fingers of scotch left in it. He held the bottle up, frowning at the label. "Huh. J and B. Well, any port in a storm." Before he said anything else, he took the time to mix himself another drink, and then held the almost-empty bottle up to Williams as if offering to share.

Kat was disgusted. "You're not going to drink even more?"

Ramsey gave her a look, then poured the remaining drops of scotch into his glass. "Look here . . . you don't seem to understand. This is my playground. If you don't want to play, you don't have to. You can always go home."

Kat was despairing. She swallowed. This visit, this torture, was the worst experience she could remember. But she swallowed her pride. "You wanted something. What is it?"

Ramsey took a sip of scotch and mumbled as he stared into the glass. "I want to know how you blew it as a neurosurgeon. I want the whole story, with all the bells and whistles. Nobody around here seems to know. I want to be the one person who does."

He took another drink of scotch and smiled at Kat. "Tell me of your shame, rich girl. Tell me of your downfall. I'm sure it must be juicy."

Kat stared at him. A line of sweat had suddenly formed on her upper lip. She could feel herself going white. "You're not serious."

Ramsey scowled, his face going hard, "I'm as serious as the bologna sandwiches I ate for three years in graduate school. Exclusively. That's my price. Take it or leave it."

Kat pursed her lips, thinking. *Oh well, what the hell?* she thought.

"And if I tell you my story, you will tell me what was in your formula?" she asked.

He shrugged. "Maybe."

"Maybe?" she exclaimed.

He grinned maliciously. "'Maybe' is all you're gonna get, girl. So either take it or leave it. I'm getting tired of all this palaver."

CHAPTER 8

For a long couple of moments, Kat didn't think she could bring herself to tell this doltish oaf anything personal about herself, especially about the gaping wound inside that could still sear and pain and throb and hurt her afresh when it stole into her mind unexpectedly.

But what was happening back in her lab was so important, so far beyond anything she could have imagined, that she couldn't see how she could keep from paying any price that this obviously unbalanced maniac wanted her to pay in order to get the information she needed. Under the lens of her one-hundred-power Zeiss microscope, she had seen a miracle. It could be described in no other way. It made her earlier success seem insignificant and puny by comparison.

Anyway, what did it really matter what she told Ramsey? Probably half the people working at the BioTech laboratory already knew. In fact, Ramsey himself probably already knew and was just interested in having the devious pleasure of hearing the story from her own lips. The scientific and medical communities were relatively small ones, and juicy bits of gossip like her failure in the operating theater would spread from hospital to hospital with the speed of light, especially given the prominence of her family in that community. There were always those who took malicious delight in seeing the mighty pulled low.

"Clock is really spinning, Doc. I can feel myself beginning to fade away. The monster is on his way. I can feel him welling up within my chest. Strangely enough, he looks like Spencer Tracy."

Kat gritted her teeth, thinking of it as one more sacrifice she had to make to obtain the secret. She told her story in a detached way, almost as if she was talking about a friend or colleague. "In my last year of neurosurgery residency, during the Iraq and Afghanistan wars, I entered an exchange program at Walter Reed Hospital to gain experience dealing with traumatic spinal injuries. Unfortunately, there were plenty of them to be had because of the ongoing offensive in the Middle East."

She paused and walked over to sit in front of the window and stared out, not noticing the sweat that had broken out on her face with the strain of remembering. "For nine weeks, I operated day and night, patching together spines that had been torn apart and shattered, trying to splice torn nerves to limbs that would never work again no matter how well I sutured them, trying to cure traumatic brain injuries and then having to face boys who were years younger than me and tell them that their lives as they knew them were over."

She wiped unconsciously at the sweat dripping into her eyes. "They would never walk, run, or make love again. They would be forever prisoners in their beds or wheelchairs, wearing dignity-defeating diapers and catheters, depending on others for their care for the rest of their lives." She sighed deeply. "Or even worse, not even recognizing their loved ones because the neurons in their brains didn't connect to each other anymore."

She continued to stare out the window, unable to meet Ramsey's eyes. "After a couple hundred such operations, my repeated failures began to undermine my confidence in my ability to help anyone, not just the hopeless cases." She glanced down at her hands, and then she clenched them into fists. "My hands began to shake, not much, just a little. But when you're working in spaces defined by millimeters, with life on one side of the line and death on the other, even a little shakiness is too much. Finally, during a rather routine subdural hematoma evacuation, I knew I was more of a danger to the patient than a savior, so I asked my assistant to take over and I walked out of the operating room."

Kat looked over at Ramsey with tortured eyes. "I never operated again. I finished my residency doing postoperative care only and never picked up a scalpel again." She finished the story with her decision to leave the practice of medicine and enter the field of research, where she felt she could still serve without fear of doing harm to others. She thought she'd told her story elegantly and simply, not sparing herself the lash of failure but making it plain that, with all the talent she'd been given, had come a responsibility that she was too young and too callow to handle.

When she was finished, Ramsey stared at her for a second. Ramsey felt the stirrings of an unfamiliar feeling: shame. "What do you mean, your hands started shaking?"

"Exactly that," Kat said with as much dignity as she could manage after feeling like she had just figuratively stripped herself naked in front of Ramsey. "My hands shook, and I lost my nerve." She drew herself up. "I've seen it happen to others, but I never dreamed it would happen to me."

Ramsey shuddered, suddenly sober. He had rarely seen such pain and suffering in another human being, and the fact that he had forced Williams to undergo telling her story and reliving the pain as a joke made him feel very small.

He got up and went to the door, looking at the floor. "Please leave. I've heard enough."

Kat stared at him in amazement. She was continually dumbfounded by Burton Ramsey. She had to keep asking herself how such a hoodlum, bully, and social misfit could have achieved a Ph.D. and risen to a prominent position in such a demanding discipline. "You owe me the knowledge of what you injected those rats with, Burton. We had a deal, and even such a man as yourself must feel honor bound to live up to it."

Ramsey now was the one unable to meet Williams's eyes. He had no intention of giving her the secret of his research and he never had, but he had not expected to feel so bad about what he had made the doctor do. He needed time to think, and he needed to do it without Williams being present. "Okay, let me think about it. I'll get back to you tomorrow with my decision."

Kat started to speak, and then she just shook her head and walked out of the office, her back straight and her head held high.

Ramsey looked at his watch. It was a quarter 'til two, and if he was lucky, he just might catch Sheila at her office in the Methodist hospital before she started seeing patients after her lunch break. He knew he needed the lift that seeing her would give him. He quickly dialed the number and waited until she came on the phone. He loved her voice. It was always so warm and soft and controlled. It always made him feel like she was standing right next to him.

He said, "What time will you be heading home?"

"Well, if it's any of your business, somewhere around half past six. Dr. Slack has asked me to see one of his patients at six, but that shouldn't take long." Then her voice took on a guarded tone. "Why?"

"Well, I'm bored here and about ready to split. I thought I'd pick up some groceries and fix us a fabulous dinner."

There was a slight sound of dismay in her voice. She said, "Oh Burton, don't cook. Dear God, please don't cook."

"Sheila, I'm offended. If a goddamn biochemist can't cook, who can? I may have been a little overly ambitious in the past, but I've learned from that. I'm thinking of bouillabaisse. That's just a fish soup. I make marvelous soups in this lab every day and then stick 'em in rats."

She sounded desperate. "Burton, please don't cook. Let's go out. It's not just your, uh, unusual dishes. It's the mess you leave. The last time you cooked, I couldn't bring myself to face the kitchen for three days. Promise me you won't cook."

"Goddamnit, Sheila, there you go again. Just because you're the love of my life does not allow you to impugn my skills as a culinary artist. I'm the big dick around here and don't you forget it."

"I'll agree you're a big dick, though I wish I could say the same for your penis." She paused, and then she added suspiciously, "You're not drunk, are you?"

"At this time of day? Don't be ridiculous."

"What have you been doing?"

"Well, that's something I want to talk to you about, but not over the phone." His voice got a little hoarse. "I need some TLC right about now and I need you."

"I know you do, Burton." She sighed. "Okay, come on over tonight and do your worst with my kitchen, and then, if we're able to after eating what you cook, we'll talk."

"There is more truth in that than you know, my girl. Get home as soon as you can. Bouillabaisse is best served fresh from the stove." He hung up the phone and mixed himself another drink, a very weak one, already starting to plan the dinner he was going to create.

Kat went back to her lab and into her office and closed the door. Kevin was recording some data at the computer, but Kat paid him no mind. She sat down heavily in her chair and stared into space, thinking. It was hard to imagine, she thought, but her whole future might well be in the hands of Burton Ramsey, an obvious drunk and a neurotic.

She could not quite come to understand how such a circumstance could have entered her well-ordered life. She did not associate with people like Burton Ramsey. They were not allowed to be a part of her life. And yet, this man was not only in her life, but he practically had control of it, and all without knowing—or caring.

That was what puzzled Kat—Ramsey didn't seem at all interested in anything she, Kat, had to say. For all Ramsey knew, she could be offering him the next Nobel Prizes in both Medicine and Chemistry. But Ramsey didn't even bother to listen. He had stated flatly that his work was done and that was that. Most scientists would have been at least a little curious about why Kat was so interested in their work. Maybe it was the alcohol. He must have been too drunk to realize how serious Kat was.

As unpleasant as the confrontation had been, the news that the rats had been previously injected with *something* had been exhilarating. It had answered all of her questions about why the NeurActivase had finally worked. She had barely been able to wait for Ramsey to leave that morning before she'd taken one of the blue rats out and run him through the maze.

The improvement had continued, and it was clearly obvious that some sort of symbiotic enhancement existed between her serum and Ramsey's. She had taken one of the precious six test rats and, after killing it in the usual manner, had taken a specimen from the animal's brain. She had prepared a slide and, with trembling fingers, slid it into the microscope.

She was prepared to be surprised, but not quite to such an extent. Not only was the specimen tissue packed with neural cells, but they were all healthy and young-looking. The amazing spectacle to her had been how young *all* of the tissue looked. It simply wasn't consistent with that age of a rat. To verify her point, she had sacrificed a three-year-old control rat and taken a sample of brain tissue. The two tissue sections were almost comparable except for the much-increased neural cells in the five-year-old. Either the five-year-old rat had been mislabeled, or *something* was making the animal's tissues seem younger and healthier, not to mention the improvement in intelligence that accompanied the other changes.

And that *something* had to be whatever Ramsey had obviously perfected. Kat had sat back and put her hand to her forehead. Ramsey stood directly in her way, right in her path to greatness, blocking her progress. No, that was not right, she thought. It was not her greatness or her fame that was at stake . . . It was the millions of people who could be helped or cured with such a formula, if only Ramsey would cooperate.

Now she sat, lost in thought, searching for a way through the Ramsey bulwark. Through the glass partition of her office, her eyes strayed to Kevin, who was still working on the computer. She sat up straighter, an idea beginning to form. Among her other accomplishments, Kat was a computer expert and was as much at home with them as any other equipment she used. It would be, she thought, the perfect way to cut Ramsey out of the picture.

She couldn't burglarize Ramsey's office, but she might be able to break in to his files electronically. She got up, left her office, and went into the small bathroom contained in the lab. She smoothed her hair and then opened her compact and blotted on a little extra makeup. She looked into the mirror and practiced a smile.

There was a silly young man down in the records room who appeared to her to get the stutters every time she came around. She might just be able to induce him to give her the phone number of the biochemist's computer and let her take a peek into Ramsey's personnel file. People habitually used some piece of personal baggage, such as their birth date or their middle name or their wife's maiden name, as their access code or the password to their computer's records. With

Ramsey, she expected it to be something as unimaginative as his initials.

If she could get the young man in the records room to let her get some of that sort of information, she had no doubt she could successfully hack Ramsey's system. The files would probably be in code, but she was willing to bet that it would be a simple code, and cryptography had been one of her hobbies for years.

The secret of Ramsey's serum would involve chemistry, and she was no chemist, but she knew a number of people who were, including her lab assistant, Kevin. Ramsey had embarrassed her terribly, sneering at her and forcing her to tell the story of her failure. She expected it was already the gossip of the laboratory, especially after the unceremonious way Ramsey had ushered her out of his office.

Well, she thought, time would tell just who would be embarrassed last.

She glanced over at Kevin, still inputting data into the computer. She had to get him out of the office so she could work her wiles on the boy in the office. She glanced down at Angus in his bed next to her desk. Of course . . .

"Kevin," she called, motioning him over when he glanced up at her.

"Yes, Doctor?" he said.

"I need a huge favor."

He got up and walked over to stand in front of her desk. "Yes, ma'am?"

"I've got some work to do down in the front office, and today is Angus's day to go to the vet for his arthritis shot. Would it be too great of an inconvenience for you to run him over there for me? I've noticed he seems a lot more stiff than usual, and I'm afraid he may be in pain."

Kevin smiled and shook his head. He cared for Angus almost as much as Kat did. "No, ma'am. I'll take him right over and see that he gets his shot. We can't have him hurting, can we?"

"Thank you, Kevin. Just tell Dr. Washburn to put it on my bill."

Kevin grabbed Angus's leash from the desk and bent over to pick the dog up.

"*Ugh*," he grunted with a smile. "The old boy's getting kinda heavy, too. I might just ask about putting him on a diet."

Kat grinned. "Too many cookies, I guess."

At the word *cookie*, Angus perked up his ears and barked.

Kevin laughed and patted Angus's head, then walked out the door.

As soon as they'd left, Kat got up and followed them out into the hall. She was about to attempt to be charming, and she didn't know if she remembered how.

Moments after Kat left her office, the door opened and a man entered. He moved directly to the cage where she kept her experimental rats. After observing them for a few minutes, he moved to the computer on her desk and turned it on.

When it was booted up, he scrolled to the pages devoted to the results of her experiments. "Holy shit," he exclaimed softly to himself when he saw the maze results she'd recorded for the newly injected rats.

He quickly took a thumb drive from his pocket and inserted it in the USB slot of the computer, then copied her data onto it, shut the computer down, and left the room.

CHAPTER 9

When he left the laboratory, Burton planned to go to a fish market, but a wiser thought prevailed and he headed for Pier One, his favorite seafood restaurant. He was well-known there, and he went back into the kitchen and talked the chef into selling him a gallon of bouillabaisse, a large tossed salad, and two loaves of garlic bread already prepared, so that he could just warm them in the oven.

Sheila had a large, lush apartment in the Twin Towers complex, a much-desired location that was close to the medical center and convenient to shops, grocery stores, fine restaurants, and theaters. There was, however, a corresponding higher rent to go with all that convenience. When he'd followed her to Houston from Dallas, Ramsey tried staying there with Sheila. However, less than a year after they'd moved into the place, Burton moved out, claiming that a man who only made fifty-six thousand dollars a year could not afford to live in a thirty-five-hundred-dollar-a-month apartment.

He said, sarcastically, "Maybe a doctor making a quarter of a million dollars writing little words on a prescription pad can, but an honest scientist can't."

Sheila wanted to know what that had to do with it, since their salaries were communal, but he'd answered that he was not a man to be subsidized by a woman, especially a woman bearing the title of MD.

It had hurt her at first, but then, six months later he'd made some remark about having left, and she'd said innocently, "Oh, you moved out? When was that?"

The apartment was on the tenth floor of the complex and had a sunken common room that was almost as big as his lab. It was a corner apartment, and the two sides of the combination living room and dining room were almost all glass, giving a sweeping view of the city.

Since Sheila had picked out the apartment, he made constant references to what all that open glass did to her heating and cooling bills. Of course, he personally liked the feeling of openness that the huge glass walls gave and insisted on keeping the drapes pulled back to, as he said, "Teach you a lesson about the British Thermal Unit."

In the kitchen, he transferred the bouillabaisse from the container they'd given him at the restaurant into one of Sheila's large copper-bottomed pots. As per the chef's instructions, he put the pot on the stove and turned it to very low. While the soup heated, he transferred the salad to a wooden bowl, covered it, and put it in the refrigerator. He unwrapped the bread, put it on a cookie sheet, and shoved it in the oven.

He saw by the kitchen clock that it was a little after six, so he figured he had about another hour before Sheila could fight through the never-ending evening traffic and make her way home. He found two bottles of chardonnay in the wine closet and put them in the refrigerator to chill.

When that was done, he took several clean pots and pans, along with a few useful-looking utensils, and put them in the sink, sprayed them with liquid soap, and then ran them full of water.

He stepped back and surveyed his work. From all appearances, it looked as if a neat, careful cook had been at work in the kitchen, cleaning up behind himself as he went. He smiled with great satisfaction. So much for Sheila's opinion of his neatness and culinary acumen.

Finally, he gathered up every trace of the packages and containers he'd brought with him from Pier One and consigned them to oblivion down the central garbage chute that was also part of what you got for thirty-five hundred a month, a figure he considered obscene for a place in which she mostly just slept. Why, there had been years when he'd lived on less than that figure for twelve entire months.

Finally satisfied that all was ready, he mixed himself a drink and settled down to wait for Sheila to get home. She'd play hell making fun of either his cooking or his cleanliness.

When Kevin and Angus got back from their visit to the vet, Kevin had a strange look on his face. When asked about it, he'd ducked his head and said he had to hurry and leave before the traffic got so bad that by the time he got home, it would be time to come back to the office

Kat thanked him for taking Angus and gave him a peck on the cheek, which made him blush down to the roots of his hair. As he walked out the door, he turned serious again and said that the vet wanted to talk to Kat, but that she'd call her in the morning.

Kat was puzzled, but as soon as she got Angus settled in his bed, she got back to the chase for Ramsey's computer files. She'd been trying, without success, for two hours to access Ramsey's computer and was getting frustrated.

She had easily gotten the phone number of Ramsey's computer and enough personal information from Ramsey's personnel file to access a dozen computers. The young man in Personnel had been a pushover. The most difficulty she'd experienced with him had been disengaging herself from his presence by promising to go for a drink with him someday before hastening back to her laboratory.

Finally, she was just about to give up and admit defeat. Some of the passwords she'd tried had elicited responses from Ramsey's computer such as "SORRY, WRONG NUMBER," or "WASHING MY HAIR," or "OUT WITH STING," whatever that meant.

Mostly, she'd just gotten a blank response and a blinking screen that meant nothing was happening between the two machines. She had written down a list of at least fifty possible passwords, and she began to slowly and patiently try them again, using every conceivable combination of the information she could think of.

It was about ten o'clock and they had finished dinner and were sitting on the couch before the window that led out onto the terrace. At least Sheila was on the couch. Burton was sitting on the floor at her feet, leaning back against her legs—one of his favorite positions, especially after a few glasses of Chivas had mellowed him out enough to forget that she was a dreaded MD.

She was holding a glass of white wine in one hand and teasing his hair with the other. "Burton, I think you should take up a new occupation," she said out of the blue.

He half-looked around. "Yeah?"

"Yes. That bouillabaisse is every bit as good as they have at Pier One. In fact, it tasted remarkably like what we had there just last week."

He looked a little uncomfortable and covered his discomfort by taking a large sip of his Chivas before answering, "Bouillabaisse is bouillabaisse. It all tastes alike. I told you, it's nothing but fish soup. It's child's play."

Above his head, she smiled slightly. She had changed when she'd gotten home from the business-cut suits she wore at work to a loose, colorful silk lounging gown. Sheila Goodman was five years younger than Burton Ramsey, but in some ways, she felt very motherly toward him. She had loved him almost as soon as she'd penetrated the supposedly angry, swaggering, defiant personae he presented to the world and had seen the sensitive, good-humored, and dedicated man within. She figured she was the only person in the world he'd let see that deep inside him.

Sheila had blondish hair, and her face was more pleasant than pretty. She was small, almost too small for Burton's massive size, but she had a trim figure and prominent breasts and the kind of metabolism that didn't run to fat. At times, Burton called her "Sheena of the Jungle," because as calm and reserved as she appeared in public and in her business life, she underwent a wonderful loss of inhibition in bed.

She was a warm, caring, forgiving person, and Burton Ramsey would have loved her if she'd been fat and ugly. He'd once told her so, but quickly, before there was any chance it might sound like he was paying her a compliment, he'd said, "But that doesn't mean I want you to go all the way on this thing. You've nearly got the ugly down pat. No use adding fat to it."

But he hadn't fooled her. She'd just smiled secretly to herself. She was secure with Burton, but she did wish he'd grow up a little faster.

"No, I mean it. I think you should apply to Pier One as a consulting chef," she repeated.

He turned around and looked her full in the face, suspicious that she hadn't fallen for his little trick. "What's the matter with you? By God, this time you can't possibly claim I left a mess. I did everything but put the big stuff in the dishwasher, and I would have done that if I'd known how."

"Oh no. It was fine." She took a sip of wine. "In fact, some of the pots and pans looked like they hadn't even been used."

"And what's that supposed to mean?"

"Why, nothing, dear, except that you must have done such a good job of scrubbing them out."

He squinted his eyes and scowled at her. "I smell some sort of crack coming. Some snide remark."

"Oh no, dear."

He gave her another hard look. "A fine state of affairs this is. A man fixes his wife dinner after he's worked hard all day, and his thanks is some sort of smirking attitude. A wife, by the way, who won't even take her husband's last name."

She sighed. "Now, Burton, you are going to keep telling that story until you begin to believe it. It was you who requested I go back to my maiden name. If I remember, you said you did not want your vaunted name attached to an MD. I did it reluctantly and only after you threw one of those fits you ought to have patented. Besides, I've never even had it legally changed."

"You really mind, don't you? Tell you to do something and you do it halfway."

"I keep expecting you to come to your senses one of these days. Burton, you've been keeping up this MD nonsense so long it's become a habit. People think you're strange enough as it is. I know you were hurt, and I know how much you wanted to go to medical school. But if you continue with this fetish—"

"Fetish!" He turned around and glared at her. "Damn it, Sheila, don't call such a strong passion of mine a 'fetish.'"

"I was an MD when you married me."

"You're different."

"Burton, you don't feel that way anymore, and you know it. And for God's sake, get rid of the silly, personalized license plate. That's disgusting and undignified."

"FUMD?"

"Yes."

He smiled slyly. "Nobody knows what that means."

"Oh right! Nobody under the age of ten. Especially around a medical center."

"Listen, my girl, I'm about to get rich, and then we'll see just how often you climb up on your high horse of acceptable social beha—"

"'High horse'! When is anyone allowed to climb up on any kind of horse around you? Even a pony. If they try, you just take that big baseball bat of a tongue of yours and knock them off. Or wave one of those big bully fists around."

"Speaking of bullies . . . do you know Kaitlyn Williams, ex-neurosurgeon, presently at BioTech pretending to be a researcher?"

"I've heard of her. Hers is a big name in medical circles. At least her family's name is." She looked at Burton and narrowed her eyes. "For God's sake, don't tell me you've managed to have a run-in with her? Burton, from what I hear, she's shy and gentle and wouldn't hurt a fly."

He told her the whole story, beginning with Williams's visit to his lab on Saturday morning to take a dozen of his rats, and ending with the final episode, in which he'd forced Williams to recount her disgrace.

"Well, I can't say she acted very professional, but you didn't have to treat her like that. Damn it, Burton, why do you persist in acting so in opposition to your true character? Do you take some sort of perverse pleasure from it?"

He scrunched up his shoulders as she rubbed his neck. "I used to think I hated that silly bitch. That smug, silver-spoon-in-the-mouth bitch. I'd pass her in the hall and she would drop her eyes, like she didn't want to look at someone as lowly as I."

Sheila shook him a little. "Why do you call her a 'silver-spoon-in-the-mouth bitch'?"

He shrugged against her hands on his shoulders. "Well, you said her family was very prominent in medical circles, and they obviously paid her way through medical school . . ."

"Oh no, you've got it all wrong, Burton. Her dad was a general practitioner and her mom was an internist. Back in the day, they opened a clinic in the Fifth Ward in Houston—probably the worst and most dangerous area of the city at that time. They treated everyone who came through their doors, regardless of ability to pay. They even lived above their clinic in a two-room apartment. Their memory is so revered because of what they did, not because they were wealthy or from the high society."

He craned his neck to look back at her. "Then, how did they afford to send their daughter to college and medical school if they were so poor?"

"They didn't, Burton. Word is, Kaitlyn joined the navy and paid them back two years for every year of college and medical school she attended. That's why she is just getting started in her research career, even though she's in her mid-forties."

With that, she gave him an extra-tight squeeze on his shoulders.

He moaned a little. "Right there, don't stop," and then he continued his thought. "Well, maybe I did misjudge her if that's the case. But it's weird that she did that to me 'cause I'd finally begun to respect her—although only just a little," he hastened to add before she got the idea he'd gone soft. "She's got a lot of pluck, and in the monthly meetings she's never kowtowed to Captain Sunshine and she gave him back as good as she got."

"Uh-huh, kinda like me, huh?"

He turned to look at her with a hurt look on his face. "You do know I really do respect and admire your gumption and drive, don't you?"

"You didn't hate her, Burton. You don't really hate anybody. But you've been playing this game so long you're starting to get confused. I know you didn't move out because I'm an MD. You moved out because you insisted on paying the rent and you couldn't afford it. It was my fault. I should never have picked this place out while knowing how you are. But I thought that since we loved each other, our money was communal and that we could afford this place with both our salaries. But never mind. As soon as the lease is up, we'll live wherever you say. In a Motel Six if that will make you happy."

It was a dark night, and toward the east, storm clouds were rolling in. Now and then through the wall of windows they could see a thrust of lightning zigzag its way through the black clouds. He smiled. "My girl, very shortly, we will not have to worry about money. I am going to make us very, very rich."

"You keep talking about that. This doesn't have anything to do with all those trips you've been making to Mexico, does it?"

"Better brush on up your Spanish, my girl."

"Oh no. I've no intention of living in Mexico."

"Wherever I goest and all that. Says so right there in the Bible."

"It's a woman who says that. Ruth. And she says, 'Whither thou goest.' And I'm not saying, 'Wherever thou goest to Mexico.' Listen, why do you have to be such a bastard? If you can help Dr. Williams, why don't you just do it? You would be surprised how painless it is to be nice for a change."

He shook his head. "Oh no. Not on this. I'm not showing this serum to anyone except somebody with a check in hand that's got a lot of zeros on it. A whole lot of zeros."

She heard the fervor in his voice and grabbed him by his short-cropped hair and pulled his head back so she could see his face. "Have you got something good, Ramsey? Something really good? Important?"

He smiled as well as he could, considering the position his head was in. "More important than you could believe."

"Are you still working on the serum to improve the dialysis machines?"

He answered, "Have I told you any different?"

She looked closely at him. "Why do I have the feeling that the laboratory you are contracted to, BioTech, may have to read about this in the newspapers?"

His eyebrows raised. "Because you have a suspicious mind?"

She let go of his hair. "You'll never get away with stealing the formula from BioTech and selling it as your own. It's been tried before by people greedier than you and it hasn't worked. You may be a hell of a researcher, Burton, but a lawyer you most definitely are not, and it's lawyers who draw up those contracts, and it's lawyers who make them stick."

"Well, we'll just have to see, won't we?"

"And then there's that satellite office business. Conroe, isn't it? I know you've been paying rent on another office there. What is that all about?"

He got up from the floor, lay down on the couch, and put his head in her lap. "How do you know about Conroe? What have you been doing? Snooping?"

"Ramsey, I balance your checkbook."

"Why do you do that?"

"Because you like to pretend to be the absentminded professor type."

"Oh yes. I forgot." He was examining her breast, massaging the nice large nipple through the thin material of her silk dress.

She was very conscious of his roving fingers. "Plus, you can't add or subtract. Which makes it difficult to balance a checkbook."

"Well, BioTech is welcome to everything they find at Conroe. And it won't be insignificant, I can assure you that. They'll feel very lucky they caught me cheating and very fortunate to have had an association with the eminent blood man, Burton Ramsey, Ph.D."

"But they aren't going to get the real goods, is that the idea?"

He continued playing with her breast. "Now you are getting the idea, sweetie."

"Meanwhile, after having dazzled them with your footwork, you are going to steal quietly off into the dark in Mexico with the sho' 'nough stuff."

"There ya go. And nobody the wiser."

"Bullshit, Ramsey. You won't fool the lawyers at Bio-Tech any more than you fooled me with that dinner."

He raised his head off her lap and gave her a hard look. "What's that supposed to mean? You trying to start a scene?"

"Ramsey, a scene is what you do in front of other people. You're thinking of a fight."

"What do you call it if you have it in the bedroom?"

"A hell of a lot of fun if you do it right."

CHAPTER 10

Ramsey didn't get to his office until early afternoon the next day. He'd been busy with phone calls to Monterrey, Mexico, and phone calls to Mexico were more difficult and complex than calling Australia. He had spent a frustrating three hours trying to get some needed information on the whereabouts of a dialysis machine, most of which had been spent simply trying to reach Dr. Garza.

When he finally got to his lab, he saw that Dottie was at the computer. She turned, frowning as he entered. She said, "Dr. Ramsey, have you been fooling with the computer?"

He stopped short of his office door. "Me? Fooling with that thing? I'd just as soon touch a live snake. Why?"

"Because someone phoned it and spent from about six p.m. until nine fifty trying to access your information and research file."

"What do you mean, 'someone phoned it'? Does my computer have a telephone number?"

"Oh yes."

"What? Why?"

Dottie rolled her eyes as if she couldn't believe anyone didn't know about this. "Say you were in some other loca-

tion and you wanted some information out of your files.
You'd just get to another computer, dial your number, and
then access your information files with the password."

"How do you know somebody 'phoned up' my computer?"

"Because I programmed a trap into it that would tell me
when the computer is turned off and on. And I shut it down
yesterday before lunch, when you let me have the afternoon
off. So, if you didn't do it, who did? Someone tried awfully
hard to discover your password, tried for four hours almost.
Until almost ten o'clock."

"What, does that thing have a clock in it, too?"

"Oh yes."

"What will they think of next? Does it give head?"

She blushed, deeply, even though she should have been
used to Burton Ramsey's unrestrained language. "The code
words they tried for passwords all had to do with you. Obviously, someone who didn't know that you never use a computer was trying to break in. They were very determined, but
they never had a chance, because they didn't know that I
programmed the machine and devised all of the passwords.
Who do you think it was, the progress committee?"

He shook his head. "Nah. They can get at my files any
time they want just by asking. It's in my contract. Besides,
at ten o'clock last night they were all at home pretending to
have sex with their wives."

"Then who could it be?"

He thought for a moment and then smiled grimly. "Sounds
to me like the work of the rat thief."

"Dr. Williams?"

"Haven't you heard? Dr. Williams is extremely interested in what I'm doing down here in this little ol' laboratory. I thought it was the talk of BioTech."

Dottie said, hesitantly, "I think I did hear something."
Then she looked up at Dr. Ramsey. "What are you going to
do, report her? We can't really prove it unless I put a trace

on the computer that will cause her computer to identify itself."

He was starting to smile. "No need for that. I'm fairly
certain of who the culprit is." He knelt over the workbench
by the computer and quickly scrawled out, on a blank sheet
of paper, a long, four step chemical equation. He handed it
to Dottie. "Can you put that in the computer, separate from
the other stuff? Make it look like the big casino? Put some
kind of program in that leads her straight to this?"

She looked at the paper uncertainly. "I suppose so. You
want her to see this? It looks quite important."

"Oh, it is. It is. It's one of the three major medicines in
the world."

"What are the other two?"

"Sex and alcohol. Don't you know what that is?"

She studied the paper and shook her head. "No. But I'm a
biology major."

"Yes, I forgot that. God forbid a biologist should learn
some chemistry. But you can put this in that Rube Goldberg
invention and lead our good Dr. Williams to it? Correct?"

"Sure, but what shall I label it?"

He thought a moment. "Call it the X-Factor Serum."

"What does that mean?"

He shrugged. "Beats the hell out of me. Just sounds mysterious."

He waited while her chubby little fingers nimbly worked
over the keyboard. After a few moments, she looked up.
"Anything else?"

"Yes. We've baited the trap. Now we've got to guide our
rat to its mouth."

"Huh?"

He walked around, thinking and jingling the change in
his pants pocket. "I think it's pretty common knowledge that
I'm leaving BioTech in less than a month. That supposedly
puts you out of a job."

"But I thought you had it fixed where I'd be the assistant to whomever takes over your lab?"

"I do. But that's our little secret. Dr. Williams doesn't know that. And she won't know it when you go down and ask her if she might not have an opening for a lab assistant."

"But she's already got a lab assistant."

He grimaced and grabbed his hair with both hands. "*Argh . . .* Dottie, I am trying very hard not to strangle you. Fine. We both know she's got a lab assistant. But she knows you've been my lab assistant and I've got something she badly wants and you're going to let on you know where it is. Not directly, you understand, like you were selling out completely, but obliquely. You're going to tell her that I can't use a computer, that you do all the programming for me from my notes. And you're going to keep on telling her that until she finally figures out that it has to be you who put in the passwords, which you are going to change to your first name right now . . . 'Dottie.'

"And you keep saying your name, over and over, *Dottie, Dottie, Dottie.* Maybe she'll get it, maybe she won't. Maybe she'll ask you what you know about my work, and you'll just tell her only what's in the notes I give you, and they're all about chemistry and you're a biology major. Just be yourself, Dottie. Just act like you're really going to her for a job. Now, can you do that?"

She mulled it over in her mind a moment. "I think so. But isn't it dishonest?"

"Not if you put yourself down for twenty hours of overtime this week."

Her lips rounded. "Oh!"

"Yes. Oh! Just remember, you own the computer and all the goodies are stored in it. Tell her I have a ritual of burning my notes every evening and dancing around them buck naked and smeared with paint. She'll probably believe it."

"When should I do this?"

"Anytime Dr. Williams is in and her assistant is out. Maybe this afternoon. The sooner, the better. I think her assistant leaves at five and Williams usually works late. What do you think?"

She studied on it for a moment. "I think she deserves it. Dr. Ramsey, do you know she lied to me? She told me that you and she were good friends and she knew all about your research."

"Why, that cur!" Ramsey laughed delightedly. Williams's attempt to break in to his computer had relieved Ramsey of all of his guilt about forcing her to tell her story under false pretenses.

Kat Williams was waiting with ill-concealed impatience for Kevin to arrive. It was nine in the morning, and usually, unless he had a school schedule interference, Kevin was right on time. On this morning, of all mornings, he had decided to be late. But Kat was feeling so satisfied and relieved that she was willing to overlook the young man's minor transgression. Still, she was impatient to get on with the information she now had in hand.

The night before, thanks to Ramsey's ditzy assistant, she had easily accessed the computer using Dottie's name as the password. Her first name, she'd thought, now, that was certainly clever thinking—and so original. Of course, she had no intention of hiring the young woman when Ramsey left, but it wouldn't hurt to let her think the job was going to be hers. There was no telling what else she might be able to glean about Ramsey's formula before he was gone for good.

When her phone rang, she answered it, thinking it was probably Kevin calling to explain why he was running so late.

"Hello, Kevin . . . ?"

"Hello, Kat. This is Dr. Diane Washburn."

"Oh, hello, Diane."

"Did Kevin talk to you about my visit with Angus yesterday afternoon?"

"No, not really. He did say you wanted to talk to me, though."

"Kat, this is a very hard call to make, but I think we need to talk about when we've let Angus suffer enough."

"What?"

"Kat, Angus has very severe arthritis in both of his hips, and it is progressing into his spinal vertebrae. I'm afraid before long he is going to lose control of his bladder and bowel functions."

Kat felt her heart sink as she glanced over at Angus sleeping in his bed. "Are you talking about putting him down?" she fairly sobbed.

She could hear the doctor sigh over the phone. "Not immediately perhaps, but, Kat, I think the time is not far off. After all, Angus is thirteen years old, and that is a very advanced age for a Scottie."

"But . . . but . . ."

"All right, Kat. I can see you are not ready for this right now . . . but I want you to start thinking about it, for Angus's sake. I don't know how much longer I can control his pain."

"Okay, Diane," Kat sobbed. "I will, I promise."

When she hung up, she went right to Angus's bed, sat down, and pulled him into her arms, sobbing into his fur.

After a while, Kat got control of herself. She took Angus for a short walk in the park and told him over and over how much she loved him and how much he meant to her. From the look in his adoring brown eyes, she knew he understood.

Now Angus was back in his bed, chewing contentedly on a Greenie, and Kat was examining the data she'd stolen from Ramsey's computer files the night before.

She was certain she had what she was looking for. Once she had gotten into the computer, the programming had led her straight to a complicated-looking chemical equation that

Ramsey had dubbed, in more blazing imagination, the "X-Factor." Kat could only conclude that Ramsey had seen too many early 1950s science-fiction movies.

She did not know what the chemical equation was, but she knew it was important by the devious path she'd had to follow to find it. Her chemistry was weak, but it didn't matter. Kevin was a doctoral candidate in physical chemistry, which was one of the reasons Kat had chosen him as her assistant.

She'd gained the information just as she had begun to despair. To make certain that Ramsey's serum had been the catalytic factor in her rats' much-improved behavior, she'd ordered a group of rats of the same strain as those she'd taken from Ramsey's lab, and of the same age. She had inoculated them with exactly the same serum as she had the original six rats from the Ramsey group. The results had been the same old failure she'd experienced before, except the brain cell deterioration had occurred faster because, as she'd expected, of the rats' age.

The six rats of the Ramsey group that she had been using as a "control" she'd realized were not control subjects at all, since they, too, had been injected with Ramsey's serum. She had run them through the maze along with a control group of normal five-year-olds. Even without her NeurActivase serum, Ramsey's rats had done better than the new control group.

And then there had been the breeding. To her surprise, she'd noted that all of the rats of the twelve she'd taken from Ramsey's lab were actively breeding. Five-year-old rats occasionally bred, but with nothing like the activity she'd been seeing. These rats were acting like teenagers in a testosterone storm!

The progress of the original group had continued until they seemed to have settled down to running the maze in a little over three and a half minutes, a phenomenal time that indicated the rats were at least three times as smart as rats were supposed to be. But Kat's elation at how well the du-ally injected rats were doing was tinged by worry that she would not be able to learn what Ramsey had originally in-jected the rats with.

But now Kat was almost certain she was holding the an-swer in her hand in the form of the four-step chemical equa-tion she'd written out on a sheet of paper. In a little while, she would know.

Kevin finally showed up at a little after ten, offering an excuse that he'd been called into consultation with his thesis professor. Kat brushed it aside and thrust the piece of paper into her assistant's hands. She said, "Fine, fine. Now, take this and go down to Supplies and make sure we have the necessary chemicals to compound this formula."

Kevin took the paper and walked toward the door, read-ing it. Kat got up from the computer desk and stretched her arms over her head. Kevin stopped at the door. He looked back at Kat, a funny look on his face. "Dr. Williams . . ."

Kat lowered her arms from their stretch and said, impa-tiently, "What's the matter, Kevin, forget your way to the supply room?"

"No, ma'am." He hesitated. "It's just that this for-mula"—he motioned with the paper—"it's acetylsalicylic acid."

Kat wasn't really listening. "So what? I didn't ask you what it was. Just please get it."

"But it's aspirin, ma'am. I've got some in my desk if you need it."

Kat stared at him blankly, her brain taking in the infor-mation but her mind not wanting to accept it. "It's what?"

"Aspirin, ma'am. Plain old aspirin. The kind that Bayer claims nine out of ten doctors prefer."

Kat felt her heart sink in her chest. Her stomach gave a flip, and she thought she was going to be sick. She'd been suckered—and not only suckered, but taken in by a silly little fat girl and a hulking oaf. They had deliberately let her into Ramsey's computer, deliberately given her the pass-word, and deliberately let her know that they knew she was trying to break in to Ramsey's files. She sat down heavily in the stenographer's chair.

At that instant Burton Ramsey suddenly appeared in the lab door. He said, "Why, hello, *Doctor*! Did my little pre-scription help your headache?"

And then he had disappeared down the hall, laughing wildly.

Kat put her head in both of her hands. She was defeated.

Sometime later, with the dying sun sending shadows through the windows of the cafeteria where Kat sat thinking over a cup of coffee, she finally reached a conclusion and an admission. The admission was that she had never planned to work with Ramsey. That she had intended to steal whatever data Ramsey had about whatever it was that had enhanced her serum, and then work alone, taking all the credit. She might have told Ramsey that they needed to talk, but what she'd meant was that Ramsey should talk and tell her all about his own serum. Never, never, had she intended to be put in a position of having a man like Ramsey as her scien-tific equal and partner. But now that had all changed.

The conclusion she'd reached was that she had to find some way to get Ramsey to work with her and share equally in the stupendous breakthrough her research was indicating. But that appeared as if it was going to be easier said than done. She had heard that there was only one person whom Burton Ramsey would listen to, and that was his ex-wife, Dr. Sheila Goodman.

Kat glanced out the window, watching the parking lot empty. She didn't know much about Dr. Goodman. She could only hope she was nothing like Burton Ramsey, because, for all practical purposes, she was her last hope.

Kevin walked up and interrupted her reverie. "Dr. Williams, I've finished cleaning up the lab and I've put the rats in their cages. Everything is ready to shut down for the night."

"Okay, Kevin, thank you."

"Uh, Dr. Williams, do you mind if I ask what that asshole Ramsey meant when he taunted you from the door?"

She looked at him and couldn't help it. She teared up and just shook her head.

Surprisingly, he moved to her, pulled her to her feet, and put his arms around her, squeezing gently. "Dr. Williams . . . Kat, I know something is going on that you're not telling me about. I know the new test rats have been doing much better than ever before, and that you've had some sort of break-through. The rats act younger and smarter. Now, I know that I am only a lowly lab assistant, and if you don't want to talk about this with me, just say so and I'll go home and forget all about it."

His kindness affected her in ways she couldn't under-stand, but she did know his arms felt great around her, and so she sat him down and told him the entire story, up to her humiliation at being tricked by Ramsey's computer joke.

He took her hands in his. "If you want, Kat, I'll go and beat the truth out of him."

She laughed and shook her head. "No, I don't think that will be necessary, Kevin. I've got something else in mind."

He nodded. "Okay, but from now on, will you promise to tell me everything and let me help you?"

Touched, she nodded. "Of course."

CHAPTER 11

It took Dr. Williams two days of discreet inquiries to learn Sheila Goodman's schedule well enough to drop in on her unannounced. She had not wanted to call her in advance, for fear that she would discuss it with Burton Ramsey first and either refuse to see her or have her mind already fixed against her before she could say her first word.

Sheila received her in her consulting office in the Methodist hospital. Sheila's first knowledge that the doctor in the lab next to her soon-to-be ex-husband's was coming to visit her had come when her assistant had buzzed to say there was a Dr. Williams to see her, and that she only needed a moment of her time. Her first inclination had been to say no, for fear of angering Burton by appearing to be interfering in his business. But then curiosity got the better of her and she told her assistant to send the doctor in.

Sheila's first impression of Williams as she came through the door was that she could certainly see why she and Burton didn't get along. They were very unalike in both speech and in mannerisms. Where Burton was brusque and abrasive to most people, Dr. Williams was quiet and self-effacing . . . almost shy. She was the complete opposite of Burton Ramsey, and this was a case where opposites most certainly didn't attract.

She walked into the room, took a second to look around, and then stuck out her hand to Sheila. "Hello, Dr. Goodman. I am Dr. Kaitlyn Williams, but I hope you'll call me Kat like all of my friends do."

Sheila grinned as she shook the doctor's hand. "And are we to be friends, Kat?" she asked with raised eyebrows.

Kat shrugged, blushing. "I sincerely hope so, Dr. Goodman."

Sheila waved her to a seat. "Come now, Kat. If we are to be friends, you must learn to call me Sheila."

"Okay, Sheila," Kat said hesitantly.

"Good. Now that we've got that settled, would you like some coffee, tea, or perhaps a soft drink?"

Kat smiled ruefully. "Some coffee would be great. I haven't been getting a lot of sleep lately."

Sheila punched a button on her intercom and asked her assistant if she would bring them both coffee, then she looked up at Kat. "Working late on something earth-shattering in your lab, I suppose?"

Kat looked surprised. "Has Dr. Ramsey said anything to you about my work?"

Sheila hesitated, then she shook her head, not wanting to repeat what Burton had told her about Kat trying to steal his formula. "No, not really. I just assumed that if you've been missing sleep over it, then it must be very important to you." But that wasn't what you wanted to see me about."

Before Kat could answer, Sheila's assistant came in with a carafe of coffee, two cups, and a small bowl of packets of creamer, sugar, and artificial sweetener.

After she put the tray down on Sheila's desk, Sheila poured them both cups and gestured toward the bowl on the tray.

Her eyebrows raised and she grinned when she saw Kat add four packets of sugar to her cup.

After Kat took a deep draught of the coffee and sighed

contentedly, she glanced up at Sheila. "You are right, of course, Sheila. I didn't come here to talk about Dr. Ramsey, but about what I think we have stumbled upon."

Sheila pursed her lips. "And that is . . . ?"

"Of course, it's much too early to tell, but I believe we're on to one of the most important discoveries in medical history."

Sheila looked at her blandly, with a slightly skeptical expression on her face. "Then, what is the trouble?"

Kat swallowed, then she drank down the rest of her coffee in one long gulp, as if to give herself courage to go on. "There seems to be a personality conflict between your husband and myself. In fact, he refuses to even discuss the matter with me."

"Do you blame him?"

She shook her head. "No, not really. I'm afraid I abrade Dr. Ramsey. And I haven't been particularly honest with him. We got off to a very bad start, most of which was my fault."

She looked up, locking her eyes with Sheila's. "But, Sheila, I cannot overemphasize the importance that Dr. Ramsey and I reach some degree of cooperation. The combined results of our serums could be stupendous."

Sheila sipped her coffee and stared at Kat for a moment. "Why don't you tell me how you happened to come to this remarkable conclusion, Kat?"

Kat took a deep breath and began. "Some short time back, about ten days, I happened to come into possession of twelve of your husband's rats that had been injected with a blood serum I believe he's been working on."

Sheila cocked her head to the side and raised her eyebrows. "'Happened to come into possession of'?"

Kat bowed her head and blushed crimson. "Yes . . . I mean, no. My assistant forgot to order replacement rats for our lab, and since it was during the weekend, I borrowed some from Dr. Ramsey's office without asking his permission, fully intending to replace them the following Monday. I knew he rarely worked on the weekends, and I didn't think there would be any harm done."

"But," Sheila said, "Burton found out about your 'borrowing' his rats and if I know him, it infuriated him."

Kat nodded quickly. "Exactly. And to make matters worse, not knowing Dr. Ramsey's rats had been inoculated with his serum, I injected six of them with a neuron accelerator *I've* been researching for three years. The results have been nothing short of phenomenal."

"Oh? How so?"

"It appears that there is a symbiotic relationship of a very positive kind between his serum and mine."

Sheila leaned back, looking at the younger woman. She could see how Burton would take an immediate dislike to her, and she wondered if Kat was subduing her normal personality to gain her acceptance. Once a neurosurgeon, always a neurosurgeon. She doubted if Kat could maintain this humble approach very long if she was being dishonest. But Sheila didn't have a cruel streak, and she could very easily guess why Kat had come to see her.

"And you want me to bring you together with Burton, is that it?"

Kat stared at Sheila for a moment. "I believe I read that you are a specialist in internal medicine?"

Sheila nodded. "With subspecialties in endocrinology and geriatrics."

Kat reached into a leather portfolio she had in her lap. She withdrew a sheet of paper with a long list of names on it. She glanced at it, and then she handed it across to Sheila. "Dr. Goodman, if Dr. Ramsey and I could pool our research, I believe we have an excellent chance of curing every one of the previously incurable diseases on that list."

Sheila read down the paper and handed it back, impressed in spite of herself. "That's quite a page full."

"There's more."

"More?"

Kat looked down at the floor. "All of the test results so far—and you realize we are talking about laboratory experiments only on rats—indicate that the dual serums seem capable of retarding aging."

Sheila stared at her in disbelief. "What?"

Kat was still looking at the floor. "Perhaps even reversing it."

She had spoken so softly Sheila wasn't sure she'd heard her correctly. She leaned toward her across the desk. "Did you say 'reversing' aging?"

"Yes, I did."

CHAPTER 12

John Palmer Ashby was as old as he was rich, and he was very rich. He had been born in a tar-paper shack in a small, dusty West Texas town in the shadow of the very oil derricks that would later make him one of the ten richest men in the United States.

From his earliest days, he had fought and clawed his way through life, expecting and giving no quarter. He quit school at the age of twelve to work the oil fields, and he surprised everyone by waiting until he was eighteen to kill his first man, and that by accident. He beat the man to death with a whiskey bottle after an argument over the number of spots showing on a pair of dice. Afterward, Ashby drained the whiskey bottle, picked up the cash from the floor, and went back to work like nothing had happened.

He had won his first oil lease in a stud poker game, and quickly parleyed that first strike into a dozen producing wells by the time he was twenty-two. He drove his men as hard as he drove himself, making many enemies and few friends on his road to riches. He was fond of saying that you couldn't find oil without spilling some blood, and few of his wells came in without at least one unmarked grave near the sludge pool. He paid top dollar, and his foreman and top crewmen got a percentage of the wells. No one much cared one way or the other about the men who got in Ashby's way and died for their trouble, as long as his checks cleared the bank.

When a young man, he had been called J.P., and even today, the initials alone were enough to tell anyone in the state whom was being referred to. Once barrel-chested with arms like tree limbs, age and illness had shrunken and withered his body—but not his spirit, or his temper.

Beverly Luna, his day nurse, entered his room on tiptoe, hoping to check his IVs and escape without awakening him. She bent over the bed and tapped the clear plastic reservoir on the IV bottle with her index finger, checking the level of the fluid within.

"Goddamnit, Beverly! Don't sneak around like that," growled Ashby out of the side of his face that still worked. He scooted up in the bed and turned his head to look at her as he talked. "Walk in here with a little authority so a body can hear you coming, without being startled out of a sound sleep."

Beverly started backing toward the door, mumbling, "Yes, sir. I'm sorry, sir. It won't happen again, sir."

As she turned and hurried out the door, Ashby just waved a limp hand at her in dismissal. He couldn't tolerate anyone he could dominate, and that was just about everyone.

He lay there, eyes roaming the room that had become his prison since his stroke. It looked more like a hospital infirmary than a bedroom. There were IV bottles, medicine bottles, and several machines that beeped and wheezed and clicked as they went about their business of keeping J.P. Ashby alive.

He reached for the bell hung next to his bed to summon Beverly back, and he was still surprised when his left hand didn't obey his command, even though it had been almost a year since the stroke that had robbed him of the use of the left side of his body.

Angry at his body's refusal to obey his will, he rolled on his side and grabbed the bell with his right hand, ringing it furiously.

Beverly rushed into the room, breathless. "Yes, sir. Yes, sir. What do you need, Mr. Ashby?"

"Unhook this goddamn oxygen. I want to have a cigar."

"Now, Mr. Ashby, you know what the doctor said . . ."

Ashby jerked the oxygen tubes out of his nostrils and threw them at the terrified girl. "I don't give a shit what that goddamn doctor said. I'm not going to lie here and waste away without even the comfort of a good smoke! Now, turn that blasted machine off and get me my cigar."

At that moment, a man walked through the door, a lopsided grin on his face. He was dressed in a suit that cost more than most men made in a year, and had coal-black hair and a dark complexion.

"You'd better care what your 'goddamn doctor said,' you old reprobate, or I'm gonna quit coming around here trying to keep your sorry ass alive," the man said wryly.

One side of Ashby's face turned up in a rare attempt at a smile. "Why, Dr. Tom, what the hell are you doing here?"

Dr. Tom Alexander glanced quickly at the nurse, Luna, and then he just shook his head. "I've been hearing reports from reliable sources that you've been a bad, bad boy and haven't been taking the meds that I ordered."

Ashby cut his eyes at the terrified nurse and pointed an index finger at her. "Goddamnit, Beverly, you've been talking out of school again. You're fired! Now, get your bony ass out of my house!"

Alexander held up both hands, palms out. "Now, J.P., just cool your jets. The nurse is only doing what I told her to do . . . namely, trying to keep an ornery old fart alive so I can keep living in the lifestyle to which I've become accustomed."

He inclined his head at the nurse. "Go on now, Beverly, and don't pay this grumpy old goat no nevermind. Maybe you could fix us both a cup of coffee—decaf for the grump and leaded for me."

Ashby nodded his assent and Beverly scooted out of the room, her face flaming scarlet.

Alexander shook his head again at the old man in the bed. "Now, J.P., you'd better be nice to Beverly. She's the third nurse I've had to hire this year, and with the word getting around, pretty soon we won't be able to get anyone to take care of you."

"Alright, alright," Ashby grumbled. "I'll try to take it easy, but damn it, what's the use of staying alive if I can't even enjoy an occasional cigar?"

"Occasional is okay. Ten a day is overdoing it," Alexander replied with a smile.

As he took a seat next to Ashby's bed, the doctor thought back to their first meeting two years previously. Alexander had been walking through the emergency room of the heart hospital in Corpus Christi when he heard a nurse shout, "Code blue! Code blue!"

He entered the nearest treatment room, where an elderly man on a stretcher was writhing, gasping for breath, and slowly turning blue.

Alexander, a cardiologist, quickly went to work, and after a touch-and-go thirty minutes had the man stabilized, though it was obvious that he had suffered a massive stroke.

Over the next fifteen days, the two men had become fast friends, primarily because John Ashby had finally found a man he could not intimidate and who seemed to be immune to his constant carping and bluster.

When Ashby had recovered as much as he was going to, he moved back to his favorite city, Houston. He bought a two-million-dollar home in River Oaks and had it fitted out as completely as any first-rate hospital suite.

He also put Dr. Alexander on a six-figure annual salary to be at his beck and call, and he gave him the use of his private jet so that the doctor could continue his practice in Corpus Christi while still traveling back and forth to Houston at least once a week to keep tabs on Ashby.

Their friendship had deepened over the past two years, to the point that they were as close as brothers.

Alexander set up a bed tray and thanked Beverly as she placed two china coffee cups on it, one with a glass straw in it so Ashby could sip the coffee without it running down his chin.

After the nurse had quickly left the room, Alexander took a drink of his Colombian brew and smiled. "You have the best coffee in Houston, J.P., even better than Starbucks."

"It oughta be," Ashby grumbled around his straw. "The damn stuff costs more per ounce than gold."

Alexander chuckled. "You can afford it, you old skinflint."

The corner of Ashby's mouth turned up again. "Yeah, I can, can't I?"

"By the way," Alexander said, glancing over his shoulder to make sure Beverly wasn't within earshot, "I heard something interesting from my sister this morning when I took her to breakfast."

One of Ashby's eyebrows rose. "That the one whose kid I'm putting through graduate school?"

"Yes, Kevin's mother."

"What did she have to say?"

Alexander pursed his lips, his eyes gleaming. "Well, it seems Kevin's working for a research scientist over at Bio-Tech, a neurosurgeon who is working on a formula that might be of interest to us."

"Yeah, what kind of formula?"

"Kevin told his mother that they have had some recent success in making older rats act young again, and, in fact, it even seems as if the rats not only act younger, but they act smarter, too."

Ashby wagged his head, a look of disgust on his face. "So

fuckin' what? I don't have any old rats I want made younger or smarter."

Alexander finished his coffee and set the cup aside as he leaned closer to Ashby's bed. "Listen, J.P., I've done about all I can to keep you alive, but I know this kind of life is unsatisfactory to you. If this formula does all that Kevin says it does, it might just be a way for us to get you up and out of this bed. Making rats smarter means the formula affects the brain in a positive way, and it might just mean it would help reduce the symptoms of your stroke."

Now he had Ashby's full attention. "Yeah, but if they're just now working on rats, human trials are probably years away."

Alexander nodded slowly. "In the normal course of events, that is probably true. However, most researchers I know are starved for cash, especially now that government funds are so scarce."

Ashby's eyes narrowed. "So, if someone with more cash than the government were to offer some to this starving researcher, you think they might part with the formula for some reasonable consideration?"

Alexander shrugged. "With the right amount of persuasion, anything is possible."

Ashby lay back on his pillow, his eyes wet. "Tom, whatever it takes, whatever Kevin needs, I want you to find out if this fountain of youth is real, and if it is, I want to try it."

"It might be dangerous, J.P. Just because it works on rats doesn't necessarily mean it will work on humans, and even then we don't know what effect it will have on a damaged brain."

Ashby rose off the pillow, his eyes hard. "Then, whatever it takes, get this researcher to try it on someone else first, and if it works on them, then by God, I'm gonna be the second one to use it!"

Alexander nodded. "Okay then. I'll take Kevin to dinner

and let him know that the sky is the limit as far as what it
will take to get his boss to do a human trial as soon as possible, and to let him know that his future is secure if he can
manage to get us some of it if it works."

"Not only his future, Tom, but yours, too, if you can get
me out of this fuckin' bed."

He put his good right hand out and grasped Tom's. "You
know what this will mean to me, don't you?"

"Yes, J.P., I do, and I'll get to working on it right now."

"Good, then get that lazy nurse in here with a bottle of
champagne and two of my Montecristos and we'll celebrate
in style."

Alexander smiled. It was the first time he'd seen J.P.
happy in over twelve months.

CHAPTER 13

Kaitlyn Williams arrived at Sheila's apartment exactly at the agreed-upon time of eight o'clock. She had dressed to impress, donning her one and only dressy outfit—the typical "little black dress," covered by a fox fur coat, and a stunning Hermès scarlet scarf. This wardrobe was a relic of her much earlier days as a respected neurosurgeon and was slightly too large for her, as she'd lost weight in the marathon sessions she'd spent working in her lab.

While waiting for Sheila to answer the door, she self-consciously rubbed the fur, trying to gain some solace from the soft feel of the coat.

Sheila let her in and showed her to a seat at the dining room table, where she had set out a glass of white wine for her and Williams, and a bottle of beer for her husband.

Burton Ramsey stood at the window looking out over the city, watching the lights of downtown Houston twinkle in the darkness, and he didn't bother to turn and look at Kat when she entered. He was angry and bored, and was doing nothing to hide his displeasure from his wife. They'd had a righteous row about her inviting Williams to a sit-down dinner to discuss their serums, and he was still smarting at the way Sheila had stood up to him. She'd finally told him to sit down, shut up, and act like a grown-up. He was still pouting over the remark.

Sheila poured Kat a glass of wine, then she glanced up to see Ramsey's scowl reflected in the glass of the window. "Burton, come over here and sit down. Dr. Williams has come here to discuss your serums and the possible beneficial effects that might come from combining them. The least you can do is listen to her."

She'd purposely refrained from telling him what Kat had told her about the effects the combination might have on the aging process.

Ramsey turned, his scowl deepening. He stared at Williams for a moment, relishing her hangdog look. "Sheila, I've told you that my serum is complete as it is. I don't need *Dr.* Williams's serum, or *Dr.* Williams herself!"

Kat looked up at Ramsey, then around at the apartment. She shook her head, thinking to herself, *I can't believe any man is stupid enough to give up this apartment—or a woman like Sheila. A man that dumb is going to be hard to deal with.*

Ramsey strolled over to the dining room table and picked up his glass of beer, staring into the bubbles as if they could tell him how to get through this evening and put Williams in her place without completely alienating his wife.

He gave Kat a disdainful glance. "As far as I'm concerned, this meeting is a complete waste of time and effort." He raised his glass to her in a mocking toast, then he drank the beer down in one, long convulsive swallow.

Williams turned to Sheila, raising her eyebrows for permission to speak.

Sheila shrugged as if to say, *It's your one and only chance*, and sat back, sipping her wine.

"Dr. Ramsey, if you'll just hear me out, I promise you that it won't be a waste of your time. In fact, it might be the most profitable time you'll ever spend."

Ramsey's ears perked up at the word *profitable*. He took off his wristwatch and laid it on the table as he sat down. "Okay, Williams, you have exactly ten minutes to get my attention, then it's out the door with you."

Kat took a quick drink of wine, marshaling her thoughts, then she leaned forward and began to talk. She outlined in abbreviated fashion her experiments, noting the initial success and eventual failure of her serum to continue to cause the antiaging and intelligence-building effects. Finally, with mounting excitement, she told of the differences in the rats after her serum was combined with Ramsey's.

Finally, exhausted with the effort, she leaned back in her chair and finished her wine, never taking her eyes off Ramsey.

Ramsey put his hands behind his head and leaned back, staring at the ceiling, thinking. After a few moments, he looked over at Sheila. "What do you think? Do you believe any of this?"

Sheila steepled her hands in front of her face. "Burton, from what I know of your serum, and from what Kat has told me of hers, I think you two may have stumbled onto the find of the century."

She reached over and poured herself another glass of wine. "I have been thinking about this ever since Kat told me about the experiments. I believe her serum has caused the brain cells to begin to divide and grow, thus increasing intelligence and reversing some of the effects of aging on the central nervous system. However, the increased metabolic rate this induces causes a rapid buildup of toxic byproducts and free radicals, which then cause even more rapid aging and deterioration."

She spread her hands. "When combined with your serum, which greatly increases the body's ability to handle and dispose of these toxic metabolic by-products, the effect becomes permanent and additive."

Both Kat and Ramsey stared at Sheila, their eyes wide

and their mouths open at the depth of her knowledge of the way their serums could be interacting.

After a moment, Ramsey frowned as he thought about what she'd said. And then he snapped his fingers. "Of course! As the cells continue to grow and divide, and the body continues to eliminate the free radicals and toxins, the organism tends to regress in age."

He slammed his hand down on the table, looking back and forth from Kat to Sheila. "Jesus! We've got the fucking fountain of youth here!"

Williams smiled uncertainly at the coarse language, then she grinned widely. "Of course, we'll need to do more testing to determine the best ratio of the serums to use, and to further determine whether there are any negative side effects, but I do believe you're right, Burton." She cringed inwardly at her inadvertent use of his first name, and hoped it wouldn't alienate him further.

A sly expression crossed Ramsey's face. "And just how do you propose we do all of this without the government finding out about it?"

"Why . . . uh . . . I don't know. I suppose I haven't given it much thought one way or the other."

Ramsey got up and went to the refrigerator. He pulled out another beer and twisted the cap off. At the table, he refilled his glass and then, after taking a quick drink, he sat down and leaned forward. "Kat, how long has it been since you've read your contract of employment with the center?"

Williams rubbed her face with her hand. "I don't understand what you're getting at, Burton."

"Just this. If we go through the center with this breakthrough, we'll be lucky to ever see a dime from it other than our usual salary. The first thing the progress committee will do is classify it, and bury it, and that's the last we'll ever see of our serums. We'll get a slap on the back and maybe even a nice letter of commendation for our records, but otherwise it'll be zip, *nada*, bupkes, while they continue to test and develop it for their own use!"

Kat glanced from Sheila to Ramsey. "You really think so?"

"I know so. What we have to do is create a little diversion, a computer smoke-screen, for want of a better analogy. You need to go into your computer and erase all evidence of the successes you've had, and make 'em think that every road has been a dead end."

Kat lowered her eyes and thought about this for a moment. When she finally looked up, she asked, "What about you? What are you going to do about Dottie, and your computer data?"

Ramsey leaned back and smiled. "Oh, don't worry about me. I'm way ahead of the game. Dottie knows nothing about my experiments, and her computer knows even less.

He hesitated. "What about your assistant?"

Kat grimaced. "Kevin is pretty much up on what is going on. He is fully familiar with the chemical composition of my formula. In addition, he knows that our rats are doing much better, and he knows that I accidentally combined our serums. Of course, he has no knowledge of what your serum is or what it is intended to treat."

Ramsey nodded slowly. "Okay, there are a few ways of getting around that. Now, here's what we'll do . . ."

The rest of the evening was spent deciding how the two scientists were going to do their combined testing without the supervisors at the center suspecting what was going on.

As Kat left Sheila's apartment, dawn was breaking over the Houston skyline. Ramsey's parting words to her were not to expect him at the center before noon, because he had some serious planning to do.

The next day, each of the researchers prepared for their upcoming deception. Ramsey told Dottie that he had decided to help Dr. Williams with some of her experiments, which caused Dottie to shake her head in wonderment at the ever-changeable moods of Dr. Ramsey. For the rest of the day, she wandered around the lab mumbling to herself and casting strange looks at Ramsey.

In her lab, Kat told Kevin that Dr. Ramsey would be doing some work in their lab, attempting to help her find the answer to her rats' earlier deterioration and to try to figure out why their serums worked so well when combined. Although he thought she had lost her mind to invite such a cretin into their lab, Kevin's only verbal response was to ask whether Dr. Ramsey was going to be smoking in the lab, and if so, could he be excused when Ramsey was present. Relieved, Kat said that of course he could. She told Kevin he could retire to the center's library to catch up on his studies when Ramsey was in the lab.

Kat then spent most of that next day spreading smoke and fog throughout her computer program, obliterating any evidence of success in her previous experiments. Acting on Ramsey's suggestion, she started a separate notebook detailing her actual experiments and their results. Ramsey had suggested a small notebook that Kat could keep with her at all times, to forestall any chance of detection by the powers that be at the center.

Ramsey strolled into Kat's lab at four thirty, a cigarette dangling from his lips. Kevin took one look at the smoke eddying around his head, scowled, and left the lab.

Ramsey walked around the lab, picking up several pieces of equipment and looking at them for a moment, then putting them down. He bent over and peered into the rat cages, smiling at the daub of dye on their backs. "Quite a setup you have here, Kat. Very professional."

Kat, uncertain whether Ramsey was being sarcastic, didn't answer. She had decided that the best way to deal with Ramsey was to say as little as possible and try to extract as much information out of him as she could. In spite of his vow to work with her, Kat still trusted the man about as far as she could throw him.

Finally, Ramsey sat next to Kat's desk and, finding no ashtray, crushed his cigarette out on the bottom of his shoe. He put the butt in his lab pocket, then turned to her. "Kat, we need to set some ground rules for our collaboration."

Kat nodded, not trusting herself to speak, for she had absolutely no idea what was about to come out of the man's mouth.

"First, I don't think either one us trusts the other very much." He raised his eyebrows in silent interrogation, and when Kat just shrugged, he went on. "Therefore, I think it best if we keep the formulae of our own serums to ourselves. I will make up my serum in my lab, and you will make up yours . . . without either of us knowing just what is in the other's serum."

Kat frowned. "But how will we know whether there's some conflict in the ingredients?"

Ramsey waved his hand in dismissal. "We'll know if the serums work together, and that's all we really need to know." He smirked. "If there's a conflict and they aren't compatible, that's all we need to know . . . right?"

Unconvinced, Kat nodded. "Okay. But if they don't work, then at some point we're going to have to compare notes on the formulae to figure out how to fix the problem."

"Okay, then we'll cross that bridge when and if we come to it. Now, let's get to work. I propose that we scrap all the previously used ráts and start fresh with new controls and new experimental animals."

"I agree. We'll start over from scratch so that there'll be no question of any contamination of our experiment with any others."

"Great. So, let's do it!" Ramsey withdrew a vial of clear liquid from his lab pocket and held it out to her.

Kat took one of her vials out, reached up, and clinked the vials together. "To us, and to the Serum of Youth."

Ramsey grinned, and said, "Amen, sister, from your lips to God's ears."

After they combined the serums, they injected six rats taken at random from the rat cage and put blue dye on their backs.

Once that was done, they agreed to meet at the lab at nine o'clock the next morning, and they each headed home.

Kat had no idea that eyes were watching her leave the lab. As soon as her car pulled out of the parking lot, a man entered the lab and went straight to her computer.

While it was booting up, he rummaged through her desk, looking for any notes or other written documents that might pertain to her experiments.

Finally, the computer was ready, and he entered the database of her experiments that he'd copied before to see if anything new had been added.

His eyes widened, and he snarled angrily when he saw completely different progress notes than what had been on the computer last week.

"That little bitch!" he exclaimed, slamming the laptop lid closed.

Whirling around, he stormed out of the lab and into the hall.

Kevin, tired of studying in the dining room, headed back to the lab. He turned the corner in the corridor just in time to see Captain Sohenshine leaning over and locking the door to their lab.

He quickly stepped back around the corner and waited for a few moments. When he peeked around the corner, Sohenshine was headed the other way.

What the hell was he doing in our office? Kevin asked himself.

He hurried down the hall and went into the lab. After looking around for a moment, he put his hand on Kat's laptop and noticed it was still warm.

That son of a bitch is spying on us, he thought, vowing to tell Kat about it first thing in the morning.

CHAPTER 14

It took Dr. Tom Alexander two weeks to clear his surgery and on-call schedule to the point that he could fly Ashby's jet back to Houston and arrange a dinner meeting with his nephew Kevin Palmer.

Tom picked Kevin up at his apartment near the University of Houston in his Mercedes 500SL. He kept the vehicle at the private airport where Ashby's jet was hangared to use on his frequent visits to Houston. Since the evening was balmy, he had the top down.

Kevin slipped into the passenger seat and gave a low whistle of approval at the fancy ride. "Wow, Uncle Tom, this is some sweet automobile."

Tom glanced at him as he pulled out of the parking lot. "You like it, huh?"

Kevin laughed. "Who in their right mind wouldn't?"

Tom nodded. "Well, after dinner, I might just have a way for you to get one just like it."

"What?"

"Never mind, that's a tale for dessert."

Kevin stared at his uncle for a moment, then asked, "Where are we going for dinner?"

"The Reef. The chef is an old acquaintance of mine, and they happen to have the best seafood in the state, outside of Corpus Christi, of course."

When Tom tossed the keys to the Mercedes to the valet, he said, "Try to park it where it won't get dinged and I'll double your tip."

"Yes, sir!" the valet exclaimed as he got behind the wheel with a wide grin.

When they approached the hostess, she inquired, "Do you have a reservation, sir?"

Tom shook his head and handed her a one-hundred-dollar bill. "No, but could you let Chef Bryan Caswell know that an old friend is here and would like to tell him hello?"

The hostess made the bill disappear, grabbed two menus, and said, "Certainly, sir. Shall I give him a name?"

"Just tell him Dr. Tom is in town for the evening and is starving."

She smiled and led them to a corner booth near a wide window with a spectacular view of downtown.

After they were seated, a waiter appeared and asked if they would like something to drink.

"I believe we'll start with a bottle of Veuve Clicquot La Grande Dame," Tom said.

"Very good, sir!" the waiter said.

Kevin, who was perusing the wine menu, raised his eyebrows. "Jesus, Uncle Tom, that's two hundred dollars a bottle."

Tom smiled. "Yeah, it works out to about fifty bucks a glass."

Kevin shook his head. "I knew doctors made a lot of money, but this is ridiculous."

"Don't worry about it, Kevin. A patient of mine is treating us to this meal."

"Oh?"

"Like I said, that's a story for dessert."

Just then, a man dressed in chef's whites appeared at the table and spread his arms wide, grinning.

Tom stood, and the two men embraced, then spent five or six minutes catching up on what the two of them had been doing since they'd last seen each other.

Finally, Tom gestured to Kevin. "Chef Bryan, this is my favorite nephew, Kevin Paxton."

"Very happy to meet you, Kevin," Chef Caswell said. "I want you to know, your uncle saved my life a few years ago, when I was down in Corpus shopping for some fresh fish for my restaurant."

"Now, Bryan," Tom said, a depreciating smile on his face, "I did nothing of the sort. It was just a minor arrhythmia . . . easily corrected."

Caswell placed both hands over his heart. "Bullshit, my friend. It was a miracle you performed, and you know it."

He stepped back and added, "And since the hostess told me you were 'starving,' I will leave you to your dinner and perhaps we can get together afterward for an espresso and some more gabbing."

As he left, the two men read the menu and then ordered. Tom ordered seafood and andouille sausage gumbo as an appetizer while Kevin chose the jumbo crab cake. For their entrées, Tom had grilled swordfish with crispy fries and Siracha remoulade, and Kevin picked the spice-crusted snapper and fried mac and cheese.

Before the waiter left to turn in their orders, he poured them both generous goblets of champagne.

As Kevin sipped, he frowned momentarily.

Catching the expression, Tom asked, "You look worried about something."

"I am trying to remember the Bible classes Mom made me take as a youngster," Kevin replied.

"Bible classes?"

Now Kevin grinned. "Yeah, I'm sure in there somewhere

was a parable about a 'fatted calf' and what he was being fattened up for."

Tom laughed and raised his glass in a toast. "Nothing bad, I assure you, Kevin." He took a sip and then added, with a mischievous grin, "In fact, it is just the opposite." He held up his hand before Kevin could reply. "Remember, for dessert only."

When their food finally came, Kevin couldn't help but moan with delight at the delicious fare. He pointed his fork at Tom and said, "This is absolutely the best meal I have ever had . . . bar none."

Later, over bananas Foster for Tom and cherries jubilee for Kevin, Tom finally got to the purpose of his invitation to dinner.

"A couple of weeks ago," he said, around a mouthful of bananas, "I was in town visiting a patient and took your mother out to lunch."

Kevin nodded, still chewing.

"At lunch, in talking about you and your work and school and other activities, she happened to mention that you had told her that your doctor employer had been making major breakthroughs in the science of life prolongation, as well as increasing mental acuity—and even that you all had had some success with reversing various effects of aging."

Kevin frowned and put his fork down forcibly. "Damn it, I knew I shouldn't have told her anything about our research." He shook his head. "I signed a nondisclosure document, and I will be in severe legal trouble if Kat . . . I mean, Dr. Williams finds out that I told anyone about our work."

Tom held up his hands. "Don't worry about that, Kevin. No one needs to know you mentioned your research project to anyone."

Kevin wiped cherry juice off his chin and replied, "Then just why did you bring it up, Uncle Tom? I am not a fool, and I know this wonderful dinner and champagne is leading up to something."

Tom pursed his lips. "Okay, you are right. I do have a proposal to put to you, and I hope you'll let me finish my speech before you comment . . . okay?"

Kevin just nodded, a suspicious look still on his face.

Tom signaled the waiter and asked him for two espressos, then he got right down to it.

"I have this patient, right here in Houston, who happens to be one of the ten richest men in the country, and probably no worse than twentieth in the entire world."

He paused while the waiter placed two cups of thick dark coffee in front of them, along with a tray of cinnamon, cream, chocolate shavings, and lemon rind.

After their coffees were prepared to their satisfaction, Tom took a small sip and continued. "A few years ago, this man, who is in his late seventies, had a rather severe stroke. I was nearby and treated him, and in his opinion, I saved his life. He was left paralyzed on the left side and is essentially bedridden."

Kevin nodded, beginning to see where this was headed.

"Now, in gratitude, this gentleman pays me almost a million dollars a year and provides me with his own personal jet so I can fly back and forth from Corpus Christi to here to continue to care for him."

Kevin smiled wryly. "No wonder you can order fifty-dollars-a-glass champagne."

"Among other things. Now, when your mother told me about your progress, I mentioned the same to this man."

"Damn it, Uncle Tom, you had no right to do that!"

Tom nodded. "You're right, Kevin. I had no right to do that, but I owe this man a great deal and I thought that if there was any hope that your project might help him to live a life worth living, then I had an obligation to see what he thought about it."

"And what did this mystery patient say?"

Tom leaned back and took another sip of his espresso, looking at Kevin over the rim of the cup. "He essentially said that if you could provide him with this formula, he would see to it that you never had to want for anything for the rest of your life, and that he would make both of us incredibly rich."

"What?" Kevin asked with a sneer. "He's going to make us millionaires?"

Tom wagged his head. "No, Kevin, more like *billionaires*."

Kevin sank back in his seat. "Holy shit!"

Tom laughed. "Holy shit, indeed, my boy."

"But listen, Uncle Tom," Kevin began, and he explained that the serum so far had only worked on rats, and the successful experiments had only been going on for a few weeks.

"I know it is early times yet, Kevin, and that much more experimentation will have to be done, including at least one human trial before I can recommend this treatment to my patient, but I wanted to know if you are on board with working with me to push the research trials as quickly as you can. Especially the human trial aspect of it."

Kevin spread his arms. "But I'm just a lab assistant. I have no power to get Dr. Williams to speed up her research . . . plus, she's now working with this other doctor, a real asshole, and he would never take any suggestions from me."

Tom leaned forward and put his elbows on the table, talking low to make sure no one could overhear him. "Money, especially huge amounts of money, has a way of turning assholes into pussycats, Kevin. What if you went to your Dr. Williams and told her you had a relative who was fabulously wealthy and just looking for a place to invest untold millions of dollars—if the project was worthwhile."

As Kevin started to protest, Tom held up his hand. "No, you don't have to tell her we know about the project yet. Entice her and Dr. Asshole with the possibility of their project being generously funded by someone who would never look over their shoulders and would give them complete freedom to continue as they wished, as long as they moved rapidly. If I know anything about medical researchers, they are always champing at the bit over inadequate funding and overzealous interference with their work."

Kevin stroked his chin. "I could tell them that this fabulously wealthy individual is elderly and has a poor quality of life, and that when you told me about him, I immediately thought that he might be interested in funding their research, but that I knew not to say anything until I asked if they were interested . . ."

"Exactly right!" Tom exclaimed.

Kevin finished off his espresso, licked his lips, and said, "Give me a few days to ease into the subject, and I'll let you know if they are interested."

Tom put his hand on Kevin's arm. "Make sure to let them know that we are not interested in controlling or owning the formula, just so long as my patient is the second human to get to use it, assuming, of course, that the first human subject survives and is benefited by the formula."

The same night that Kevin and Tom were out at dinner, Sheila opened the door to her apartment to find Williams and Ramsey sitting at her dining room table. The two were wearing party hats and had a magnum of champagne set out on the table with three glasses.

As she stood in the door and took in the scene, Sheila thought she'd never seen anyone who looked as quite out of place there as did Dr. Kaitlyn Williams . . . She had a party hat on and a glass of champagne in front of her, but her expression was more one of embarrassment than of frivolity.

Well, Sheila thought, if anyone could make someone more uncomfortable than her husband, Burton, she had yet to meet him.

Sheila shook her head and smiled, then set her briefcase down and sat at the table. "To what do I owe the pleasure of two such . . . er, happy and carefree people plying me with champagne?"

Kat sighed and nudged Ramsey's shoulder. "You tell her, Burton," she said with a hiccup, and Sheila knew that the two had started without her. "After all, she's your wife."

Ramsey grinned a silly grin. "We've done it, babe. We've hit the mother lode. Over the past two weeks, we have tested dozens of rats with our combined formulas, and after a couple of false starts, we finally have the correct proportions of each formula so that our rats are getting not only younger and smarter, but healthier and more disease-resistant, as well!"

While he talked, Ramsey popped the cork on the champagne, spewing bubbles all over them, and refilled all three glasses. Ramsey dissolved in laughter, and Kat and Sheila grinned. He handed Sheila her glass, and then, after clinking their glasses in a toast, they all began to drink the sparkling liquid.

Finally, Sheila held up her hand, a tiny golden mustache of champagne on her upper lip. "Okay, guys. Tell me all about it. I want all the details of this magical brew you two have cooked up."

With much bantering and interrupting by Ramsey, he and Kat told her of their work. How they had tried different quantities and mixtures of the two serums until they had arrived at the optimal dosage of each component. And then they described how the serum seemed to regress the rats back in age to early adulthood, and how after that, they began to age again at a normal rate, but to be much more intelligent and healthy. They even seemed to have an increased resistance to diseases and illnesses, Kat informed her seriously, forgetting that Ramsey had already mentioned it.

"So," asked Sheila, "that's it, then? You've done it . . . you've perfected the serum. Now what?"

The pair looked at each other, momentarily sobered. "Well, uh . . . I don't know," said Kat, looking into her champagne as if the answer were in the glass. It was obvious to Sheila that Kat and Burton had had some disagreements on the next course they should take.

Ramsey scratched his head. "Christ, I guess first we'll have to test it on higher mammals, like dogs or monkeys. See if it works on them like it does on the rats, and if it does, I suppose the next step would be to try it on humans."

When he said this, Kat again lowered her gaze, showing her disapproval without saying a word.

Sheila held up her hand. "Wait just a minute, guys. To do human experiments, you'll have to get the FDA involved."

Ramsey sat up, his face blossoming scarlet. "No way! There is no way I'm going to involve those pricks. To do that, we'd have to give up the serums to the center, and then they'd cut us out of it."

Sheila glanced at Kat. "Do you agree with Burton, Kat?"

"Yes," said Kat, "I agree that to notify BioTech of our discovery would be the wrong thing to do, but not for the reasons Burton has."

As Ramsey glared at Williams, Sheila cocked her head to the side, "Oh, and what are your reasons for stealing the work that BioTech paid you to do for them?"

Kat blushed and looked again at her glass of champagne as she answered. "Burton is afraid BioTech will take our discovery and only pay us a pittance for all of our work, while they make millions off of the formula. I don't care about the money, but I'm afraid all of our work would be for nothing, because BioTech would take years and years and thousands of trials before anyone would be able to benefit from our serums, and then they'd probably sell it to the government and only certain important people would be allowed access to the formula."

Ramsey thought for a moment, trying to figure out some way to spin this so he wouldn't sound like such an asshole to Sheila. "Kat is right, Sheila. If BioTech gets its hands on something this revolutionary, there is no way they'll be able to keep the government out of it, and we all know what happens when the Feds get involved in medical innovations."

He glanced from Sheila to Kat. "We'll just have to figure

out some other way, some way that no one but us will know whether it works or not."

Sheila stood up, holding her hands out in front of her. "Wait a minute. I don't think I want to hear this." She turned and started to leave the room. "Don't talk to me about stealing someone else's work and doing unauthorized experiments on human beings. I can't go along with that."

After she left, Ramsey put his finger to his lips. "Shhh," he whispered drunkenly. "We'll talk about this tomorrow."

Kat stood and walked unsteadily toward the door, a worried look on her face. "Yes. The only trick now is to find some way to get the higher mammals on which to run our tests without BioTech finding out about it."

Ramsey opened the door, leaning on the doorjamb. "Yeah, and we're gonna have to do it without the help of our assistants, too, 'cause loose lips sink ships."

Kat nodded as she walked down the sidewalk, but she knew she'd never leave Kevin out of her plans. He'd been too good of a helper to her, and she trusted him implicitly, though she knew she'd have to reemphasize to him the importance of secrecy about their upcoming experiments.

When Kaitlyn got home, she stood in the doorway for a moment after she turned on the light and waited for Angus to come running to greet her as he always did when she'd been away.

After a moment, frowning when he didn't appear, she gave a short whistle and walked through the living room toward the bedroom, where she kept his bed.

She took a deep breath when she turned on the light and saw him lying in bed, his big brown eyes fixed on her, his mouth open and panting while his tail wagged back and forth.

She rushed over to kneel by his bed, took his head in her hands, and rubbed her face against his. "What's the matter, big fellow?" she crooned. "Your arthritis keeping you in bed tonight?"

He moaned around his panting, which Dr. Washburn had told Kat meant he was in pain.

"Oh baby," she whispered, tears coursing down her cheeks. "I know you're in pain, but I just can't think about what Dr. Washburn wants me to do."

Angus gave her a big wet kiss to show her he agreed with her.

She put her arms under him, picked him up, and gently placed him on her bed, where he could sleep next to her.

While she showered, something Burton had said suddenly ran through her mind. *What was it . . . ?* she thought. *Oh yeah, he'd said their next step was to use their serum on dogs or monkeys and then on to human experimentation.*

"That's it!" she exclaimed out loud. "We can use the formula on Angus, and hopefully it will take him back to before he got the arthritis."

And if Burton objects, she thought, *then I'll just tell him that's the way it's going to be or he can damn well find another partner!*

As she dried off, she began to run through the things she would have to do to get the serum ready for Angus. First of all, she'd have to see whether Dr. Washburn could get her some fetal dog brains for the slurry she would need. Other than that, all of the ingredients would be pretty much the same for rats, dogs, or humans.

When she slipped into bed, she glanced at the clock. Too late to call the veterinarian tonight. First thing in the morning would have to do.

She leaned over and gave Angus a snuggle, saying softly, "I'm gonna make you better, big guy, I promise."

She stepped over to him and placed a hand on his arm. "That's part of what I want to talk to you about. Keep my coffee warm and I'll be back soon. What I have to say won't take long."

She strode out of her office and walked down the hall and around the corner to Burton Ramsey's lab. When she opened the door, he was standing next to Dottie's desk, going over a list of equipment for her to requisition from BioTech.

He glanced at her and actually smiled, just one of the several changes that had occurred in their relationship since they'd started working together with their combined formulas.

She smiled back, ignoring the scowl on Dottie's face. "Burton, I need to have a word with you, if you have a minute."

"Sure," he said in his brusque voice. "Dottie, why don't you go down to the cafeteria and get me a couple of sausage egg, and cheese taquitos? And get two for Dr. Williams ... o for yourself, too. Just tell them to put it on my tab."

Dottie looked at him, then at Kat, and then she just gged and walked out of the lab.

amsey gestured for Kat to sit in a chair next to his desk ked, "Would you like some coffee, Kat?"

shook her head and sat down. "Burton, you know dog, Angus?"

maced. "Yes, and to tell you the truth, I don't think longer to live."

what I want to talk to you about. Last night you out time for us to try our serums on larger ani- nkeys or dogs. I would like to give Angus the if it will work on him like it does on the rats."

s eyebrows. "You realize the risk in him ge animal we try it on? We won't have the figured out yet, and I would imagine there s that you might have to change in going

ut I've already made arrangements to

CHAPTER 15

Kat knew she was making the right decision the next morning when she had to carry Angus outside and practically hold him up while he did his business. Even then, he groaned with pain when he hunched his back for a bowel movement.

"That's all right, Angus," she said as she picked him up and carried him toward her front door. "You'll be chasing rabbits and howling at the moon again before you know it."

As soon as she had Angus settled in his bed, Kat placed a call to Dr. Washburn at her veterinary clinic.

"Hello."

"Hello, Dr. Washburn," Kat said.

"Oh, hi, Kat. Have you made a decision about Angus yet?"

"Yes, but it's not the one you think," Kat replied.

"Oh?"

"There is a new therapy, not available to the general public yet, that I would like to try before going the final step."

"A 'new therapy'?"

"Yes. It's come up at the research facility that I'm working at, but I'm going to need your help to give it a try on Angus."

"Well, of course, Kat. Anything I can do to help, you know I will. Remember, I love Angus almost as much as you do. He's a fine little fella, and he deserves all we can do for him. Now, just what do you need from me?"

Kat hesitated. "Um, I'm gonna need some fetal dog brain tissue. It doesn't have to be from a Scottish terrier—any fetal dog brain tissue will do."

Dr. Washburn said, "So, is this some sort of stem cell therapy?"

Kat hated to lie, but she had no choice. "Yes, Doctor, it is something like that, but it's being used in a completely new way."

"Hold on a moment, and let me check my surgical schedule."

Kat held her breath until Dr. Washburn came back on the line. "We're in luck, Kat. Tomorrow I'm doing a spay on a bitch that is four weeks pregnant, and so I should be able to get you the tissue you need. I should be through with the surgery around two o'clock, if all goes as scheduled."

"Oh, Dr. Washburn, Angus and I are so grateful."

"One thing, Kat."

"Yes?"

"If this doesn't work, and Angus remains in pain, you have to promise me to let me help take him out of his misery."

"Of course, Doctor. Now, I've got to go and get everything ready for the procedure."

"Okay, and I'll give you a call right after the surgery and you can come and pick up the tissue at my office."

"Great. And—thanks."

After Kat hung up the phone, she took a deep breath. Now all she had to do was convince Burton Ramsey that their next experimental subject should be her dog, Angus.

She glanced at her watch. It was already after eight o'clock. She quickly dialed Kevin's number.

When he answered, she said, "Kevin, I'm going to be late

to the clinic this morning. If Dr. Ramsey drops by, let him know that I'll be there by nine or nine thirty."

"Is everything all right, Dr. Williams?" he asked, concern evident in his voice, since Kat had never once been late to the clinic before.

She sighed. "It's Angus, Kevin. He could barely walk this morning, so I had an early consultation with Dr. Washburn."

"Uh-oh, she's not still trying to get you to put him down, is she?"

"Kevin, I've got to get ready and get on the road, or with Houston traffic I won't make it before noon. When I get there, you can fix me some of your wonderful coffee and I'll tell you all about it. I have an idea I want to run by you get your opinion on."

"Sure thing, Kat . . . uh, Dr. Williams."

She laughed. "I think it's about time you sta me Kat, Kevin. Especially when we're alon company, it can still be Dr. Williams, but Kat will do nicely."

"Okay, Kat. I'll have the coffee rea the door, and I'll have Angus's bed too."

It was nine fifteen wh wrapped in a blanket a

Kevin rushed to gently laid him i a heating pad h

He stood

She frown word with Dr. R

He shook his hea started working with t fine by ourselves."

procure those, and, in fact, I will have them by tomorrow afternoon. If you don't have to change any of your ingredients, and if we work really hard today and tonight, we should be able to get a close approximation of the changes necessary in amounts to use the serum on a dog. Most of the changes should be easily figured by simply increasing the proportions by the differences in weight."

He nodded slowly. "I agree, it is time, just so long as you are willing to accept the very real possibility that we might do more harm than good in our first canine patient."

Her eyes welled with tears, and she gave a low sob. "I don't have time to try it on other dogs first, Burton. I'm afraid he has only a few days left, and he is in constant pain."

Ramsey was flustered and embarrassed by her tears. He had never been a very compassionate or sympathetic man, and he simply had no idea of how to react to a crying woman. He leaned forward and awkwardly patted her shoulder. "Okay, Kat. As soon as we've finished our breakfast, we can get down to figuring out just what adjustments we need to make to our serums for Angus."

She shook her head and stood up. "I'm too nervous to eat just now, Burton, but thank you anyway. Besides, I've got to go to my lab and explain what we're going to do to Kevin."

He frowned and said, "I told you, Kat, we need to keep some separation between our work and our assistants. The fewer who know what we've accomplished, the better."

"You might as well know right now, Burton. I trust Kevin with my life, and I have no intention of keeping him in the dark about this. His knowledge of organic chemistry has been an enormous help to me in formulating my serum, and I think he will be a great asset to us going forward, especially if we run into any problems as we transition to larger and more complex animals."

He sighed and held up his hands, palms out. "Okay, okay, if you are sure he can be trusted."

"I am! And that brings me to another subject."

He raised his eyebrows.

"I think you should endeavor to get Sheila involved in our project. With her knowledge of both medicine and geriatrics, she, too, will be invaluable to the success of our work."

He pursed his lips. "I don't know. She was pretty adamant about our not using humans in our experiments, and you know that would be the next step."

"Burton, I think she will come around if we show her our success with dogs and monkeys, and if we do with humans like we are doing with Angus and find a subject that is so near death or that has such a terrible life that she will agree to the experiment."

He snapped his fingers and grinned. "I think you've hit the nail on the head, Kat. While we're working on Angus, I'll see if a suitably miserable human subject can be found and see about getting him or her in to see Sheila so she can see that our serum would be the poor soul's only hope."

Just then Dottie entered the door with her arms full of taquitos.

Kat nodded and winked at Ramsey and said, "I'll head back to my lab. You two enjoy your eggs."

As soon as Kevin saw her enter the lab, he went to the Keurig, popped in a K-Cup, and fixed her a steaming cup of coffee. He added three teaspoons of sugar and had it on her desk just as she sat down.

"Now," he said, leaning back in his chair next to her desk, "you said you had some things you wanted to talk about."

She sipped her coffee and smiled at him. "Perfect, as always."

He grinned. "Quit stalling, Kat. Please get to it . . . the suspense is killing me."

"Okay, here goes . . ." Kat began at the beginning and

told him how her serum had first showed great promise, only to finally lead to further disintegration and death in her rat subjects, until the fateful day when she had borrowed some of Ramsey's rats that had been injected with his formula.

"I know the rats began to do better right after you accidentally combined our formula with Ramsey's, but since I don't know what his formula does, I have no idea why."

She nodded. "At first, I thought the rats were simply doing better because of the changes I'd made in our formula, but when I tried our new formula on rats that weren't from Ramsey's lab, they didn't do nearly as well—in fact, they all died. Finally, Ramsey discovered that I'd taken his rats and braced me about it . . . That was when I finally had to accept the fact that it was the combination of our formulas that made the difference."

Kevin shook his head. "And I'll bet the asswipe wouldn't tell you anything about his formula, would he?"

Kat grinned. "Yeah, and I had no idea what to do. I knew he would never reveal the details of his formula to me, him being, as you say, a total asswipe."

"So, what did you do?"

"I did what any self-respecting woman would do . . . I went straight to his wife."

"No shit?" Kevin asked with a laugh.

"No shit," Kat replied, laughing with him. "In fact, I threw myself on her mercy, telling her how I'd 'borrowed' her husband's rats and how the resultant error had led me to believe we'd stumbled upon one of the most important findings of this century, one that could possibly cure any number of neurological diseases."

"Do you really believe that?" he asked, a skeptical look on his face.

Kat narrowed her eyes. "Well, what do you think, Kevin? Here we have a serum that not only reverses the physical changes to the body and brain caused by aging, but also somehow enhances the mind, not only making it younger but also increasing its intelligence."

Kevin whistled. "I knew the rats were acting younger and could run the maze faster, but I had no idea the changes were so profound."

Now Kat looked embarrassed. "That's because, at first, Dr. Ramsey and I decided to keep you and his assistant in the dark about the progress we were making."

When he started to protest, Kat held up her hand. "I know; it wasn't my finest hour. But just to let you know, I just told Burton that from now on, you are going to be in all the way, no secrets, and no funny business. I told him I trusted you with my life and that as far as I am concerned, we are partners all the way in this."

Kevin's eyes filled and he looked away. "You really said all that to him?" he asked in a low voice.

She put her hand on his arm. "Yes, and I meant it, Kevin. I could not have come this far without your help, and I certainly do not intend to proceed without you beside us."

He covered her hand with his and nodded. "Then, I am all in, to the very end."

"Good," she said, and got to her feet. "Now, for the next surprise, I am going to go to Dr. Washburn's office and get some fetal dog brain tissue, and then you and I and Dr. Ramsey are going to figure out a way to make our formulas work on Angus."

He stood up. "Okay! I'll get on the computer and see if I can quantify the changes in each of the components we'll need to make to account for the difference in weight between Angus and the rats."

She hesitated and stared into his eyes. "Figure it good, Kevin. We're only going to get one chance at this, and Angus's life depends on us getting it right the first time."

CHAPTER 15

Kat knew she was making the right decision the next morning when she had to carry Angus outside and practically hold him up while he did his business. Even then, he groaned with pain when he hunched his back for a bowel movement.

"That's all right, Angus," she said as she picked him up and carried him toward her front door. "You'll be chasing rabbits and howling at the moon again before you know it."

As soon as she had Angus settled in his bed, Kat placed a call to Dr. Washburn at her veterinary clinic.

"Hello."

"Hello, Dr. Washburn," Kat said.

"Oh, hi, Kat. Have you made a decision about Angus yet?"

"Yes, but it's not the one you think," Kat replied.

"Oh?"

"There is a new therapy, not available to the general public yet, that I would like to try before going the final step."

"A 'new therapy'?"

"Yes. It's come up at the research facility that I'm working at, but I'm going to need your help to give it a try on Angus."

"Well, of course, Kat. Anything I can do to help, you know I will. Remember, I love Angus almost as much as you do. He's a fine little fella, and he deserves all we can do for him. Now, just what do you need from me?"

Kat hesitated. "Um, I'm gonna need some fetal dog brain tissue. It doesn't have to be from a Scottish terrier—any fetal dog brain tissue will do."

Dr. Washburn said, "So, is this some sort of stem cell therapy?"

Kat hated to lie, but she had no choice. "Yes, Doctor, it is something like that, but it's being used in a completely new way."

"Hold on a moment, and let me check my surgical schedule."

Kat held her breath until Dr. Washburn came back on the line. "We're in luck, Kat. Tomorrow I'm doing a spay on a bitch that is four weeks pregnant, and so I should be able to get you the tissue you need. I should be through with the surgery around two o'clock, if all goes as scheduled."

"Oh, Dr. Washburn, Angus and I are so grateful."

"One thing, Kat."

"Yes?"

"If this doesn't work, and Angus remains in pain, you have to promise me to let me help take him out of his misery."

"Of course, Doctor. Now, I've got to go and get everything ready for the procedure."

"Okay, and I'll give you a call right after the surgery and you can come and pick up the tissue at my office."

"Great. And—thanks."

After Kat hung up the phone, she took a deep breath. Now all she had to do was convince Burton Ramsey that their next experimental subject should be her dog, Angus.

She glanced at her watch. It was already after eight o'clock. She quickly dialed Kevin's number.

When he answered, she said, "Kevin, I'm going to be late

to the clinic this morning. If Dr. Ramsey drops by, let him know that I'll be there by nine or nine thirty."

"Is everything all right, Dr. Williams?" he asked, concern evident in his voice, since Kat had never once been late to the clinic before.

She sighed. "It's Angus, Kevin. He could barely walk this morning, so I had an early consultation with Dr. Washburn."

"Uh-oh, she's not still trying to get you to put him down, is she?"

"Kevin, I've got to get ready and get on the road, or with Houston traffic I won't make it before noon. When I get there, you can fix me some of your wonderful coffee and I'll tell you all about it. I have an idea I want to run by you and get your opinion on."

"Sure thing, Kat . . . uh, Dr. Williams."

She laughed. "I think it's about time you started calling me Kat, Kevin. Especially when we're alone. In front of company, it can still be Dr. Williams, but when it's just us, Kat will do nicely."

"Okay, Kat. I'll have the coffee ready when you walk in the door, and I'll have Angus's bed nice and warm for him, too."

It was nine fifteen when Kat walked into the lab, Angus wrapped in a blanket and cuddled in her arms.

Kevin rushed to take the dog from her and turned and gently laid him in his bed next to Kat's desk, first removing a heating pad he had placed there to keep the pillow warm.

He stood up and turned. "I'll get your coffee now, Kat."

She frowned. "Not just yet, Kevin. I need to have a quick word with Dr. Ramsey first."

He shook his head, scowling. "I don't know why you've started working with that asshole, Kat. We were doing just fine by ourselves."

She stepped over to him and placed a hand on his arm. "That's part of what I want to talk to you about. Keep my coffee warm and I'll be back soon. What I have to say won't take long."

She strode out of her office and walked down the hall and around the corner to Burton Ramsey's lab. When she opened the door, he was standing next to Dottie's desk, going over a list of equipment for her to requisition from BioTech.

He glanced at her and actually smiled, just one of the several changes that had occurred in their relationship since they'd started working together with their combined formulas.

She smiled back, ignoring the scowl on Dottie's face. "Burton, I need to have a word with you, if you have a minute."

"Sure," he said in his brusque voice. "Dottie, why don't you go down to the cafeteria and get me a couple of sausage egg, and cheese taquitos? And get two for Dr. Williams two for yourself, too. Just tell them to put it on my tab."

Dottie looked at him, then at Kat, and then she just shrugged and walked out of the lab.

Ramsey gestured for Kat to sit in a chair next to his desk and asked, "Would you like some coffee, Kat?"

She shook her head and sat down. "Burton, you know about my dog, Angus?"

He grimaced. "Yes, and to tell you the truth, I don't think he has much longer to live."

"That's what I want to talk to you about. Last night you said it was about time for us to try our serums on larger animals, like monkeys or dogs. I would like to give Angus the serum and see if it will work on him like it does on the rats."

He raised his eyebrows. "You realize the risk in him being the first large animal we try it on? We won't have the exact proportions figured out yet, and I would imagine there are some ingredients that you might have to change in going from rats to a dog."

"Yes, there are, but I've already made arrangements to

procure those, and, in fact, I will have them by tomorrow afternoon. If you don't have to change any of your ingredients, and if we work really hard today and tonight, we should be able to get a close approximation of the changes necessary in amounts to use the serum on a dog. Most of the changes should be easily figured by simply increasing the proportions by the differences in weight."

He nodded slowly. "I agree, it is time, just so long as you are willing to accept the very real possibility that we might do more harm than good in our first canine patient."

Her eyes welled with tears, and she gave a low sob. "I don't have time to try it on other dogs first, Burton. I'm afraid he has only a few days left, and he is in constant pain."

Ramsey was flustered and embarrassed by her tears. He had never been a very compassionate or sympathetic man, and he simply had no idea of how to react to a crying woman. He leaned forward and awkwardly patted her shoulder. "Okay, Kat. As soon as we've finished our breakfast, we can get down to figuring out just what adjustments we need to make to our serums for Angus."

She shook her head and stood up. "I'm too nervous to eat just now, Burton, but thank you anyway. Besides, I've got to go to my lab and explain what we're going to do to Kevin."

He frowned and said, "I told you, Kat, we need to keep some separation between our work and our assistants. The fewer who know what we've accomplished, the better."

"You might as well know right now, Burton. I trust Kevin with my life, and I have no intention of keeping him in the dark about this. His knowledge of organic chemistry has been an enormous help to me in formulating my serum, and I think he will be a great asset to us going forward, especially if we run into any problems as we transition to larger and more complex animals."

He sighed and held up his hands, palms out. "Okay, okay, if you are sure he can be trusted."

"I am! And that brings me to another subject."

He raised his eyebrows.

"I think you should endeavor to get Sheila involved in our project. With her knowledge of both medicine and geriatrics, she, too, will be invaluable to the success of our work."

He pursed his lips. "I don't know. She was pretty adamant about our not using humans in our experiments, and you know that would be the next step."

"Burton, I think she will come around if we show her our success with dogs and monkeys, and if we do with humans like we are doing with Angus and find a subject that is so near death or that has such a terrible life that she will agree to the experiment."

He snapped his fingers and grinned. "I think you've hit the nail on the head, Kat. While we're working on Angus, I'll see if a suitably miserable human subject can be found and see about getting him or her in to see Sheila so she can see that our serum would be the poor soul's only hope."

Just then Dottie entered the door with her arms full of taquitos.

Kat nodded and winked at Ramsey and said, "I'll head back to my lab. You two enjoy your eggs."

As soon as Kevin saw her enter the lab, he went to the Keurig, popped in a K-Cup, and fixed her a steaming cup of coffee. He added three teaspoons of sugar and had it on her desk just as she sat down.

"Now," he said, leaning back in his chair next to her desk, "you said you had some things you wanted to talk about."

She sipped her coffee and smiled at him. "Perfect, as always."

He grinned. "Quit stalling, Kat. Please get to it . . . the suspense is killing me."

"Okay, here goes . . ." Kat began at the beginning and

told him how her serum had first showed great promise, only to finally lead to further disintegration and death in her rat subjects, until the fateful day when she had borrowed some of Ramsey's rats that had been injected with his formula.

"I know the rats began to do better right after you accidentally combined our formula with Ramsey's, but since I don't know what his formula does, I have no idea why."

She nodded. "At first, I thought the rats were simply doing better because of the changes I'd made in our formula, but when I tried our new formula on rats that weren't from Ramsey's lab, they didn't do nearly as well—in fact, they all died. Finally, Ramsey discovered that I'd taken his rats and braced me about it . . . That was when I finally had to accept the fact that it was the combination of our formulas that made the difference."

Kevin shook his head. "And I'll bet the asswipe wouldn't tell you anything about his formula, would he?"

Kat grinned. "Yeah, and I had no idea what to do. I knew he would never reveal the details of his formula to me, him being, as you say, a total asswipe."

"So, what did you do?"

"I did what any self-respecting woman would do . . . I went straight to his wife."

"No shit?" Kevin asked with a laugh.

"No shit," Kat replied, laughing with him. "In fact, I threw myself on her mercy, telling her how I'd 'borrowed' her husband's rats and how the resultant error had led me to believe we'd stumbled upon one of the most important findings of this century, one that could possibly cure any number of neurological diseases."

"Do you really believe that?" he asked, a skeptical look on his face.

Kat narrowed her eyes. "Well, what do you think, Kevin? Here we have a serum that not only reverses the physical changes to the body and brain caused by aging, but also somehow enhances the mind, not only making it younger but also increasing its intelligence."

Kevin whistled. "I knew the rats were acting younger and could run the maze faster, but I had no idea the changes were so profound."

Now Kat looked embarrassed. "That's because, at first, Dr. Ramsey and I decided to keep you and his assistant in the dark about the progress we were making."

When he started to protest, Kat held up her hand. "I know; it wasn't my finest hour. But just to let you know, I just told Burton that from now on, you are going to be in all the way, no secrets, and no funny business. I told him I trusted you with my life and that as far as I am concerned, we are partners all the way in this."

Kevin's eyes filled and he looked away. "You really said all that to him?" he asked in a low voice.

She put her hand on his arm. "Yes, and I meant it, Kevin. I could not have come this far without your help, and I certainly do not intend to proceed without you beside us."

He covered her hand with his and nodded. "Then, I am all in, to the very end."

"Good," she said, and got to her feet. "Now, for the next surprise, I am going to go to Dr. Washburn's office and get some fetal dog brain tissue, and then you and I and Dr. Ramsey are going to figure out a way to make our formulas work on Angus."

He stood up. "Okay! I'll get on the computer and see if I can quantify the changes in each of the components we'll need to make to account for the difference in weight between Angus and the rats."

She hesitated and stared into his eyes. "Figure it good, Kevin. We're only going to get one chance at this, and Angus's life depends on us getting it right the first time."

CHAPTER 16

It was late that night before they had the serums combined and adjusted to what was their best guess of what the proportions should be for Angus. Kat had ground up the fetal dog brain tissue and added it to her serum in place of the fetal rat brain tissue, and she felt they were good to go.

When they finally gathered around Angus's bed in the lab, just before midnight, he looked up at them and wagged his tail. His large brown eyes stared at Kat, almost as if he knew she was there to try to relieve his pain and suffering.

Kevin gently took his right leg and shaved a bare patch over the vein, then held the leg while Kat inserted the needle and emptied the syringe containing the precious serum.

When she was done, she leaned over and hugged Angus to her breast, her eyes filled with tears.

Behind her, Burton Ramsey cleared his throat. Even he was overcome with emotion at the tender scene before him. "Whatever happens, Kat," he said, "it will be for the best."

She gently laid Angus back into his bed and said softly, "I know, Burton. Thank you for agreeing to let me treat Angus with our serum."

He reached down and patted her shoulder, then he turned and walked toward the door. "Be sure to call my cell and let me know as soon as there are any changes," he said over his shoulder.

"Do you want me to help you get Angus into the car so you can take him home?" Kevin asked.

Kat shook her head. "No, I think I'll just let him stay here for tonight. I'll make up a bed on the couch, and that way if he needs anything in the way of medicine or chemicals, I'll be here in the lab."

"Would you like me to stay?"

"No, thank you, Kevin. If it's all the same to you, I'd really rather be alone with my big guy tonight . . . whatever happens."

In spite of thinking she'd never be able to get to sleep, fatigue overtook her and within an hour she was deep in slumber.

The next morning, she awoke to Kevin gently shaking her shoulder. "I think you'd better get up and look at this, Kat."

She jerked awake, threw off the blanket covering her legs, and rushed over to Angus's bed.

He was lying there, shivering and shaking and moaning, and most of his fur had fallen out and was on the pillow next to him.

"Oh my God!" Kat exclaimed, placing her hand on his muzzle. "He's burning up with fever."

Before Kevin could answer, Ramsey rushed into the room and over to the bed. He knelt and ran his hands over Angus, shaking his head.

"Do . . . do you think he's dying?" Kat asked fearfully.

After another moment of checking Angus's pulse and feeling his muscles, Ramsey shook his head. "I'm not sure, but I think he may be just reacting to a vastly sped-up metabolic rate. That would certainly account for the rise in temperature and the shaking."

"That also might be the reason his fur fell out," Kevin added. "The faster metabolic rate would speed up the hair follicles' regular regenerative processes and increase the normal rate of his fur loss."

"Hand me that blanket on the couch, please," Kat asked Kevin.

"As high as his temperature is, I don't think he needs a blanket," Ramsey offered.

"I know, but it has my scent on it and I think it will comfort him to have it around him," Kat said.

Sure enough, once Kevin wrapped the blanket over him, Angus quit shaking and panting and seemed to relax back against the pillow. Moments later, he was fast asleep.

"Good," Kevin said. "The body heals best when sleeping."

"Okay, everyone out," Kat said, shooing them toward the door. "Check back on us after lunch, and we'll see how he's doing then."

When they had left and the lab was again empty, she took the cushions off the couch, arranged them next to Angus's bed, and lay there next to him, her hand on his flank.

"Sleep tight, big guy, and when you wake up maybe things will be different and the pain will just be a distant memory."

Four hours later, Kat awoke to the feel of Angus's tongue lathering her face.

She yawned, sat up, and blinked. Angus was standing before her, his hair fully an inch long now and coal black instead of streaked with gray. In addition, his flanks were slightly sunken, showing he'd lost his paunch. His eyes were clear and bright, and when he barked at her, the sound was higher and less gravelly than before. In short, he already looked years younger.

Kat's eyes filled, and she threw her arms around his neck and hugged him to her. "Oh, my big, handsome fella, you look so good!"

He licked her cheek a couple of times, and then he shook loose from her and trotted over to the table holding his dog food and stood up with his two front paws on the edge of the table and barked at her.

She wiped the tears from her eyes and stood up. "Oh, are you telling me you're hungry?" she asked as she moved to fill his bowl.

He watched her intently, barked again, and seemed to nod his head.

Kat stopped and stared at him, then she laughed and shook her head. "No, it can't be that you understood that."

He barked again and dropped down to nudge his food bowl with his nose, as if to say, "*Hurry up, I'm starving.*"

Kat chuckled and filled his bowl, enjoying the sight of him gulping down his food with apparent gusto. It had been years since he'd eaten with such enthusiasm.

Moments later, his bowl clean, he glanced up at her and again nudged his bowl.

"Oh, you want more?" she asked, reaching for the bag of food.

Again, he barked and seemed to nod his head.

"Jesus," Kat murmured as she filled his bowl. "Could the serum have already increased his intelligence this much?"

He stopped eating for a moment and stared at her, then he lowered his head and began to eat more slowly.

Kat set the food bag down and moved over to the phone on her desk. She dialed and then said, "Burton, you and Kevin need to come to the lab. There is something you need to see."

When the two men entered the lab, they both broke into wide grins at the sight of the new leaner, healthier Angus standing over his bowl gobbling down his food.

"Is that the same dog?" Ramsey exclaimed, his hands raised to his mouth.

"You bet it is," Kat said. "His hair is already starting to grow back without any gray, and it looks as if he burned off at least two or three pounds while he was sleeping last night."

"My God," Kevin said, shaking his head. "What a difference, and in less than twenty-four hours."

Angus finished his food, moved over to his water dish, and lapped greedily at the cool water.

"There's something else I want you to see," Kat said.

When she had the two men's attention, she turned toward Angus and said, "Angus, do you need to go potty?"

He stopped drinking and trotted over to the table holding his leash. He stood up on his hind legs, grabbed the leash with his teeth, and trotted back over to Kat. He dropped the leash at her feet, looked into her eyes, and barked while nodding his head.

"Oh shit! Did that dog just understand what you asked and then answer you?" Ramsey asked in disbelief.

Kat slowly nodded. "I think so, Burton."

He shook his head. "No, it is much too soon for that. It's just that he knows the word *potty*, and that is not so unusual for a dog to respond to."

Kat pursed her lips. "You may be right. Let's try something harder."

She leaned over to Angus and said, "No, not me, Angus. Kevin is going to take you out."

Angus looked from her to Kevin and immediately trotted over to stand before the young man.

"Holy shit!" Kevin said, grinning widely. "What do you think now, Dr. Ramsey?"

"I think Kat is right," he said, staring at Angus. "The dog is definitely smarter than any other dog I've ever seen."

"Well, the serum definitely made the rats smarter, and

they were pretty dumb to begin with," Kevin said, looking at
Angus with wonder. "And Angus was already smart, even for
a dog, so there is no telling just how intelligent he is going to
become."

Kat noticed that Angus's eyes tracked from person to
person as they spoke, as if he was listening to the conversation.

Kevin picked up the leash and fastened it to Angus's collar. "Come on, big boy. Let's go do your business."

Kat moved to take the leash from him. "That's okay,
Kevin. I just said you'd take him to see if he could understand me. I want to stay with him."

She leaned over and patted Angus on the head. "I'm
sorry I confused you, baby, but I'll take you out."

Over her shoulder as she walked out the door, she called,
"Kevin, would you fix me some coffee, please? We'll be
right back."

When they got outside, Angus led her straight toward the
grassy area where he always pooped.

At first, he sniffed around the area as usual, looking for
just the right spot. Kat watched him absently, her mind roving quickly over the events of the past few hours, until she
suddenly noticed Angus was staring at her expectantly. He
barked and turned away to face away from her, then he looked
back over his shoulder at her.

"What is it, boy?" she asked, and then it came to her.
"Oh, you want me to turn my back and not watch you go to
the bathroom?"

He barked again and continued to watch her until she
turned around to face the other way.

"Oh Jesus," she said again, "I can't believe he is embarrassed to go potty in front of me."

She turned just in time to see him lower his leg after watering a nearby tree. He glanced at her, then he trotted back
toward the building, evidently finished for a while.

She noticed he no longer moved like a geriatric dog, but

more like a two-year-old puppy. He didn't walk so much as he trotted and pranced, as if to say, *Look at me, aren't I a handsome boy?*

As she followed him back to the lab, she briefly closed her eyes and gave a silent prayer of thanks to God that He'd allowed their serum to work on her best friend.

When they entered the lab and she took off his leash, Angus trotted over to Kevin, and when Kevin lowered his hand, he licked his palm a couple of times.

After allowing Kevin to pat him for a moment, Angus yawned widely and moved over to his bed to lie down. He took the blanket with Kat's scent on it in his teeth and pulled it over him, lay back, and was almost immediately asleep.

Ramsey and Kevin looked at each other and then at Kat, their mouths hanging open.

She smiled. "And that's not all, gentlemen," she said. "When we were outside, he let me know he wouldn't go to the bathroom until I turned my back. Evidently our formula has made him a bit shy."

Ramsey looked unconvinced. "Are you sure you're not just reading more into things than is really there?"

Kevin shook his head. "I don't think she is, Dr. Ramsey. Remember, dogs are just below chimps in intelligence, and chimps and dolphins are just below humans, and that's without any artificial enhancement. If your serum does to Angus what it did to the rats, then I believe he will be right up there with an IQ about that of a young child."

Ramsey frowned, "But—"

"No, Burton," Kat interrupted. "I think Kevin is right. It has only been a few hours, and look at the differences we can already see in Angus. There is no telling how young and strong and intelligent he'll be after another couple of days."

Ramsey thought for a few minutes, pacing and rubbing his chin. Finally, he looked up. "I've got a camcorder in my office. It's small and very portable. I'm going to get it and give it to you, Kat. I want you to video-document these changes in Angus's behavior, especially the ones showing his increase in intelligence. Like they say, a picture is worth a thousand words, and I don't think anyone would believe what is happening if we don't have visual proof."

He turned to Kevin. "And since you're now a full partner, Kevin, I want you to take Kat's notebook and fully document everything we've done over the past day and night, including dosages and times and the changes that we've all noticed, like the hair and weight loss and the increased appetite and intelligence, and even the increased temperature, indicating a marked increase in metabolic rate." He shook his head. "Though I doubt if anyone will believe us unless they see for themselves what a miracle this serum has wrought."

Kevin grinned at the term *partner* and nodded his head. "Yes, sir, I'll get right on it."

Kat asked, "What about the rats we have left, Burton? Are we going to continue the experiments on them?"

He shook his head. "We're through with rats, Kat, except as a false lead for the BioTech snoops. From now on, we are on to bigger and better things."

"You mean—?"

"Yes, I mean our next step is to find a down-and-out human who is need of our assistance to lead a meaningful life." He paused. "Of course, we'll still have to mess around with the rats for a while, essentially showing poor results to our injections."

"And just how do you intend to find such a person?" Kat asked. "Are you going over to the Fifth Ward and wander the streets looking for a homeless bum to experiment on?"

He shook his head. "No, I've got a better idea. Sheila volunteers at the clinic at Ben Taub Hospital, where most of the indigent people go for their medical care. So, I'm going to follow your suggestion and fill her in on what we need and see if I can't get her to find a 'specimen' for us."

Kat smirked. "Good luck with that, Burton."

He gave a wry smile. "Thank you, Kat. I'm gonna need it."

* * *

Thirty minutes later, Captain Sohenshine sauntered into the lab without bothering to knock.

Kat looked up from where she was writing notes in her new notebook and frowned. She quickly shut the notebook and said, "Hello, Captain. To what do I owe the pleasure of your visit? I know the progress committee isn't scheduled to meet for another two weeks."

He didn't answer, but continued to stroll around the lab, hands in his pockets, his beady eyes roving over everything with a suspicious glint in them.

Finally, when he got to the corner where Angus's bed was, he stopped and stood there staring, stroking his chin. "Did your old dog die?" he asked.

Shit, Kat thought. "Uh, yes, I had to put him down. That is a rescue dog I got from the animal shelter."

He looked over his shoulder at her and grunted, "Uh-huh," with a skeptical expression on his face.

Moving over to stand in front of her desk, he said, "And how are your experiments going, Dr. Williams? Any progress to report?"

"Nothing earth-shattering, Captain. But you will have my full report prior to the progress committee meeting, and I will go into detail then."

"Okay," he said, moving around her desk and stroking his hand along her shoulders as he walked toward the door. "I do hope you have some good news for the committee."

She stared at his back, openmouthed. Had he just come on to her?

Kevin walked into the lab from the dining room carrying sandwiches and chips for their lunch. "Was that Captain Sunshine I just saw leaving?" he asked, placing the sandwiches on her desk.

"Yeah, and he was acting kinda strange."

"Oh, that reminds me. I was coming back from the dining room the other day after you and Dr. Ramsey had already left the lab, and I saw him sneaking out of your lab and locking the door behind him."

"What?"

"And that's not all. When I came into the lab, your laptop was still warm, like he might've had it turned on while he was in here."

"That son of a bitch has been snooping around, trying to see what we've been working on," she said. "I wonder how much he knows?"

"That depends on how much of what we've discovered you have in your computer," Kevin said.

"Too damn much, I'm afraid."

CHAPTER 17

Kat glanced at the camcorder Ramsey had left and then down at the sandwiches on her desk. She turned to Kevin. "Do you really want dry cafeteria sandwiches for lunch? It seems I have developed an appetite for something a little more elegant."

"Almost anything is more elegant than BioTech sandwiches," he answered with a smile.

She glanced over at Angus, still fast asleep under her blanket. "Then how about I treat you to the best deli in town . . . lunch at Antone's?"

"That's a deal! I love their tuna salad sandwiches with deviled eggs on the side."

Kat laughed. "Their po-boys ain't bad, either—especially with that chowchow they put on them."

"Why are we still here? Let's go."

After they got back, Kat sat at her desk next to Angus's bed and Kevin sat in the chair in front of the desk.

Kat yawned and then laughed. "Maybe we need to emulate Angus and take a long afternoon nap."

"Hang on a minute while I fix us an after-lunch coffee."

When he had done so, he handed a steaming cup to Kat and sat across from her. "Uh, Kat, there's something I need to talk to you about."

She stifled another yawn and quickly took a sip of her coffee. "Go ahead, but you'd better hurry while I'm still awake enough to listen."

"I had initially planned on coming at this from a more oblique angle, but here goes. I made a mistake a few weeks ago and mentioned to my mom that we had had a break-through, and that the serum we were working on seemed to be working even better than we had hoped."

Kat stopped with her cup halfway to her lips and frowned. "You talked to your mom about our research?"

His face flamed red. "Uh, yeah, but it was just kinda off-hand, and I didn't give any specifics."

Kat nodded slowly. "Uh-huh. Just what did you say?"

"Well, I said that our serum was performing better than expected and it seemed to make our rats act younger and smarter."

Kat leaned her head back and sighed. "No specifics, my ass! You did everything but tell her the chemical formula of the serum." She looked back down at him. "Kevin, you mean that after all those talks we've had about keeping our research a secret, you went and blabbed about it to your mother?"

"Uh . . . yeah, but then I told her to keep it secret and not to tell anyone."

"And did she . . . keep it a secret, I mean?"

"Well, not exactly."

"Oh Kevin . . ."

He held up his hands. "Hold on a minute, Kat. Remember I told you I had an uncle who is a famous heart doctor down at Corpus Christi?"

Kat's eyes narrowed. She felt she knew where this was heading. "Yeah, I kinda remember."

"Well, his name is Tom Alexander, and he visited her about a month ago and she just happened to mention it to him."

"So, now there are two outsiders who know about our success with the formula?"

"Uh, again, not exactly."

Kat shook her head and finished off her coffee in one long draught, then she slammed the cup down hard enough to crack it. "Come on, Kevin. Get to the point. Just how many people are we talking about who know all about our business?"

Again, he held up his hands. "Only three, I promise."

"Three? Who is the other one?"

"Well, Uncle Tom has this really, really rich patient who is super-old and who has had a stroke and is partially paralyzed and who is going to die soon unless some miracle cure can be found."

"Don't tell me," she said, dipping her head into her hands.

Kevin reached across the desk and put his hand on her arm. "Wait a minute, Kat. This is a tremendous opportunity. Uncle Tom said this guy offered not only to fund the rest of our research, but to give us millions of dollars to use the formula on him if we can prove it works."

She looked up, her mouth agape. "This patient of your uncle's offered to buy our formula for a million dollars?"

Kevin grinned and shook his head. "No, Kat. That's the best part. He doesn't want to buy or even control the formula. All he wants is for us to use it on him to make him younger and healthier. He says we never have to let the formula out of our control. All we have to do is inject him with it—and the amount is not a million dollars, it's *many* millions of dollars."

Her eyes narrowed in thought for a moment. "Are there any other conditions?"

"Just that we use it on at least one other human before we use it on him. If it works on our test case, then he will transfer whatever fee we negotiate to any bank account in the world that we want before we inject him."

"Are you sure this is legit, Kevin? Millions of dollars is a lot . . . no, it's a *hell* of a lot of money."

"My uncle says this man's net worth is over twenty billion dollars, and that a small percent of your assets isn't so much to spend to prolong your life and end your suffering."

Kat stood up and began to pace around the lab, talking to herself as much as to Kevin. "Well, several old proverbs or clichés come to mind . . . never cry over spilt milk, every cloud has a silver lining, it's always darkest just before dawn."

Kevin brightened. "So, what I did wasn't so bad after all?"

She turned to glare at him. "Yes, what you did was terrible, Kevin. You betrayed my trust, even if it does turn out okay in the long run."

He looked down at his feet, crestfallen. "Oh."

Suddenly, in spite of her anger at him, she also felt sorry for him. *After all, he is really just a kid at heart*, she thought.

"Oh hell, Kevin," she said, striding over to him and pulling him to his feet. She looked into his eyes. "I can't stay mad at you, you little shit."

When she hugged him to her, he almost gasped with relief.

She pushed him back and stared again into his eyes. "But this will not happen again, right? We need to know we can trust you or the deal is off."

He smiled and crossed his heart with his index finger. "I swear I will never again breathe a word to anyone about anything concerning our research . . ."

She pointed her finger at him. "Or about anything we do or plan to do in the future!"

He kissed his little finger and held it up in the air. "Pinkie swear!"

Kat laughed and punched his shoulder. "You really are just a little kid."

Kevin's smile faded. He didn't want Kat thinking of him as a "little kid." He wanted her to realize he was a man, a man who cared about her more than he could ever admit.

Kat turned away and again began pacing around the lab. "What do we do now?"

She sat at her desk and motioned Kevin to sit across from her. "What you are going to do, Kevin, is to buy us some time. I want you to call your uncle and tell him that we are very favorably disposed to take his deal, but that we will need a couple of weeks or so to iron out some wrinkles in the formula, and then to find and treat another human with the formula to make sure it is safe for his patient."

"Okay, but why lie to him?"

"It is not a lie, Kevin. We do need the time, and we need to be assured that while we are working on this, no one will get overly anxious and try to steal or otherwise interfere with the formula before we are ready to make the deal."

"Oh, I see."

She nodded. "We're also going to have to move our lab to someplace secure, someplace away from prying eyes like Captain Sunshine's, and we're going to have to make damn sure no one can get their hands on our formulae. Not now that we know it's worth millions of dollars."

"Anything else?"

She thought for a moment. "Moving is going to be expensive, because we can't take any of BioTech's equipment with us . . . We're gonna have to buy all new stuff. I think you should ask your uncle for a good-faith advance of about fifty thousand dollars to keep his patient first in line for our treatment."

Kevin's eyebrows raised. "You think they'll go for it?"

"Kevin, fifty thousand dollars is peanuts compared to millions. If they can't play for fifty, then I don't trust them to come across with millions later."

She thought for a moment, then snapped her fingers. "I know what will convince them." She picked up Ramsey's camcorder from her desk and held it up before him. Then she burrowed in her desk and took out a small pile of pictures. "Here are some pictures I've taken of Angus from earlier this year. We'll wake Angus up and you can take some videos of him to show how young and smart he is, and then you can take them to your uncle and show him the before pictures and the after videos of Angus, and that should give them enough evidence of what we've got to make them trust us with an advance of fifty thousand dollars."

He nodded. "I agree. After I take the videos, I'll go right home and call my uncle tonight."

She wagged her head. "No, not just yet. I've got to talk this over with Burton first before we make any hard and fast decisions. After all, we're all in this as partners."

"When will you talk with him?"

"It'll have to be sometime tomorrow. Tonight he's going over to his ex-wife Sheila's house to try to talk her into helping us find a human subject for our next experiment."

Later that night, after calling ahead, Ramsey showed up at Sheila's apartment with an armful of Chinese takeout.

She greeted him at the door and showed him to the dining room table. "What's with the Chinese?" she asked. "You usually don't eat anything but American."

He blushed as he arranged the cardboard boxes on the table and unwrapped the chopsticks. "Well, Chinese is less expensive, and I'm running a bit low on funds at the present time."

She put her hand on his arm. "Well, if you need a short-term loan, you know you can always call on me, dear."

He started to snap back at her, but when he looked into her soft eyes, he realized she was sincere in her offer of help and not trying to needle him. "Uh, thanks, Sheila, but I'll manage to get by." He gave a shy grin. "After all, I lived on bologna sandwiches for years in graduate school, and I'm not too highfalutin to do the same now if need be."

She got a wistful look in her eyes. "I remember those days, Burton. Looking back on them, it seems they were the best of times."

He put his hand over hers on the table. "For me, too, Sheila . . . for me, too."

"Now," she said brightly, "let's see what magic our Chinese chef has performed for us tonight."

Later, after dinner and over coffee taken on the balcony looking out over the Houston skyline, they talked.

He started by telling her of the remarkable changes that had taken place in Kat's dog, Angus, and how astounded they'd all been at the massive increase in intelligence the dog evidenced along with his new youthfulness.

"Oh, that's wonderful, my dear," Sheila said, squeezing his hand with hers.

"And that brings me to my second point," Ramsey said, his face reddening under her gaze.

"Uh-oh," she said, leaning back on the settee. "Why am I now afraid of what you're going to say next?"

"No, no, it's nothing like that, Sheila. It's just that I know you are opposed to us experimenting on human beings with our serum without going through FDA protocols."

"That's right."

"But you know how that is, dear. If we file an application for human trials, the procedure could take ten or fifteen years before we get approval, and by then our formula will no longer be a secret."

"But what other choice do you have, Burton? Even if you could get some person to agree to be a test subject, you'd still have to divulge the effects you would be hoping to get and your secret would still be out."

"Let me propose something to you, Sheila . . . but you have to promise to let me finish before you make up your mind."

She gave a half grin. "I have a feeling I'm going to regret this . . . but okay."

He drained his coffee, set the cup down, and took both of her hands in his. "How about if the next time you work at the Ben Taub Clinic, you keep your eye out for a truly hopeless patient? One who is on his or her last legs and for whom there is no medical treatment available that will ameliorate their symptoms or improve their quality of life in the slightest."

"But . . ." she began until he held up his hand.

"Let me finish, sweetheart. You've told me many times how working at the clinic often breaks your heart because of the many hopeless cases who come through the door. Men and women who are at the end of their lives and who are truly miserable and who are suffering greatly."

She sighed and nodded her head. "Yes, it is true that I occasionally come across patients like that, but that doesn't mean that I could in good faith offer them what is at best a crapshoot at a better life."

He shook his head. "No, that is not what you'd be offering them. If the formula works as we think it will, they would have a chance at a completely new life, one in which they are younger, healthier, and even more intelligent. And the beauty of this chance is that if our formula fails to work, they will be no worse off than they were to begin with."

She started to object, but he cut her off. "No, Sheila, I am telling the truth. Kat and I have agreed to let you see the ingredients of both of our serums so that you can see that there is no way either serum could do the patient any harm."

She sat back and looked out over the city, thinking. After a few moments, she looked back at him. "You are absolutely sure that the formula will cause no harm, even if it doesn't work as you hope?"

He nodded vigorously. "Even in the beginning, before we combined our serums, when they didn't work the rats weren't harmed—they just weren't benefited. And it is the same now."

"Okay, Burton. I won't promise anything more than that I will keep my eyes open, and if I come across such a patient, I will arrange for you and Kat to talk to him or her and make your proposal. But I will be there to make sure that you give them full disclosure that the serum has never been tried on a human before and that you make no unreasonable promises."

He grinned and leaned forward to put his arms around her in a hug. "That's all we can ask and all that we want."

When she hugged him back and gave a low moan of pleasure, he leaned his head back and stared into her eyes for a moment, then he kissed her gently on the lips.

When he pulled back, she smiled and whispered, "Would you like to stay the night, Burton?"

He sighed and nodded. "More than anything in the world."

"Good," she said and stood up, taking him by the hand and leading him into the apartment and into her bedroom.

He saw the bedcovers were pulled back and his pajamas were laid out on his side of the bed.

He smiled at her. "Did you know the evening would end up like this?"

"No, but it never hurts to hope, does it?"

"No, and I want you to know that I have never given up hoping, either."

CHAPTER 18

It was after ten o'clock the next morning when Burton Ramsey strolled into the lab. He had his hands in his pockets, and he was actually whistling and smiling, two things Kat and Kevin had never seen the man do before.

Kat and Kevin were both sitting at her desk drinking coffee. Angus's bed had been moved over to a corner of the lab, and he was sitting in it, his attention fixed on a small portable TV on a table in front of the bed.

Ramsey stopped mid-whistle and looked from Kat and Kevin over to Angus, his eyebrows raised. "Are you two trying to get the dog addicted to daytime soap operas?" he asked, his smile still on his face. "What, are you trying to make him stupid?"

Angus heard the voice and glanced back over his shoulder, then he jumped up and trotted over to sit in front of Ramsey. He sniffed a couple of times, and then with a wag of his tail, he slowly raised his right paw.

"We think that means you've been accepted as one of his pack," Kat called over to him. "Which means even though he's loads smarter, he still has poor taste in friends."

Ramsey grinned and leaned over to solemnly shake Angus's paw. "I resemble that remark," he joked. "Who wouldn't want a nice guy like me as a member of their pack?"

After the shake, Angus turned and trotted back over to his bed to resume watching TV while Ramsey fixed himself a cup of coffee and took a seat across Kat's desk next to Kevin.

Kat and Kevin glanced at each other and Kat whispered, "Kevin, who is this man and what has he done with Burton Ramsey?"

Ramsey laughed and took a sip of his coffee. "What, just because it's a beautiful day and I'm in a good mood, you have to give me jazz?"

"It's just that there have been plenty of beautiful days, and we've never seen you react like this before," Kevin said, staring at him.

As Ramsey shrugged and took another sip, Kat snapped her fingers and grinned. "Aha!"

"What's with the *aha*?" Ramsey asked.

"Your meeting with Sheila must have gone exceptionally well last night, Burton."

Now his face flamed red and his eyes left hers and wandered around the room.

Kevin looked at Kat and nodded. "I see . . . meeting with the ex-wife last night, late arrival at lab this morning, and when you add in whistling and grinning like an idiot, it can only mean one thing."

"Okay, you win," Ramsey said, setting down his cup. "We had a good dinner, a great meeting afterward, and Sheila asked me to stay the night." He smiled and spread his arms, "It seems there just might be a chance for a reconciliation in the future."

Kevin slapped him on the shoulder, "Well, good for you, Dr. Ramsey. Sheila is a great person and I wish you luck."

"Me, too," Kat said, but then her expression turned serious. "But Kevin and I have some news to share with you that is of the utmost importance, and it concerns Sheila, too."

"Oh?"

"Tell him what you told me last night, Kevin."

Kevin scooted his chair to the side so it was facing Ramsey and retold the story of his uncle's offer just as he had to Kat the night before.

At first, Ramsey's face reddened in anger at Kevin's slip of the tongue, but as the story unfolded and it got to the part about the offer of millions of dollars for the treatment, his temper cooled.

"Do you think this is a legitimate offer, or some sort of scam?" he asked Kevin.

Kevin shrugged. "I believe my uncle wouldn't lie to me. We are very close, and I do know that for the past couple of years he has had the use of a private jet to fly him back and forth from Corpus Christi to here to take care of an eccentric, rich patient. I also have noticed that he is living way above the lifestyle of most doctors. He spends money like it is nothing."

He looked at Kat. "What do you think?"

Kat shrugged. "I don't know, but I think I've come up with a way to find out if there is as much money in play as they say there is."

She went on to explain to him her idea to ask for a good-faith advance of fifty thousand dollars in exchange for videos and pictures of Angus before and after treatment."

Ramsey raised his eyebrows. "And just how did you come up with the sum of fifty thousand dollars?"

"Well, it is obvious that now that we are at the end of our experiments with rats and are moving on to bigger and better things, we are going to have to abandon BioTech and move to a new lab. There are just too many prying eyes around here for us to start to work with larger animals or even a human, and the security sucks and we definitely need to protect our formulae." She went on to tell him about

Kevin catching Captain Sunshine snooping around the lab, including his getting into her laptop.

He slowly nodded. "I knew that son of a bitch was up to no good, but at any rate, I've been thinking the very same thing. It is high time we tell BioTech our research projects are going nowhere and that we are moving on to greener pastures."

"Uh, guys, I have a suggestion, if you don't mind," Kevin said.

"Go ahead, Kevin. Like we said before, you are now a full partner in this group," Kat said.

"Captain Sunshine is gonna get awfully suspicious if two of BioTech's best researchers give up their projects and leave at the same time. It won't take much more snooping for him to find out that the two of you have been spending an inordinate amount of time together, especially since Dr. Ramsey has never been known to make friends among the other scientists here."

"Good point, Kevin," Ramsey said. "What do you suggest?"

"Well, I think one of you could say that your research has come to a dead end and that you are leaving all of your notes and journals to BioTech and are going to take a sabbatical and then start up on some other project. Meanwhile, after about a week or so, the other one can claim some sort of family emergency and ask for a couple of weeks' leave to deal with it. Then, after the two weeks is up, you can call and say that the emergency is going to last a while longer and recommend that BioTech have someone else take over your project and that you will provide them with all of your notes and journals. And if Captain Sunshine wishes, I can offer to stay on board for a couple of months and help the new guy or gal get up to speed on the project."

"Kevin, that's brilliant," Kat said. "And since the three of us will be split up as far as BioTech is concerned, they won't have a clue that we are all working together."

"Thanks," Kevin said. "The only fly in the ointment is that if two of us at first and then one of us later is going to be pretending to continue working at BioTech, the new lab is going to have to be within easy commuting distance so that we can all continue to be involved in the real project."

Ramsey smiled. "I think I have that covered." He looked at Kat, "As I told you before we started working together, I had already planned to abandon BioTech and take my formula with me. Even by itself, it was a pretty good product and would have made me a tidy sum if sold on the open market. So, in consideration of the day when I finally left Bio-Tech, I was in the process of setting up a new lab in Conroe, Texas. It's only about fifty miles from Houston and is an easy forty-five-minute drive in normal traffic."

Kat frowned. "Why did you set up a new lab so close to Houston if you were going to stiff BioTech? I would have thought you would have gone halfway around the world to South America, or at least to Mexico or some other remote location."

He nodded. "You're right, of course, and, in fact, I also have made arrangements for a lab in Monterrey, Mexico, for when I get ready to do large-scale manufacturing of my serum, but for . . . uh . . . personal reasons, I wanted to stay close to Houston for as long as I could."

Kat smiled. "I see. You didn't want to be too far away from Sheila."

"Yeah, I have been hoping we could get back together for a couple of years now, but until recently I was too consumed with anger over my perceived failures to give our relationship a chance."

"So, let me get this straight," Kevin said. "You have managed to set up two new labs in hopes of someday leaving BioTech?"

"Well, they're not really set up and ready for work. I've rented two labs under false names, but they are certainly not equipped yet. I've been too strapped for funds to finish setting them up properly. It's taken every bit of money I could scrape together just to afford the rent, especially since it all had to be in cash in order to maintain secrecy."

"So, if I can convince my uncle and his patient to advance us the fifty K, then we should be all right," Kevin said.

"That would certainly go a long way toward getting all of the specialized equipment we will need to do our experiments on humans," Kat said.

"I propose that once we get the money, we outfit the lab in Conroe first. That way, when Sheila finds us a suitable subject we will be ready to go ahead with the next step in our experiments," Ramsey said. "And the beauty of that is that it is close enough for us to use on Kevin's uncle's patient also when the time comes."

Kevin added, "And it will save the lab in Mexico to use as a bolt-hole if things go wrong and we have to hightail it out of the country in a hurry."

"So," Kat said, "the first thing to do is see if Kevin can get us the money, and the second thing to do is outfit the lab with everything we'll need."

"And the third and most important thing," Ramsey said, "is for Sheila to find us a suitable subject to experiment on."

"Okay, while Kevin is working on the money, and while you are arranging to get the lab equipment, Burton, I will get on the computer and see if I can figure out just what changes we'll need to make to use our formulae on a human instead of rats or dogs."

Kevin smiled and nodded, but he was thinking. "And I'll figure out some way to take Captain Sunshine out of play."

CHAPTER 19

Kevin got up from his chair, walked over to Angus's bed, and squatted down. When Angus looked over his shoulder and up at Kevin, he began to scratch between the dog's ears where he knew Angus liked it.

After a moment, Angus leaned his head back and gazed up into Kevin's eyes and began to lap his hand.

"I am really glad you came through the procedure so well, big guy," Kevin said softly. "You look and act great."

Angus stopped lapping and nodded his head in agreement.

Kevin laughed and gave his head another pat. "Man, you are really something, old boy."

He stood up, walked over to Kat's desk, and gathered up the photos and videos of Angus, tipped his head at Kat and Ramsey, and waked toward the door.

Suddenly Angus jumped up, ran over, and grabbed Kevin's pants legs in his teeth and pulled.

Kat chuckled. "I guess the big guy doesn't want you to leave."

Kevin squatted again and said, while looking right at Angus, "I promise I will be back, Angus. I will never leave you."

Angus released his pants and sat back on his haunches, his tail wagging slowly.

Kevin gave Kat and Ramsey another wave and walked out of the door.

Ramsey got to his feet. "I'm gonna go make some calls and start getting the lab equipment we need ordered. It'll probably take a few days, so we have some time before we need to come up with the money."

"I've got some savings that we can use if some of it comes in before Kevin has the money in hand."

Ramsey waved a hand dismissively. "I'm sure that won't be necessary, but if it is, we'll deal with it. I can probably also get a short-term loan from Sheila if we need more than you have."

He walked to the door. "I'll let you know when I find out how long it's going to take to get the equipment, and I'll also get you and Kevin some keys and directions to the lab so you can check it out when you get a chance."

After he was gone, Angus grabbed his bowl, placed it at Kat's feet, and sat back on his haunches with an expectant look on his face.

She smiled and filled the bowl with three cups of his food. "Don't get too used to all this extra food, big guy. When your metabolism gets back to normal, so will your diet. We don't want you getting all chubby again, do we?"

Kat almost fainted when Angus, with a solemn look on his face, slowly shook his head back and forth before he dipped his head and began to gobble his food.

She sat back down at her desk and said, "I don't know if I'll ever get used to your new intelligence, big guy, but I guess we'll all just have to learn to deal with it."

Opening her laptop, she pulled up the mathematical program they'd used to reconfigure the formulae from rats to a dog, and plugged in a weight of 175 pounds. While the program chugged along, she thought, *If the human we find devi-*

ates appreciably from this weight, we'll just have to refigure the proportions.

As soon as Kevin got to his apartment, he placed a call to Dr. Tom Alexander. When the receptionist answered, he asked if she could have the doctor call him in between seeing patients.

While he waited, he began to pack a small duffel bag with enough clothes for a two- or three-day stay, in case it took that long for his uncle to get the money together that they needed.

Five minutes later, the phone rang. "Hello, Uncle Tom."

"Hey, kid. What's going on? Were you able to make our offer to your partners?"

"Uh . . . yeah. That's what I want to talk to you about."

"Well, it's probably not something we want to go into over an open line."

"I agree. I'm getting packed and then I'm going to drive down to Corpus and come to see you. I should make it down there around ten or eleven tonight if traffic's not too bad."

"Don't be silly, Kevin. I figure it'll take you about an hour and a half to drive out to the airport. When you get there, follow the signs to the private air terminal. I should be able to have my jet there in just over two hours, which will give you time for a quick burger or something to tide you over until you get here. I'll meet you at the airport here and we'll go have a nice dinner and you can give me all the details in person, and then you can spend the night and head back to Houston tomorrow if you want, or you can stay a few days and get in some fishing out on the island."

"Thanks, Uncle Tom. That sounds great. I wasn't looking forward to that drive."

"I don't blame you, son. Take care, and I'll see you in a few hours. I'm not on call tonight, so we should be able to have a good, uninterrupted talk."

* * *

Four and a half hours later, Kevin and Tom were finishing up surf and turf at the Outback Restaurant in Corpus Christi. So far they'd talked in generalities, saving the important topics for when they could be assured no one could overhear them.

Finally, the meal over, Tom wiped his lips and gestured at the bar at the side of the restaurant. At this late hour, it was virtually deserted. "Let's have a coffee and cognac in the bar and you can tell me the gory details I've been dying to hear all night."

After their waiter had served them and disappeared back into the restaurant, Kevin pulled the envelope containing Angus's videos and photos out of his duffel bag lying at his feet and handed them across the table to Tom.

"Here are the results of our first non-rat patient. I've brought the unretouched videos in addition to a DVD with the same pictures on it."

He then pulled a laptop out of the duffel, opened it, and flipped it around so that Tom could see the screen. "Take a look at the photos and then play the DVD."

Tom glanced through the photos, and he inserted the DVD and watched, spellbound, as Angus ran and trotted and cavorted like a six-month-old puppy.

He shook his head. "I can't believe the changes in him. And this is just over twenty-four hours after the injection?"

"Closer to thirty-six, but you're missing the most important parts of the video." He handed a pair of earbuds to Tom and said, "Turn up the volume after you put these on. I don't want anyone else to hear the audio."

Tom frowned and shrugged, and then he put the buds in, listened, and watched the video again.

After a moment, he shook his head. "I don't believe this! This has got to be a dog trained to give those responses."

Kevin smiled and shook his head. "Uncle Tom, you have

been like a father to me . . . no, actually, you've been better than a father to me. I would and I will never lie to you or try to cheat you. Believe me when I tell you everything on that disc are genuine results of the serum we gave the dog. I've known that dog for over a year, and I guarantee it is the same dog and there was no training or tricks involved."

Tom slowly took the buds off, ejected the disc, and closed the laptop. "Jesus, Kevin, do you realize what you have here?"

Kevin leaned back, drained his cognac, and nodded. "Of course I do, Uncle Tom. It's the fucking fountain of youth."

Tom shook his head. "No, Kevin, it's a hell of a lot more than that. I don't even know where to begin to try to describe just how momentous this thing is."

Kevin grinned. "So, you'll tell your patient it's worth a potful of money?"

"Hell yes, but after seeing this I'm going to see if we can change the deal so that I get a shot at this formula, too."

"I think that can be arranged, but think about it, Uncle Tom. We can't have a bunch of people suddenly getting younger and smarter . . . It would bring entirely too much attention to us. Anyone who partakes of the serum is going to have to start life all over again . . . new identity, new life, and with no connection to their old life at all."

At first Tom looked doubtful. But after a moment of thinking about it he nodded. "Of course, I see that. I don't know if my patient will, though."

"That is nonnegotiable, Tom. Certainly with your help he can fake his death and leave all of his fortune to some obscure 'relative' for which he can afford to have a plausible life story fabricated."

"Yeah, that's what we'll have to do. I should be able to convince him of the necessity of doing that."

"The other benefit is that if he is as rich as you say, he probably has a lot of enemies who will think he is dead . . . not a bad way to get to quit looking over your shoulder for trouble."

Tom leaned back, sipped his cognac, and smiled. "You have really thought this out, haven't you?"

Kevin nodded.

"I am truly impressed, Kevin. I knew you were smart, of course, but I had no idea just how shrewd you are."

"Those photos and videos are the carrot, Uncle Tom, but there is also a stick, although it's just a little stick."

"Oh?"

"Yeah. We have talked it over, and my partners and I feel we need a little good-faith gesture. We'd like an advance of fifty thousand dollars against the millions to come later."

Tom pursed his lips and rubbed his chin. "May I ask why?"

"The short answer is that we want to make sure this man is rich enough to come through with the eventual payoff, but it's more complicated than that. The truth is that if we are going to keep experimenting on larger animals and eventually a human being, we're going to need a really secure, really remote laboratory. We obviously can't continue to work with the lab we're currently working with, because of too many eyes and too much oversight. To set up a new lab with all new equipment suitable for human treatment is fairly expensive, and neither my partners nor I have that kind of money."

Tom crossed his arms. "I could have my patient set all that up for you and you'd be able to get the best there is."

Kevin wagged his head. "No, Uncle Tom. We need to have an independent lab, and it has to be in a secret location, otherwise neither us nor our formulae would be safe." He grinned and spread his arms, "After all, we all realize just how valuable these formulae are, and we wouldn't want anyone to get . . . ideas about stealing them from us."

Tom laughed. "Well, I agree with you on that, and I know my patient well enough to know that if he ever gets the idea that he can take the formulae for himself, then he will sure as hell try to do it."

"That's the other reason for the advance. We need to take very secure precautions against anyone stealing the formula from us. Do you think your patient will agree to the advance?"

"I don't even have to ask, Kevin. Let's go to my house and I'll put you up for the night, and as soon as the banks open tomorrow, I'll advance you the fifty thousand in cash myself."

"One more thing, Uncle Tom. So far, all we've heard is generalities about what he will be willing to pay us to be the second in line for the formula. Do you think you could get him to be a little more specific?"

Alexander grinned and leaned back in his chair, sipping his coffee and staring at Kevin over the rim of his cup. "Well, do you already have a figure in mind?"

Kevin shrugged. "You said your man is worth between ten and twenty billion dollars, so let's say fifteen billion to be conservative. I figure it ought to be worth three and a third percent of his fortune to get up out of bed and be twenty to thirty years younger and smarter to boot. What do you think?"

Alexander looked at the ceiling, figuring in his head. "Uh, what's that come to? About five hundred thousand?"

Kevin laughed. "No, Uncle Tom, you dropped a couple of decimal points. It comes to exactly five hundred million dollars."

"Holy shit, Kevin! You don't think small, do you?"

"Maybe he'd take it better if you just used the three-and-a-third-percent figure."

Alexander held up his hands and laughed with Kevin. "Hell no, five hundred million it is, and I'll tell him I think it's worth every penny—if you can deliver."

"Good, then if I can impose on your jet one more time, I'll head back to Houston and get started on making preparations for our first human patient."

Tom threw some bills down on the table and said, "And

if you could, I would appreciate some before-and-after pictures and videos to show my patient."

"No problem, Uncle Tom, no problem. Just call me and let me know if he agrees to the price."

Alexander stopped and looked at Kevin. "And if he declines?"

Kevin shrugged. "Then, no harm, no foul. We'll just have to find another rich, sick old bastard and put the offer to him."

The next morning, Kevin went straight from the Houston airport to Kat's lab. As soon as he entered the door, Angus jumped up from his bed and ran over to him. Kevin opened his arms and Angus vaulted up into them, immediately lapping his face furiously.

"My God, even I don't get a welcome like that," Kat said, grinning. "Now I know you are a certified member of Angus's pack."

"Of course I am," Keven said around Angus's head. "The big boy knows I love him as much as he loves me."

After a moment, Kevin walked over and placed Angus back in his bed, then he reached into his back pocket and brought out a large rawhide bone and placed it between Angus's teeth. "There you go, big guy. No way was I going on a trip and not bringing you back a present."

Angus dipped his head as if to say "*thank you*," and then he began to gnaw on the bone in earnest.

"If you are quite through with the damn dog, perhaps we can find out what happened in Corpus," Ramsey growled.

"Okay, Mr. Grumpus," Kevin said, grinning. "Do you think I might get a cup of coffee before facing the inquisition?"

"I'll get it," Kat said. "You put your stuff down over there next to my desk and take a seat."

Kevin took a small case off a strap he had around his shoulder and his duffel bag, placed them next to his customary chair, and flopped down with a sigh. "I'll tell you guys, private jets are the *only* way to fly."

Ramsey snorted while Kat brought him his coffee. He took a couple of sips, smiling up at her in thanks, before he sat back and began to tell them how everything had gone with his uncle the night before. When he got to the part about his uncle getting the fifty thousand dollars in cash out of his own bank account, he picked up the case from the floor, opened it, and showed them that it was packed full of hundred-dollar bills.

"So, he was impressed with the videos of Angus?" Kat asked.

Kevin nodded. "Very. He even offered to have his patient furnish us with a new lab and state-of-the-art equipment."

"No shit?" Ramsey asked.

"Yeah, but, of course, I told him no thanks, that we realized how valuable our formulae are and that we needed our lab's location to be kept secret for security purposes."

"And what did he say to that?" Kat asked.

"He said he understood, but then he said something that kinda bothered me. He said that knowing his patient, he felt he would probably try to get control of the formulae for himself once he sees just how great the effects are and realized how valuable the formulae would be—both in terms of money and in terms of raw power."

Ramsey frowned. "So, you think we might have something to worry about from this rich guy?"

Kevin looked at Ramsey. "Burton, do you have any idea what kind of person can accumulate twenty billion dollars? I can guarantee you this guy is as hard as nails and probably as ruthless as they come, and I personally have never met a rich guy who didn't want to get richer."

Ramsey stood up and began to pace around the area in front of Kat's desk as he thought. "That settles it. We're gonna have to redouble our security efforts."

He turned to look at Kat. "We need to get new laptops

and only put on them the false data we've constructed for BioTech's eyes. They can have nothing on them concerning the true formulae."

"Why can't we just erase or delete the real stuff and not go to all the trouble of copying the fake stuff on new computers?" Kat asked.

Kevin answered before Ramsey had a chance, "Because nothing is ever truly erased or deleted from a hard drive, Kat. There are always ways to recover the data if someone is tech-savvy enough. Other than completely smashing or melting a hard drive, there is no easy or practical way to protect what was once written on it."

"But I have lots of pictures of Angus and other things on my old computer I don't want to lose," she said.

Kevin smiled. "Let me have the computer for a couple of hours and I can copy and transfer all of your personal things onto a new computer, along with the fake data you've prepared for BioTech, and then I'll remove the old hard drive and destroy it completely." He hesitated and then looked at Ramsey. "I'll do the same for you, Burton, if you wish."

He shook his head. "I don't really have any personal shit on my computer, but I would appreciate it if you could transfer all of the fake data I've had Dottie put in about my experiments. All that New Age tech stuff is Greek to me."

He looked from Kevin to Kat. "So, we're agreed that from now on, nothing is written down about the formulae or our experiments? We're gonna have to keep it all in our heads."

They both nodded.

He then took several bundles of hundreds from the briefcase and stuffed them in his jacket pockets. "Good, then I'm off to get our lab equipped. I'll leave my laptop with you, Kevin, and you can run by Best Buy and pick up a couple of cheap laptops for us to carry around with the false data on them in case BioTech wants to see them or in case your uncle's patient's thugs manage to get their hands on them."

"I've just about got the new proportions figured out for our human experiment, and I'll memorize them so Kevin can destroy those computations, as well, when he gets rid of my laptop."

"I just thought of something else," Kevin said. "Maybe I'm being too paranoid, but I think I'll pick up a couple of burner phones for us to use when we need to talk to one another. Regular cell phones can be listened to very easily, so we can use our normal cells for everyday calls and save the burner phones for communication between ourselves."

"Can't they listen to these . . . what did you call them, 'burner phones'?" Kat asked.

"Not if they don't know the phone numbers, and not if we don't use any names when we talk. There would be no way for them to pick our conversations out of the hundreds that are going on all around us, as long as we're careful and don't let them see us using the new phones instead of our regular ones."

"Do you really think all this is necessary?" Kat asked. "I feel like I'm in a spy movie or something."

"Kat, if it is not necessary, then we've spent a few hundred dollars and been put to some minor inconveniences for nothing. On the other hand, if it protects our formulae or even, God forbid, our lives from unscrupulous characters, then it will be worth it," Ramsey said.

"Oh, one other thing, guys," Kevin said, snapping his fingers. "I almost forgot the best part."

"What's that?" Kat asked.

"I told my uncle that the price for the use of the formula is five hundred million dollars."

"What?" Ramsey almost screamed. "He'll never go for that, you idiot! You've probably blown the whole deal."

Kevin smiled and shook his head. "No, Dr. Ramsey, he agreed to it without hesitation."

"Are you kidding me?" Kat hollered and threw her arms around Kevin. "We're gonna be rich!" she sang.

Ramsey just laughed and said, "Smart-ass! I'll see you two later."

As Ramsey left the office to head out to get the new lab fitted out, Kevin picked up their laptops, stuck them under his arm, and threw the briefcase strap over his shoulder.

"I'll go on over to my apartment and get to work on these, and I'll see you in the morning, Kat."

She stood and moved over to him, then leaned forward and gave him a kiss on the cheek. "You take care, Secret Agent Man," she said with a smile. "If Ramsey won't say it, I will: You done good!"

He blushed. "Uh . . . okay."

He turned and rushed out of the lab without another glance back.

Kat stood and watched him for a moment, thinking, *Hmmm, perhaps I'd better be careful with the kisses. . . . I wouldn't want to give the kid any wrong ideas.*

She heard a soft *woof*, and looked back over her shoulder at Angus, who was lying in his bed with what was left of the rawhide bone between his paws.

As she stared at him, she could swear he grinned at her.

CHAPTER 20

Things went smoothly for the next ten days, with the trio getting used to using their burner phones and watching what they said in public. Ramsey had already given BioTech his notice and had packed up his lab, given Dottie a month's severance pay, and copied all of his false data off his new computer and turned it in to Captain Sohenshine.

Sohenshine said he was disappointed in Ramsey's failure and sorry to see such a distinguished scientist leave their employ, but Ramsey could tell the man was more relieved than chagrined.

Since then, Ramsey had been spending almost all of his time shuttling back and forth between Conroe and Houston, spending most nights with Sheila, which had greatly improved his general disposition.

While this was going on, Kevin and Kat had been continuing to fake their research on rats, with little to no positive results to show for it. Sohenshine was getting increasingly strident with Kat that he expected some progress or he was going to have to take it up with the board at the next meeting, letting her know that her funding was at risk of being terminated.

Kat was discussing with Kevin the timing of her telling the man she had a family emergency back east when the very object of their discussion walked into the lab, again without knocking.

His face was full of thunderclouds when he pointed at Kevin and said in a no-nonsense voice, "You! Out!"

Kevin opened his mouth to reply, but Kat touched his arm and shook her head.

With a glare at Sohenshine, he stomped out. Curiously, he didn't slam the door but rather eased it almost shut, leaving it open a small crack.

When Sohenshine walked around Kat's desk, he again trailed his fingertips along her shoulders.

Biting her lip to keep from jumping up and decking him, she instead pushed a button on her phone, turning on the video function. Before he turned back to face her, she propped the phone against her coffee cup so the screen faced him.

"What can I do for you, Captain Sohenshine?" she asked, her voice as sweet as honey.

He stuck his hands in his pockets and stuck his chest out. "Well, I'd say it's more what I can do for you, Dr. Williams."

"And just what is that, Captain?"

He pulled a computer thumb drive out of his pocket and held it up. "A couple of weeks ago, I came into possession of this record of the data on your computer, Kat," he said, using her nickname for the first time.

She looked at him aghast. "And just how did you happen to *come into possession* of data off of my private computer, Captain Sohenshine?"

His lips curled in a nasty grin. "That is not what is concerning here, Kat. What is concerning is that the data on your computer a couple of weeks ago is completely different from the data that you have been turning in recently."

She shrugged. "That is because that data there was premature. It was more of a theory of what I hoped our experiments would show. As it turns out, the experiments showed something completely different from our theories."

"Bullshit!" he growled, approaching her desk. "I think you have been deliberately falsifying your data so that you and that bastard Ramsey can take whatever you've discovered and market it on your own."

She smiled sweetly and leaned back, crossing her arms under her breasts, pushing them up.

His beady little eyes went immediately to her chest, and he grinned maliciously.

He put his hands on the front of her desk and leaned down, his face inches from hers. "Of course, if you were to be a little bit nicer to me, I might be persuaded to forget all about what I discovered on your computer."

"Oh, so it was you who broke in to my lab and stole information off of my private computer?"

He stuck a thumb in his chest. "No! This is not your lab, Kat, it is *my* lab. I am the director of this corporation, and therefore every lab in this building belongs to me, and every bit of information is mine!"

"And all I have to do to stay on your good side is 'be nice to you'? Just what does that mean?"

"Well," he began, his lips curling into another sickly grin, "perhaps we could go out for a nice dinner, followed by a few drinks at my apartment."

"And then you'd forget all about my supposed treason to BioTech—if I allowed you to have your way with me?"

"Now, I wouldn't put it quite that way . . ."

Suddenly a hand was on his shoulder, whirling him around.

Kevin pulled his fist back and smashed Sohenshine full in the face, flattening his nose and knocking out two of his teeth.

He went limp and toppled to the floor.

Kevin bent over him, pulled the thumb drive from his

pocket, and held it up to Kat. "I told you that bastard had been in your computer."

She shook her head and reached over to turn off the phone video. "Yes, and I got him recorded not only sexually harassing me, but offering to ignore supposed wrongdoing at the same time."

She took her phone and looked up Sohenshine's cell number in her contact list, typed out a message to him, and attached the video file to it.

Looking up at Kevin, she said, "Kevin, would you please drag that piece of shit out into the corridor and dump him in the corner? Then, if you would, please wake him and tell him to heed the message I sent him or the next message will be sent to the *Houston Chronicle*."

Kevin gave her a mock salute, "Yes, ma'am," he said before doing just that.

An hour later, Ramsey walked into the lab, a worried look on his face.

"What's the matter, Burton?" Kevin asked. "Having trouble getting the lab outfitted?"

"No, as a matter of fact, I was coming here to tell y'all it's all done. I even outfitted two small rooms as bedrooms, one for one of us and the other for our human patient if we ever get one."

"Then, what is the problem, Burton?" Kat asked. "You look like someone pissed in your Post Toasties."

Kevin burst out laughing. "Why, Kat! I didn't know you had such a colorful vocabulary."

She winked at him. 'You'd be surprised at what you don't know about me, Kev."

While they were jawing back and forth, Ramsey fixed himself a cup of coffee, added a generous dollop of whiskey he had started keeping in Kat's bottom desk drawer, and drank it all down in two quick gulps, wincing as it burned his tongue.

"Okay, now I know something is wrong, Burton," Kat said. "Just what is going on?"

He took a deep breath. "On the way through the parking lot, I happened to glance at a car parked well away from the building, thinking there were plenty of closer spaces, so why would someone park way out there and have to walk two hundred yards to the offices? Then I noticed a pile of cigarette butts next to the driver's-side door, like someone had been sitting in the car for hours just waiting around."

"Was anyone in the car?" Kevin asked, a concerned look on his face.

"I didn't think so at first," Ramsey said. "But after I pulled up into the parking garage and parked on the third floor, where I usually do, I snuck over to the window and peeked over the wall. What did I see but two figures now sitting in the car? They must have ducked down when they saw me drive into the lot."

"Do you think they're watching us?" Kat asked.

Ramsey shrugged. "Well, yeah, unless there are some other scientists on the BioTech payroll who've discovered a half-billion-dollar formula."

Kevin thought for a moment, then he snapped his fingers. "You two stay put, I've got an idea." He went to the briefcase and took out a stack of bills. "You say you parked on the third floor of the parking garage?" he asked.

When Ramsey nodded, Kevin waved the bills at them and trotted out the lab door.

"What do you think he's up to?" Ramsey asked, a puzzled look on his face.

"I don't know," Kat answered, "but in case you haven't noticed, he is *really* good at this secret agent stuff."

Kat got up and called to Angus, "Time to potty, big guy?"

"What the hell do you think you're doing?" Ramsey asked.

"I'm gonna take my dog for a walk," she said with a wink, "and while I'm out there, I'm gonna take a look around and see if our watchdogs are still sitting in the parking lot."

"Kat," Ramsey said, "be careful. For all we know, these guys are just waiting for a chance to kidnap one of us."

"Don't worry, Burton. I've got my guard dog along to protect me."

Ramsey laughed and pointed at Angus. "You mean him?"

Angus squared around, lowered his head, bared his teeth, and gave a terrifying, low, rumbling growl.

"Holy shit!" Ramsey said, stepping back and holding up his hands.

Then Angus turned off the growl, gave a happy *yip*, and wagged his tail at Ramsey.

Kat laughed and pointed at Ramsey. "See, I told you he could be a good guard dog if he wanted to. As you can now see, he was just showing you his bad boy act."

Ramsey nodded, an uncertain grin on his face. "Well, he sure fooled me."

Kat bent over and snapped a leash on Angus's collar. "I know you don't need this, big guy, but we need to keep up appearances for all the other people in the office building."

While she was gone, Ramsey refilled his coffee cup, only this time he left out the coffee and just added whiskey

He was just getting up to go to the cafeteria, when she reappeared at the door.

"Well, what did you see?" he asked.

She shook her head, a worried look on her face. "They're still there. I was careful not to let them see me glance their way, but they still ducked down as if they were afraid I might see them."

"Did they make any move to come after you?"

"No. Like I said, they were careful not to be too obvious

about being there. I think what they're going to do is wait until you take off again and try to follow you to the other lab so they can find out where it is. I really don't see them making a play for the formula until after we've treated their boss, whom I assume is Kevin's uncle's patient."

Ramsey drained his cup. "Unless it is Kevin's uncle himself."

Kat disagreed. "No, I think Kevin's uncle is so close to him and his mother that if he wanted in on our formula, he would work through them to do it instead of hiring a couple of tough guys."

Just then, Kevin walked in, a satisfied look on his face.

"You look like the cat who swallowed the canary," Kat said.

He tossed them both a set of car keys.

Ramsey looked at his. "What is this?"

"It is our way of moving around without our friends being able to tail us. I took some of the money and bought a five-year-old Honda Accord, the most common vehicle and color on the road. I parked it in slot fifty on the top floor of the parking garage at the Galleria Mall next to Macy's. I also put in the backseat a woman's overcoat, a long, blond wig, and a pair of oversized sunglasses."

"What the hell . . . ?" Ramsey started to say.

Kevin held up his hand. "When you leave here to go to the lab, just head over to the mall and pull into the spot next to the Accord, switch cars, put on the coat, the wig, and the sunglasses, pull up the collar of the coat, and when you drive back down out of the garage, our two friends will be waiting for you to reappear in your car and will never notice you as you drive right by them."

"What if they go up there and check out my car?"

Kevin shrugged. "I'm sure they will, and, in fact, I'd be surprised if they don't plant a GPS device under the wheel well or bumper so they can track you without having to get too close. If they don't do that, then they are too dumb to worry about anyway."

"What will they think when I come back out of the garage in my car and go home to Sheila with nothing to show for my 'shopping' trip?"

"I thought of that. I put a bunch of empty boxes from Macy's and some other stores' bags in the trunk of the Accord. Just take them with you and they'll think you went shopping for presents for Sheila."

Ramsey's face relaxed, and he smiled and looked over at Kat. "Damn, you were right. He is excellent at this secret agent shit."

"Yeah, and over the next few days, you can let me know when you're gonna be heading to the lab and I can arrange to leave the Accord in different parking garages so we won't be going back to the same place over and over again."

"Burton, when you get home to Sheila today, ask her if she's had any luck finding a human subject. Tomorrow I'm going to tell Sohenshine I have a family emergency back east and am going to have to take a couple of weeks off."

"You think he'll get suspicious with your leaving so soon after me?"

Kat glanced at Kevin and grinned. "No, actually I think he'll be glad to see Kevin and I go."

Kevin snorted to keep from laughing and said, "I'll start getting things ready so we can leave first thing in the morning and head to the lab in Conroe."

"How will you get to the Conroe lab without our tails out in the parking lot following you?" Ramsey asked.

She thought for a moment. "I'll wait for you to come by the lab, and after a while, when you leave, Kevin will check to make sure they follow you and then we'll head on out to Conroe in the Honda. If we see anyone else following us, just in case there is another team in place, we'll abort and figure out some other way to get there unobserved."

"Okay. Tonight is Sheila's night at the Ben Taub Clinic, and I'll remind her to keep an eye out for someone we can use."

The snow mixed with sleet shot out of the darkness in a horizontal wall, coating the windshield with ice and making the wipers useless. Jordan Stone leaned over the wheel and wiped at the glass with his hand, smearing the fog and making his visibility even worse.

His wife, Mary, rocked their two-year-old daughter in her lap and softly sang her a lullaby. In spite of the cold, sweat gathered on Stone's forehead as he strained to see the road through the blizzard.

Mary reached over and put her hand on his shoulder. "I'm sorry we had to leave the party. I know how much you enjoy the faculty teas."

He put his hand on her knee and rubbed it without taking his eyes off the road. "Don't be silly. The babysitter said Megan had a hundred and two fever." He smiled, "There'll be plenty more parties, but only one Megan."

He put his hand back on the wheel as the road began a gentle curve to the left. Suddenly, out of the wall of white, came two blinding cones of light. Stone slowed as he realized an eighteen-wheeler was hurtling toward them, sliding sideways and jackknifing on the ice-slick road.

He looked frantically left, then right, but there was nowhere to go. At the last moment, he wrenched the wheel to the right, hoping to put the car and himself between the truck and his family. As the lights bore down on them, he screamed in frustration at the inevitability of the collision.

As the two vehicles slammed together, there was a horrible sound of screeching metal and a tremendous blossoming of light as the truck exploded in a giant fireball that blinded him for a moment before all became black . . .

* * *

Jordan P. Stone, Ph.D. and former professor of philosophy at Rice University, awoke screaming and thrashing, and he pulled feverishly at the tubes in his arms and nose. George Patterson, second-year resident in internal medicine at Ben Taub General Hospital, rushed into the room and grabbed Stone's arms, then began to speak to him in a soothing voice.

"Hey, Doc, it's okay. It's me, George . . . Calm down, okay? Just relax." As he talked, Patterson gently held Stone's arms away from his IV and nasogastric tubes.

Slowly, Stone's eyes cleared and focused on Patterson, then shifted to take in the hospital room and its furnishings. A dry and coated tongue emerged to lick red, cracked lips. He croaked out a garbled word, then subsided into a fit of racking, tearing coughing.

Finally, he caught his breath enough to ask, "I'm back in the hospital again, huh?"

"Yeah, you had a bad one this time. For a while there, I wasn't sure you were going to make it."

Stone's lips spread in a slow grin. "Aw, come on, Doc, you know there are more old drunks than there are old doctors."

Patterson released Stone's arms and leaned back, crossing his legs. He'd heard that old saying many times. "Now, Jordan, don't get philosophical on me. In the two years I've been a resident here, I've managed to learn more about alcoholic cirrhosis and delirium tremens from you than in four years of med school."

Stone struggled and finally managed to sit up in the bed, although he paled with the effort. "Yeah, George, I know, and don't think I'm not grateful. Why do you think I haven't charged you for all this education I'm providing for you interns and residents?"

Patterson patted him on the shoulder. "Do you think you could keep some solid food down if I ordered it?"

"If I say yes, does that mean you'll remove this infernal tube from my nose?"

"I'll make a deal with you. If you can keep breakfast down, I'll take the tube out, but if you puke it up, the tube goes back down. Okay?"

Stone shuddered, then shivered violently. "Okay, but I think you'd better give me some more Librium, or a shot of Night Train, before you try to feed me. The shakes are starting, and I'd rather not have any more of those blasted seizures."

The doctor reached up and pressed the NURSE CALL button. "Okay, I'll increase the dose to fifty milligrams every four hours, but I'm going to keep the IV going so we can push some vitamins and antinausea medicine. I'd like to build you up a little more this time before we let you go."

Stone stuffed his shaking hands under his arms to keep them still, then leaned his head back and closed his eyes. "Okay, Doc, whatever trips your trigger. Maybe this time I'll fool all of you and stay on the wagon after I leave here."

Patterson gave him a wry grin. "Now, don't promise anything rash. If you do that, how do you expect me to train these interns in the fine art of bringing someone back from the brink of an alcoholic coma?"

When Patterson walked out of the room to order the increase in Stone's tranquilizers, he found Dr. Sheila Goodman standing there reading Stone's chart.

"Uh, is everything okay, Dr. Goodman?" Patterson asked, worried that maybe she'd found some fault with the way he'd been treating Stone.

She smiled up at him over her half glasses. "Yes, Dr. Patterson, everything is fine. I was going over your patient's past history and lab results."

She closed the chart. "Rather a sad case. A long history of chronic alcoholism, liver and kidney functions in the cellar, and obvious signs of incipient heart failure on his chest X-ray and EKG readings."

Patterson just nodded. He knew the chart well.

"I'd say it would be a miracle if the man lives another month," Sheila said.

Patterson nodded again. "Did you have time to really look at his past history?" he asked.

"Just the list of past hospitalizations. Why?"

"The man has a doctorate in philosophy and was a tenured professor at Rice University until his wife and daughter were killed in a car wreck while he was driving. He had no history of drinking until then, but evidently that knocked the slats out from under him and he went off the deep end. It's been downhill ever since."

Sheila pursed her lips. Perhaps this was the man she'd been looking for. His case was certainly hopeless enough; the only question was whether it was too late for Kat's and Burton's magic serum to work its miracles on him.

"It is an interesting case, George," Sheila said, handing the chart back to him. "Please keep me informed and be sure to let me know before he is discharged. I might like to have a word or two with him."

CHAPTER 21

The next morning, Sheila met George Patterson outside the door to Jordan Stone's room. Sheila had asked Patterson to have him transferred from a ward bed to a private room. When he asked her why, she just shrugged and said she was contemplating putting him in a research project and needed to get a better idea of his past history, both medical and social.

They entered the room to find Stone staring at his breakfast, a wistful look on his face.

"Hey, Jordan," Dr. Patterson said. "How're you doin' this morning?"

Stone turned red, bloodshot eyes to Patterson. "Thinking back to when I could eat steak and eggs for breakfast and never look back. Now I look at this oatmeal—if that is what this concoction before me truly is—and I wonder what the chances are that I can keep it down long enough to digest it."

Patterson ushered Sheila over to Stone's bedside. "Jordan, this is Dr. Sheila Goodman. She is head of the department of internal medicine's geriatrics department."

He leaned over, put his hand up next to his mouth, and stage-whispered, "She is also one of my bosses, so be extra-nice to her or I might get canned."

Sheila laughed and playfully punched Patterson on the shoulder. "Now, don't go telling him that, George. He'll think I'm a dreadful martinet."

Stone stared at her for a moment, and she had the strangest feeling he could see all the way down to her soul.

"No, Dr. Goodman, I would never think that. I can see right away that you are a gentle, compassionate doctor filled with the milk of human kindness."

He glanced at Patterson. "And, George, you and I both know the good doctor here thinks you are one of the best residents in the department. Otherwise they would never have put you on such a difficult case like mine."

Sheila laughed. "Now I can see, Mr. Stone, why George said you had a line of bullshit a mile long and twice as wide."

Stone held up a hand. "Please, Dr. Goodman, call me Jordan. I like it when beautiful women call me by my first name . . . makes me feel decades younger."

"Then you must call me Sheila."

He shook his head. "No, ma'am. While in the hospital, protocol must be followed, so I shall call you Dr. Goodman." And then he winked. "Until such time as I feel well enough to ask you to dinner, since I see you are not wearing a wedding ring."

She laughed again and signaled to Patterson he could leave. Then she pulled up a visitor's chair and sat next to the bed. "I am here to ask you some rather personal and probing questions—if you don't mind, of course."

Stone looked around and spread his arms. "Is that why I was transferred from the dungeons of ward life to the presidential suite?"

This man is still mentally sharp, Sheila thought. "Yes. I thought we might do better with some privacy for our discussion."

He grinned, exposing yellow, dirty teeth that hadn't seen a toothbrush in quite some time. "Oh, thank goodness. I was afraid for a moment that you'd put me here so that you could have your way with me in secret." He ran his hands down his chest to his stomach. "Because I do realize that I am fairly irresistible in this oh-so-sexy hospital gown with no back to it."

Sheila leaned back and crossed her legs. She found to her surprise that she not only liked this man, but she was enjoying the interplay quite a bit.

"I will try to restrain myself, in the interest of good medical ethics, of course," she replied, drawing a chuckle from Stone.

She leaned over and pulled out a small, handheld recorder from her purse. "Do you mind if I record our discussion?" she asked. "Like most doctors', my handwriting is so bad I can scarcely read it myself."

He waved a hand. "Not at all, Doctor. In my previous life as a professor of philosophy at Rice University, I was used to students recording my golden words for posterity."

Sheila clicked the recorder on and said, "Let's begin by talking about your previous life, Jordan."

For almost two hours Sheila interviewed Stone, though, truth to tell, he elicited as much personal information from her as she did from him. Before long, she knew that they had become fast friends rather than mere acquaintances.

Before she ended the interview, she decided she would try to find out what had happened to send him so far off the normal course of his life.

"Jordan, before I go, would you mind my asking just what caused you to go completely around the bend and turn to alcohol as you evidently did? I know you lost your wife and child in an auto accident, but was there more to it than that?"

Jordan turned and glanced out the window before he answered. "Oh yes, there was more," he said, his voice filled with sadness.

"Do you mind sharing it with me?" she asked.

"The evening of the accident, my wife, Mary, and our two-year-old daughter, Madison, and I were attending a faculty tea at Rice University. We received a call from our baby-sitter that our one-year-old daughter, Megan, had a very high fever and was acting lethargic, so we decided to head home to see whether or not she needed to go to the emergency room. As it happened, Houston was in the midst of one of its rare winter storms. The roads were icy, and sleet and freezing rain was blowing in a gale-force wind."

He paused, his face pale at the memory, and took a sip of water. "On the way home, an eighteen-wheeler lost control and hit us head-on. There was just no way I could avoid the accident."

Sheila reached over and took his hand. "I'm truly sorry, Jordan."

He nodded, but his eyes were far away. "It was several days later when I awoke in the hospital to find that my wife and Madison had been killed instantly in the crash." He turned to stare at Sheila. "But that wasn't the worst of it . . . I also learned that my younger daughter, Megan, had died of bacterial meningitis while I was unconscious in the hospital. The babysitter hadn't known to take her to the emergency room until it was too late."

"Jesus," Sheila whispered, wondering whether she could have withstood a double blow like that herself.

Jordan continued, speaking low. "So, it appeared to me that God had bitch-slapped me with the death of Mary and Madison, and then He had backhanded me with the death of Megan." He shook his head. "When I recovered, I contemplated suicide many times, but I just didn't have the courage to take my own life, so I just dove into the bottle and I've never come up for air."

He laid his head back on the pillow and stared at the ceiling. "When I'm drunk is the only time I don't see their faces or think about how life was so sweet until that night."

Sheila shook her head. "I am so sorry I made you relive

that night, Jordan. That kind of blow would have been hard for anyone to survive."

He turned his head to look at her. "I *didn't* survive it. I have been dead inside since that day."

Finally, she glanced at her watch, surprised that so much time had passed. "Oh my goodness, I'm going to be late for my office patients. May I see you again, Jordan, if I promise not to bring that subject up again?"

Stone reached over and placed a rough, gnarled hand gently over hers. "Please come again, Dr. Goodman. I haven't enjoyed someone's company so much in more years than I care to remember."

She clicked off the recorder and patted his hand. "Me either, Jordan, me either."

And, for the next three days, she did return and spent considerable time both interviewing and just talking with Jordan Stone. She found him to be a very intelligent, engaging man and someone whose company she found quite enjoyable.

After the third day, she called Burton and asked if he and his partners could come to her apartment that evening for coffee and pastries and a discussion of the man whom she thought should be their first experimental patient.

That same night, John Palmer Ashby was having a meeting of his own. Present were the two men he'd had tailing Ramsey—Matt Gomer and Doug Johnson—both ex-marines. They were working for the other man present, a private investigator named Harold Gelb, whom Ashby had hired to find out everything he could about the scientists to whom he was entrusting his life.

Once Beverly Luna had shown the men in, Ashby told her to turn off his oxygen, serve them coffee, and then make herself scarce. When she closed the door behind her, Ashby pulled a cigar out from under his blanket and stuck it in his mouth. "Light me up," he ordered Gelb.

Once his cigar was going to his satisfaction, he leaned back against his pillow and said, "Give me your report, Harold."

Harold, a chubby man with a corona of hair surrounding a bald pate, inclined his head at Matt Gomer, the senior operative.

Gomer took a small spiral notebook out of his jacket and opened it. "The subject we were assigned to tail, Dr. Burton Ramsey, has spent most of his time going back and forth from the lab at BioTech Laboratories to the apartment of his ex-wife, Dr. Sheila Goodman. Other than a few trips to various malls, where he shopped and bought various packages he took home to her, and a couple of nights out at restaurants with her, he has not left town or gone to any other locations, especially not any that could be used as a satellite laboratory, which we were told to look out for. Last week, he gave his notice to BioTech, telling them his research project had been unsuccessful and that he was going to take a sabbatical for a few months and then try a different research project, as yet undetermined."

Gomer closed the notebook and put it back in his pocket. "A detailed, typewritten report was turned in to Mr. Gelb."

Ashby narrowed his eyes and used his good arm to point the cigar at Gomer. "How did you find out what he told his superiors at BioTech?"

"Mr. Johnson and I broke into the offices at BioTech one night and found the personnel file on Ramsey, and that was what his boss, Captain John Sohenshine, had entered into it. It further stated that his failed research project had concerned an attempt to find a chemical way to cleanse the blood of toxins, whatever that means."

"And you are sure he hasn't managed to elude you and set up some other laboratory?" Ashby asked.

Gomer shook his head. "Not unless he walked to it. We planted a GPS monitor on his car and we have never lost its position. Even when he went to the malls to shop, we maintained visual sight on his car while he was in the stores."

"Did you follow him into the stores while he was shopping?"

Gomer shook his head. "Too dangerous, sir. There is no way we could do that and not be observed following him, and we were told not to let him become aware he was under surveillance."

"Okay. What about the other subjects, Kaitlyn Williams and Kevin Palmer?"

"We also put a GPS monitor on Dr. Williams's car, but we have not maintained visual surveillance. Her car has only gone back and forth from the lab to her apartment with a few side trips to grocery stores or small restaurants. Her car has also not left the city limits." He grinned. "She evidently doesn't have much of a life outside of her work, as there are no indications of any close friends or boyfriends."

"And the boy, Kevin?"

Gelb interrupted. "I did not assign any surveillance on the young man, since he is only a lab assistant and not intimately involved in their research. Spot checks have confirmed that he pretty much spends all of his time either at the lab, his apartment, or at the University of Houston, where he currently attends college. Gomer and Johnson did ascertain that his attendance at his classes has been good, with no unexplained absences, and his grades are excellent."

Ashby nodded. "Any idea why Ramsey has been spending so much time at his ex-wife's apartment instead of his own?"

Gomer smiled again. "From what we have been able to learn by using a parabolic microphone to listen to some of their conversations, they are attempting a reconciliation. They have been very lovey-dovey and have had sex on most nights he spends there. There have been no suspicious conversations that we have overheard and no mention of his work."

Ashby took a deep draught of his cigar and blew a perfect smoke ring at the ceiling. He looked at Gelb. "Well, Harold, it looks like you have the situation well under control."

"Yes, sir. Do you want us to continue with 'round-the-clock surveillance?"

Ashby thought about it for a moment. "Not at this time. Continue to monitor the GPS readings and maybe do spot checks once or twice a week, unless the GPS shows something suspicious. I think once the subjects go to ground at night, we can let them go."

"Yes, sir," Gelb said. "I'll continue to provide you with weekly reports unless something suspicious turns up."

"Good. Thank you, gentlemen, and congratulations on a superb job. Now, on your way out, tell my nurse it is time for my nightly bath."

CHAPTER 22

When the group gathered at Sheila's house, she offered them all drinks and cookies. Kevin took a beer, Burton took a whiskey over ice, Kat asked for white wine, and Sheila made herself a rum and Coke, with lime making it officially a Cuba libre.

Because Kevin and Kat had come straight from the lab, they had Angus with them. Sheila threw a bath towel down on the floor and put a couple of cookies on it for him. He gave her a soft bark and settled right down, munching on the cookies.

As the rest of her guests settled themselves around the living room, Sheila took out some notes she'd made after listening again to her tape-recorded interviews with Jordan Stone.

Before she could begin to talk, Kevin held up his hand and put a finger to his lips.

When Sheila raised her eyebrows at him, he quickly bent to the briefcase at his feet, opened it, and took out a small black plastic box. After going to all of the windows overlooking the city and pulling the drapes shut, he pulled a silver antenna out of the top of the box, flipped a switch on the side, and then began to walk around the room. He waved the box at the windows, light fixtures, and walls, humming to himself as he did so. A small green light on the front of the box remained green.

After a few moments, Kevin grinned and put the box away. He sat down, took a swig of his beer, and explained, "Since we know the bad guys are having us watched, and since we know they've put GPS trackers on all of our cars . . ."

"What?" Sheila asked.

He nodded. "Yep, I checked ours earlier today and I checked yours when we pulled into the parking garage, Sheila. It's located under your right front wheel well, attached there by a small magnet."

"Shit!" Ramsey exclaimed. "Now, what do we do? We can't have them learning everywhere we go."

Kevin shrugged. "It's no problem, really. Now that we know they are there, if we want to go someplace private, we can either use the Honda safe car, or just remove the tracker device and stick it against a metal pole in the garage. As long as they don't have actual eyes on us, they'll never be the wiser."

"And just what was that little dance you just did with the curtains and black box for, Kevin?" Kat asked.

He held the box up. "I bought this today at the Spy Shop in the Galleria. It is guaranteed to find any bugs the bad guys might have placed in our offices or apartments. It sure as heck found the GPS devices when I used it on our cars. As for the drapes, it's possible to listen to everything said in a room by using a laser device to read the vibrations on windowpanes. Closing the drapes prevents that."

"I assume that since the little green light didn't change color, we are safely debugged in here, then?" Ramsey asked.

Kevin nodded.

"You did good, Kev," Kat said, patting his leg, causing him to blush furiously.

"Okay, go ahead, Sheila," Ramsey said, sitting back in his chair and sipping his whiskey.

She consulted her notes and began, "I think I have found a suitable candidate for our human trial with the formulae. He is just over sixty years old, and he is going to die in the next few weeks unless a miracle occurs, which I am counting on Kat and Burton to provide. He is very smart and has a kind, generous disposition, but he has been brought down by circumstances in his life beyond his control."

She went on to tell them what she knew of Stone's life and the occurrences that had turned him from a respected academic to a down-and-out alcoholic. She also tried to give them some sense of the man as a human being, one whom she had grown to care for as a friend.

Ramsey, feeling just a few twinges of jealousy, frowned. "Okay, so he is a great man, but do you think his medical condition is so severe that even our formulae won't be enough to help him?"

Sheila looked over at him, smiling, for she knew just why he was irritated. "I really don't know, Burton, not having had any experience with your formula under these circumstances before. I do know that his liver and kidney functions are barely high enough to keep him alive, and that he also has advanced cardiovascular disease and even some pulmonary dysfunction from multiple bouts of pneumonia."

Ramsey glanced at Kat. "What do you think, Dr. Williams? Do you think he is too far gone to even attempt to save him?"

Kat shook her head. "No, Burton. In fact, this is the very type of patient I had in mind when trying to perfect my formula. After all, what good is it if it only works on healthy, middle-aged people? The ones who really need our help are patients just like this, whose only chance for a better life is our formulae."

Kevin stared at Kat, thinking, *God, what a woman. No wonder I can't get her out of my mind.*

Sheila nodded. "Okay, then. Jordan should be ready for discharge in the next few days, so I'll go by tomorrow and visit with him to see if he is interested in a drug trial that might help keep him alive for a few more years."

"You mean you're going to ask his permission? What if he says no?" Ramsey asked, an astounded expression on his face.

Sheila glared back at him. "Of course I am! I am not all that enthused with the idea of trying a potentially fatal treatment on anyone, no matter how near death they are, and I am certainly not going to consider it without their permission and their full awareness of the dangers."

"I agree," Kat said, looking at Ramsey with disdain, "and I wouldn't have it any other way, either."

Ramsey glanced over at Kevin. "And I suppose you agree with the ladies?"

Kevin nodded. "Fully."

"Okay, okay. Just please ask him not to tell anyone else about our little experiment, even if he refuses."

"Certainly," Sheila said, ice in her voice.

"Not to change the subject," Kat said, "but is the lab about ready for us to proceed with Mr. Stone if he agrees with Sheila?"

Ramsey nodded. "The last of the equipment just arrived, and as we planned, there are two rooms fitted up as guest quarters: one for us and one for our patient. That way someone can stay there full-time to take care of him as he recovers from the treatment."

"You don't think he will respond as quickly as Angus did?" Sheila asked Kat.

At the sound of his name, Angus's ears perked up and he looked over at Kat, obviously listening to what she was saying.

Kat shook her head. "I doubt it. After all, Angus was old, but he was healthy, other than the severe arthritis in his hips. Not only is Mr. Stone much sicker and much more frail, the differences between a human and a dog are such that I would expect at least a few more days of recuperation in a human subject."

Then she smiled and shrugged. "But then again, who knows? This is all cutting-edge stuff we're doing here, and as you all know, we are flying by the seat of our pants with our first human patient, so just what will happen is anybody's guess."

Ramsey got to his feet. "Okay, so since we all have a busy day tomorrow, I suggest we get to it. Kat is going to start her leave of absence from BioTech in the morning, and then she and Kevin are going to head out to the Conroe lab to meet me and make sure everything she needs is there. And, Sheila, you are going to try to convince Jordan to let us experiment on him."

As they all got up and gathered at the front door, Angus got to his feet and pranced over to stand in front of Sheila. With a solemn look on his face, he picked up his right front leg and held it out to her.

She looked over at Kat, a puzzled look on her face.

Kat grinned. "I think he is thanking you for the cookies," she said.

Angus glanced over his shoulder at Kat and gave a soft bark, showing that she was correct.

Sheila laughed, then bent over and shook Angus's paw. "You are quite welcome, . . . what is it you call him? Oh, I remember . . . you are welcome, 'big guy'."

With that, Angus turned and trotted over to follow Kat and Kevin out the door.

After everyone was gone, Burton went over to Sheila and put his arms around her. "I'm sorry, darling."

"For what?" she asked against his shoulder.

"For not realizing that you would never experiment on anyone without their permission."

"Good. I'm glad you are starting to understand me—finally."

"Then you're not angry with me?"

"Umm, not too much," she said softly, putting her arms around him and giving him a squeeze.

The next morning, Dr. Patterson walked into Jordan Stone's room and stood next to the bed. As he perused the chart, he asked, "How are you feeling this morning, Jordan?"

Jordan smiled, held up a hand, and waggled it back and forth. "Oh, so-so, I guess. The shakes have about gone, and I've been able to keep my last two meals down, so no complaints from me."

Patterson glanced up with an apologetic expression. "That's good, 'cause the hospital administration is climbing all over my back about using a private room for a nonpaying patient."

"So, you want to move me back to the ward?"

Patterson pursed his lips. "It's worse than that, I'm afraid. They want me to discharge you. They say we've done all we can for you, and it's time to make room for someone who needs the room more."

"Okay, that's fine by me. I'm kinda tired of breathing this stale hospital air anyway. I'm ready for the great outdoors."

Patterson handed him an envelope. "I had Social Services put together a packet for you with all of the homeless shelters and food kitchens in the area listed, so you'll have a place to go and somewhere to find good food."

Jordan laughed. "I'm afraid you're stretching the truth with that 'good food' description of the food kitchens' fare."

"Okay then, let's just say 'healthy food,' all right?"

"Well, we can agree on that at least," Jordan said as he climbed out of bed and went over to the closet. When he opened the door, he sniffed at his clothes and then turned to look at Patterson.

Patterson blushed. "I took the liberty of having the hospital laundry wash and press your clothes. They were in pretty sorry shape."

"Thank you, Dr. George, you are both a scholar and a gentleman," Jordan said as he climbed into the ragged but clean clothes.

As he walked Jordan to the front door, Patterson pressed a twenty-dollar bill into his hand. "Promise me you'll use this to buy food, not wine."

Jordan's eyes brimmed with tears. "Doc, you don't have to do that. I'll manage. I've been on the streets for over three years, and I've become something of an expert at survival."

"Take it, anyway, just spend it on protein, not the kind of carbohydrates you find in a pint of alcohol."

The bill disappeared into his ragged coat, then he waved and passed out the double doors of the hospital and was immediately lost in the crowd of people walking along the sidewalk.

Patterson shook his head, knowing he would probably never see the professor again—unless it was in the morgue—and he moved back down the hall to finish making his rounds.

It was just over two hours later when Sheila walked into Stone's room and was surprised to find a middle-aged woman in the bed instead of Jordan Stone.

She excused herself to the patient and went looking for George Patterson. She finally found him exiting the line in the employees' cafeteria, tray of food in hand.

"Oh, hi, Dr. Goodman," he said cheerfully. "Would you care to join me for lunch?"

She nodded, then went to the coffee bar and poured some hot water over a Lipton's tea bag, grabbed a couple of packets of Sweet 'N Low, and joined him at his table.

"George," she said as she sat down before he had a chance to speak, "I was just over to Jordan Stone's room and found he'd been moved."

Patterson shook his head and said around a mouthful of hamburger, "Not moved, Dr. Goodman, discharged."

"Oh no. I thought you realized I was in the process of trying to enroll him in a drug trial."

He nodded. "I did, and when the administrator's office told me he had to go, I tried to call your office, but they said you were not on call and they refused to page you for me."

"Damn!" she exclaimed. "Those fools have standing orders to always call me for a fellow physician, no matter the day or time."

He smiled and shrugged. "Maybe they forgot."

"Never mind that. Do you know where Stone lives?"

He shook his head. "Nowhere, as far as I know. My sense is that he lives on the streets and only takes shelter in one of the homeless places when the weather gets really bad. I did have Social Services make up a list of shelters and soup kitchens and I gave it to him, but I doubt if he even bothered to keep it. These street people are very independent and rarely take advantage of all the services that are out there for them."

She took a final sip of her tea and set the cup down. "George, I need two favors."

He shrugged and held his hands out. "Anything, Dr. Goodman."

"Make that three favors, actually. First, when we are alone, please call me Sheila. We've worked together too long to be so formal."

He grinned. "You got it, Sheila."

"Second, I need a copy of Stone's chart, especially the lab and X-ray results, and I don't want to go through official channels to get it."

He pursed his lips and narrowed his eyes. "So, this drug trial is . . . uh . . . kinda 'unofficial,' is that it?"

"Very perceptive, George. It is something I am pursuing on my own, without any sanctioning by the FDA."

He nodded. "No problem. And the third thing?"

"I would like you to ask around of any of the other street people in the hospital now or who come in over the next few days and see if you can find out where Stone hangs out—if there are any particular neighborhoods where he is likely to be found."

"It must be pretty important that you find him, then, huh?"

She nodded. "You have no idea how important."

He picked up his tray and stood. "Then I'll get right on it."

Four hours later Sheila received a call from George Patterson.

"Hello, George, what do you have for me?"

"First, I put a copy of Stone's chart in your box in Medical Records, and no one saw me copy it."

"Thank you. Anything else?"

"Yeah, I just admitted an old drinking buddy of Stone's. Before I sedated him, I managed to find out that Stone's friends hang out along Navigation Boulevard. That's a street in the Fifth Ward that runs along the ship channel. Specifically, they stay pretty close to a liquor store there named the Bottle Shop. Seems the owner has a soft spot for alcoholics and extends them credit when they get short."

"Hang on a minute while I write this down. Navigation Boulevard, ship channel, and the Bottle Shop . . . right?"

"Yes, ma'am."

"George, I am forever in your debt."

He laughed. "Just remember that when I ask you for a recommendation letter for my fellowship year."

She smiled into the phone. "I won't forget, believe me."

She hung up the phone and turned to Burton Ramsey, who was sitting in her kitchen sipping on a whiskey and water.

"Are you ready to go looking for our subject?"

"What? Now? Hell, Sheila, it's almost seven o'clock.

Can't we wait until morning and look for him in the day-light?"

She frowned. "Sure, if you think he'll still be alive by then. Remember, he just got out of the hospital and several days of forced sobriety. What do you think is the first thing he is going to do?"

He snorted. "Get as drunk as he can as fast as he can."

"You've seen his liver and kidney tests. How many more benders do you think it will take until both organs shut down for good?"

"Okay, okay. I see your point. But did I hear you say Navigation Boulevard and the ship channel?"

"That's right."

"Do you have any idea how dangerous that area is, especially at night?"

"Yes, I do. How about we call Kevin and Kat and ask them along for reinforcements?"

He shook his head. "Can't. Kat finally broke down and told me one of the ingredients in her serum is fetal brain tissue. Not too hard to get for rats and dogs, but damn near impossible for humans. So I sent her and Kevin to Monterrey to see a doctor contact of mine who said he could get her whatever she needed—for a price, of course. They won't be back until day after tomorrow."

"That'll be too late. We'll just have to do it ourselves."

"But Kevin took the undercover car to the airport. If we use your car, the guys following us will know where we went."

"So what? Their patient knows we're going to need a subject to test the serum on, so what if he finds out we went to the worst part of town to find one? We're going to have to share Stone's medical history and general condition before and after with him at some point. And Kevin said we could just remove the tracker and leave it in the garage and they'll never know we left."

"Okay, my dear. But do you mind if we drop by my

apartment on the way, so I can pick up my pistol? I'd feel naked in that part of town without some kind of protection."

"Not only do I not mind," she said as she moved to the door to her bedroom, "but I think I'll take my own gun with us, too."

He raised his eyebrows. "You mean you own a gun, too?"

"Of course, silly. I've got a nice little Browning stainless-steel .380 semiautomatic pistol, and I've even got a concealed-carry permit in case we get stopped by the police."

When she came out of the bedroom putting the pistol in her purse, he put his arm around her and said, "Saddle up, Annie Oakley, we got us an hombre to corral."

She shook her head, picked up the keys to her Mercedes-Benz, and said, "What a truly awful imitation of an Old West accent."

"Why, ah donn know what ya mean, pilgrim," he drawled, hitching up his belt.

CHAPTER 23

Sheila put the liquor store, the Bottle Shop, into her dashboard navigation system, and in less than an hour, they were cruising Navigation Boulevard at twenty miles an hour checking out the neighborhood.

Ramsey glanced over at her as she drove and was surprised to see a sheen of sweat coating her face. "Hey, babe. Are you nervous about the neighborhood?"

"No," she answered in a hoarse voice. "I'm nervous about what we are doing, the whole kidnapping and unlawful-experimenting-on-a-human-being thing."

"Jesus, Sheila. We're not going to kidnap anybody. We're simply going to find a wino and offer him some food and shelter in exchange for him helping us with our serum experiment."

Sheila glared at him. "Yeah, right! We're not going to do anything wrong. We're just going to perform unauthorized medical experiments on a human being without fully informing him of the risks he's going to be taking, because we have no idea ourselves what the risks are of injecting an untried mixture of chemicals into his body."

"Look, Sheila, honey, we've been over this a dozen times.

We've analyzed every separate chemical in our mixture, and there's nothing in there that hasn't been used in research on humans before."

"What about the fetal brain tissue that Kat has gone after? What if it's impure, or has the AIDS virus, or something else we don't know about?"

Ramsey thought about Kat and how she was even then in Monterrey, using his medical contact, Dr. Humberto Garza, to obtain fetal tissue from abortion clinics there. She was to bring the tissue across the border in a thermos bottle, praying that the border guards wouldn't check the contents. The plan was for Kat to separate out the fetal brain tissue and introduce the slurry into her serum just before injecting it into their subject, Jordan Stone.

He reached across the seat and put his hand on her arm. "Sheila, relax. I told you, Dr. Garza is obtaining the tissue from private clinics that serve only upper-class clientele, the richest of the rich in Monterrey. All of the mothers were checked for AIDS and venereal diseases before the procedures were done."

"Yes, but . . ."

"But nothing, darling! We have done everything possible to make this experiment as safe as we can for Mr. Stone. And don't forget, you yourself said he is as good as dead in the next couple of weeks if nothing is done. At least this way, he has a fighting chance for a better and longer life."

Finally, she nodded. "I know what you say is true, it's just that I have grown to like this man, and I want to be sure that everything is done properly, including getting his informed consent as much as possible."

The discussion was interrupted as the car pulled up in front of the Bottle Shop liquor store. They sat in the car for a few moments and watched as a fairly steady stream of patrons shuffled in and out of the store.

Ramsey said, "Jesus, what a sorry-looking group of people."

"Yes," Sheila said, "one thing's for sure. If the serum will work to reverse the ravages of alcoholism and disease represented here, then it will surely work on anyone, and we will have truly made a great discovery."

As they talked, a man stumbled out the door, a bottle wrapped in a paper sack clutched to his chest like a life preserver.

He staggered over to a nearby street lamp and leaned against it as he began to unscrew the bottle in the sack.

"I'm going to go over there and ask that man if he knows Jordan."

"No, you'd better let me go," Ramsey said, putting his hand in his pocket and wrapping his fingers around the butt of his pistol.

She shook her head. "No, you're too big and you'll probably just scare him. Let me try first. A woman is much less threatening at night."

"Okay," he said, pulling his pistol out of his pocket and holding it in his lap. "But I'll be keeping an eye out for trouble."

She eased out of the car and walked slowly over toward the man.

When he looked up from taking a deep draught of his liquor and saw her, he started and looked like he was getting ready to run.

Sheila held up her hands and began to talk to him in a low voice. After a few moments, he seemed to calm down and nodded at her a couple of times.

Finally, he turned and pointed over across the street toward a group of ship containers and a couple of dumpsters stacked haphazardly in an empty lot next to an alleyway.

She thanked him, pressed a bill in his hands, and trotted back toward the car.

After she got in, she said, "He knows Jordan. He said they call him 'the Professor,' and that he stays over there near those old containers."

Her face screwed up in distaste. "The man said they sometimes spend the night in them to get out of the cold and that they use the dumpsters to find food."

Billy heard a car at the end of the alley, but there were no headlights. A light rain and the Houston ship channel's fog made it hard to tell in the gauzy darkness.

"Prob'ly the cops," Billy muttered, nudging Clyde with an elbow. "Toss that empty bottle in the dumpster over there. They only got one reason to be here, that's to roust us. Wake Jordy up, if you can find him. He was in that second dumpster a while ago lookin' for somethin' to eat."

Clyde jerked upright from a slump against a steel wall. "The fuckin' cops?" he mumbled drunkenly, blinking, turning his head back and forth. "Ain't no cops, Billy. It's darker'n shit an' a cop's got lights."

He looked down at an empty bottle of Thunderbird wine lying between his legs. "You got the fuckin' DTs again, seein' shit that ain't there. There ain't no cops 'cause there ain't no lights . . ."

Billy struggled to his feet, ignoring the stench of his own urine in dampened pants clinging to his bony legs. He threw an empty bottle of Mogen David 20/20 into the dumpster beside him and belched just as the glass shattered.

"Go find the Professor." He swayed to remain upright, peering into the misty fog, resting an unwashed palm against the rear of the ship's container they were lying against.

"Jordy's more scared of goin' to jail than any of us. He claims it's 'cause they'll find out who he is. I never did b'lieve all that shit, 'bout him bein' a college professor one time, or almost gettin' the fuckin' Pulitzer Prize. He's jus' another drunk like you an' me, livin' in a stinkin' container like a fuckin' stray dog . . . but he's still our friend, so's we gots to look out for him."

His eyes narrowed. "Yonder Jordy is. I can see his feet stickin' out from between the dumpster an' his container. Go wake up him so the cops don't get him. I'd go, but my bad leg's killin' me."

Clyde managed to make it to his hands and knees, trembling with the beginnings of his own delirium tremens as he gave the end of the alley a closer examination. "Them's Jordan's feet, all right," he said. "I'd have stole his shoes, only his feet's so goddamn big they won't fit me. He's passed out, Billy. Won't do no good to tell him 'bout the cops, only I don't see no cops, just all those fuckin' snakes 'round Jordan's feet. See 'em? I never seen so many fuckin' snakes in my life . . ."

"There ain't no snakes, Clyde. You're comin' down, is all it is. We need us 'nother jug, but we gotta keep them cops from gettin' Jordy. He's the best panhandler I ever did see. He'd ask the pope for d'rections to a whorehouse. Go wake him up so's he can hide."

"Fuck him," Clyde groaned, shaking more violently now. "I got my own troubles. Let Mr. Jordan whatever go to jail for all I care. I gotta have a drink or I'm gonna be sick."

Billy watched two shadowy shapes pause at the mouth of the alley, turning their way, barely visible in a shroud of humidity blanketing everything in Houston's summer heat. "One's a woman, Clyde," he whispered, throat clotted with phlegm. "What the hell is a man an' a woman doin' down here so late at night? Somebody is liable to stick a dick in her. They ain't dressed like cops."

"I tol' you there wasn't no cops," Clyde croaked before his stomach muscles convulsed. He collapsed on his chest, making soft, retching sounds.

Billy saw the man and woman take a few tentative steps into the alleyway—it appeared they were talking to each other. "It ain't the cops," he said again, weaving, fighting the pull of bad balance and a swimming sensation inside his head. "Whoever the hell they are, they's headed straight for Jordy like they already know he's there. Maybe they can see his damn feet."

Clyde was unable to answer, caught in the throes of a series of dry heaves.

Billy remembered Jordy . . . Jordan, when he first came to the streets, rambling on about some car wreck that had killed his wife and daughter, telling everybody he was a Ph.D. in something or other. And, of course, nobody believed him because *everybody* in the alley had been "somebody special" a long time ago, before wine and vodka, or both, turned them into street people. But Jordy was different. He knew big words, and when he was sober he could talk about real scientific-sounding shit. When he wasn't crying.

The man and the woman stopped where Jordy was lying between what he called "his" dumpster and "his" container.

"They found him," Billy muttered quietly. "Poor ol' Jordy. Wonder what they want with him?" Jordy didn't have any money, so they couldn't rob him. It was hard to figure what they were doing.

The woman bent down near Jordy's legs. Billy couldn't hear what she said because Clyde was still retching, but the woman did say something to the big guy with her. "She'll smell where Jordy pissed his pants an' they'll leave him alone." Jordy couldn't stop pissing his pants when he was drunk, Billy remembered.

To Billy's amazement, the heavyset man leaned over to pick Jordy up, cradling him in his arms like a limp rag doll. "What the fuck are they gonna do?" Billy asked himself aloud, but not loud enough to be heard at the other end of the alley.

Jordy was carried around a corner, the woman walking beside the guy holding him like an infant. "I gotta see what they're gonna do with the poor bastard, so's I can tell everybody when they ask what happened to the Professor."

Billy staggered away from the steel wall, almost falling until he caught himself, stumbling down slippery concrete littered with garbage until he came to the end of the alleyway.

He saw the guy putting Jordy into the trunk of a dark car, a dark blue or black Mercedes sedan, his sleeping face momentarily lit by a small lightbulb in the trunk lid until the trunk was closed. Both the man and woman seemed in a hurry to get back in their car as soon as Jordy was locked in the trunk.

Billy heard the motor start. Tail lamps and headlights came on, and a license plate light illuminating numbers he couldn't quite read. There was a white sticker on the rear window of the car, and he managed to read part of it before the Mercedes was in gear, pulling away from the curb down an empty street.

"Hey, Clyde!" Billy shouted. "They kidnapped Jordy, an' the guy's car had a parkin' sticker on it sayin' Physician Parking Permit, Ben Taub Hospital. Wonder who the hell at that hospital would snatch ol' Jordy? I'll bet that guy stole some doctor's car tonight, so he could take his bitch ridin' around in a fancy Mercedes, only I can't figure why he'd wanna steal Jordy. Looks like he coulda smelled how Jordy always pissed all over himself . . ."

Clyde's answer was another bout of gagging on his own bile, and it was beginning to make Billy feel sick himself.

"I gotta get my hands on a bottle," Billy muttered, putting what had happened to Jordan Stone from his mind. Nobody would remember him after a while. He was just another stray dog, a lost soul among the street people of Houston. Someone would come along to take his place. There was always someone new showing up with a story to tell, about how he used to be somebody special until booze got its claws in him.

"Too bad 'bout Jordy," Billy said to himself, reeling down a dark sidewalk toward the ship channel's wharfs, where he might beg a few swallows of wine from the River Gang . . . It wasn't a gang in any real sense, just a community of street people who claimed the bounty from dumpsters in another part of town, their "territory."

He reminded himself to tell the River Gang about Jordy, that a man and a woman had snatched him in a doctor's stolen car. In all his years living on the streets, he'd seen some mighty strange things, but nothing quite like this. Who the hell would want to kidnap an old drunk like Jordan Stone, even if he was who he said he was, almost winning the Pulitzer prize, whatever the hell that was. The only prize Jordy was capable of winning now was for pissing in his pants more often than anyone else in Houston.

John Palmer Ashby scowled at the bedside clock when his phone rang just after ten o'clock that night. He grabbed the receiver and growled, "This had better be damn important to call me at this time of night!"

"This is Harold Gelb, Mr. Ashby, and it is."

"Okay, Harold. Tell me."

"The lady doctor, Williams, and her lab assistant got on a plane for Monterrey, Mexico, this afternoon. My man Johnson, who was following them, just managed to get on the same flight, and he is tailing them to see where they go and who they talk to in Monterrey. It may just be there that they are planning to set up that other clinic you were wondering about."

Ashby pursed his lips, then shook his head. "Nah, I doubt that. Traveling across an international border would be too cumbersome for them to have a satellite lab there. It must be something else. Tell your man to keep a close eye on them, expense is no problem."

"Okay, Mr. Ashby. Also, Dr. Ramsey and his wife took off early this evening and drove down toward the waterfront. I have Gomer following them."

"The waterfront? What the hell would they be going down there for?"

"I don't know, boss. 'Bout the only thing down near the ship channel this time of night is stray dogs and homeless bums."

Ashby nodded. "Of course," he said, realizing they were probably looking for a suitable specimen to try the formula on. "That's alright, Harold, I think I know what they are doing. Call Gomer off, I don't want him to interfere with their mission."

"Are you sure, Mr. Ashby?"

"Goddamnit, just do what I say, Harold!" Ashby growled and slammed the phone down.

He laid his head back against the pillow. *At last*, he thought, *things are finally progressing*. Maybe soon he'd be out of this damn bed and in possession of a formula that would make him king of the world.

CHAPTER 24

While Kevin and Kat were standing in the long Customs line at Houston International Airport, he glanced at her and thought, *Oh shit!*

Her face was covered with a fine sheen of sweat, and he could see the whites of her eyes as she glanced rapidly back and forth. She was obviously terrified that Customs would look into the thermos sticking up out of the backpack she wore.

Casually, he put his arm around her shoulders, pulled her close, then bent down and kissed the side of her neck.

She jumped and turned to stare at him. "What are you doing?" she demanded in a hoarse whisper.

He put his lips next to her ear and whispered back, "I'm trying to make you relax and think about something other than that thermos. You look about as guilty as someone with a kilo of heroin in their luggage, and the Customs agents are trained to recognize nervousness."

She leaned away from him and tried to smile, but it didn't quite come off. *Oh well, here goes nothing*, he thought.

He put his hand behind her head and drew her to him,

kissing her full on the lips with all the built-up passion he had been experiencing.

After a few moments, he felt her relax into him and even felt the touch of her tongue against his for a second.

She leaned back and now had a genuine smile on her face. "There, is that better?" she asked.

He grinned. "Damn straight!"

"Of course, now the Customs agents are thinking I'm some old grandmother molesting a child," she said self-consciously.

"Did that feel like a kid's kiss?" he asked, his face serious.

She took a deep breath and stared into his eyes, for perhaps the first time since she'd known him. "Now that you mention it, definitely not!"

Now he smiled and put his arm around her shoulders again. "Good, 'cause now we're at the front of the line."

"Passports," the Customs man behind the kiosk said, holding out his hand while giving Kevin a sly wink.

By the time they got to their car in the long-term parking lot, Kat was a different person. It was as if breaking the law and getting away with it had freed her from some constraints of conservatism and now she felt like some flower child of the sixties, reveling in her new "outlaw" status.

"God, I'm wired," she gushed as Kevin put their luggage in the trunk and then got behind the wheel. "Smuggling that thermos through Customs was a real rush."

Kevin glanced over at her in the passenger seat as they exited the airport parking lot and pulled out onto the freeway leading to downtown Houston.

"Is this the first time you've ever broken the law?" he asked, the corners of his mouth turning up slightly.

She narrowed her eyes and pursed her lips, thinking about it. After a moment, she nodded. "Yep."

Then she looked over at him. "How about you?"

He laughed. "Hell, no. I smoked pot all through junior and senior high school and shoplifted gum and candy bars in elementary school. But other than that, I've always been pretty straight, too."

As she nodded, he added, "Of course, today I broke another law besides smuggling."

"Oh?"

"Yeah, I kissed my boss. In some places, that counts as sexual harassment."

She blushed. "Well, I won't tell if you don't."

"What if I want to do it again?" he asked.

"Kevin, doing that to get me to calm down and take my mind off of the Customs officers was one thing, but making a habit of it—"

He glanced at her and interrupted. "Making a habit of it is exactly what I want to do."

She shook her head and put a hand on his arm. "Kevin, I am too old for you, and a relationship between us just wouldn't be proper."

"Bullshit," he said. "I have cared about you—cared deeply since almost the first moment I met you, Kat. And age just doesn't figure into it."

She sat back, stunned. She turned her head to look out the window, thinking back to all the hints of his feelings for her that she should have picked up on. Would have picked up on, if she hadn't been so damn obsessed with her research.

"Kevin, I never knew . . ."

He smiled, less serious now. "I know you didn't, Kat. When we were working together, you were so intense about the work you hardly noticed if it was day or night. In fact, your dedication to the project was one of the things I liked best about you."

"Kevin, I don't want to hurt you, but . . ."

He took one hand off the steering wheel and held it up. "I know, I know that you don't feel the same way about me . . . yet," he said. "So let's just table this discussion for the present and pretend it never happened. I'm a patient man, and I can wait until things are less turbulent to see whether a relationship is in the cards for us."

She started to respond, but then she realized she didn't really know what to say, so she just kept quiet and spent the rest of the trip looking out the window and wondering just what the hell she'd started.

After picking Angus up from the dog sitter who lived in an apartment down the hall from Kat's, they drove to Sheila's building. They parked on the top floor of Sheila's parking garage and took the elevator to her apartment. After they rang the bell, the door was opened about two inches and a bloodshot eye peered at them from over the safety chain.

The door shut, the chain was pulled back, and then Ramsey opened the door again, barely enough for Kat and Kevin to squeeze through.

"What's with the cloak-and-dagger routine?" Kevin asked.

Ramsey pointed over his shoulder toward the door to Sheila's bedroom. "We've got a guest, and I just wanted to make sure you weren't those private eye fellows coming to check up on us."

Kat held up the thermos. "I got the human fetal brain tissue from your friend, Dr. Garza."

Ramsey frowned. "He's not a friend, just a useful contact. How much was he able to provide?"

She shrugged. "Depending on the weight of the subjects, enough for six, maybe seven doses."

Kat glanced over as Sheila appeared in the bedroom doorway, wiping her face with a hand towel.

Kat immediately went to her. "Sheila, are you okay?"

Sheila nodded. "Yes, I'm just tired is all. I'd forgotten how difficult it is to care for a severely sick patient, especially without a group of nurses to help."

Ramsey bristled and walked over. "What do you mean 'without help'? I've been helping, or did you forget who changed all those bedpans and cleaned up after him?"

"Uh," Kevin said from the doorway where he stood holding Angus in one arm and the dog's bed in the other. "Do you mind if I put the big guy down somewhere? He feels like he's gained ten pounds since we left."

Sheila distractedly pointed toward a corner of the living room.

Kat looked from her to Ramsey. "Is he that bad?"

"Come and see for yourself," Sheila said, leading her into the bedroom.

Kat saw an extremely emaciated male lying on Sheila's bed, an IV in his arm and his wrists tied to the bed frame with cloths. She moved to look closer and saw further that his skin was tinged yellow and he looked to be about eighty years old.

"Jesus, couldn't we find someone younger? I thought the chart you showed us said he was only in his mid-sixties."

Sheila chuckled. "He is sixty-four years old, but he has a lot of miles on him."

"Yeah, he looks like he's been rode hard and put up wet," Kevin said over Kat's shoulder.

Suddenly, Jordan's eyelids fluttered and opened wide, his eyes flicking back and forth rapidly. Low-pitched mewling sounds came from his lips, and his nose began to run.

"Holy shit!" Kevin exclaimed, stepping back. "He's not going to die, is he?"

Sheila shrugged. "I hope not. A dead body in my bed would be hard to explain to the apartment house manager."

"Not to mention to the police, since he didn't exactly come in answer to an invitation."

Kat grabbed Ramsey's shirt and pulled him out into the living room. "You mean you kidnapped him?"

He grinned sourly. "Actually, it was more like a rescue

operation." He went on to explain how they had found Stone passed out and severely dehydrated, lying in his own vomit in an empty lot. "I have little doubt that if we hadn't brought him here, he would not have survived the night."

Sheila moved up beside him. "Burton is right, Kat. It has taken all the skills I possess to keep him alive here in my bed. I've poured gallons of saline and electrolytes and potassium and vitamins and antibiotics into him, and it hasn't seemed to make a whole lot of difference. He's still going in and out of DTs, in spite of massive doses of Librium given via IV."

"DTs?" Kevin asked.

"Delirium tremens," Kat replied. "It's the body's response to rapid detoxification from alcohol. Primarily shaking, drooling, muscle spasms, and occasionally seizures."

"Yes, and it is about twenty-five percent fatal even in a hospital with 'round-the-clock care," Sheila chimed in.

"When will he be coherent enough to gain his permission for the experiment?" Kevin asked.

"I'm hoping another twelve hours of IVs and vitamins and a few more doses of Librium and he'll wake up."

"Is there anything we can do?" Kat asked.

"Are you tired from your trip?"

She shook her head. "No, at least I'm not. I slept on the plane, and we got a good eight hours' sleep last night before heading back."

"Good," Sheila said, handing her the washcloth. "'Cause I'm dog tired. If you can make sure his IV doesn't run out and clean him up if he vomits or soils himself, then I'm going to get some much-needed sleep."

"Why don't you get some shut-eye, too, Burton?" Kevin said. "Your eyes look like the inside of a tomato sauce can."

Ramsey yawned and said, "You should see them from this side."

He put his arm around Sheila's shoulders. "Come on, darlin', I'm too tired to be a danger to you."

She snorted. "As if I couldn't handle you, even if you weren't too tired to tango."

He laughed and slapped her bottom gently. "Oh, is that so? Well, maybe I'll just make a supreme effort to see if I can't make you change your mind about that," he said as they shut the door behind them.

Kevin, watching them, shook his head. "I just hope they don't start making a lot of noise in there. That would be TMI."

"TMI?" Kat asked.

"Too much information," Kevin answered.

CHAPTER 25

John Ashby leaned his head back against the pillow and ran his Montecristo cigar back and forth under his nose while he watched the men standing in front of him. He considered himself an expert at evaluating men and knowing when they were telling the truth and when they were lying. In the many years of his early days in the oil fields, it had often meant the difference between life and death.

Harold Gelb and his two minions were standing at the foot of Ashby's bed, a fine sheen of sweat beading their brows. This in itself meant nothing—most men tended to sweat under Ashby's steely gaze. Gelb himself had a stellar reputation both for getting the job done and for being discreet about it afterward; Ashby wouldn't have hired him otherwise.

Finally, satisfied he was getting the truth, Ashby moistened the cigar with his lips and pulled a gold lighter from beneath the covers and lit up, his eyes steady on Gelb as he rotated it to get it burning evenly. As he replaced the lighter under his bedcovers, he felt the cold steel of the Beretta forty-caliber semiautomatic pistol he kept next to him, hidden from view.

He'd named the piece his "Enforcer," and he had only needed it once. A foreman on one of his numerous projects had been skimming from the expense budget, thinking that the bed-bound Ashby would never find out. When called into Ashby's bedroom and informed that he was being fired and would never be allowed to work in construction again, the man had lunged at Ashby and had gotten so far as to climb up on the foot of the bed before the Enforcer blew him head over heels to land flat on his back, bleeding profusely from a massive chest wound.

Ashby had calmly replaced the gun beneath his covers, lit a cigar, and waited for the bleeding to stop before he let the house staff call for an ambulance and the police.

Ashby had never had the rug cleaned, and he delighted in telling anyone who asked about the stain exactly what it was, using it as a lesson to never, ever think about crossing him.

Now he motioned at Gelb with his cigar. "Go on, Mr. Gelb. Tell me what you've found out about the subjects of your investigation."

Gelb licked his lips and began, glancing at notes in a small notebook he carried. "Each of the subjects is a well-respected citizen, and none of them have any sort of criminal history."

He went on to give a brief synopsis of the lives of Kat, Ramsey, Kevin, and Sheila Goodman. "In short, Mr. Ashby, none of the subjects has significant financial resources, other than Dr. Goodman, whose net worth is probably a little over two hundred thousand dollars. Doctors Williams and Ramsey live hand to mouth, and Kevin Paxton, as you know, is a grad student dependent on his uncle, Dr. Alexander, for his living and college expenses."

Ashby pursed his lips. "So, what you are telling me is that without my financing, these people do not have the resources to double-cross me or to run and hide if they feel threatened?"

"That's correct, Mr. Ashby."

Ashby inclined his head toward Johnson and Gomer standing slightly behind Gelb. "Have you two found anything when you searched their laboratories and homes?"

Both men shook their heads. Johnson spoke up, "Nothing as relates to any chemical formulas, which you asked us to look for, boss. We even copied their computers' hard drives and had the professor you recommended look 'em over. He said the stuff on the drives was rather routine and didn't represent any breakthroughs in medical treatments of any kind."

Ashby grinned. "They are smarter than I gave them credit for. They knew I'd come looking, and they've managed to hide the formula from me."

He suddenly frowned. "Are you sure they haven't made you two? You're sure they don't know they're being followed?"

Both Johnson and Gomer nodded vigorously. "We're sure, Mr. Ashby. We've been very careful not to let them see us, and we switch cars a couple of times a day so they won't see the same one following them."

Ashby nodded. "Okay, so what did you find when you followed Williams and Palmer to Mexico?"

Johnson pulled a small notepad from his shirt pocket. "They flew directly to Monterrey, and met with a lawyer named Felix Navarro and a doctor named Humberto Garza. At the meeting, the doctor handed Dr. Williams a thermos container, and she handed him a wad of cash."

Ashby leaned forward, a look of intense anticipation on his face. "Did you find out what was in the thermos?"

"Not right then," Johnson said. "But later, after crossing Dr. Garza's hand with five hundred dollars, he told us the thermos contained human fetal brain tissue."

Ashby's eyes widened for a moment. "Aha," he said, while thinking to himself the formula was at least in part using fetal stem cells. Not wanting to give the detectives anything else to think about, he changed the subject.

"And what about the lady doctor and her husband? I assume you have had them under surveillance."

This time Gomer nodded and consulted his own small notepad. "The couple went out the other night and drove to a really seedy part of town down near the ship channel . . . Navigation Boulevard, I believe," he said.

"What the hell were two yuppie doctors doing in that part of town at night?" Ashby asked, eyebrows raised.

"They were looking for someone," Gomer answered. He checked his notepad again. "Someone whom the locals called 'the Professor.' A longtime drunk and homeless man who evidently used to be some sort of college teacher."

"What did they do when they found him?"

Gomer smiled. "According to another homeless drunk named Billy, they stuffed him in the trunk of their car and took off."

"The hell you say!" exclaimed Ashby.

Gomer nodded. "I can only assume they took him to their apartment, since I lost track of them by staying behind to question Billy and other witnesses."

"I see," Ashby said in a distracted voice. He suddenly realized that this man must be the human patient the doctors were going to try their serum on to see if it worked. "Okay, Mr. Gelb, I want you and your men to back off the surveillance temporarily. Continue to monitor the GPS trackers on their phones, but I want all audio and visual surveillance to cease until I tell you otherwise."

Gelb looked puzzled but slowly nodded his head. "Okay, Mr. Ashby, if that is the way you want it."

"That is exactly the way that I want it, Mr. Gelb, and," he added with narrowed eyes, "if I find out you are doing otherwise, you and your men will face dire consequences."

Gelb held up his hands, palms out. "No need to make threats, Mr. Ashby. We work under your orders, and if you want us to back off, then of course we'll back off until you tell us otherwise."

"Good," Ashby said, nodding. "Now, take off and I'll call you with further orders unless you see something out of the ordinary on the GPS tracking devices."

As they nodded and filed out of the bedroom, Dr. Tom Alexander stuck his head around the doorjamb and waved. "Mind if I come in, John?"

Ashby smiled and waved the doctor in. "Not if you will reach me one of my Montecristos and turn on the exhaust fan so I can have a smoke."

Alexander wrinkled his nose. "Smells like you've already had a smoke or two recently."

"Come on, Doc. I'm about to become younger and smarter, so a couple of cigars won't hurt me any."

Alexander turned on the exhaust fan next to a window and cracked the pane so the smoke could be drawn out, then he picked a cigar out of a box next to the bed and handed it to Ashby.

As he got the cigar going, Ashby raised his eyebrows and said out of the corner of his mouth, "So, did you hear what those idiots said?"

The doctor nodded, a concerned look on his face.

"What's the matter, Tom? You look worried about something."

"I am just wondering why you have placed the doctors and my nephew under surveillance, and I am also a little worried about what you might be planning, John."

"What? Why?" Ashby asked, his face a mask of innocence, at least half of it anyway.

Alexander smiled grimly. "Let's not kid each other, John. I know you as well as anyone on earth, and I know you are a shrewd and ruthless and greedy bastard. In fact, those are the things I like about you. You don't pretend otherwise, and generally you tell me the truth 'cause you know I am on your side and in your corner."

Ashby nodded. "Uh-huh, but how about this time, Tom?"

Alexander shook his head slowly. "This time I am conflicted, John. I don't particularly care about the doctors, but I love my nephew Kevin dearly, and I would hate for anything . . . untoward to happen to him."

"First, let me assure you that I do not plan for anything 'untoward' to happen to either the doctors or to your nephew, Tom. Of course, I cannot just ignore the unbelievable opportunity having this serum would provide, not to mention the power-wielding potential such a formula would give a man. However, other than eventually controlling and owning the formula, I have no dastardly plans for the doctors or your nephew. Hell, even if they wanted to, they couldn't tell anyone that I'd stolen a formula from them that they, in fact, had stolen from their previous employers."

Alexander leaned forward in his chair. "So I can rest assured that no matter what happens with the formula, Kevin will be taken care of appropriately?"

Ashby nodded. "You have my word as a friend that Kevin will come out of this so rich that he will never have to work again as long as he lives . . . and you, too, pal. I won't forget it was you who brought this formula to my attention."

"Speaking of the formula, John, there is something that we need to talk about."

"Oh?"

"Unless you want everyone in the world to know of the existence of the serum, you are going to have to fake your death and take on a different identity."

Ashby laid his head back on his pillow and blew smoke rings at the ceiling, staring at them as he thought. Finally, he said, "I see what you mean, Tom. The formula is much more valuable if no one knows of its existence."

"With your contacts, it shouldn't be too difficult to arrange a false identity, one that could be mentioned in your will as a sole-surviving relative who would inherit all of your assets," Tom suggested. "That way you could start fresh, with all of your 'inheritance,' without having to look over your shoulder for old enemies who might be coming after you."

Ashby smiled. "I can see you've given this some thought."

Alexander shook his head. "No, actually it was Kevin who suggested it. He is much shrewder about all of this than I am."

"I can see that, Tom. Perhaps I should think seriously about inviting this young man into my employ. I can always use a man who can think on his feet."

Alexander laughed. "You could do worse, John."

Ashby squinted and stared at the doctor. "Tell me something, Tom. Everyone else in the world calls me J.P., yet you persist in calling me John. May I ask why?"

"Everyone else you know is either an employee or an underling of some sort, John. They call you what you order them to call you. I, on the other hand, consider us to be friends, not an employer and employee. That's why I call you John and not J.P."

"You don't consider yourself my employee, yet you take my money to provide care for me. How is that different?"

Alexander smiled. "As I said, I consider us friends, John, and the difference is that I would continue to care for you if you lost every cent you owned and were destitute and could pay me nothing. I do take your money 'cause it means little to you and it is a great deal to me, but the money is not why we are friends. It is just a convenient by-product of our friendship."

Ashby grinned, tears in his eyes, and pointed his cigar at Alexander. "Maybe we could make hiring Kevin a package deal, Tom. After all, it shouldn't be too difficult for the doctors to make two doses of serum instead of one. How would you feel about joining me in taking the serum?"

Alexander nodded and smiled, not bothering to tell

Ashby he'd already decided to do just that. "How about I pour us a nip of that Napoleon brandy on your side table and we'll drink to it?"

"Sounds good . . . partner."

When he stood and went to the table and poured the brandy, Alexander didn't notice the small camera and parabolic microphone attached to the top of the window drapes behind Ashby's bed.

Two hundred yards away, in a vacant house next door to Ashby's sprawling mansion that had a FOR SALE sign in the yard, two FBI agents sat watching a monitor and listening to the voices in Ashby's bedroom.

One turned to the other, a quizzical look on his face. "What the fuck do you think that is all about? Mysterious doctors importing human fetal brains and kidnapping homeless bums down near the ship channel?"

The other answered, "Yeah, and then there's this supersecret formula Ashby keeps harping about. Maybe we'd better reach out to the boss and see what he thinks about these latest recordings."

"Yeah, won't hurt to cover our asses in case it's something important."

CHAPTER 26

Kevin stood in the doorway and watched as Kat checked the sleeping Jordan Stone's vital signs, fiddled with the IV fluid bottle, and generally acted like a nurse in a hospital intensive care unit. It bored him to tears, even though he did enjoy the sight of her bustling around the room.

He yawned, covered it with his hand, and said, "Well, if there's nothing I can do to help, I think I'll go play with Angus."

Without turning around, she waved a hand in the air and said, "Good, 'cause you're making me nervous standing there watching me."

He smiled and shrugged; making her nervous was an improvement over being totally ignored, he reasoned.

When he went into the living room, Angus sat up in his bed, his ears perked and his tail wagging furiously.

Kevin pulled the dog's favorite ball from his pocket and held it up. "I bet you thought I forgot this, didn't you, big fellow?"

Angus barked softly, as if he knew others were asleep and he didn't want to wake them.

Kevin sat on the couch and waved the ball in the air. "Are you ready?"

Angus practically jumped up and down in excitement.

Kevin flipped the ball toward the dining room, and Angus whirled and chased after it like a whirlwind.

Just before he caught it, the ball hit the dining room wall and caromed back over Angus's head. He watched the ball fly over his head and stopped and looked at the wall and then at the ball as it bounced back toward the living room. After a second or two, he whipped around, chased it down, and grabbed it in his mouth.

Prancing proudly, he carried the ball back to Kevin and dropped it gently in his lap.

Kevin again waved the ball in the air and then pitched it toward the dining room again.

Angus took off after the ball, but instead of following it all the way to the wall, he stopped and waited. Sure enough, the ball bounced off the wall and straight into Angus's waiting jaws.

"Holy shit!" Kevin exclaimed, not believing what he'd just seen.

When Angus again brought the ball back to his lap, Kevin thought he'd try a little experiment. This time, he threw the ball in a different direction toward the kitchen archway.

Once again, Angus followed, but he veered off halfway to the archway and moved sideways to the exact spot where the ball bounced when it hit the kitchen wall.

When he dropped the ball into Kevin's lap this time, Kevin rubbed his ears vigorously. "I cannot believe how friggin' smart you are, big guy. Hell, you figured out the exact angle the ball would take off the wall and you've never even had one lesson in trigonometry."

Angus's lips curled in what could only be a smile and he licked Kevin's hand, as if to say thanks for the rub.

* * *

In the bedroom, Kat was adjusting the blanket on Stone's bed, when she felt a hand cover hers gently.

Startled, she jumped back, her hand to her chest.

A low, gravelly voice said, "Oh, I am sorry, miss. I did not mean to startle you."

Kat grinned sheepishly. "That's all right, Mr. Stone. I just wasn't expecting you to wake up so soon, that's all."

Stone returned the grin. "Or at all, perhaps, since I must look like I have one foot in the grave and the other on a banana peel?"

Kat blushed at the accuracy of his self-description. "Oh, you're not that bad."

He gave a dry chuckle. "As they say, 'don't kid a kidder,' miss . . . I am afraid I do not know your name."

"Oh, excuse me, Mr. Stone. I am Kaitlyn . . . Kat Williams. I am a doctor, and I am one of several people who are involved in your treatment."

Stone, with some effort, pushed himself up in the bed and managed to fluff the pillows behind his back so he could semi–sit up. He glanced around the room at the fine furnishings and expensive wallpaper.

"Unless I have, in fact, died and gone to heaven, I do not believe Ben Taub Hospital has such a luxurious room in its environs. So, if I may be so bold as to ask, just where am I, and how did I come to be in the care of such a beautiful creature as yourself?"

"Mr. Stone, if you would be so kind as to hold off on your questions for just a little bit, I would like to have my compatriots with me before we undertake to answer all of your concerns."

Stone grinned and shrugged. "So be it, Miss Kat. However, whilst we are awaiting your compatriots' arrival, I find that I have awakened with a mighty appetite for the first time in recent memory. Is there, by any chance, a kitchen nearby that could provide me with eggs and ham or bacon and perhaps some coffee, if my present state of health permits?"

Kat nodded vigorously. "Of course, Mr. Stone. I'll see to it immediately. Coffee first, then sustenance."

Kat rushed from the room and waved urgently at Kevin.

When he jumped to attention and came over to her, she said, "Kevin, Mr. Stone is awake and quite coherent . . . and hungry. Both great signs that he is not quite as ill as he looked. Could you go into the kitchen and whip him up some coffee, scrambled eggs, and ham or bacon while I wake up Burton and Sheila?"

"Sure, no problem. I'll get right on it."

"And, Kevin, don't answer any of his questions until we can all be there, okay?"

"Absolutely."

As Kevin walked into the kitchen and Kat rushed to begin knocking on Sheila's bedroom door, Angus got up from in front of the couch and ambled into the bedroom where Stone lay.

Stone noticed the Scottish terrier walk into his bedroom and smiled. He had always been an animal lover, and one of his main regrets about living on the street was his inability to keep a pet.

He gave a low whistle and patted the bed next to his legs. "Come here, fella. It's okay to come up into bed with me."

Angus looked over his shoulder, as if to make sure no one was watching, for he knew that one of Kat's rules was no dogs in the bed, unless invited on special occasions.

After a moment, he took a couple of quick steps and jumped up onto the bed, where he sat near Stone's feet, staring at the man with quizzical eyes.

Stone nodded once. "Good boy." He held out his hand, palm down so Angus could sniff him without fear, and waited.

After looking again at the door, Angus eased forward and lowered his head to sniff at Stone's hand. Seconds later, he put his head under the palm and gave a little jerk.

"Oh, so you want me to scratch those big, beautiful ears, huh, boy?" Stone asked.

He was astounded when Angus looked up at him and seemed to nod.

"Hoo boy, you are a smart one, aren't you?" Stone said as he began to scratch and rub Angus's ears.

Moments later, with a soft groan of pleasure, Angus scooted up in the bed, sat on his haunches, and stuck out his right paw for Stone to shake.

Stone raised his eyebrows in wonder, when Kevin said from the doorway, "That means he accepts you as one of his pack."

Kevin walked into the room and handed Stone a large mug of steaming coffee. In his other hand he held a tray with a pitcher of half-and-half and packets of sugar and artificial sweetener.

"Hello, Mr. Stone. I am Kevin Palmer, and I hope we will become fast friends."

"If that is cream in that pitcher, young man, you have made an excellent start."

Kevin grinned and poured a generous dollop of cream into Stone's mug. "How about sugar?"

"By all means, young Kevin. Coffee, when living on the street as it were, is rare enough, but coffee with cream and sugar is often only encountered in one's dreams."

Kevin put several spoonfuls of sugar in the coffee and then said, "Eggs and bacon coming right up. It'll just be a couple of minutes. Scrambled okay?"

"Scrambled would be delightful, Kevin, and I knew you were a scholar and a gentleman the moment I saw you."

As Kevin left, Stone held out the mug toward Angus. "I do not suppose you partake of coffee, do you?"

He laughed out loud when Angus wrinkled his nose and shook his head.

"Jordan, my boy, I do believe you have fallen down

the rabbit hole, so to speak," he said to himself, smiling at Angus.

Kat and the others waited until Stone had finished his eggs and bacon and was on his third cup of coffee before they all entered the room. Kevin and Burton brought in dining room chairs and they arranged themselves around his bed.

Stone smiled and nodded at Sheila. "I do believe I see a familiar face. Good evening, Dr. Goodman. I surmise it is evening as the drapes are pulled and the room lights are on."

Sheila grinned and glanced around at the others. "I told you he was sharp as a tack."

"I have met Mr. Kevin and Miss Kat, and I know Dr. Goodman from previously, but I do not believe I have had the pleasure, sir," he said, looking at Burton.

Ramsey stood up and offered his hand. "Dr. Burton Ramsey—but not the medical kind," he could not resist adding, to Sheila's chagrin.

As Stone shook Ramsey's hand, he looked around at the group. "Unless you all belong to some weird religious group bent on saving homeless denizens off the street, I cannot imagine what I am doing here."

As he spoke, he gently rubbed Angus's neck, who was still sitting next to him in the bed.

Sheila noticed this and said, "Perhaps I can best explain by showing you some pictures and videos, Mr. Stone."

He smiled and shook his head. "Please, call me Jordan. I do believe we are all to be friends here, are we not?"

Sheila got up, strode into the living room, and came back moments later with a stack of pictures and the video camera that had been used to film Angus both before and after his injection.

She handed them to Stone and watched as his eyes widened with wonderment at what he was seeing.

After a while, he put the pictures and video down and stared at Angus, who merely nodded.

"Am I to understand that this is the one and same animal pictured in those photos and videos?"

Angus whined and cocked his head at the word *animal*, whereupon Stone laughed and said, "Oh, excuse me. I meant to say, is this the same fine specimen of canine masculinity as is pictured there?"

Angus grinned and barked, his tail wagging happily.

When the group all nodded, Stone just said, "Oh my!"

No one spoke for a moment, until Stone gave a small chuckle. "I think I can see where this is headed. You good people have come up with a compound that caused those changes in . . . just what is this young fella's name?"

"Angus," Kat said.

"Okay, so this compound made an elderly, quite normal dog into this young puppy and evidently also markedly increased his native intelligence. Is that correct so far?"

Sheila looked around and shook her head. "Mr. Stone . . . uh . . . Jordan, you have a remarkably quick mind."

"In spite of the alcohol abuse, you mean?" he asked, a smile on his lips.

"No, I mean you have a remarkably quick mind for anyone, much less someone as physically ill as you are."

"That is not all that I surmise, Dr. Goodman, and gentlepersons."

Ramsey narrowed his eyes and asked. "Oh?"

Stone nodded. "Yes. I further surmise that, because I am not in a medical institution surrounded by interns and residents, and am instead in a private dwelling, that you all are doing these medical experiments bereft of official sanction . . . on your own, and off the books, so to speak."

Kat laughed, in spite of herself. "Oh, Jordan, you are a peach!"

"And you are entirely correct," Ramsey said, shaking his

head. "We *are* off the books and on our own, for various and sundry reasons that there is no need to go into at present."

Sheila stood and moved to sit on the edge of Stone's bed, taking his hand in hers. "Jordan, as a medical doctor, I am absolutely opposed to experimenting on humans without their full knowledge and also without prior years of animal trials to make sure the experiments are as safe as possible."

He reached over and patted her hand with his. "But in this case, for various reasons," he said cutting his eyes at Ramsey, "that is not possible."

She dropped her eyes and didn't reply.

"Don't worry, Dr. Goodman. As you say, I have a quick mind, and I know that when a delightful, compassionate doctor comes to see me in the hospital and after seeing my lab and X-ray results can hardly bear to look me in the eyes, that it means just one thing. That I have used up just about all of my nine lives and am on the brink of facing my Maker in the very near future."

As Sheila nodded, a tear escaped from her eye to roll down her cheek.

"I see," Stone said, watching her intently. "It is that bad, is it?"

She nodded again, without speaking.

He glanced around at the group surrounding him. "I want you all to know that I have lived a full, and I think a relatively righteous life, and that I am not in the least afraid of facing whatever comes next."

He paused and pursed his lips. "However, after meeting young Angus here and seeing what a joy of life he has, I would not be averse to casting the dice and giving this compound of yours a try. After all, the worst that can happen is that I take the final journey across the River Styx a couple of months early."

As the others smiled and grinned, Sheila held up her hand, her eyes on Stone's. "Are you completely sure, Jordan?"

He thought for a moment and then said, "Yes, I am. You

see, Dr. Goodman, while I have, as I said, always lived a righteous life, it has not been an adventurous one. I think after all of these years it is about time for me to spread my wings and try something totally outrageous."

Sheila laughed and leaned forward to give him a hug, while everyone else gathered around the bed to shake his hand and clap him on the back.

After a moment, he held up his hands. "Just a minute, friends."

Kat said, "Yes, Jordan?"

"Does this magical compound that is going to transform me have a name?"

"Uh, I called my part NeurActivase," Kat said.

Ramsey shrugged. "I just called mine the Scrubber, from blood scrubber, which is what it did."

Stone shook his head. "That won't do . . . that won't do at all. Give me a minute to think of something appropriate . . . and while I am thinking, young Mr. Kevin, might I have another mug of your delightful coffee?"

Everyone stayed silent until Kevin returned with a steaming mug and put it in Stone's hands.

Stone nodded and held up the mug, "I give you . . . the Phoenix Formula!"

Everyone looked at one another with quizzical expressions on their faces.

Stone shook his head, a woeful look on his face. "I can see that none of you has had a classical education. In Greek mythology, a phoenix was a long-lived bird that was periodically reborn. Some said the bird died in flames and was reborn from the ashes. Some also said the bird could live for fourteen hundred years before becoming reborn again."

He spread his hands with a grin. "In other words, friends, the phoenix is a symbol of rebirth and immortality . . . just like I am going to be."

When he laughed, it became infectious and everyone joined in.

CHAPTER 27

FBI special agent in charge Nicholas Fowler's administrative assistant stuck her head in his office door and said, "Got a phone call holding for you, boss. Line one."

"Who is it, Betty?"

"It's from the surveillance team you've got assigned to that rich oil man, J.P. Ashby."

"Okay, I'll take it."

He grabbed his phone and punched line one. "Yeah, Fowler."

"Hey, boss," special agent David Butler said. "Got a couple of interesting sound recordings and videos we think you should hear."

"Interesting how?"

"Well, to begin with, this is not about Ashby's usual tricks of bribing low-level employees of Exxon or Mobil to give him advance notice of oil field acquisitions or paying labor union officials so he can overwork his oil field employees. It's something completely out of the ordinary for him, so I thought you ought to take a look sooner rather than later."

"So, Ashby is branching out and learning new ways to break federal laws?"

"Uh, I'm not sure yet, boss, but I am sure that this is something weird and strange and completely out of character for the way Ashby's been operating for the past six months that we've been listening to him."

Fowler threw his pen down on the desk, leaned back, and put his feet up on the corner. "Give me a brief overview before I listen to the tapes."

"A couple of weeks ago, he hired this private eye to put surveillance on a team of doctors and scientists who were working over at the BioTech Research Facility near the medical center. This was right after he'd been visited by his own personal physician, Dr. Alexander."

"And, of course, we don't know what, if anything, Alexander's visit had to do with that, do we?"

"No, 'cause, as you know, our warrant allowing the surveillance of his house specifically excludes us from being able to listen to his personal doctor or lawyer visits."

"Goddamn judges," Fowler exclaimed. "Okay, so Ashby hires a couple of private dicks to follow some doctors. So what?"

"Last night the detectives checked in, and it seems that two of the docs went to Monterrey, Mexico, and came back with human fetal brain tissue in a thermos. Then two other of the docs went down to the ship channel area, kidnapped a homeless wino, and took him back to their apartment."

"Holy shit!" Fowler exclaimed, dropping his feet off his desk and sitting straight up in his chair. "Send me those tapes and videos right now."

"You want us to drop a bug in the local law's ears about the kidnapping?"

"Hell, no, not until we know what's going on. Besides, if we act on any of this Ashby is liable to figure out that we've got eyes on him."

"Okay, I'll send the digital files to your desktop computer as soon as we hang up."

"And, Butler, no one else in the Bureau hears about any of this until I say so."

"You got it, boss."

Fowler hung up and buzzed his assistant. "Betty, no calls or interruptions for a while."

After watching and listening to the videos, Fowler leaned back in his chair, put his hands behind his head, and stared at the ceiling, thinking. He couldn't tell from the tapes just what in the hell this serum or formula or whatever it was was going to be used for, but if Ashby was spending this much time and effort on it, it had to be worth a shitload of money. In any event, this was the first thing they'd caught on tape that had any potential of profit for him, so he'd better take advantage of it right now.

He was coming up on his sixty-fifth birthday, and that meant mandatory retirement from the FBI. He was a little under six feet in height, weighed almost two hundred and fifty pounds, and suffered from hypertension and acid reflux. In fact, the only reason the FBI doctor had passed him on his last physical was that he was due for retirement in several months.

Special agent in charge of the Houston FBI office was a plum assignment, but he should have been a deputy director by now, and the fact that he'd been passed over his last two promotion dates rankled him. It had evidently rankled his wife, too, because the last time he'd been passed over, she had said enough, packed her bags, and left him for her Pilates instructor.

In short, he only had a few months in which to make a major bust or he was going to be retired into ignominy. This was his last chance for a big score. He figured his only two options were either to catch Ashby in a huge crime, bust

him, and become famous, or to catch him in something ne-
farious that he could use to blackmail Ashby into hiring him
as head of his security forces. God knew he had no other
skills other than what he'd learned in thirty years as an investigator for the FBI.

He sat forward and transferred the videos and tapes to a
thumb drive, then erased them from his computer. He was
going to have to play this very carefully until he found out
exactly what Ashby was up to. That meant he needed to get
rid of any other witnesses to Ashby's activities if he was
going to be able to take full advantage of it without any interference from the FBI.

He picked up his phone and called Special Agent Butler's
cell phone.

When he answered, Fowler said, "Hey, David. I've got
some bad news. I passed on what you sent me to the deputy
director, and he said that since we stumbled upon a possible
kidnapping and international smuggling operation, he wants
to send in a special operations crew to take over the Ashby
surveillance."

"But, boss"—Butler started to say.

"Hey, I know, it pisses me off, too, David. But I'm being
cut out of the loop, too, so just pack up your personal gear
and report to me tomorrow for another assignment."

Butler agreed sullenly and Fowler hung up the phone, a
smile on his face. This meant that he'd have to review all of
the surveillance tapes himself every night after he left the
office, but what the hell—with his wife gone, he had nothing else to do.

He just hoped the prize was worth the aggravation.

Kevin and Kat, with Angus in tow, all arrived at Sheila's
apartment exactly at eight o'clock in the morning as they'd
agreed the night before. Sheila had drawn a battery of blood
tests from Stone, and she'd said she wanted to get the results

before proceeding with the injection of the Phoenix Formula, as they'd begun to call it.

While Kevin fixed her and him some coffee in the kitchen, Kat took Angus and went directly to the bedroom where Stone was staying.

"Hey, big fella," Stone called when he saw Angus.

Angus barked once, then immediately hopped up in the bed next to Stone, his tail wagging furiously and his tongue lathering Stone's face.

"I know, I know, I'm glad to see you, too, big guy," Stone said happily as he rubbed Angus's ears vigorously.

"I think you have made a new friend, Jordan," Kat said, sitting in the chair next to his bed.

Stone smiled and switched to rubbing Angus's flanks. "I hope I have made more than one, Miss Kat."

Kevin entered and handed one of the two coffee mugs he was carrying to Kat. "I know of at least four more, Jordan," he said, and raised his mug to him in a toast.

Before he could reply, Sheila and Burton Ramsey entered the room. Sheila was holding a sheaf of lab reports and was studying them intently, a pair of half glasses perched on her nose.

"Is that good news, Doc Sheila, or am I to be thrown back on the mean streets of the ship channel?"

Sheila looked up as she removed her glasses and chuckled. "I swear, Jordan, I don't know how you do it. You live on a diet of nothing but raw carbohydrates contained in cheap wine, and yet you still manage to come back from the dead each time you leave the hospital." She held up the lab reports. "Your test results, while not even close to normal, are still remarkable considering all you have done to try to kill yourself."

"It's me pure heart that keeps me goin', lass," Stone said in a terrible attempt at an Irish accent.

Burton snorted and smiled. "More like the luck of the Irish," he said.

In a normal accent, Stone said, "While it is true that I am of Irish descent, I regret to say that I am only half Irish, on my father's side."

"The half that is full of blarney, no doubt," Kat said with a grin.

Stone laughed. "It is true that I have been accused of bending the truth on occasion, but only in jest and never to harm."

Sheila walked around the bed and sat in a chair opposite from Kat's. "Jordan, it is time for us to talk seriously."

Stone nodded and watched her intently.

"From your tests, it is clear that you have advanced cirrhosis of the liver, at least one gastric ulcer that is bleeding and keeping you very anemic, and your heart is in mid-stage heart failure."

"In short, I should not endeavor to buy anything on time payments?" he asked, the corners of his lips curled in a slight smile.

When Sheila started to respond, he held up his hand. "That is quite all right, dear Dr. Sheila. While I have no formal education in medicine, nevertheless I am, as you say, quick of mind. I have realized for some time that my poor body could not much longer endure the torture through which I was putting it. In fact, due to a rather long-standing melancholy, I have been looking forward to shuffling off this mortal coil and joining my dear wife and children in the afterlife."

When Angus sensed Stone's mood, he whined and leaned in to lick Stone's face. Stone smiled and patted his head. "That is, until recently. After meeting you good people, and especially Angus here, I have decided that helping you in your quest to help others like me would give my life some meaning that it is otherwise lacking. In short, if I am a suitable candidate, bring on the Phoenix Formula and let us see what transpires."

Sheila looked around at Kat and Burton and shrugged. "I

am afraid Jordan is as healthy as he is going to get without a liver and heart transplant, and I think the formula is his only chance of living even a relatively normal life."

Burton put his hand on her shoulder. "So, dear, you are okay with us going ahead with the formula?"

She nodded, staring into Stone's eyes. "It is truly your only chance, Jordan, or I would never agree to its use."

He reached over and patted her hand. "I know, dear lady." Looking up at Kat and Burton, he asked, "Now, just what might I expect to happen after the injection?"

Burton moved to stand at the foot of the bed, where he could talk directly to Stone. "We don't know . . . exactly. In Angus's case, for a couple of days he had a high fever due to an increased metabolic rate, he burned off a few pounds of excess fat, and all of his hair fell out and was then replaced with darker, younger-looking hair."

Stone patted his distended belly and then rubbed his few sparse hairs. "Well, at least the fat and the old hair I will not miss."

"Due to your greater size and less healthy status," Kat said, "I expect the transformation to take longer than it did with Angus, who was healthy except for severe arthritis. Perhaps as long as a week or more."

"During that time, will I be in pain?"

Burton shook his head. "No, at least Angus didn't seem to have any discomfort. In fact, for most of the transformation, Angus slept through it."

Stone pursed his lips. "Perhaps, just for your protection, I should sign some sort of disclaimer, stating that I have been fully informed of all risks and that I accept full responsibility for whatever might happen?"

Sheila smiled grimly and shook her head. "Not necessary, Jordan, and, in fact, it would do no good. What we are doing is completely illegal, and if it goes badly there is nothing that will protect us from facing the consequences of our actions."

"And yet you are willing to go ahead anyway?"

"Yes, because if it works, this formula may be the cure for any number of horrible diseases that at present have no suitable treatment."

Stone laid his head back on the pillow and said, "Then let us carry on posthaste."

Kat and Burton had already figured out the doses of each of their formulas and had them mixed in a syringe, which she handed to Sheila. "Would you do the honors, Dr. Goodman?" she asked.

Sheila took the syringe, fixed a rubber tourniquet on Stone's left arm, found a nice vein, and injected the formula.

Burton took out a small notepad and made a note of the time.

"What now?" Kevin asked.

"Now, we wait, and we pray," Kat said.

Angus barked once and lay down with his head on Stone's stomach, his brown eyes looking up into Stone's.

Stone laid his hand on Angus's neck and closed his eyes, content to see what tomorrow would bring.

After the group had filed out of the bedroom, Burton noticed Sheila looking pensive.

"What is going on in that marvelous mind of yours, dear?"

She shook her head. "I think we're making a mistake, trying to treat Jordan here."

"Why?" Kat asked. "After all, we're near the medical center in case things start to go wrong."

"Yes, there is that," Sheila conceded, "but my neighbors are bound to notice all of you coming and going, and this apartment has to be known to Ashby's men. What is to keep them from coming in here, taking Jordan, and using him to force us to give them the formula?"

"Damn, you're right!" Burton exclaimed.

"I agree," Kevin said. "It would be much safer all around to take Jordan to the lab house in Conroe and watch him there, where Ashby and his minions will have no idea where he is."

"And Conroe does have a first-rate hospital in case of a medical emergency," Burton added.

"So, we're agreed?" Sheila asked. "We should move him to Conroe?"

The other three all nodded, and it was decided.

CHAPTER 28

The decision to move Stone having been made, the group trooped back into the bedroom.

Stone opened his eyes and watched as Sheila sat in the chair next to the bed, reached over, and pulled the IV needle out of his arm. Then she stuck a bandage on the wound and began to pack up the other medical paraphernalia in the bedroom.

Angus sat up and looked at Kat, wondering what was going on.

Stone glanced down at the bandage and then up at Sheila. "I take it from the way you are cleaning house that I am to be moved to another location?"

"Yes, Jordan. It is too dangerous to keep you here any longer. Sooner or later my neighbors would notice the extra number of visitors coming and going and would begin to ask questions, which we definitely don't need."

"Are you sure we'll have time to transport him before the formula takes effect?" Kevin asked.

"Pretty sure," Sheila answered. "Angus didn't begin to show changes for at least twelve hours, and I believe for a human, it will take even longer due to their greater size."

Burton interjected, "Yeah, and the trip to Conroe should only take about two hours at this time of day."

Stone plucked at the hospital gown he was wearing. "I assume I will not be walking down the halls of your apartment building in this stylish but immodest garment, with its rear air-conditioning. Have the clothes I was wearing when you brought me here been cleaned?"

"Uh . . . about that, Jordan," Burton said hesitantly, "your clothes were beyond cleaning, and so after I put you in the hospital gown that Sheila borrowed from Ben Taub, I put them out in the apartment incinerator."

Stone actually blushed. "I am truly sorry that you had to deal with my . . . uh . . . unfortunate lack of personal hygiene, Burton. It is a fact of life on the street that cleanliness is difficult if not impossible to maintain without access to proper bathroom or shower facilities."

"Don't worry about it, Jordan. Kevin stopped at a Walmart on the way here from the airport and picked up some sweatpants and a shirt for you. They will have to do until we can get you better supplied after the formula has done its work."

"Oh?"

"Yes," Kat answered. "Remember, we told you that Angus burned off several pounds under the increased metabolic rate induced by the formula. We expect you will do the same, and so we won't know what size clothes to get you until then."

Kevin stepped over and laid the sweat clothes on the edge of the bed, "We'll step out and let you change."

When they arrived at the Honda sedan parked in Sheila's garage, Kat opened the rear door and said, "If you wouldn't mind, Jordan, I am afraid we're going to have to ask you to lie down on the backseat out of sight."

"What?"

"Yeah," Kevin said. "We'll explain on the way, but for now, that's the way we have to proceed."

Stone chuckled. "Well, as they say, in for a penny, in for a pound. I feel like I am in a spy movie."

After he was situated lying on the backseat with Angus cradled in his arms, Kevin covered the two of them with a blanket. While he was doing that, Kat donned the blond wig and sunglasses kept in the car. Finally, ready to travel, Kevin sat in the front passenger seat and slumped down as far as he could get.

When they were out of downtown Houston traffic and on the highway headed to Conroe, Kat pulled the car over at a roadside rest stop. Stone was able to sit up and Kat removed her disguise, while Kevin stood watch to make sure they weren't being followed.

When Kat pulled back onto the highway, Kevin turned around in his seat and told Stone the entire story about J.P. Ashby, how they were using him to finance their experiments with the formula, and about how he had hired private investigators to follow them in hopes of stealing the formula for himself.

"It seems you have made a deal with the devil to advance your cause," Stone said, a disapproving expression on his face.

Kevin nodded. "Yes, we did, Jordan. But only out of necessity. None of us, not even Sheila, had the financial resources to fund the development of the formula."

Kat said over her shoulder, "And if we had depended on the lab we were working at to develop the formula, chances are it would have taken years and years and then the government would have gotten involved and who knows what a bunch of Washington bureaucrats would have done with something this valuable."

"We were afraid they would keep the formula for the exclusive use of the rich and powerful, and the common people would never get to benefit from the disease-curing effects of the formula," Kevin added.

Stone peered out the window for a moment, finally nodding his head. "Yes, you are most certainly correct in assuming that the government would not act in the common people's best interests, since it rarely has in the past."

Kevin noticed a fine sheen of sweat on Stone's forehead. "Are you feeling okay?"

Stone smiled and wiped his forehead. "Yes, Mr. Kevin, quite all right. I do not think this is due to a premature effect of the formula, but rather due to the absence of any intake of spirits. In short, I do believe I am still in a bit of withdrawal from my abrupt cessation of partaking of alcohol."

"Well, the trip to Conroe only takes a couple of hours. If you can last that long, Sheila gave us some Xanax to give you that should help alleviate the withdrawal symptoms."

Stone waved a dismissive hand. "Do not worry, young man. I shall be just fine. After all, I have gone through this many times in the past."

Stone was surprised when Kat pulled the Honda into a residential neighborhood about a mile from Lake Conroe. "I thought you said you were taking me to your new laboratory location?"

Kevin looked back over the seat. "We are, Jordan. We decided to rent a regular house in a typical residential neighborhood instead of a lab in a commercial building. Like I told you earlier, we are being hunted and followed by some very good private investigators. If they somehow get wind that we've located our lab in Conroe, the last place they'll look is here."

"Plus, it has the added advantage that we knew we'd need to live here while our subject, you, is going through the transformation. Typical labs have very few amenities for long-term inhabitance."

"Yeah, this place has three bedrooms, a full kitchen, and even a small office space we can use for our computers."

"We've set up one of the bedrooms as a makeshift lab and one we've set up for you, complete with IV poles, a variety of medications Sheila thought we might need, and even a small TV so you can keep up with the news, should you desire."

Stone got a wistful look on his face. "The TV I don't need. But if I might be so presumptuous, if I give you a list of my favorite authors, do you think you might be able to pick up some of their latest tomes?"

"I don't know whether the local Barnes and Noble has a section on philosophy," Kevin said doubtfully.

Stone laughed. "The heck with philosophers. Give me Robert Crais, Ridley Pearson, David Baldacci, or Vince Flynn any day."

"So, no philosophers?" Kevin asked.

"Young Mr. Kevin, I read nothing but philosophy for eight years of college and graduate school, and, besides, who said the authors I mentioned are *not* philosophers?"

Kevin held up his hands in defeat. "Okay, okay, so popular authors it is, then."

Kat turned into the driveway of a house that sat on nearly an acre of fairly wooded landscape. "Here we are, Jordan, home sweet home for the next few weeks."

Stone glanced around. The nearest house was almost a mile away. "Why so isolated, Miss Kat? Afraid I'll cry out in anguish and bring the neighbors running?"

She laughed. "No, Jordan. Burton just didn't want a bunch of prying eyes seeing all of the lab equipment he hauled in here. Even so, he did most of the moving in during the dead of night."

"Well," Stone said as he took Angus and set him gently

down on the driveway, "I hope he hauled in lots of food-stuffs, because I am famished."

Kat glanced at Kevin. "I do believe the Phoenix Formula is already speeding up the professor's metabolic rate. It's only been a couple of hours since he ate a huge breakfast."

Stone rubbed his hands together and took off at a fast walk toward the front door. "Whatever the cause, I am all for checking out the kitchen . . . what about you, big guy?" he asked Angus, who was trotting by his side.

Angus barked happily, and the duo passed through the door as soon as Kevin unlocked it.

While Stone and Angus were rummaging through the re-frigerator, Kevin brought in the suitcases and duffel bags from the car.

Once inside, he dumped them on the bed of the room designated for the scientists to use.

"Hmmm," he said, looking around. "Only one bedroom with one bed for the two of us to use. Which side do you want?"

Kat punched him playfully on the shoulder. "Both sides, silly."

She turned him around and pushed him toward the living room. "Burton thought of that and made sure the couch in the living room was a sleeper sofa. It folds out into a queen-size bed."

Kevin laughed and pulled a quarter out of his pocket. "How about we flip for it? Heads, I stay in the room with you; tails, I sleep out here all alone."

She shook her head. "If you are that concerned about sleeping alone, I could ask Angus to bunk with you."

Hearing his name, Angus stuck his head around the corner and barked, his tail wagging furiously, before he whirled around and disappeared back into the kitchen.

"See," Kat said. "He won't mind at all."

With that, she turned and followed the dog into the kitchen.

Stone was already seated at the table, a plate containing two huge sandwiches, several large pickles, and a pile of potato chips in front of him. Angus was sitting in the chair next to him, a plate of ham slices before him.

Around a mouthful of food, Stone said, "Burton seems to have done well with his provisions; however, we could not find any staples for young Angus here, so put that on your list of things to buy, if you do not mind."

Kat snapped her fingers. "Darn, Jordan is right. I forgot to tell Burton to get some kibble for Angus."

When she looked back at the table, Angus's plate was empty and he was licking his lips.

"My guess is he did not mind too much," Stone said, rubbing the dog's ears.

"How about I make us a couple of sandwiches and we can chow down before we unpack everything?" Kevin asked Kat.

"Sounds good to me," Kat said. Watching Stone and Angus eat had made her hungry, too.

As Kat and Kevin were finishing their sandwiches, Stone got a funny look on his face and put his hand to his chest.

"Oh my," he said in a strangled voice. "I am afraid something untoward is happening."

Kat jumped up from the table and rushed to his side. She took his wrist in her hand and looked over at Kevin.

"I think the formula is beginning to work. His pulse is like a hundred and twenty and is very full."

"Should I be alarmed?" Stone asked, his eyes wide.

Kat shook her head. "No, Jordan, I don't think so. I believe the formula is doing what it is supposed to do, which is to vastly speed up your metabolism. That is why your heart is racing, and I also detect a slightly warmer temperature."

"I am feeling rather shaky. Perhaps I should lie down for a while."

Kat nodded at Kevin, who got up, put his arm around Stone's shoulders, and escorted him to the bedroom designated for their patient.

He grinned when Angus jumped up on the bed as soon as Stone was under the covers. The dog lay down next to him, his head on Stone's stomach.

Kevin reached over and patted Angus's head. "I do believe the big fella has taken quite a liking to you, Professor."

"And I to him, dear boy," Stone said, laying his hand on Angus's flank. "I believe you may leave us to our much-needed rest. We shall be fine."

Kevin nodded. "You be sure to call us if you get to feeling bad, Jordan. We'll be in the room right next door."

As the day progressed into evening, Stone's symptoms intensified. His fever climbed to 104 degrees, and he began to shake and quiver so much that Angus jumped down off the bed and stared at Kat with concerned eyes.

Kat continued to monitor Stone's vital signs every fifteen to thirty minutes and checked in with Sheila by phone on several occasions to determine doses of the various medications Sheila had left in the medicine cabinet to combat the symptoms of a vastly increased metabolic rate.

By the morning of the next day, all of Stone's grizzled hair had fallen out and been replaced by a fine black stubble.

Kevin had gotten him up twice to change his sweat-soaked bedclothes and take cool showers to help lower his body temperature. On these occasions, Stone had been conscious, but he seemed slightly mentally confused and had to be reminded several times of where he was and what was going on.

Finally, around ten o'clock in the morning, his fever broke, and he fell into a deep sleep. Angus moved from his bed in the corner of Stone's bedroom and jumped back up into the bed next to Stone. He gave Kat a baleful glance, as if he blamed her for his friend's discomfort, and then he once again laid his head on Stone's stomach and relaxed next to him.

Kat and Kevin, exhausted from a sleepless night, checked in with Sheila to reassure her that the crisis had passed, and then they both fell onto the bed in the second bedroom fully clothed, too exhausted to argue about who would sleep where.

CHAPTER 29

On the fourth morning following the injection of the Phoenix Formula into Stone's body, Kat woke up to the smell of coffee and frying bacon. She leaned her head to the side and saw that Kevin was no longer in the bed. He had finally worn her down two days before by stating that the pull-out bed in the living room was ruining his back.

She had relented and said he could sleep in the same bed as her, but they were both to wear full pajamas and there was to be no hanky-panky, either implied or assumed. Kevin had agreed, reluctantly, figuring half a loaf was better than none at all.

She yawned, rubbed her eyes, and walked into the kitchen.

Standing at the stove was a man who appeared to be in his late thirties, with coal-black hair and a trim build. The sweat clothes he was wearing hung loosely on him as if they were two sizes too large.

Angus was sitting on his haunches next to the man, his attention riveted on the frying bacon in the skillet on the stove and his tail slowly wagging.

Kat glanced at the kitchen table and saw Kevin sitting there in his pajamas, drinking a cup of coffee, and smiling at her.

She looked back to the man at the stove. "Who are you, and what have you done with my elderly professor?" she asked, grinning.

Stone turned around, his arms held wide. "What do you think, Dr. Kat? Do you approve of what your formula has accomplished?"

Kat, who up until now had only seen Stone lying in the bed under covers with just his head sticking out, was amazed at the transformation.

She moved quickly to embrace him, then stepped back and held him at arm's length. "You look great, Jordan. Really great."

He gave a short bow. "Thank you, Dr. Kat. And more importantly, I feel great."

Angus gave a short bark and inclined his head toward the stove.

Stone turned back to his cooking. "You are correct, Angus, lad. If I don't pay attention to what I am doing, I will surely burn the bacon."

He waved back over his shoulder. "Dr. Kat, by the time you have showered and changed, breakfast should be ready. We are having eggs à la Stone, along with bacon, pancakes, and home-style fries with onions and bell peppers."

Kat laughed. "Remember, Jordan, not everyone has had their metabolism kicked into high gear. Kevin and I will have to be careful not to gain twenty pounds if we are to let you do all the cooking."

She turned and rushed toward the bathroom to get ready, her mouth watering at the thought of breakfast.

Angus lay on his side next to Stone's chair at the breakfast table, his belly distended from several pieces of bacon and a small helping of scrambled eggs.

While she drank a post-breakfast cup of coffee, Kat looked at Kevin. "How about I clean up the kitchen and do the dishes while you take Jordan to Dillard's and get him some new clothes?"

"That sounds like a plan," Kevin answered. "And after I bring him back here, I think I'll take the Honda to Houston and see about picking up Burton and Sheila and bringing them back here. They deserve to see this in person."

"Why can't they just come here in their own cars?" Stone asked.

"You forget, Jordan, we are being watched. Kevin found GPS locators affixed to all of our cars a few weeks back, so any time we want to go someplace secret, we have to use the Honda," Kat said. She held up her mobile phone. "We have even begun to use so-called burner phones so that our calls can't be listened in on."

Stone nodded. "More cloak-and-dagger stuff."

Kat leaned across the table and put her hand on his. "But necessary, Jordan. I'm sure you can see that. The Phoenix Formula is so . . . so revolutionary that if its secret got out, men would do anything to obtain it."

"And most would not want to use it to do good, but to gain power and control over others," Kevin said.

"Like the reclusive billionaire with whom you have promised to do business."

"Yes, just like him," Kat answered. "And forgive me, Jordan, but you don't have to sit there with your ivory tower background and be so judgmental about what we have had to do to get this far with our research."

Stone looked stricken. "I am truly sorry, Dr. Kat. There is great merit in what you say, and I must confess to having some doubts about the character and intentions of the man we are talking about, but I would never presume to look down upon you or your compatriots, whom I know have only the best intentions in your hearts."

"Thank you for that, Jordan," Kevin said. "If there was any other way, we would take it, but original research is very expensive, and almost impossible without getting the government involved."

"I may have some thoughts on that, which I shall share with you later," Stone said. "But first, away with us, young Mr. Kevin. My new attire is waiting for us at the nearest men's store," he added, obviously attempting to lighten the mood in the room before it got out of hand.

It was almost five o'clock before Kevin managed to return with Burton and Sheila. He had used every trick he could think of to make sure they weren't being followed. He'd even gone over the Honda with his electronic checker to assure himself there was no GPS tracker on it.

Burton sniffed as he entered the front door. "My God, whatever that is, it smells delicious."

Stone appeared in the dining room archway, a dish towel slung over his shoulder. He was wearing new black Levi's, a purple and black Izod shirt, and black tennis shoes.

"I discovered this afternoon that the house you rented came equipped with a gas grill on the back patio, Burton, so I took the liberty of grilling some of those rib eye steaks you had so thoughtfully provided in the freezer."

Kat appeared next to him. "He also baked potatoes and cooked corn and green beans."

Stone shrugged. "Simple food, but then, I am a simple man."

Sheila put her hands to her cheeks, eyes wide. "My God, is it you, Jordan?"

He laughed. "In the flesh, Dr. Sheila."

"Holy smoke!" Burton exclaimed. "It actually worked."

"You look thirty years younger, and . . . and so healthy," Sheila said, moving closer to him to put her palms on his shoulders.

"And more importantly, I *feel* thirty years younger, Dr. Sheila," Stone said, placing his hands over hers.

Angus appeared in the kitchen doorway and barked loudly, looking back over his shoulder to the kitchen.

"Ah, young Angus is correct," Stone said. "The steaks are going to get cold if we do not make haste to the dining room."

As the group took seats around the dining room table, Stone speared a rib eye, cut it into small pieces, and placed them in Angus's bowl next to his bed in the corner of the room.

Angus settled down and began to eat the steak, groaning low in his throat in delight.

Everyone at the table laughed and began to dig into their own food, with much talking back and forth about the formula and what Stone had experienced during the transformation.

"Well, since I slept through most of it, there is not a lot I can tell you that you do not already know," he said in answer to the questions. "It was kind of like having the flu . . . chills, fever, shakes. All in all, not too unpleasant."

J.P. Ashby was getting impatient. He'd heard nothing from the researchers since he had given them the fifty thousand dollars, and since he'd told his investigators to back off, he had no new intel on their actions or whereabouts.

He angrily hit the speed-dial on his phone and soon had Harold Gelb on the phone. "Do you have any news for me, Gelb?"

"Uh . . . no, sir. Since you told me to have my men back off, all I've been doing is monitoring the movements of the subjects' automobiles."

"And have there been any unusual movements to report?"

"Not at all. None of the vehicles has made any unusual trips, and especially not out of the city. In fact," he added, "let me check right now."

After a moment, he came back on the line. "Yes, all of their vehicles are in their various parking garages as we speak."

"So I can assume they are all currently in their apartments?"

"Uh . . . again, sir, I have no way of knowing that without going to each location and physically checking on them."

Ashby took a deep breath and thought for a moment. "Okay, then I suggest you send your men to do just that. I need to know where they are right now."

"Well, Johnson is on another assignment, but I'll get Gomer on it right away."

"Gelb," Ashby said in a dangerously low voice, "do not ever think me a fool. I know you are charging me almost double your usual rates. Now, I don't mind that, and, in fact, I expect it, since no one in their right mind ever gives a billionaire a discount. However, at these rates, I do expect that you will keep all of your operatives available to me twenty-four/seven. Do I make myself clear, or should I peruse the yellow pages for other private investigative firms?"

"No, sir! I will get my men on it immediately. There might be some problem with Dr. Goodman's apartment, since it has rather good security that keeps unknown or unwanted visitors at bay, but the others' apartments are all rather Spartan and I can have my men approach as salesmen and see if anyone answers their doors."

"And, Gelb, forget what I said about backing off. From now on, I want eyes on these people at all times as long as your men can do it and remain out of sight."

That night, after he had gotten off work, showered, and eaten a tasteless microwave TV dinner, FBI SAIC Nicholas Fowler listened to the tape of Ashby talking to Gelb with interest. Though he could hear only one side of the conversation, he knew things were heating up with Ashby and his mysterious scientists.

"I think things might just be coming to a head with Mr. J.P. Ashby," he said to himself as he sat before his recording equipment. Not wanting to leave the recordings unattended all day in case he might miss something important, Fowler decided to call in sick for a few days and monitor the equipment continuously.

He pushed the appropriate dials to have the video- and tape-recording feeds forwarded directly to his home computer, then he headed home, locking the door behind him.

He figured he could monitor things from home, just in case someone from the office called him to make sure he was really home sick. Not likely, but not impossible, since the FBI would be watching him closely in his last few months on the job before his upcoming retirement.

As he drove toward his apartment, he wondered just what in the world Ashby was doing messing around with these rather low-rent doctors. He'd had their records checked, and none of them had tripped any bells.

Well, he figured, now that he was listening on his own without any other agents looking over his shoulder, he might just wrangle a way to listen in himself on Ashby's talks with his doctor and lawyers. Perhaps that would give him the answers he was looking for.

CHAPTER 30

After the group finished dinner, Sheila told Kevin he needed to take her and Burton back to Houston before they were missed and Ashby's investigators began looking for them.

"Sure thing, Dr. Sheila," Kevin said. "Just give me ten minutes, okay?"

When she nodded her assent, Kevin went into the bedroom and dug through his duffel bag for a moment. Finally, he pulled out the video camera he'd used to document Angus's transformation.

He came back into the living room and addressed the others. "When you first picked up Jordan and took him to your apartment, I took the opportunity to make some video recordings of him while Burton was getting him undressed and into bed."

Kat said, "Kevin—"

"Oh, nothing dirty, Kat. I just mainly wanted to show his deteriorated condition and how much older and frailer he looked than his chronological age. Now, if he doesn't mind, I'd like to show the 'after' pictures of him since the injection of the Phoenix Formula."

Stone arched an eyebrow. "I presume this is to document the formula's effectiveness for your rich client?"

Kevin nodded. "We told him we would test the formula on someone else first to make sure it was safe, and then, when he was satisfied, we would inject him and earn our fee."

Sheila stepped forward. "We know this is a gross violation of patient confidentiality, Jordan, and if you'd rather not pose . . ."

Stone shook his head. "No, Dr. Sheila, after all that you have done for me, I feel that helping you in this endeavor is the least I can do. And the added bonus is that the sooner you collect your fee, the sooner the formula can be made available to others to help ease their suffering."

"I do have one suggestion," Kat interjected. "To protect Jordan's identity, I think he should wear a mask."

"But Ashby will have to be able to determine that this is the same man in both videos," Burton argued.

Kat laughed. "Burton, do you remember what Jordan looked like when you and Sheila brought him home? His face already looks completely different due to the age regression and weight loss."

"If I may," Kevin said, "I agree with Kat about hiding his new face, since we have no idea who else may get to see these videos. However, I noticed during the original video I took at Sheila's house that Jordan has a rather distinctive strawberry birthmark just below his waistline on his back. If he doesn't mind showing a little butt cheek in the video, the birthmarks will both be seen and it will prove that he is the same man."

"Then let us proceed," Stone said. He pulled a handkerchief out of his rear pants pocket, folded it into a triangle, and placed it over his mouth and nose like an old-time bandito. Moving to the center of the room with his back to a bare wall, he stripped off his shirt and lowered his jeans a few inches.

The group was amazed at the lean, ropy musculature of his body and how vibrant he looked shirtless. Even though he now appeared to be in his thirties, he had the body of a much younger man.

"I am here next to this blank wall so that there will be no clues in the video to lead anyone to this place," he explained. And then, leaning over and flexing his arm muscles in a classic weight lifter's pose, he said, "Shoot away, young Mr. Kevin."

As everyone broke into laughter, Kevin shot photographs for the next five minutes, having Stone walk, do jumping jacks, and perform various other exercises to show off his new, youthful vitality.

Even Angus watched intently from his bed in the corner, his tail wagging happily to see his friend dance about.

Finally satisfied, Kevin packed up his camera and started to leave with Sheila and Burton to head back to Houston, when Stone stopped him and handed him a folded-up piece of paper. "Read that when you get to Houston, please," Stone said.

Kevin nodded and followed Sheila and Burton out the door.

Kat moved over next to Stone as he was pulling his shirt over his head. "I am sorry you had to go through that, Jordan."

He tucked in his shirt, a wry look on his face. "Do not be silly, Dr. Kat. How often does an old codger like me get a second chance at life? Maybe in this life I will be able to do something to make a difference that I was never able to do in my last one."

"What do you mean, Jordan? You've taught thousands of young men and women when you were at the university."

He waved a dismissive hand. "Bah, philosophy. A bunch of meaningless words never long remembered by those to whom they were taught."

She shook her head. "I think you are being too hard on yourself."

Suddenly his face took on a serious mien. "Let us repair ourselves to the kitchen for a nice cup of coffee and a chat."

She gave him a puzzled glance, but nodded and walked into the kitchen.

Minutes later, Angus had a snack of crumpled-up breakfast bacon in his bowl and Kat and Stone were sitting at the table nursing steaming mugs of coffee.

After a moment, Stone began. "Kat, I know that you and Burton and young Kevin went into this affair with only the best of intentions . . . meaning to help people with heretofore incurable diseases to get well. Am I right?"

She gave a nervous laugh. "Well, Kevin and I did, that's for sure. Burton, at first, was only interested in how much money he could make from his blood-scrubber and he gave little thought to the people with kidney failure whom it would help."

"You said 'at first'?"

"Yes, for now Burton has changed. Since he and Sheila have gotten back together, he is happier and has lost much of the bitterness that so pervaded his life before. Now he sees the good that the Phoenix Formula can do and he is fully behind its development."

Then she laughed and put a hand on his arm. "But don't get me wrong. None of us are saints, and we are all looking forward to having enough money not to have to worry about where the next rent check is coming from."

Stone sighed and took a long draught of his coffee, as if to fortify himself for what he was about to say.

"What is it, Jordan? You look worried about something."

"Dr. Kat, I suppose you know that among the other changes the Phoenix Formula brings about is a marked increase in intelligence?"

She sat back, a surprised look on her face. "Of course we

knew, but the physical transformation was so impressive that I'm afraid we all temporarily forgot about that."

He smiled gently. "And, of course, you did not put me through those mazes like you did your rats."

"Of course not." She laughed.

"Dr. Kat, would you be surprised to learn that my IQ prior to my rather precipitous fall from grace was in the 'genius' level?"

She shook her head slowly. "I hadn't really thought about it, but . . . no, I am not surprised."

"Actually, I had been tested to be in the high one hundred and sixties."

He held up his hand when she started to speak. "No, do not say anything, Dr. Kat, for I am not telling you this to brag, but to emphasize that since I received the formula, my mind has seemed to explode with what I believe is more of a gain in efficiency than a true makeover of the brain cells."

He hesitated. "I believe that if I was tested now, my IQ would be well over two hundred."

She was stunned. "That's . . . that's amazing."

"Again, I tell you this not to brag, but to bring meaning into what I am about to talk to you about."

"Which is?"

"Dr. Kat, I am afraid that you and your compatriots have not fully thought through the implications of your formula."

She looked at him over the rim of her cup as she drank. "Which are?"

"As it is now, you cannot possibly release your Phoenix Formula to the public for general use."

"But—"

He held up his hand. "No, Dr. Kat, please hear me out."

She sat back, crossed her arms over her breasts, and stared at him. "Okay."

"First of all, you should understand that another attribute of your formula is that I no longer need more than a few hours of sleep, so while you and Kevin have been sleeping, I have used my extra time awake to peruse your notes about the chemical structure of the formula. At first it was simply out of idle curiosity, but later it was to make sure of what I came to believe about the formula."

She uncrossed her arms and leaned forward, looking at him with interest. "And what have you come to believe, Jordan?"

"That you all have produced a miracle formula that has, at its core, four main attributes."

He held up his hand and began to count off on his fingers as he spoke. "One is to cleanse the blood of all impurities much more efficiently and completely than anything else available; two, is to repair and to help the body itself repair damaged or ailing neurons and other neurological structures; three, is to markedly increase the brain's efficiency and mental acuity, thus increasing what we call intelligence; and finally, four, the most problematic of all of the features of the formula, to cause the body to regress in apparent age and to become much more healthy than previously."

"But, Jordan," Kat argued, "those are all good things."

"That's just it, Dr. Kat. They are all good things, indeed, things that everyone would want for themselves."

She smiled. "And things that we all want to give them."

He shook his head. "You are not thinking through the consequences of making your formula available to everyone, dear Kat."

Again, she looked puzzled.

He leaned forward, his gaze intent. "Let me give you a little history, Kat. During World War Two, the Allies invaded many islands in the Pacific. At that time, the population suffered from massive deaths due to malaria, and many of those who didn't die were incapacitated from the effects of the disease. When the Allies invaded, they sprayed extensively with DDT to prevent their soldiers from coming down with the disease and they also introduced and made available chloroquine, which both prevented and cured the disease if it was contracted. Can you guess what happened next?"

She shook her head.

"So many fewer people died from malaria that the islands' populations exploded, outpacing the islanders' ability to grow enough food for the increased population, or to provide work for the masses of young people being born. Soon the islands' economies were in shambles, and they had to be rescued by other, richer nations across the globe."

A thoughtful look came into Kat's eyes. "I see where you're going with this, Jordan. But our formula wouldn't be for everyone, only for those suffering from one of the renal or neurological diseases. Therefore, there wouldn't be a huge explosion of new people to have to take care of."

Stone reached across the table and put his hand over Kat's. "Dear Dr. Kat, you once accused me of being naïve. If all your formula did was to cure those illnesses, of course it would be a good thing. But, remember, it does two other rather remarkable things. It makes people smarter and younger, things that will be hard to hide and things that almost everyone on the earth will want for themselves."

She slowly nodded her head.

"Your first problem, once the effects of the formula become known, will be to keep the formula out of the hands of the government, which will almost certainly want to restrict it to its own exclusive control. Even if you made the formula public so that anyone could use it, then you would soon have massive overpopulation—with all of the problems that entails."

"But what if we maintained exclusive control of the formula ourselves? That way we could decide who really needed it and who didn't."

He smiled and shook his head. "Do you really want that responsibility, Kat? To be the one who decides who is worthy of becoming younger and smarter and healthier, and who should be consigned to growing old and feeble? And how long do you think you could control a formula that is priceless, both in monetary value and in the power that the owner of such a formula would exert?" He shrugged. "Men have actually killed for much less, my dear, probably including your Mr. Ashby."

She put her hand to her mouth. "You don't think . . . ?"

"I think that once your Mr. Ashby finds out that the formula really works, none of our lives will be worth a plugged nickel. If he is ruthless enough to have attained many billions of dollars in wealth, he is more than ruthless enough to want to control completely something as valuable as your Phoenix Formula."

She suddenly looked frightened and jumped up. "I've got to call Kevin and keep him from showing that video to Ashby!"

He put his hand on her arm and pulled her back down. "It is too late, Kat. Too many people already know about the formula." He gave a low chuckle. "Someone once said that two people could keep a secret, as long as one of them was dead."

"You're right, Jordan. Ashby will never give up trying to get his hands on the formula, especially because he is so desperate to get it for himself."

"Oh?" Stone said.

"Yeah, we haven't told you this yet, but he has had a stroke. He is almost totally paralyzed and is bedridden."

He nodded. "You are correct—such a man will not give up easily."

"Well, what can we do?"

He thought for a moment. "First, we must buy ourselves some time. I suggest we go ahead and give Ashby the formula injection. That will tie his hands for at least a week or two while he regresses."

"And then?"

"And then we take precautions, such as putting the chemical structure of the formula in the hands of multiple lawyers with instructions to release it to the press and the government if any of us disappears or dies."

"But couldn't he torture us in order to determine the locations of the lawyers?"

Stone shrugged. "Admittedly it is not a foolproof plan, but it would be a start, once again to buy us time to take further precautions."

"Such as?"

"Such as, I plan to use my new intelligence to work on the formula—to try to separate its effects so that it will still cure disease but not necessarily cause increased intelligence or youthfulness."

"But what do you know of biochemistry and medicine?"

He laughed. "Nothing yet, but that note I gave Kevin was a request for him to bring me every book on biochemistry and aging that he could find. I intend to give myself a crash course in those fields and then try to modify your formula to make it more selective in its actions."

"Jordan, you have given me much to think about. Now I need to talk to the others and make them also understand what is at stake here."

He held up a hand. "Just be careful to do it where there is no chance of your being overheard. We must not let Ashby know that we suspect him of trying to get control of the formula until we have a plan in place to thwart him."

CHAPTER 31

Kevin sat at his computer desk in his small apartment thinking. He was waiting for his uncle, Dr. Tom Alexander, to show up so that he could show him the video and give him a copy to take to J.P. Ashby.

Okay, Kevin, let's think this whole thing through, from beginning to end, he told himself.

He pulled a yellow legal pad across the desk and began to make notes on it. *First*, he thought, *there is the problem of getting the formula to Ashby so that he can use it, while at the same time making sure he cannot have it analyzed to see what the components are in order to make his own batch.*

Second, we have to figure out some way to transfer five hundred million dollars from Ashby to us without either the government or anyone else noticing such a large movement of funds.

Third, we have to do all of this from a safe and secret location, so that neither Ashby nor his henchmen can kidnap us to get the secret of the formula from us.

Fourth, after all of this is over, we have to find a safe way to disappear forever, while at the same time deciding just how we are going to be able to control the formula while remaining anonymous.

He reached up and scratched his head with the pencil, trying to think of any other problems the group faced, as if these were not enough.

After staring at the wall behind his desk for several minutes, he finally nodded. Maybe they could find a chemical compound to add to the formula after it was in the syringe so that if the formula was exposed to air, it would destroy the key components, rendering it useless. That way, if Ashby or his uncle tried to have the formula analyzed, it would be destroyed the moment it left the syringe. At the moment, he couldn't think of any such compound, but maybe the other doctors could. He put a check mark and a small question mark next to number one.

Moving on to the second problem, he turned to his laptop computer and Googled *"Anonymous bank accounts."* A range of choices was displayed and he picked one entitled *"Open an Anonymous Banking Account Online."*

As he read the article, he decided this was the best way for them to go. He read down the page to the *"NO ID Option/Invisible Man Option"* and began to read: *If you open a personal bank account, the bank secrecy will protect your privacy to a certain level, but to get a 100 percent Anonymous Offshore Bank Account, you will need to register or incorporate an offshore company. This offshore company should be registered with a foreign nominee director who will also act as the sole shareholder. You will need him to sign the documents for the opening of the offshore bank account, for you to remain invisible and have your name appear nowhere. Once your account is opened, you will receive your business debit card, along with a portable electronic device (generating six-digit security codes) that will allow you to log on and safely address your online banking, and only you will have access to your new Business Bank Account; no one else will have access to your funds.*

He read on to learn that after the account was opened, the funds would be transferred to various tax haven countries that had not signed the new international banking agreements and so were still completely anonymous. He also found out the entire process would take ten days to two weeks to complete. The initial fees were high, but not exorbitant. After the accounts were set up, the fees increased markedly, but that was to be expected; after all, anonymity was expensive.

He quickly logged on to the website mentioned in the article and got the process started, opening an account for each of them in their own names, four in all, each under the umbrella corporation he named the Phoenix Corporation. After thinking about it for a moment, he went back into the website and added Jordan Stone's name to the other four, feeling sure the others would agree that the professor deserved at least a share of their fee.

He used his own personal credit card to pay for the initial fees, figuring that by the time the bill came due, he would have enough money to pay it off. Now all they had to do was to stall Ashby until the accounts were set up, a matter of a couple of weeks.

Once that was done, he looked back at his legal pad. Numbers three and four were problematic: He had no idea how to find a secret place or to disappear completely once the deal was done, especially if they still wanted to administer the usage of the Phoenix Formula.

When his doorbell rang twenty minutes later, he put the legal pad into his desk drawer and answered the door.

Dr. Tom Alexander stood in the hall, looking expectant. "Hey, Kev. I hope you have good news for me, 'cause Ashby is getting rather impatient."

Kevin grinned. "Come on in, Uncle Tom, and I'll let you judge for yourself."

"Okay," Alexander said, and he looked around at the sparse furnishings and small room as he entered. "Jesus, Kevin. I didn't know you were living like this. You know all you had to do was to let me know, and I'd have given you more money for a better place."

"No need, Uncle Tom. This is plenty good enough for a grad student, and besides, from what Mom says, you had it much worse working your own way through medical school."

Alexander grinned. "Well, yeah, but I didn't have a rich uncle who was willing to help me."

"We'll talk about that later, but for now I want you to have a seat and take a look at this," Kevin said, handing him the video camera. "Would you like a cup of coffee while you watch?"

Alexander arched an eyebrow. "Is it safe?" he asked, glancing around at the disorder in the room.

Kevin pointed to a corner where a brand-new Keurig coffeemaker sat. "One of the first purchases with the fifty thousand dollars you advanced us."

"Then, by all means, let me try it out."

Minutes later, Kevin handed his uncle a mug of steaming coffee and watched as the doctor observed the video of Stone bending and stooping and exercising like a man twenty years younger than his chronological age.

After the video was over, Alexander took a drink of his coffee and shook his head. "Amazing, Kevin. Just amazing, though I am a little worried because the man has a mask on. Ashby may feel they are two different men, the before and the after."

"Run it again, Uncle Tom, and notice the strawberry birthmark below the waist in the rear just above the buttocks. I think you'll agree this is the same man."

After Alexander ran it again, he nodded. "I believe you, Kevin, but Ashby is a very suspicious man."

Kevin took a seat on the bed next to the chair where Alexander was sitting. "Then explain it to him, Uncle. We are not big con men trying to flummox him; we are just a group of everyday, ordinary doctors and one grad student. Does he really think we are dumb enough to try to con one of the richest, most dangerous men in the world? How in the world would we get away with it—where could we hide where he couldn't find us and seek retribution? For that matter, where could we hide millions of dollars where he couldn't get to it with his battalion of lawyers and detectives?"

Alexander smiled grimly. "You are more right about that than you think, Kevin." He hesitated and then looked directly into the young man's eyes. "You know I love you, Kevin, and I am telling you right now not to cross J.P. Ashby. As good of a friend as I am to him, that would not stop him from doing terrible things to you and your friends if things don't go as you've stated them."

"I promise you, Uncle Tom, on my honor, the formula works just as we've shown you. There is no trickery involved in this video."

"Okay, then. If you don't mind, I'll take the chip out of this camera and show it to J.P."

"A couple of things first," Kevin said.

Alexander took another sip of his coffee and leaned back, crossing his legs. "Okay, let me hear them."

"First, we are going to need another installment of fifty thousand dollars. It was more expensive setting up the lab than we thought, and we also need some funds to set up bank accounts where he can transfer the funds when we hand over the formula."

"That should be no problem. I can give you a check for that amount right now."

"Okay, good. And second, we are a little worried that Ashby might try to . . . um . . . take control of the formula for his own uses, and that he might even possibly try to do us harm to keep us from revealing the secret of the formula, so we are going to take precautions to make sure he can't take the formula and have it analyzed in order to make more of it."

Alexander raised his eyebrows. "How are you going to do that?"

"Mix a little something in the formula that is harmless but that will destroy the mixture if it is exposed to air instead of being directly injected into Ashby."

His uncle laughed. "Very good, Kevin. I told Ashby you were a shrewd businessman. Anything else?"

"Yes, we prefer—for obvious reasons—not to be available when we hand over the formula to Ashby, so we are going to give it to you at a secret location and then disappear before Ashby can come after us."

"But you've already said that disappearing from a man like Ashby is impossible."

"That's if he really wanted us badly 'cause we'd conned him. In this case, the formula will work and he will have no reason to try to hunt us down, unless he intends to steal the formula once he sees how effective it is."

"And if he does intend to do just that?"

"We have taken precautions against that also. We have given the precise chemical formula to a number of lawyers and other people we trust, with orders that if any one of us does not check in with them on a precise schedule, they are to release the details of the formula to the press and other scientific persons whom we have named. That way, if Ashby does manage to snag one or two of us, the others will make sure the formula is given out free to the world, and thus will be useless to him."

Alexander frowned. "Have you really done that?"

Kevin shrugged. "It is a process in the midst of being carried out. And none of us will know to whom the others have sent their packages, so unless he was able to corral us all at one time, the others would have a chance to get the formula out."

"Wow, you really don't trust Ashby, do you?"

Kevin stared at his uncle for a moment before asking, "Would you?"

Alexander laughed out loud. "Hell, no, Kev. I wouldn't for a minute."

He took his checkbook out and began writing a check. "Uh, there is one other thing I'd like to ask," he said.

"Yeah?"

"Would it be possible to get two doses of the formula for the same price as you are charging for one?"

"So you have decided to partake of the formula also, huh?" Kevin asked.

"Yes," Alexander answered. "I find that as I enter my sixties, I am rather bored with my life. The chance to start over younger and healthier and rich is a very powerful dream. There are a lot of things I have given up over the years in order to be a successful doctor, and I would relish the chance to travel and see the world and not to have to work eighty hours a week while doing so."

Kevin smiled. "While I cannot promise anything until I talk to my partners, I can promise I will do everything in my power to get the formula for you, Uncle Tom. I owe you much more than that for all you have done for me."

Alexander's eyes filled as he stood and handed Kevin the check for fifty thousand dollars. "Thank you, Kevin."

Three hours later, Alexander sat sipping brandy in Ashby's bedroom as the billionaire watched the video for the third time. Finally, he looked up. "And you are sure this is not a fraud?"

Alexander shook his head. "As Kevin himself told me when I asked him the same thing, these are three rather ordinary scientists and one young grad student. How in the world would they expect to get away with conning a man with your wealth and rather . . . dangerous reputation? After all, they know that you could easily track them to the ends of the earth if you thought you'd been wronged."

Ashby grinned wryly, "There is that."

"Actually, John, they are much more worried about you trying to get the formula from them for your own private use, and they are also worried that you might actually do them some harm in order to accomplish that."

Ashby blushed, for that was exactly what he was planning on doing, but he knew he couldn't let Alexander suspect that because of the involvement of his beloved nephew. "But, Tom, you know we haven't planned on doing that."

Alexander laughed. "I know I haven't planned on doing that, but I'm not too sure about you, John. I am not sure that being given an entirely new lease on life and being made younger and smarter and healthier is even enough for you, considering just how valuable the formula would be to a man willing to exploit its use for personal gain."

Ashby frowned. "Tom, after this . . . uh . . . transformation, I'll be, as you say, younger and healthier and still worth over nine billion dollars. Don't you think that is enough for anyone?"

"Sure, I think that, John. I'm just not sure of what you think."

Ashby waved his good hand in dismissal. "Forget about all of that, Tom. When did they say I . . . uh . . . we can get the injection?"

"They want to watch the subject they injected for two more weeks to make sure there aren't any unexpected late side effects of the injection, and then they'll present us with two syringes of the formula for injection."

Ashby looked disappointed. "That long?"

Tom smiled. "Oh, there's more than that. They are also working out how to get the money transferred without causing a stir in the financial markets and without alerting the government to the transfer, and they are working out a way that we can't take the formula to have it analyzed and replicated for our own use."

"What?" Ashby exclaimed, his face flaming red, for that was exactly what he'd planned on doing.

"Yeah, and they also are working out a way for them to give me the syringes in a secret place—unknown by you—and then to have me bring the syringes to you for injection while they are many miles away . . . for their own protection."

"Why, those dirty—"

Alexander held up his hand. "Now, John, try to tell me you'd do anything different if you were in their place."

After a moment, Ashby relaxed and smiled. "And I'll bet most of this was your nephew Kevin's idea, right?"

Alexander grinned and nodded. "I told you he was sharp."

"All the more reason to try to get him to join us after all this is over," Ashby said, a glint in his eye that Alexander didn't like.

He leaned forward in his seat. "John, there will be no 'us' after this is over. We'll both be young and healthy, and I intend to spend my new life traveling and enjoying life, not trying to make another million or two dollars."

"Of course, Tom, of course. I understand, but your young Kevin may have other ideas, and I do intend to offer him employment of some kind. He has too much talent to waste on being a run-of-the-mill biochemist."

Alexander sat back and nodded, but he was still concerned that John Ashby was planning a double cross of his nephew and his friends.

CHAPTER 32

As soon as she neared the Houston city limits, Kat called Kevin on his burner phone. "Kevin, we need to meet as soon as possible . . . the entire group."

"Okay, how about at Sheila's apartment?"

"No, we need someplace very secure. I know—let's meet at that new steak house on Bellaire Boulevard that's not too far from your apartment, the Longhorn Steak House, I believe is its name."

"Okay . . . but wait a minute. Where are you?"

"Just pulling into the city limits."

"How did you get here? I drove the Honda home and you didn't have a car when I left Conroe."

"I took a taxi to downtown Conroe and rented a car, but don't worry, I used Jordan's driver's license. It was expired, but the rental guy didn't notice. Good thing Jordan can be either a male or female name, huh?"

"What about the picture?"

Kat laughed. "Kept my thumb over it while the man copied down the license number."

"What are you gonna do about Sheila and Burton? Their cars both have GPS monitors on them."

"I'll arrange to pick them up at the Methodist hospital parking garage. It's so busy that there is no way anyone could follow them in and see them get in my car without being obvious about it. Besides, the detectives will just think it's normal for them to be going to Methodist hospital in the middle of the day."

Nicholas Fowler woke with a crick in his neck due to falling asleep in a chair while trying to keep track of what J.P. Ashby was doing. *Damn, for one of the richest men in the world, he leads a damn boring life*, Fowler thought as he keyed up the videos and tapes to watch what he'd missed while asleep. *Of course, being partially paralyzed and bedridden limits his choices for fun*, Fowler mused while chuckling to himself.

He suddenly sat straight up in the chair when he saw Ashby's doctor, Tom Alexander, enter the bedroom.

After twenty minutes of watching the same video Ashby was perusing, Fowler muttered, "Holy shit!"

So that's what all of the excitement concerning the doctors and scientists was all about, he thought. *These damn people had discovered a veritable fountain of youth, if the video Ashby was watching was legitimate. What am I thinking?* Fowler realized. *Who in their right mind would try to con a man as powerful and dangerous as J.P. Ashby was. Hell, they'd never live to enjoy any money they extorted out of him if the formula didn't work.*

When the doctor finally left, Fowler shut down the video, went into the bathroom of the safe house, and began to scrub his face and prepare to shave and shower. He needed to wake up and gather all of his wits about him if he was to figure out some way to profit from what he had just found out. He no longer had any thoughts of busting Ashby and bringing him to justice; the formula was simply too valuable of a commodity for that.

He realized that if he could get even a piece of what the formula was worth, he'd be set for life, assuming he could do it without making a mortal enemy of Ashby—that kind of trouble he definitely didn't need. Nope, he figured his best chance was to somehow get the formula from the scientists and then make a deal with Ashby to cut him in on the profits, even a small percentage of which would be worth millions, if not billions.

Since it was still mid-afternoon, the group requested a booth in the rear of the Longhorn where they could talk without fear of being overheard

"Okay, Kat, you requested this meeting, so get down to it," Burton said crossly.

"Yes, please do," Sheila added, "I left an office full of patients who aren't going to be too happy to have to wait for my return."

Kevin merely nodded.

"All right," Kat said. And then she proceeded to tell them what she and Stone had talked about, especially his ideas about how impossible it would be to market or use the formula as it now stood. She emphasized his point that they would never be able to keep total control of such a valuable formula, especially when people began to realize there was a fountain of youth in existence.

"I agree with Jordan about this," Kat said. "Everyone—and I mean, everyone—from Ashby to the government will want to control this breakthrough, and there will simply be no way to limit its use to those who really need it."

Burton slowly nodded. "I do believe she has a very valid point. In our excitement about the formula proving successful, we didn't stop to think through all of the implications of its eventual use."

Sheila shook her head. "They are correct. The formula works too well to ever be kept a secret. Even if we only used it on the truly needy, the ones with neurological or renal diseases who would not survive without it, there is simply no way to hide the rejuvenation and intelligence-enhancing effects from their friends and families."

"And trying to get them to all form new identities just wouldn't be practical. Few would be willing to cut off all contact with their friends and family, even if the alternative was death," Kevin added.

"And we are forgetting the most important person in all of this," Kat said, looking from one to the other. "J.P. Ashby is not a man to let something this valuable escape his control, no matter what he promises Kevin's uncle. He is bound to come after us with a vengeance once he sees what the formula is capable of."

Kevin shook his head. "And it will be damn near impossible to hide from a man with several billion dollars to spend to try to find us." He looked around the table. "I am afraid Jordan was right. We've made a deal with the devil."

Burton slammed his hand down on the table, drawing a reproving glance from their waiter across the room. "Well, hell. What if we forget about all of our do-gooder ideas and just tell Ashby we are going to give him the formula for the half billion dollars, then go on our way? Then he would have no reason to come after us and we'd at least be safe, and with more money than we could ever spend to boot."

Sheila gave him a dirty look and was about to object, when Kevin shook his head and interrupted. "It's no good, Burton. Even with that offer, Ashby would just consider us loose ends that had to be dealt with. There is no way a man like him would ever let us live, knowing what we know about the formula. It would be too big of a risk that we'd reconsider and let the secret out of the bag, ruining his chance to make yet another fortune from selling the formula to the rich and powerful."

Sheila turned to look at Kat. "Assuming we can figure out some way to deal with Ashby, do you think Jordan is right that with his new intelligence he will be able to separate the formula's effects and make it to where it just cures the neurological and renal diseases alone without the rejuvenating effects?"

"But the man has no knowledge of biochemistry, let alone medicine," Burton objected.

Kevin shrugged and pointed to a duffel bag on the chair next to him. "That's why he requested that I bring him all available books on the subjects in question. He figures he can learn enough from the books and from our notes on the formula to at least make some progress along those lines."

"Bullshit," Burton blurted. "No one can learn all that in the time we have left before we have to put up or shut up with Ashby."

"Perhaps not by himself, but what if we all worked together?" Kat asked. "After all, we have a fully equipped lab in the safe house, along with some very powerful computers that Kevin provided us. Heck, we'll never know if we don't try, and it does seem the only way that the formula will ever be used for good instead of greed."

As the others all began to talk at once, Kevin held up his hand. "Just a minute, folks. While we cogitate on those questions, I have some news I'd like to bring before the group."

When he had their undivided attention, he brought forth his legal pad from his backpack. He set it on the table in front of them and began to go over the four things they needed to do to get the formula to Ashby and still remain safe.

Once he'd gone over all of the objectives, he said, "I've managed a way to do the first. I told my uncle that we would include a chemical in the syringe that would destroy the formula if it was subjected to air. That way they couldn't risk trying to have the components of the formula analyzed for the purpose of making their own."

"That's brilliant, Kevin," Kat said. "What chemical did you come up with for us to use?"

He shrugged. "I haven't the faintest idea. I was hoping you geniuses would be able to figure something out, but if not, perhaps the bluff alone would be sufficient. I don't see Ashby risking his rejuvenation on the chance that we might be bluffing."

"That's something else that we could put our heads together to try to figure out while working with Jordan," Burton said, a look of approval on his face at Kevin's ingenuity.

"I have also made some progress on the second issue, getting the money into our hands in a manner secret from both Ashby and the government."

He went on to explain the anonymous banking website and how he'd signed them all up for it. "I also took the liberty of adding Jordan's name to the list. I hope that meets with your approval."

"What?" Burton exclaimed. "Why, the man had nothing to do with developing the formula. Why should he get a share? Isn't saving his life and making him younger and smarter enough?"

Sheila put her hand over Burton's. "Dear, even with Jordan getting a full share, you'll still come out with a hundred million dollars instead of one hundred and twenty-five million. Don't you really think that is enough money?"

Burton had the grace to blush. "Well, sweetheart, when you put it that way, I guess so."

"Two other quick points before we get to issue numbers three and four," Kevin said. "I pushed my uncle for another fifty thousand dollars seed money. I thought we'd use it to set up the anonymous corporation for the offshore bank and to buy another couple of cars use to escape Ashby's detectives. It is just too cumbersome to try to transport all of us in the Honda, especially as we get closer to the deal with Ashby. I do expect him to double up on the surveillance."

Everyone glanced at one another and nodded. "Good idea, Kevin. Thank God you're right on top of things," Kat said, affection in her voice.

He frowned. "Thanks for the vote of confidence, Kat, but I'm afraid I'm drawing a blank on the last two points—getting the formula to my uncle from a safe place where we can't be trapped or taken, and disappearing afterward to someplace secure where we can't be found."

When everyone looked concerned and it was clear that no one else had any ideas, Kat said tentatively, "I may just know someone who could help us with those two problems."

"Who is that, dear?" Sheila asked.

"My father used to tell me stories of a second cousin of mine who was a mercenary pilot and jack-of-all-trades who sort of lived on the edge of society and made his living by flying into and out of danger zones, transporting everything from arms to people to other questionable cargo. If I can locate him, it might just be that he could be the answer to these two problems."

"How old is this jack-of-all-trades mercenary?" Burton asked skeptically.

Kat shrugged. "A little older than me, I think. He'd probably be in his early sixties by now."

Kevin pulled his laptop from his backpack and opened it. "What is his name?"

"Jackson Dillard, but I doubt if he's going to be easy to find, not with his background."

Kevin opened up Google and typed in Dillard's name. After a moment, his eyes flashed and he grinned. "Well, I'll be damned. He has his own website."

He made a few more clicks and then looked up at the group. "Seems he's gone at least partly legitimate, Kat. It says here that he operates a flying service out of Galveston, Texas, flying freight and 'sundries' from Texas to Mexico and the Caribbean."

"Legitimate, my ass," Burton said, smiling. "Sounds suspiciously like a smuggler advertising right out in the open."

Kat pulled a small notebook from her purse. "Give me that number, Kevin, and I'll call him and set up a meeting.

After we all get to know him a little, we can take a vote on whether we trust him enough to ask him to help us."

"Even if he can't help us, perhaps he can give us some ideas of how to proceed to solve our problems," Sheila offered.

Burton scowled. "As long as we don't give him too much information until we all agree he's our man."

Everyone agreed and they left the restaurant. Out in the parking lot, Kat got in her rental and the others piled into the Honda. After Kat dropped the rental car off at a Houston branch of the rental car company, she got in the Honda and Kevin drove them to a large used car lot on the 610 Freeway. There they bought two additional cars with cash, using fake names. Kat drove off in one, and Sheila and Burton took the other one.

Before they left, Kevin cautioned them to use care in parking the cars so that anyone trying to keep tabs on them would not see them.

They promised to talk the next day by their burner phones to find out what Kat had learned about Jackson Dillard. Sheila said she would see about getting coverage for her practice so she could work with all of them on separating out the effects of the formula.

As he was driving the safe car toward their apartment, Burton glanced over at her and said, "Dear, I hate to mention this, but it looks like from our discussion that we are all going to have to disappear for good once this is over. Perhaps you'd better think about either selling the practice or giving it to someone you trust who will take good care of your patients." He shrugged. "Because we may have to move very fast when the time comes, and I know you'd not want to leave your patients in the lurch without coverage."

She placed her hand on his arm. "Oh Jesus, Burton, you're right. I guess I just didn't want to face the fact that my career in medicine is soon to be over."

"Well, maybe not over, sweetie. There may be some way you can still practice medicine wherever it is that we come to roost."

She choked off a sob. "I don't know if I would have agreed to all of this if I'd known all the changes it would mean in our lives."

He took his hand off the steering wheel and put it on hers. "At least it has brought us back together, and for me that is worth any cost."

She squeezed his hand and smiled through her tears. "Oh, it is for me, too, sweetheart."

CHAPTER 33

FBI special agent Nicholas Fowler emerged from the safe house bathroom feeling like a new man. He now had a purpose that was driving him—to steal the rejuvenation formula from the scientists before they could give it to Ashby. He'd teach his fucking wife a lesson for leaving him—he'd become super rich and stick it in her face. Hell, once he had control of the formula he might just decide to take some himself and become thirty years younger, like the guy in the video Ashby had watched.

He checked his cell phone to make sure it was still forwarding calls from his home, just in case someone from the FBI office called to check on him.

He fixed a cup of coffee using the old Mr. Coffee in the kitchen and sat down at the desk containing the computer monitors used in the surveillance of Ashby's bedroom.

He thought for a moment, then dialed the number of the intelligence division at FBI headquarters. When the phone was answered, Fowler gave another FBI agent's name and badge number and asked for the license plate numbers of everyone involved with the formula. Just in case anyone thought to check, he didn't want it known he still had an interest in the case.

After he wrote them down, he took one last look at the computer monitor to make sure nothing was going on at the Ashby mansion. Ashby was still asleep, so he left the safe house and headed for the parking garage of Dr. Sheila Goodman. He knew that her estranged husband, Burton Ramsey, was staying there most nights now, so he figured he could check out both of their cars at the same time. He'd leave the college student, Kevin, and Dr. Williams for later.

When he got to the garage of the Twin Towers apartment complex, he finally found both Goodman's and Ramsey's cars parked next to each other on the third floor. Smiling, he pulled a black plastic cube from his pocket and pushed a button on the side. When a green light began to flash, he slowly walked around both cars. The Sniffer, as it was called, beeped once near the front wheel well of each car.

Good, he thought. The GPS trackers he'd heard the detective Gelb say they'd put on the cars were still active, and now their signal was going to be sent to Fowler's computer also. That would serve two purposes: It would make keeping track of their whereabouts much easier, and when the time came to corral them all and steal the formula for himself, he would know exactly when and where it could be done.

As he walked down the stairs of the parking garage, he pulled a notepad from his coat pocket and checked the address for Dr. Williams's apartment. He would go there next, leaving the less-important college kid for last.

Kat got up early and pulled up Jackson Dillard's website on her computer. Summoning up her courage, she dialed the number listed under CONTACT US.

After three rings, a gruff, gravelly whiskey-and-cigarette voice growled, "Yeah, Dillard."

"Uh . . . Mr. Dillard, this is Kaitlyn Williams. I don't know if you rem—"

The voice changed from gruff to happy. "Why, of course, I remember you, Kat. After all, your dad and I had some business in the good old days."

Kat was astounded. Her dad had talked to her and told her some tales about Dillard. "You and Dad worked together?"

"Yeah," he said, chuckling, "but I bet he never told you about it, did he?"

Unconsciously shaking her head even though he couldn't see her, she answered, "No, but I'd love to hear about your . . . adventures."

Now he laughed out loud. "And I'd love to tell you sometime, since the statute of limitations has probably run out on our . . . adventures, as you call 'em."

Statute of limitations? Kat thought. *What in the world could Dad have gotten mixed up in to rate worrying about legal limits on prosecution?*

"But," Dillard continued, "I'm sure you didn't call me at this ungodly hour of the morning to talk about old times, so what can I do for you, Kat?" Suddenly his voice became more concerned. "Nothing has happened to your dad or mom, has it?"

"Oh no," Kat replied. "They're still retired up in Boston and doing fine."

In a relieved voice, Dillard said, "Yeah, your dad said that after thirty years of the Houston heat, he couldn't wait to get somewhere that had four seasons. He said Houston only had two seasons: summer and almost summer."

Kat smiled, remembering her dad saying just that on many occasions.

"So," Dillard continued, "what's goin' on that you need to call an old reprobate like me, Kat? Are you in some sort of trouble?"

"You could say that, Mr. Dillard."

"Now, Kat, when we were kids you used to call me Jackie. Well, I'm a little long in the tooth for Jackie, but how about calling me Jack instead of Mr. Dillard?"

"Okay, Jack. I do need your help, if you are available."

"I am always available for friends and relatives, Kat, and you are both. So, why don't you tell me just what it is that you've gotten yourself mixed up in that you needed to call in the marines."

Even though she was calling from a burner phone, Kat didn't want to go into specifics over the airwaves. "Uh, I'd rather not talk about it on the phone, Jack. Is there any way you could come up here to Houston? I'd be glad to pay you for your time even if you decide there is nothing you can do for me."

He chuckled again. "Kat, unless your circumstances have changed since the last time I talked to your dad about you, you can't afford my rates. But let's not talk about money— at least not yet. How about I fly my little plane on up to the big city and meet you about"—he hesitated as he checked his watch—"about two hours from now. I'll be flying into the private air terminal at Bush International. Do you think you can pick me up, or should I rent a car?"

"Oh no. I'll pick you up. And Jack, thank you."

"You got it, kid. I'll see you in a couple."

Kat hung up and immediately called Ramsey. "Hey, Burton. Jackson Dillard is going to fly up here from Galveston. I'm to meet him at the airport in two hours. Do you think you and Sheila could be ready to interview him by then?"

"Yeah, I think so, Kat. Sheila was able to get one of her on-call doctors to cover her practice for the next two weeks by telling them she was going on a vacation. As a matter of fact, we are just having breakfast in her apartment right now."

"Good. Listen, there is an IHOP out on Highway 45 about a mile before the turnoff to the airport, and I think they have a private dining room that we can use. I'll call Kevin and have him ready for you if you don't mind picking him up on the way to the restaurant, and we'll meet there in . . . say . . . two and a half hours."

"Okay, Kat. Do you really think Dillard can help us?"

"If he can't, Burton, then we are out of luck, because I can't think of anyone else who will come to our rescue."

A half hour later, Sheila and Burton got out of the elevator on the third floor of the parking garage. "Should we take the safe car?" Burton asked.

Sheila shook her head. "No, I don't see why we should. After all, we're not leaving town—and we are just going to meet some friends for breakfast. I don't think that will raise any alarms if the detectives are monitoring our car's movements."

"Okie-dokie," he replied and he opened the door to her Mercedes sedan for her, then got in the passenger seat.

From her parking space in the FBO (Fixed Base Operations) arrival area two hours later, Kat watched as a sleek twin-engine airplane came in for a smooth landing.

Ten minutes later, a man walked up to her car, a wide grin on his face. He was a shade under six feet tall, had iron-gray hair cut in a flattop and high and wide on the sides, was well-muscled with not an ounce of extra fat on his body, and had steel-gray eyes that matched his hair.

Watching him move, she was reminded of a large jungle cat: no wasted motion and fluid, even strides. She noticed his eyes were never still, but moved back and forth as if he was checking in all directions for any danger that might be lurking in the vicinity.

He put his hands on her window and leaned in to look at her closely. "You haven't changed a bit in twenty years, Kat. Still as pretty and bright as ever."

"You haven't, either, Jack, except maybe just a touch grayer up top."

He grinned and brushed his hand over his brush cut. "Don't

remind me. Father Time is working its magic on me like he does on everyone."

She smiled and thought, *Not everyone, Jack, not everyone.*

He moved around the car, pitched the large duffel bag he was carrying into the backseat, and climbed into the passenger seat. "Okay, what now, Kat?"

She put the car in gear and pulled out. "Now we go to meet my friends, and we'll tell you just what is going on and see if you have any ideas on how to help us."

"Before we get there, does this help include protecting you from physical danger?" he asked.

When she hesitated and finally nodded, he reached over the seat and pulled his duffel bag onto his lap. He unzipped it and pulled a small semiautomatic pistol and holster from inside.

Throwing the duffel back over the seat, he clipped the holster to his belt and pulled his shirttail out to cover it. Grinning, he faced forward and said, "Better safe than sorry."

Thirty minutes later, all introductions having been made, they were seated in a private dining room at the IHOP restaurant.

Dillard looked around at the group. "If you folks don't mind, I'm gonna order breakfast, since Kat called me this morning before I'd had time to eat."

After the waiter had brought them all coffee and taken their orders, Kat said, "Jack, I have known you all of my life, but my partners have no idea who you are or what you do for a living. Would you mind terribly telling them a little about yourself?"

"Okay, Kat. Here's the short version. I'm an ex-marine . . . uh, scratch that. There are no ex-marines—once a marine, always a marine. For the past thirty years I have been flying people and cargo into and out of some of the worst hellholes in the world. I have also, on occasion hired on as a mercenary if I thought the fight was worth fighting. I once spent about six months working as a private investigator, but the work was too boring—nothing like on TV. I fly a Cessna 425, otherwise known as a Conquest I, and I am an expert in electronic surveillance, as well as an expert with just about any weapon known to man. I do not hire myself or my expertise out unless I am in full sympathy with whomever needs my help."

He looked around the table and spread his arms. "Is that enough?"

When everyone nodded, he smiled and said, "Good, 'cause I think our waiter is on the way with our grub. So why don't we eat while you all tell me something about yourselves?"

When they had finished eating and Dillard had heard each of their stories, he took a sip of his after-meal coffee and said, "So, let me summarize. Kat is a medical doctor who quit medicine to do research, Burton is a Ph.D. who has pretty much always been in research, Sheila is an internist who specializes in old people and people with endocrine problems, and Kevin is a student studying organic chemistry who evidently has quite a crush on Kat. Is that about right?"

"Uh . . . I don't . . . that is . . ." Kevin stammered, his face flaming red.

Dillard grinned and held up his hand. "Oh, don't worry, Kevin. I told you I've had to live by my wits for the past thirty years, and being observant is part of that. I just noticed the way you look at Kat and how you moved your chair a little closer to her, as if to protect her if need be. Your feelings are nothing to be ashamed of, 'cause I noticed the same look in Kat's eyes when she looked at you."

"I don't . . ." Kat started to object when Dillard held up his hand.

"Save it, Kat, it's not important. Now, why don't you good people tell me just what kind of mess you've gotten yourselves into?"

It took three refills of coffee before Kat finished telling Dillard about their situation and what was going on. She didn't give any specifics about the formula, only that it cured certain diseases that Ashby was afflicted with and that it was extremely valuable, also leaving out the exact amount he was willing to pay for the formula.

"So, the other player in all of this is your experimental subject, an ex-professor and current drunk?"

Sheila shrugged. "We needed someone who had nothing to lose and everything to gain by the use of our formula."

At this point, Kevin pulled out his legal pad and showed Dillard his four bullet points.

"We've got one and two covered, but it's three and four we cannot figure out," he said.

"So, the bottom line is that you need to find some way to hand this magic formula over to the go-between, Dr. Alexander, and to do it in a way that you cannot be trapped or captured by the detectives that this rich guy Ashby has hired, and then you all want to disappear forever and live to spend the money Ashby is going to pay you?"

"That about sums it up, Jack," Kevin said.

"Well," Dillard said, leaning back in his seat and staring at the ceiling, "one way would be for me to kidnap the doctor, blindfold him, and fly him to some remote location where you could hand him the syringes and then blindfold him again and fly him back to Houston."

"Do you think that's the best way?" Burton asked, excitement in his voice.

Dillard laughed. "No, of course not. How about FedEx?"

"What?" Kat asked.

Dillard shook his head. "You guys are so caught up in this that you can't see the forest for the trees. Just package the syringes up and drop them in a FedEx box with a label with Alexander's address on it. I assume the syringes aren't heat-sensitive?"

Burton slapped his forehead with his palm. "Why didn't we think of that? It is a simple and elegant solution."

Dillard held up his hand. "That's only a solution to Kevin's point three. For point four, disappearing with a shit-load of money and staying off of everyone's radar, including the government's, is a lot more difficult."

"Mr. Dillard," Sheila asked, "do you think you can help us? Like you say, we are scientists and doctors, not secret agents or people experienced in this sort of cat-and-mouse game."

Dillard stroked his chin and looked around at the group. "Ordinarily, I'd say no and get up and walk away from all of you. In my humble opinion, you have about a ten percent chance of getting away from this with your lives, not to mention the big payoff you're expecting."

"But, Jack—" Kat started to say.

"Hold on, Kat," Dillard interrupted. "I said 'ordinarily,' meaning if my favorite cousin wasn't involved." He chuckled. "I ought to have my head examined, but I guess I'm in for the duration, with a couple of nonnegotiable demands."

"What is it you want?" Burton asked.

"First, I at least have to be paid expenses—that plane I mentioned cost me eight hundred seventy-five thousand dollars and costs several hundred dollars an hour to operate, and then there is the business I am going to lose working with you guys twenty-four/seven."

Kat looked around and the others nodded. "How about this, Jack? If you can wait until we get our payment from Ashby, we'll guarantee you two million dollars plus any and all expenses."

Dillard grinned. "That payoff I was talking about must be very healthy for you to offer me that much, but hell, yes, that will do nicely."

"What about the other conditions?" Burton asked, giving Kat a dirty look for offering so much to Dillard.

"First and foremost, you must all agree to do exactly as I tell you, without deviation. If any of us are going to get out of this with our skins intact, we need to all be working from the same playbook."

Burton shrugged and nodded. "I think we can all agree on that."

"Don't agree too soon, Burton. It is definitely not going to be easy. First of all, as of right now, each one of you will drop off the grid, and I mean completely off. We are going to go directly from here to rent two or three safe houses. We'll all stay together in one, and if that one becomes compromised, we'll go to the next, and so on. There will be no going back to your old residences ever again, so if there are things there that you absolutely cannot replace or live without, make a list and I'll go in and get them for you."

"But, why . . . ?" Burton started to ask.

Dillard laughed. "See, Burton, I told you it would not be easy. Listen to me, all of you. If the men Ashby hired are worth their salt, they've already got your cars bugged, your houses under surveillance and probably bugged, and your cell phone numbers tagged and bugged, so they know everything you've said and probably every place you've been for the past several weeks."

"But we've been using burner phones," Kevin said.

"Did you take the batteries out of your regular phones, and did you carry them with you?"

Kevin's face flared red. "Oh shit! I forgot about the batteries." He looked at Dillard and then dropped his eyes. "I told everyone not to use their phones, but I forgot about the damn batteries."

"Crap," Burton exclaimed. "That means they probably know about the lab house in Conroe."

"We'd better call Jordan and have him clear out," Kat said.

Dillard shook his head. "Uh-uh, too late for that. They've probably got the house under surveillance."

He thought for a moment. "Evidently, they're not quite ready to grab you or they would have already done it. Ashby is probably waiting for you to give him the injection and to make sure everything goes well before he makes his move to take you all out and get the formula for himself."

"But," Sheila interjected, "how can you be sure he is going to double-cross us? Maybe he's just going to get the injection and be satisfied to be cured of his medical problems."

Jack laughed. "Dr. Goodman, that is probably what you and ninety percent of normal, decent people would do. They'd thank God for their second chance and go on with their lives. But, and it is a big *but*, we are not dealing with a normal, decent human being here. We're dealing with a very rich man who has gotten rich, most likely, by never accepting half a loaf when he could take the whole loaf by force."

He sighed and took a breath. "Okay, I could be wrong, but think about it. If I am wrong and Ashby means you all no harm and does intend to go through with the deal as planned, what have we hurt by taking the precautions I'm advocating? Nothing. Then the deal will go through, you'll get your money, and you will have wasted only some of it by paying me."

He paused and looked around at the group, staring into each of their eyes one by one. "But if I am right and he plans, as Sheila says, a double cross, then the two million you are paying me will be the best money you've ever spent."

CHAPTER 34

Dillard looked from one member of the group to the other. "My money is still betting that Ashby is planning a double-cross. Otherwise why would he hire detectives to track your every move?"

"Maybe he's just trying to protect the fifty thousand dollars he paid us up front," Kevin said.

Dillard shook his head. "I don't think so, Kevin. He knows you guys are amateurs, so he knows that with his resources he could have you tracked down no matter where you tried to run. No, the only reason I can come up with to put at least two agents on you at all times along with electronic tracking devices, is so that he can find out where all your hidey-holes are, and when he's ready, he can have you picked up wherever you might try to go to ground."

"Then you are sure he does not plan to go through with our deal?" Kat asked.

He shrugged. "*Sure* is too strong a word, but I think it is a distinct possibility that as soon as he is convinced that you have given him the formula, he will do all that he can to make certain that it is in his control, and then he has no choice but to eliminate you."

"You mean you think he will try to have us killed?" Sheila asked, a horrified expression on her face.

Dillard reached over and put his hand over hers to calm her. "Dr. Goodman, people have been killed for far less than this formula of yours is worth. Like I say, I have never met Mr. Ashby, but from what I've read about him in the past, he is certainly ruthless enough and has enough power to do whatever he thinks he needs to do to gain complete control of your formula."

When no one had anything further to add, he nodded. "Like I say, you all are paying me a lot of money to keep you safe and to help you get through this process with both your skins and your formula safe."

He bent over and reached down into the duffel bag lying next to his chair. "Which I am going to start earning right now." He held up a flash drive. "This is designed to fit most burner phones. Plug it into the charging port and a screen will come up on the phone. Download the app on the screen, and it will automatically encrypt all of your phone calls and also bounce them off of several different satellites so that your location cannot be tracked. Only another burner phone with the same app can hear and understand your calls."

He glanced over at Kevin. "And Kevin, since I assume you are the cyber expert for the group, you can download the same app onto your laptops and it will scramble all of your Wi-Fi transmissions so that they cannot be hacked or used to locate your computers. It will also have a feature where you can hit a key combination and it will immediately wipe your hard drives so that they cannot be recovered, in case the computers are in imminent danger of being stolen. That means you should save a copy of important documents in the cloud so you can recover them later if you have to wipe the laptops."

While they were each in turn downloading the encryption app, he handed a piece of paper to Burton. "Pass that around, please. It's my secure phone number and I want each of you to put it as number one on your speed-dial."

While they were busy downloading the app and putting in his phone number, he got up from the table and walked around the room until he found a window that looked out on the parking lot in front of the restaurant. He stood slightly to the side of the window and peered out for a good five minutes before returning to their table.

"I understand from what you told me that each of you has a regular car and you also each now have a car that is not under your names and you are fairly sure have not been bugged or tagged with GPS trackers?"

When they all nodded, he went on, "Now, Burton and Sheila and Kevin came here together. Did you come in your regular car?"

Sheila nodded. "We figured that coming out to dinner in town would arouse no suspicions, and we didn't want to risk being seen in an unknown car in case we were being watched."

He smiled. "Good thinking, and it also gives me a chance to get a line on who is following you, since they almost certainly followed your car's GPS tracker here. Since Kat and I got here first, they don't know which car is ours and they haven't seen my face yet."

"Uh, how do you know they haven't come into the restaurant and seen us together?" Kevin asked.

Dillard grinned. "Because I've been watching the door. No one other than couples or people with children have entered, at least no single or paired men, so I am fairly certain the men who followed you are waiting out in the parking lot to see who you met here. They've probably got a camera with a telephoto lens on it trained on the entrance right now."

"But that means when we leave they'll find out what kind of car I'm driving," Kat said, alarm on her face.

Dillard shook his head. "No, they won't, Kat. I'm going to take care of that right now. Why don't you all have another cup of coffee and a pastry? I'll be right back."

He moved from the window and walked back down the hall toward the kitchen. Once there he asked to talk to the head cook.

A thickset man in a white apron with a chef's hat on his head walked over, a scowl on his face at this interloper in his kitchen. Dillard handed him a hundred-dollar bill and asked if he could borrow an apron and slip out the back door.

The man's face went blank and he palmed the bill and shrugged, inclining his head toward a rear wall, where several aprons hung next to the back door.

Moments later, Dillard slipped out of the rear door, wearing an apron and chef's hat. Next to the door he found a garbage can, which he hefted up on his shoulder, and he sauntered across the parking lot toward a dumpster in a corner.

As he walked, he used the can to shield his face and he scanned the cars in the lot, looking for someone just sitting in a vehicle. To his surprise, he found two such cars. One was parked in the second row and held two men, one of whom had a camera equipped with a telephoto lens resting on the dashboard pointed toward the entrance.

The other car was parked a couple of rows behind the first and was an obvious government-issue automobile . . . plain black sedan with tiny, cheap hubcaps and no frills at all. Hell, it even had a small radio antenna on the rear bumper— some undercover operative with no sense at all.

The man sitting in that car was wearing a rumpled suit and looked as if he hadn't slept for several days. *Typical government type*, thought Dillard as he walked by a few cars over.

As he emptied the garbage can in the dumpster to maintain his cover, Dillard's mind raced. What to do? He could easily take out all of the men, but that would tip Ashby off that they knew about the surveillance. And what about the government-issue man in the black sedan? He would need to find out just which agency was watching, and whether it was watching Ashby's men or whether it was watching Dillard's clients.

On the way back into the restaurant, Dillard made a mental note of the government sedan's license plate and then reentered through the back door.

When he got back to the table, he waved at the waiter to bring him more coffee and then he addressed the group, who were watching him anxiously.

"Bad news, but just as I figured. There are two men out front with a camera watching the entrance. They've got to be Ashby's men. Problem is, there is another man watching who is an obvious government type, and I don't know if he's watching Ashby's men or if he is here to watch you guys."

"What?" several of the group exclaimed at the same time.

Dillard nodded. "I've no idea which governmental agency is involved in this, but it does make our job considerably more difficult. Private dicks are easy to handle, but governmental types have a lot more power and have access to much more sophisticated surveillance equipment."

"So, what do we do?" Kevin asked.

Dillard shrugged. "Like I said, our first priority is to obtain a few safe houses and then to move into them and disappear off the grid, though that's gonna be a bit more difficult now that Uncle Sam is involved."

He thought for a moment while the waiter poured his coffee. After the waiter left, he said, "Okay, here's what we're gonna do. Burton, you and Sheila and Kevin leave the restaurant just as you entered and head back to your apartments as if nothing is going on. I'll make sure our tails all follow you guys, and then Kat and I will go about getting some safe houses ready for us to move into when the time comes. We'll also see about getting your professor safely out of the house in Conroe. When we're ready, probably sometime after midnight, I'll call you on the encrypted burner phones, and you can sneak out of your apartments, get into your safe cars, and come to the safe house."

"What about the detectives following us?" Burton asked.

Dillard grinned. "I'll be there to make sure they don't see a thing."

As Sheila, Kevin, and Burton went out the front door, laughing and talking as if they hadn't a care in the world, Dillard slipped out the rear door and made his way to a corner of the restaurant where he could get a good look at both of the cars that were tailing them.

When Sheila drove her Mercedes sedan out of the IHOP parking lot, both of the trailing vehicles followed, showing Dillard that the men had no idea that Sheila and the others had met someone else for lunch.

As soon as the vehicles were out of sight, Dillard hurried back into the restaurant and motioned to Kat for her to follow him.

Moments later Kat was pulling out of the parking lot in her safe car while Dillard pulled a tablet notebook out of his duffel bag.

"Are you going to use that to rent us some safe houses?" she asked.

"Yeah. Google is great about listing all of the Realtors who have rental property available in the area."

"So, you're gonna rent here in Houston instead of Conroe, where our other safe house is?"

He nodded. "Yeah, 'cause the detectives probably already know about Conroe, and that city is just too small for the five of us to hide in for very long without being spotted."

"What are you going to rent—a house, condominium, or town house?"

He smiled and looked over at her. "Well, they all have their advantages and disadvantages."

She raised her eyebrows and glanced over at him. "Such as?"

"Well, a condominium building is good, because once

you're in the doors, you could go to virtually any apartment in the building and it would be very hard to follow you to find out which one without becoming obvious. On the other hand, the disadvantage is that your car would be easy to watch and there are usually only two entrances, front and rear, that have to be watched, so they are hard to sneak out of without being observed."

"What about town houses?"

He shrugged. "Depending on the layout, both good and bad. If it is a gated town house community, it would be difficult to follow you onto the grounds to see which unit you live in, unless there is a good line of sight from the fence surrounding the property. If there is, then a good pair of binoculars would be all that was needed to track you to your unit. Another disadvantage is that individual units are easier to kidnap someone from without causing a disturbance. Then it would depend on just how good the guards are who man the gate."

"And houses?"

"If I can find at least two next to one another and another within walking distance of the first two, and if they have enough land to keep them apart from their neighbors, that would be perfect. That will be hard to find in a town like Houston, but hopefully with a large budget, not impossible."

"Why do you want two next to each other? I would think you'd want them far apart."

He shook his head. "No, just the opposite. If we find that our first house has been discovered, it'll be fairly easy to slip next door without being seen, and the people following us will think, just like you, that we would never have a second house so close to the first."

"Okay, so which way do you want me to drive?"

He looked up from his tablet and motioned with his head toward a roadside park. "How about pulling in there and give me a few minutes on the phone to see what is available?"

When she'd pulled up next to a concrete picnic table, he got out of the car, stretched his legs, and pulled out his burner phone.

It took him three phone calls before he found a Realtor who had what he considered were strong possibilities.

He arranged to meet the real estate agent at the first address and told Kat to drop him off at the nearest rental car agency.

"Why not just use my car?" she asked. "Ashby's men don't know about it."

"I know, and I want to keep it that way. There is no need to let the real estate person see either your face or your car. I'll rent a car using a fake ID that I always carry and give the agent the same name. Once the houses are rented, both the ID and my rental car will be discarded."

CHAPTER 35

While Dillard was meeting with the Realtor, Kat drove her safe car to Conroe, parked it in a local theater parking lot, then jogged three blocks over to a small strip mall. Only then did she call a cab and have it take her to the safe house where Professor Stone was staying.

Knowing the house was probably under surveillance made it very hard for her to keep her gaze on the front door and not look around to see who might be watching, but she managed, though it didn't stop sweat from pooling under her armpits.

When she got to the front door, she gave the coded knock Kevin had arranged so Stone would know it was one of them at the door.

He flung the door open, a wide grin on his face. "Kat, you won't believe the progress—"

She frowned and shook her head, making a *shush* sound with her lips.

Thankfully he got the hint and immediately shut up, though he wasn't cool enough to keep from sticking his head out of the door and peering around.

"Jesus, Professor," Kat said with exasperation as she

brushed by him into the living room. "Could you possibly be more obvious?"

His face burning with embarrassment, he shut the door and turned. "Well, I am sorry, Mata Hari, as I am not used to being in a spy movie."

Kat's frustration vanished when Angus rushed up to her, his tail wagging furiously. He put his paws up on her legs and barked several times to show his joy at seeing her.

"Oh, my big boy . . . you are as handsome as ever," she cooed, squatting down to put her arms around his neck and give him a big hug.

Finally, she stood, took a dog cookie out of her purse, and handed it to him. Instead of snatching it out of her hand like most dogs would, Angus took it very gently in his lips and sat on his haunches, staring at her for a moment. Then he nodded his head as if to say thank you and began to crunch the cookie.

Kat took a deep breath and told herself to relax, that it wasn't the professor's fault. They'd just had a bit more time to realize what danger they were all in. "I'm sorry, Jordan," she said, moving to give him a hug and a peck on the cheek. "It's just that things are moving very quickly, and I'm afraid there is some bad news."

He hugged her back and used a hand to her back to gently guide her toward the kitchen. "Well, I am sure that a bracing cup of caffeine with lots of sugar in it will have you feeling better in no time."

He sat her at the kitchen table and began the process of making them both cups of Colombian Supreme coffee. When her cup was ready, he looked over his shoulder at her and grimaced as he added the requisite four teaspoons of sugar.

"What?" she asked, actually smiling for the first time in hours. "You don't like sugar?"

He shook his head. "Used to, but life on the street taught

me to drink it black, since sugar was in short supply to homeless people."

Moments later, after he had thrown a few bits of kibble into Angus's dish in the corner, he sat across the table from her and leaned forward, whispering while he smiled, "Do you think it is safe to talk here or might 'they' be listening?"

She took a sip of her coffee and spoke in a low voice, just above a whisper. "You're joking, but that is what the bad news is about. Ashby's men are not the only ones watching us—now there seems to be a government man of some sort also on the case."

He raised his eyebrows. "Oh?"

"And that is not all. They probably have managed to track us to this safe house and are likely watching as we speak."

"What? How? I thought you all made sure all of your safe cars were not bugged and Kevin even had you turn off your phones."

She grimaced. "That's just it. It seems that turning off and not using the phones is not enough. With new, sophisticated equipment, the phones can be tracked as long as their batteries are connected, even if the phone is turned off. In fact, I'm told that the government can even turn the phones back on and use them as listening devices without your even knowing it."

He wagged his head. "So, since they probably know where we are, what are we going to do?"

"There is a new player in town, a friend of mine named Jackson Dillard."

She went on to tell him all about Dillard's past and about the meeting at the IHOP and Dillard's plan for them to go "off the grid."

"But if they are indeed watching the house, how will we do that?" Stone asked.

He was interrupted by a deep growl from Angus, who

was squared off staring at a man standing in the door to the kitchen.

"Easy enough, if we're careful," said the man, who then knelt down and held out his hand, palm down toward Angus.

Kat gasped and grasped her chest. "Damn, Jack, don't do that! You almost scared me to death."

Stone glanced at the doorway, his mouth open, as Angus moved slowly to sniff at the man's hand.

Angus glanced over his shoulder at Kat, who grinned and nodded once. Angus seemed to relax, and he sat on his haunches and raised his right paw to Dillard.

Dillard grinned and held out his hand to shake Angus's paw.

"That's his way of welcoming you to our pack," Kat said proudly.

"I am honored, Angus," Dillard said.

"Mr. Dillard, I presume?" Stone asked, rising with his hand out.

"In the flesh," Dillard replied and shook his hand.

"How in the world did you get in here?" Kat asked.

"There are men watching both the front and rear entrances, so I climbed in through a bedroom window so they wouldn't get a look at me."

"But the windows are all locked," she said.

"Please," he said, waving a hand dismissively. "Child's play for an old reprobate like me."

"Would you like some coffee before you whisk us off the grid?" Stone asked, rising.

Dillard nodded. "A cup'a joe would be great, thanks. I've been on the move so fast this afternoon I haven't had time to caffeine up."

"I'd like another, too, please," Kat said, handing Stone her cup.

While he attended to the Keurig machine, she turned to Dillard. "Speaking of being on the move, did you manage the new safe houses?"

"Yeah, and to tell the truth it wasn't so hard," he said, taking a seat at the table while reaching down to rub Angus's head between his ears. "Seems the rich have fallen on hard times and quite a few homes in the Memorial Park area are up for rent, and most of them come furnished."

"The Memorial Park area?" Kat asked. "That means they must have large yards, as those homes are mostly what I would call mansions."

He nodded. "Yes, they are, so they are perfect for our purposes. Of course, they come at a steep price, but I figured our safety is more important than extra profits."

Stone handed them both cups of steaming brew. "A sound decision, if my opinion counts," he said.

Dillard saluted him with his cup. "Of course, your opinion counts, since I'm told you are now the most intelligent one of our small group."

Stone grinned and nodded his head toward Angus, who was sitting next to Dillard's chair watching him with interest. "Yes, except for Mr. Angus there, who seems to be getting more intelligent with each passing day."

Dillard chuckled and gave Angus another pat on the head.

Stone snapped his fingers. "That reminds me, Kat. You interrupted me as I was about to tell you that I believe I have made tremendous progress in separating the effects of the serum."

Dillard drank most of his coffee in one gulp and held up his hand. "Excuse me, Professor, but I must also interrupt. We need to get a move on and make our escape before the next shift comes on duty."

Kat glanced at him. "I am sure there is a good reason for that."

He nodded. "Yeah. It is getting near the end of the evening shift's time on duty, so they will be tired and less vigilant than the new boys about to show up. Also, I plan to dart them and put them to sleep while we slip away. Since they've been on duty almost twelve hours, hopefully they'll think they just dozed off for a few minutes and won't raise an alarm until we are well on our way to our new digs."

"How do you know their schedule?" Stone asked, finishing his cup of coffee.

Dillard shrugged. "I don't, for certain. But since I often set up surveillance like this, it's how I would schedule the men watching, so we'll just have to hope they did it the same way."

He stood up. "Professor, pack everything you need into one duffel bag that you can easily carry and leave the rest. We'll resupply later."

"Roger," Stone said, giving a small salute.

"Kat, you make sure all of the electronic gear—laptops, tablets, smartphones—and even handwritten notes are picked up and taken with us. They will for sure go over this place with a fine-tooth comb when they realize we're gone for good."

"What about fingerprints?" she asked. "They'll be able to identify the professor if we don't wipe the place down, and I don't think that would be a good idea."

He laughed. "What, 'wipe the place down'? Did you see that in some movie?"

She blushed. "No, but in all the romance novels I've read . . ."

"We're more high-tech than that now," he said, shaking his head and smiling. He pulled a quart-sized canister from the duffel bag that was always at his side.

"And that is?" she asked, arching an eyebrow.

"Aerosolized bleach," he answered. "Just before we head out, I'll spray a fine mist of bleach over all of the surfaces that might have been touched, and then I'll also connect the canister into the air conditioner so that it will spray the mist over every surface in the house."

"Very nice," Stone said from the doorway, as he began to pack Angus's food and water bowls into the bag in his hand.

"Yeah, in the olden days we'd just burn the house down to destroy evidence, but that often led to a lot of collateral damage with neighbors' houses and property."

He looked over at Kat. "While you're gathering up the electronics and any notes the professor made, I'll go make sure the guards get a nice little nap. I'll be back in ten, so be ready."

Matt Gomer was still smarting from the ass-chewing he and Doug Johnson had received from Harold Gelb for not getting a picture of whomever the scientists had met at the IHOP earlier. After they'd followed the scientists back to their apartments, they had called Gelb to check in. Gelb had asked whom the scientists had met at breakfast, and he'd tried to explain that to get close enough to get a picture would have blown their cover, but Gelb had just cursed him for an incompetent idiot.

"Just for that, I want you to get your asses out to the location in Conroe that their phones had pinged and find out what in the hell is going on out there. And don't bother to come back unless you have some answers for me!" he'd screamed at them over the phone.

They'd tried to explain that they'd been on duty for almost eighteen hours already and were dragging, but Gelb had just laughed. "You can sleep when you're dead, Gomer," he'd said, "which might be sooner than you'd like if Mr. Ashby and I don't get some results—and sooner rather than later!"

Now, here they were, sitting in bushes in the middle of the night, getting eaten by mosquitos, and trying to get a peek into the windows to see who was in the house where the scientists' phones had pinged.

He was near the front door while Doug was similarly placed to watch the rear door.

He looked down and fiddled with the settings on his

Canon Rebel camera. He was going to make damn sure if anyone came out the door, he'd get them on camera.

He thought he heard a rustling in the bushes to his right and was just turning his head to take a look, when he felt a sudden sharp sting in his neck. "Damn mosquitoes," he exclaimed as he slapped at his neck.

Twenty seconds later, he slumped over and slid face-first into the bushes, dead asleep.

Dillard slipped up and gently removed the dart from the detective's neck, and moved his body into a more comfortable position lying on his side.

"Wouldn't want you to get a crick in your neck, old boy," he murmured.

Grabbing the camera from the man, Dillard quickly scanned through the photos on the memory card. When he saw that there were none that were important, he put the camera back down next to the man's hand, as if it had slipped out when he "fell asleep."

Dillard took out a small penlight and checked the ground to make sure he'd left no telltale footprints, then he moved quickly to the door and opened it.

"Come on, guys," he called softly into the living room. "Time to boogie on out of here. Our watchers are fast asleep, but they won't be for long."

He was just putting his dart gun back into his duffel bag when Kat and Stone came hurrying out of the front door, followed closely by Angus.

Kat glanced down at the bag. "Is there anything you don't carry in that thing?" she asked.

He laughed. "I once had an assistant who said that I could either live out of this bag for six months, or start World War Three with its contents. He was probably right."

Kat shook her head. "No doubt. Well, come on, you can drive us to my car in your rental. It'll save us having to jog two miles."

* * *

An hour later, they'd dropped Dillard's rental car off in the agency lot and had ensconced themselves in the first of the new safe houses.

Stone stood on the front porch for a moment and looked around at the Houston skyline that surrounded them on all sides. "Right in the middle of the city, with the bad guys and unknown government agents hot on our trail." He shook his head. "I am beginning to believe your Mr. Dillard is a genius, Kat."

She placed one arm through his while she petted Angus with the other hand. "I sure hope so, Jordan. We're gonna need a genius to get us out of this mess alive and healthy."

CHAPTER 36

While Kat and Jordan Stone and Angus were getting settled into the new safe house on Memorial Boulevard, Dillard made a trip across town to get Sheila and Burton and Kevin out of their apartments without either Ashby's men or the government agents being able to follow them.

He figured that Kevin would be seen as the least important member of the team and thus would have the least amount of surveillance attached to him.

He was right—there was only one man watching Kevin's apartment, and he was strategically parked so he could also keep an eye on Kevin's car.

Knowing that soon it would be too late for subtlety, Dillard pulled up right behind the operative's auto and put his lights on bright, effectively blinding the man.

Dillard opened his door and called out, "Okay, get out of the car with your hands up. . . . This is the Houston Police Department."

As the detective climbed out of his car with his hands in the air, he was already beginning to make excuses. "Sorry, officers. I am a private detective working on—"

Dillard didn't wait for the man's eyes to adjust to the

blinding glare. He stepped up and smacked him in the side of his head with a blackjack.

The man went down like a load of bricks.

Dillard looked around to make sure no one was watching, before he lifted the man up and laid him gently on his back-seat. He patted his cheek. "Hope your headache isn't too bad, pal, but you've got to learn when you're working for the bad guys, bad things happen to you."

He got back into his car and called Kevin on his burner phone. "Hey, Kevin, this is Jackson. The coast is clear for you to head to the new safe house. Did you get the text I sent with the address, and are you all packed and ready to go?"

"Yes, sir, Mr. Dillard."

"It's Jack, Kevin. Mr. Dillard was my father. Get a move on, and I'll pick up Sheila and Burton and meet you at the house in about an hour."

Dillon knew there would be more than one agent on Sheila and Burton, which would make getting them out clean much more difficult, especially if the government also had them covered.

When he got to their parking garage, he parked his car on the street nearby and called Sheila on her burner phone. "Sheila, this is Jackson. I'm set and ready to go, so you and Burton bring your bags, get into your Mercedes, and drive out of the garage, go around the block, and then come back to the garage and park near your safe car."

"Okay, Jack," Sheila said. "Will do."

While he was waiting, Dillard poured some whiskey out of a bottle from his glove compartment and splashed it on his face and neck. Then he took up station near the parking garage entrance but just out of sight behind some bushes.

When Sheila and Burton pulled out of the garage fifteen

minutes later, a nondescript sedan followed them a few moments later. When he was sure there were no other cars following, he got ready.

Five minutes later, Sheila pulled back into the garage and headed up the ramp.

As the sedan began to follow the Mercedes into the garage, Dillard stumbled out of the bushes and onto the driveway, singing a drunken tune and waving the whiskey bottle around.

The sedan slammed on its brakes and as the fender nudged Dillard, he screamed and flung himself to the side, landing on the grass next to the entranceway.

"Oh shit!" he heard the driver of the car exclaim as he jumped out of the driver's side door and ran over to lean over Dillard, who lay facedown. "Damn, I think the bum is dead. He must be drunk as a skunk . . . he smells like a brewery."

The passenger joined him, and as they grabbed Dillard's shoulders to roll him over, he swung a fist into one's face and rebounded with an elbow to the other's nose.

Both men went down, lights out.

Dillard pulled them to the side of the driveway and rolled them into the bushes there. Then he climbed into their car, pulled it into the garage, and parked it on the first floor. After he exited the car, he moved to the front wheel well and felt under the fender. Sure enough, he found the GPS tracker right where he'd expected it.

As Sheila and Burton came down to the exit in their safe cars, he gave them a thumbs-up and ran to get into his own vehicle.

Instead of following Sheila and Burton to the safe house, Dillard stopped off at a KFC and bought two large buckets of fried chicken, ignoring the sour looks from the counterperson at his pronounced whiskey odor.

When he entered the front door of the safe house, Angus greeted him like a long-lost brother, putting his paws up on Dillard's thighs and wagging his tail like an airplane propeller.

But then he stopped, sniffed twice, wrinkled his nose, and barked loudly.

Dillard laughed and held the buckets of chicken over his head and out of Angus's reach. "You don't fool me, big guy. It's the chicken you're glad to see, not me."

"Oh, thank God," Kat said, as she rushed to him and helped him with the chicken. "We've been about to starve, since no one has had time to provision the larder."

"This will have to do for a while. I thought we could eat while I go over some news you all need to hear."

Then Kat stopped, sniffed, and looked questioningly at him, her eyebrows raised.

He laughed. "Don't ask. A bit of subterfuge to fool the men following Sheila and Burton into thinking I was a drunk."

She smiled back. "I'll tell the others so they won't think you stopped off to have a few."

Twenty minutes later, Dillard had washed off the whiskey smell and they were all seated around the house's huge formal dining room table.

"I don't know who owns this house," Sheila said around a mouthful of mashed potatoes, "but they must have been entertainers. This table could easily seat fifteen people."

"Like Jack said," Kat added, spooning more coleslaw onto her paper plate, "even the rich have come upon hard times lately."

Dillard swallowed the last of his cup of coffee and knocked on the table with a fist. "Okay, while you guys finish up the feast, I'm gonna go ahead with the latest news."

He paused as Angus came over and put his paws up on

his leg. Shaking his head, he took a piece of chicken, pulled the meat off the bone, and handed it to Angus. "Good thing Kat told me your metabolism has sped up, fella, or you'd weigh about fifty pounds by now."

Angus took the meat gently and nodded his thanks, before trotting over to his bed in the corner of the kitchen and settling down to eat.

Dillard turned his attention back to the group. "I just heard back from my contact at the Galveston Police Department. I gave him the license plate number of the government vehicle that was following the two men following Sheila and Burton, and he hit pay dirt."

"Whose car was it?" Burton asked, buttering another biscuit.

"It is an FBI car, currently checked out to an agent named Nicholas Fowler."

"Oh shit," Kevin said, then quickly apologized to Kat for the language. "I mean, oh darn. The last thing we need is for the FBI to be involved in this affair."

Dillard stroked his chin. "I'm not so sure the Feebs are officially involved."

"What do you mean, 'officially,' Jack?" Kat asked.

"Well, after I got Agent Fowler's name from my contact, I Googled him, both to get a look at him and to find out just what his job is at the FBI. Turns out he is not just a special agent for the FBI—he is, in fact, an SAIC, and he is definitely the man who was driving the car I saw at the IHOP."

"What the hell is an SAIC?" Burton asked irritably.

"It means special agent in charge," Dillard answered. "That means he is probably the agent in charge of the Houston FBI office, or at least one of them. He's also over sixty years old and only a few months away from mandatory retirement."

He paused to take a bite out of a chicken leg, and while he chewed he continued, "And trust me on this guys, sixty-year-old SAICs do not ever go on stakeouts or get tailing duty from the FBI."

"Did you find out anything else?" Kat asked.

"Yeah. I took a chance and called the Houston office of the FBI and asked to talk to Agent Fowler's secretary. When I got her on the line, I told her I was one of Agent Fowler's informants and that I had some information for him."

Burton laughed. "That was ballsy, Jack. What would you have done if she had put him on the line?"

Dillard smiled. "I'd have hung up—quickly."

He got up and fixed himself a cup of coffee while talking to the group over his shoulder. "Fortunately, she didn't do that. She just asked, 'Does this have to do with an active investigation? If so, there is another agent in charge of the office while Agent Fowler is on sick leave.' "

" 'Sick leave'?" Kevin asked. "What was he doing following either us or the detectives Ashby had hired if he was on sick leave?"

Dillard shrugged. "I'm not sure, Kevin, but that is why I said I don't think the FBI is officially on the case. I think Agent Fowler is running a show of his own."

"But why would he—?" Kevin started to ask.

Dillard leaned forward. "Think about the amounts of money involved, guys. I think this Fowler was in charge of a team surveilling Ashby, for whatever reason the FBI is interested in him, and through that surveillance he got wind of Ashby's plan to use your formula. And he learned not only what it might do, but what Ashby was willing to pay for it. I think that once he thought about the millions of dollars we're dealing with, not to mention the vast potential profit to whoever owns your formula, he decided to try to cut himself in on it."

Kevin looked confused. "So, he calls in sick and begins to follow the detectives he knew Ashby had hired, hoping they would lead him to us."

Dillard nodded. "I confirmed that . . . I found a GPS tracker on the detectives' car similar to the ones the detectives put on your cars, but of a different make. So my guess is it was put there by Fowler."

"But," Kevin continued, "why would he do that? Like you say, Jack, he's the man in charge of a team. Why wouldn't he just have the team do the following instead of doing it himself?"

Dillard shrugged. "I can only guess, but the only thing that makes sense is that he cut his team out of this part of the investigation so that he could make his own play. Must be that the FBI retirement pay isn't looking so good to him now that he has this other prize in his sights." He hesitated and then added, "Or maybe he just wants to make a big, splashy arrest prior to his retirement. It could be either motive."

"But you think he's gone rogue?" Burton asked.

"Probably, and the good news is that makes him a little bit easier to deal with than if we had the entire structure of the FBI to contend with."

"So," Sheila asked, frowning, "what do you advise that we do next, Jack?"

"If I know the FBI, they've got Ashby's house wired from top to bottom, including his cell and house phones. Even if Fowler has cut his team out, he will still be monitoring those wires in hopes of getting to us and the formula. That means we need to warn your uncle, Kevin, that everything he and Ashby talk about is being overheard by the Feebs."

"Yeah, so they can rip those bugs out!"

Dillard held up his hand. "No, you must warn your uncle not to let Ashby do that. They've got to let the bugs remain in place so Fowler doesn't know we're on to him. That way, Ashby and your uncle can use the bugs to spread misinformation to Fowler and keep him from interfering in our project."

"Oh," Kevin said, grinning, "right."

* * *

Fowler finished his shower, shaved, and headed back out to check in on the detectives Ashby had following the scientists. He'd hated to leave them unattended, but his personal hygiene had gotten so bad from spending the last couple of days in his car that he could hardly stand himself.

Now, refreshed, he was ready to get back on the job.

He checked his laptop, and it showed the GPS signal of the detectives' car to be located at the husband and wife's apartment building garage. Good, he thought, that meant the two were probably in for the night. If so, he might be able to get a few hours' shut-eye while the detectives kept watch.

He wasn't worried about watching the young man or the other woman doctor so much. He figured where the husband-and-wife team went, the others would follow.

When he got to the garage, he drove slowly past the detectives' car. He was surprised to see that no one was in it.

Damn sloppy work, he thought. One of the men should have stayed with the car at all times in case the couple decided to leave on short notice.

He parked his car a couple of spaces over from the detectives' car and decided to take a stroll around the garage to see if he might be able to spot them.

As he was walking down the ramp, he heard a muffled moan from the entrance to the garage.

Trotting over, he saw a disheveled man come crawling out of the bushes next to the doorway. His nose was bent to the side, and he had dried blood streaking his face.

Uh-oh, Fowler thought. *This doesn't look good.*

He stepped behind a nearby pillar and watched as the man moved back to the bushes and half-lifted another man up by his armpits.

"Matt, wake up. Are you okay?" the man asked, lightly slapping the groggy man on the cheeks.

"Doug? Is that you?" the man stuttered. "What happened?"

Johnson answered angrily, "That drunk suckered us! The bastard pretended to be drunk so he could take us out."

"But why?" Gomer asked, rubbing the knot on the side of his head.

"Five will get you ten the subjects have flown the coop," Johnson answered.

Gomer looked at him in alarm. "Oh shit. Gelb is gonna kill us."

Johnson shook his head. "Forget about Gelb—it's that fellow Ashby I'm worried about. All Gelb can do is fire us, but Ashby is liable to really kill us if we've lost them."

Fowler shook his head in disgust. "How could these men be so incompetent?" he asked himself as he ran to his car.

He immediately checked his laptop and saw that the icons for the husband-and-wife team's cars were still located in the parking garage.

That meant they either had other cars without bugs in them, or they had been taken away by the new player, the man who took out the detectives.

He decided to do a black-bag job and enter their apartment. Maybe that way he could find out where they'd taken off to. Otherwise he'd just have to monitor Ashby's bugs and see if the billionaire could lead him to the group.

As he walked up the ramp toward the elevator that would lead to the couple's apartment, he had a sinking feeling that things were getting out of his control.

CHAPTER 37

Dr. Tom Alexander sat at his desk after seeing his last patient of the day and took a deep breath—it had been a hectic and trying day. Jeannie, his head nurse, brought him a cup of coffee and set it on his desk in front of him.

"What's this?" he asked as he arranged his call slips on his desk blotter so he could call back doctors and patients who had left messages for him to return.

Jeannie grinned. "That's a little reward for working so efficiently that it looks like we may actually get off work on time today . . . for once!"

He held up his hands. "Message received, loud and clear. In fact, you may tell the receptionist to cease making any appointments for the next couple of weeks, and please get Dr. Madry on the phone. I've decided I need a break and I'm gonna see if he'll take my calls for the next couple of weeks."

Jeannie smiled again and patted him on the shoulder. "You have been looking tired, Dr. Tom. I think it's a good idea that you take a little time to recharge your batteries. Let me know if Dr. Madry agrees, and I'll go through your schedule and make new appointments for those already scheduled."

"Thank you, Jeannie, and don't worry about the surgeries . . . I've already rescheduled the routine ones and the urgent ones I'll kick to Dr. Madry."

Before he could pick up the phone to make his first callback, his cell phone rang with the ringtone "Bad to the Bone," the one he'd reserved for his nephew Kevin.

He grabbed it and said, "Hello, Kevin. I've been waiting to hear from you. Ashby is getting—"

Kevin interrupted him. "Uncle Tom, stop and listen to me!"

"Uh, sure, Kevin," Alexander replied.

"As your tech adviser, I am advising you that it is time to upgrade your cell phone. I need you to go to the nearest Walmart and buy one of the Straight Talk models—and be sure and get the model that has no GPS chip in it. As soon as you've done that, give me a call back . . . but don't take too long, okay?"

Alexander's heart began to race. He could tell by Kevin's tone that this was some sort of emergency. "Okay, Kev, I'll go immediately."

He hung up and called Jeannie back into his office. "Jeannie, I've just had an emergency call. Would you take care of these callbacks? Please refill any meds the patients need and tell the docs who called that I'm off for two weeks and to refer any patients they're calling about to Dr. Madry?"

It took Alexander almost an hour and a half to get to a Walmart, buy a phone, and get it set up before he could return Kevin's call.

He called him from the Walmart parking lot. "Okay, you have officially scared the bejesus out of me, Kevin. What the hell is going on?"

"First take out your regular phone and pull the battery," Kevin said.

"You're kidding."

"Uncle Tom, do I sound like I'm kidding?"

"No, you sound as frightened as you are making me."

"That's because I am. Now, is the battery out of your smartphone?"

"Um . . . wait a minute . . . yes. But why—?"

"Because the FBI can turn anyone's smartphone on and make it into a microphone to eavesdrop on you with."

"The FBI? What have they got to do with me?"

"You mean 'us,' Uncle Tom."

Kevin went on to tell Dr. Alexander about their discovery that the FBI was monitoring Ashby's residence and phones, and how they knew about the detectives he'd hired and were following them trying to get to Kevin and his friends. "And," he added, "if they're monitoring Ashby this closely, it stands to reason that they may be targeting you also, so you need to always be aware that hostile ears may be listening when you speak."

"FBI? Detectives? What the hell is going on, Kevin, and why the hell don't I know about it already?"

"As for why you don't know about it, maybe you should ask your good friend Ashby why he's hiring detectives to shadow us without your knowledge—if it is without your knowledge, Uncle Tom."

"Kevin, I swear to you that I knew nothing about this, and I will speak to Ashby about the detectives, but tell me more about the FBI and just what their involvement in this is all about."

"We found out there is a special agent in charge, or SAIC, named Fowler who has bugged the detectives' car that Ashby had following us, and he personally was following them to try to get to us. We think he has gone rogue and is acting as a lone wolf to try to get our formula or the money Ashby is going to pay us for it, or both."

"But how did they get involved in the first place?"

"Again, our theory is that they have been surveilling

Ashby about something else and perhaps overheard him and you talking about our deal. Hell, they might even have video surveillance and could have seen the video of Angus and our subject that we sent to you. At any rate, Fowler knows more than he should and has been dogging the detectives to try to locate us."

"Are you safe from him now?"

"Yes, we have taken the precaution of going off of the grid to escape both Ashby and the FBI. Uncle Tom, you can understand that now there is no trust between us and Ashby, so the transfer of the money is going to have to precede the transfer of the formula. In addition, we will transfer the formula in such a way that we remain off the grid and safe from Ashby's henchmen, or the deal is off."

"I don't know if he will go for that, Kevin. He is a very paranoid man."

"Fine, then we'll just sell the formula to someone else, repay him his hundred thousand, and let him die in his bed. The choice is up to him, Uncle."

"Jesus, Kevin! I had no idea you were this hard-nosed."

"Got to be hard-nosed when you've been betrayed, Uncle Tom, and make no mistake—we consider Ashby's hiring of these detectives to follow us a betrayal of our trust."

Alexander sighed. "Yeah, I can see why you would believe that. Okay, let me get to him and tell him you're pissed about the detectives and how the FBI is listening in. I'll see what he wants to do about that and then we'll see about the formula."

"Oh, Uncle Tom, whatever you do, don't let him take down the bugs and surveillance devices. The FBI must not be allowed to find out we know about them, or we will lose our advantage over them. Instead, you and Ashby can make the FBI believe anything you want to and they'll never be the wiser."

"Got it, Kev. Good idea, and just to let you know, I'm taking the next couple of weeks off. I am going to go directly to the airport and fly up to Houston to talk to Ashby tonight."

"And, Uncle, if you're gonna partake of the formula, too, then you'd better be getting your new ID ready for your new life. I have a feeling we'll be ready to send the formula in the next couple of days, and after that, it's *adios*."

After he hung up from his call to his uncle, Kevin got in his safe car and made a run to the post office box he'd rented at a UPS facility under a fake name. He found a large manila envelope waiting for him with the banking website's name in the upper left corner.

Back at the safe house, he gathered his friends around him while he opened the envelope. A thick sheaf of papers came out, along with five debit cards with numbers on them instead of names. As they read through the papers together, they found that the initial bank account was set up and ready to go. As soon as money was deposited into it, the money would be immediately transferred through a series of other banks in varying countries, until it was finally settled in five equal portions in banks in countries that had no banking relations with the United States.

Kevin explained, "I set it up this way so that once the money was delivered, each of us would have control of his or her own account, which you can access using the number on your debit card. That way, if you want you can set up your own passwords or even immediately move the money to another account that none of the rest of us knows about, for safety's sake. Then, if eventually Ashby or the FBI or anyone else captures one of us, we won't be able to point to where the others' money is. I also recommend that we keep our new identities secret from one another, as much as possible. We can still keep in touch through our burner phones, and I've also set up with the anonymous banking website a way for messages to be forwarded to anonymous e-mail accounts that we can check periodically to see whether we need to get back in touch."

Dillard stepped up to the table the group was gathered around and shook his head. "Kevin, I cannot believe how good a job you've done with all of this. I do not know any seasoned professionals who could have set things up better than you have. I feel the group's security is in excellent hands with you."

He held his hand out and grinned when Kevin blushed a bright red as he shook it.

"Bravo, bravo," Stone said, clapping lightly, laughing as the others all joined in.

When the clapping died down, Dillard said, "I also have some good news." He pulled out a packet of five passports, along with driver's licenses and credit cards.

"All of your IDs are ready with the names you gave me earlier for your future lives. I agree with Kevin that, generally speaking, you should share these new names with as few people as possible. Of course, I know all of the names, but I am going to provide each of you with the name and contact information of my source for the documents, so that if you desire to change your identities again at some time in the future, you will have the information you need to do so. Everything will hold up to anything less than a full National Security Administration checkup. I also checked all of the national databases, and none of your fingerprints are on file, except for Kat's. I am working on finding a hacker who can get into the armed services database and delete hers, but it's taking a little more time than I thought it would."

"But what about our pictures?" Burton asked. "You haven't taken any new photos for the IDs."

Dillard pulled out a chair. "That's another thing I wanted to talk to you all about."

He took a swig of the coffee he'd been holding in his hand, and then he said, "No matter how well I may change your IDs, you will never be safe without drastically changing your appearances. Both the National Security Administration and the Department of Homeland Security have excellent facial recognition software, not to mention Interpol. So, no matter how good a job I do on your identification documents, every time you go through an airport or any international border, you will be at risk."

"But can't we use wigs and makeup and other means to disguise ourselves?" Kevin asked.

Dillard shrugged. "Sure, that'll help somewhat, but if someone with extensive resources, like the FBI or John Palmer Ashby, comes looking for you, it may not be enough."

"So," Burton asked, a disgusted look on his face, "just what do you recommend? Extensive plastic surgery for us all?"

Dillard laughed. "No, something a lot simpler and less painful. I think you should each take a dose of your own formula."

Everyone looked around at the others, until Sheila said, "But . . ."

Dillard held out his hands. "But what, Dr. Goodman? Each of you is of at least middle age, you have access to the formula, and who among you wouldn't love to be younger, healthier, and most importantly, more intelligent?"

As they all quieted down and looked thoughtful, Kevin spoke up. "But what about me, Jack? I'm only thirty years old. I don't want to go back to being a kid again."

He looked at Kat as he said this, and Dillard knew what he was thinking. The young man didn't want to lose his potential to be with her.

Dillard looked over at Kat, and he could see the same expression on her face—she didn't want to lose Kevin, either. "Kat, when you explained the way the formula worked to me, you said it would take someone back to their optimum age, depending on their state of health."

She nodded slowly. "Yes, that is what we surmised from the rat experiments."

"So, just as an example, you and Kevin are both relatively healthy, and you are now only about ten or so years apart in age . . . right?"

She blushed, but nodded. "Yes, that is true."

"Then, the way I figure it, if you both took the formula, you'd both end up at your optimum age, or somewhere in your late teens or early twenties, is that right?"

She frowned. "Well, theoretically that may be true, but we cannot know that for sure until we do more experiments. After all, we've only used the formula on two organisms: Angus and the professor."

Upon hearing his name, Angus barked and stood on his hind legs, tail wagging furiously.

"Well, I'd suggest you start checking it out immediately, 'cause Kevin will never be safe unless he takes the formula and radically changes his appearance like the rest of you."

"And if we all do this?" Burton asked.

"Then, when you're recovered and stable, I'll take new pictures of you and place them on your passports and other documents. You'll be as safe as can be."

Kat reached over and put her hand on Dillard's. "What about you, Jackson? Want to be young again?"

He smiled gently and shook his head. "No, Kat, I don't think so. At sixty years old, I've earned every gray hair on my head, and there is lots about my life I would not want to relive. Besides, all of my old friends, like your parents, are my age." He shook his head again. "No, I think I'll stay sixty and sexy for a while yet."

Everyone laughed and stood up to pat him on the back.

"Also, I figure that you'll need someone to look after you for the few days it takes for the Phoenix Formula to do its magic."

After a moment, Kat held up her hands. "Okay, everyone, we've got a lot of work to do. We've got to get the ingredients to make at least six more doses of the Phoenix Formula, and we've got to go back to the drawing board to try to figure out how to dose Kevin so he won't go back to wearing diapers."

"Six doses?" Sheila asked.

"Yes," Kat answered, "one for each of the four of us, one for Ashby, and one for Kevin's uncle, Dr. Alexander."

Kevin spoke up, "Kat, I think if we're gonna make six more doses, we might as well make an even ten."

"Ten? Why?" she asked.

He shrugged. "Well, we know we're gonna need at least six, but having an extra four could be insurance against any unforeseen emergencies."

"What kind of emergencies are you worried about, Kevin?" Dillard asked.

"I don't know, Jackson, hence the word *unforeseen*. I just think it wouldn't hurt to have a couple of extra doses lying around in case we need them."

Dillard nodded. "I think you are right, Kevin. Extra never hurts, and who knows, it might just come in handy." He grinned, "Like the Boy Scouts say, always be prepared."

Kat laughed. "Okay, boys, we'll make a few extra doses just in case."

Sheila shook her head at the byplay, smiled, and reached over to take Burton's hand. "How about it, dear? Do you feel like starting over . . . with me?"

He covered her hand with his. "Of course, darling, and maybe this time we'll go to medical school together!"

Kat's eyes brimmed with tears watching Sheila and Burton, until Kevin moved over next to her and leaned down to whisper in her ear. "How about you, Kat? Would you like me to be a part of your new life?"

She leaned back and looked up into his eyes. "Oh yes, Kevin, I most certainly would!"

CHAPTER 38

Nick Fowler finally finished searching Kevin's apartment, which he'd gone to immediately after searching Sheila and Burton's place. "Damn," he muttered in frustration. He'd found absolutely no clues as to the current whereabouts of any of the scientists involved with John Palmer Ashby. Either they were very good, or they were very lucky. It was not often that amateurs like these could leave a room completely without any clues that a veteran FBI agent like Fowler could find.

Exhausted from the search, Fowler sat on Kevin's threadbare couch and took some deep breaths. He had to get in shape, he told himself. That damn desk job had caused him to put on thirty or forty pounds since his glory days when he was a field agent. He laughed, thinking he'd been lean and mean in those days, instead of fat and sloppy like he was now.

When he finally got up, he happened to glance at his reflection in a wall mirror—his face was red and blotchy. Fuckin' blood pressure probably sky-high, he thought.

He decided, *what the hell*, and he made himself a cup of Kevin's coffee and sat at the small kitchen table.

Taking out his cell phone, he scrolled through the contacts list until he came to one labeled DEPARTMENT OF HOMELAND SECURITY. He dialed the number and asked for Agent Sam Coburn.

When Sam came on the line, Fowler spent a few minutes catching up with his old friend from their early days in their agencies, and then he got to the point. "Sam, I need a huge favor."

"Yeah, well, you know I'll do anything I can to help you, Nick, as long as it doesn't put my ass in a sling."

"Nah, this is nothing like that," Fowler replied. "I'm working a deep-cover case, and I need to know if any heavy hitters from out of town have been caught on your surveillance tapes entering Houston in the past couple of weeks."

"You mean like terrorists or bomb throwers?"

"No, no. I mean ex-spooks or ex-agency types, maybe working as a PI now or something on the fringes. This guy I'm tracking has some serious skills and he took out a couple of agents I had tailing some suspects like they were newbies."

"You mean took out, as in killed?"

"No, but he neutralized them without doing any permanent damage, which as both of us know, is even harder than simply killing them."

"So, you're thinkin' ex-CIA or ex-NSA, something like that?"

Fowler shrugged, even though Coburn couldn't see him over the phone. "Probably, or maybe some sort of special forces, but all I really know is the guy is talented, and he knows how to go underground. My suspects have dropped off the face of the earth."

"Okay, pal, I'll dig around and see if anyone has popped up on our radar lately."

"And, Sam, could you check with that friend of yours over at the NSA? I don't have any current contacts there whom I can ask."

"Sure, we share stuff like this all the time. I'll get back to you within the hour. Take care, Nick."

Fowler grunted his thanks and hung up. Before he took his last sip of coffee, he pulled out one of his blood pressure pills and swallowed it with the coffee.

Now it's time to go and review the latest tapes from the Ashby home surveillance, he thought. Maybe he'd get some clue as to the scientists' new location from them.

It was almost eight o'clock before Alexander arrived at Ashby's house in the limousine the billionaire had sent to pick him up at the airport.

When he entered Ashby's bedroom, Ashby didn't waste any time. "Goddamnit, Tom, when the hell am I . . . ."

Alexander held up his hand and shook his head slightly. "Now, John, calm yourself before you have another stroke."

Ashby stopped, openmouthed; Alexander had never spoken to him in that tone before.

Alexander moved to his bedside and leaned over, his face close to Ashby's ear as he pretended to fluff his pillow. "Keep your mouth shut—we're being bugged," he whispered.

After a moment, he straightened up. "There, that better?" he asked. "You looked a little uncomfortable."

Ashby stared at him through narrowed eyes. "Yeah, it is. My neck was getting a little stiff until you fixed it."

"You know, John, it is a great night, nice and cool for a change. I think I'll have your nurse put you in your wheelchair and take you out on the patio. While she's doing that, I'll go to the bar and fix us both a drink. How about it?"

Ashby nodded, his head canted to the left from the weakness of the neck muscles on his affected side. "Sure, why not? I haven't been out of this bed for at least a week, 'cept for my daily sponge baths."

Thirty minutes later, Ashby was bundled into his wheelchair with a blanket over him, even though the Houston weather was warm.

As soon as they were settled, each with a drink in their hands, Ashby got right to the point. "Okay, Doc, what's with all the whispering, and what do you mean we've been bugged?"

He made a downward motion with his hands, "Keep your voice down, John. We're probably safe out here, but I don't know how sensitive the microphones are. Kevin called me earlier today, and he said they're being followed, and not only by the detectives he said you'd hired, but also by the FBI."

Ashby had the grace to blush when Alexander mentioned the detectives he'd hired, but the mention of the FBI really got his attention. "What? How has the FBI gotten involved in this affair?"

Alexander smirked and shook his head. "Yeah, well, we'll talk about you hiring detectives to follow my nephew and his friends later 'cause the important thing is the involvement of the FBI. Kevin and his friends think the FBI has been surveilling your house and phones for some time, and when I brought Kevin's proposal to you about the Phoenix Formula and showed you the videos of the dog and later the test subject, he thinks it sidetracked the FBI off of whatever they were watching you for originally, and it got them onto the Phoenix Formula and all that entails."

"Son of a bitch!" Ashby exclaimed. He wagged his head vehemently. "Those bastards have no right to bug my house and phones. Just wait till my lawyers get ahold of their sorry asses!"

Alexander took a deep swig of his drink and held up his hand. "No, John, that is just what we can't do. Kevin reminded me that if we let the Feebs know that we are on to them, we will lose a great advantage."

"What advantage?"

"The advantage that we know about their surveillance

but they don't know that we know. It's a perfect opportunity to tell them just what we want them to know and to keep them from knowing our true plans."

"So, I'm supposed to just let the bugs stay where they are? How the hell am I supposed to conduct my business, not to mention go through with the formula thing without them hearing and maybe even seeing what we're doing? Hell, you saw that it took almost half an hour to get me out to this patio. We sure as hell can't do that every time we want to have a confidential talk. That alone would let them know that we are on to them."

Alexander finished off his drink and set the glass on the patio table. "That is why I think it's time for you to take a little vacation. How about I mention that you're looking pale and drawn and that I think you should take some time at your house up in Maine? As I recall, your cabin is on an isolated lake with no neighbors for miles around, and if we plan it right, we can have your people precede us out there to secure the place and make sure the Feebs can't get in to plant more surveillance equipment."

When he saw Ashby nodding, he added, "Plus, it will get us out of this fucking Houston heat and will also be a perfect place for us to use the formula and keep our changes from being seen by anyone in the government. You can have enough men coming and going that when we're younger-looking we'll just blend in with the other employees when we're ready to leave."

"What about my supposed death? How do we manage that?"

"I've got that covered. There are plenty of old cemeteries up in that part of Maine. We just dig up a couple of recently buried bodies, place them in the cabin, and have an accidental fire kill both of us. Those small towns don't have real medical examiners, and it should be easy enough to bribe the local mortician to certify that the bodies in the fire belonged to us."

"Damn, Tom. That's a great idea. And the best part is that the cabin is insured for more than it is worth, so I'll come out okay on that."

Alexander laughed. "You cheap bastard, who cares about the damn cabin? The important thing is we'll be free to start our new lives without having to look over our shoulders for the FBI or anyone else who might be looking for us."

Ashby laughed, too. "Yeah, that's right."

"Speaking of our new lives, has your man got our new identities all worked out?"

"As a matter of fact, the paperwork came in yesterday. We are all set."

"And you've got your will all set up so your new identity will inherit all of your property?"

"Yeah, all of that is ready. Now, if your nephew will come through with the formula . . ."

"That's the other thing we need to discuss, John. Kevin now says that since you've betrayed them by hiring detectives, they will not send the formula until all of the money is paid in advance."

"What? Why those dirty—"

Again Alexander held up his hands. "Don't even go there, John! You brought this on yourself, and after you promised me you wouldn't try any double-crossing on my nephew and his friends."

"I only hired those detectives so that I could make sure they didn't try to get the money and not deliver the formula."

"Yeah, right," Alexander said sarcastically. "And stealing the formula for your own use never occurred to you, did it?"

Ashby held up his good hand. "Tom, I swear . . ."

Alexander laughed again. "You wily old bastard. I guess ten billion dollars just isn't enough for you, is it?"

Ashby, too, laughed. "Uh-uh, nine billion and change after I pay off Kevin and his friends."

When Alexander just shook his head, Ashby added, "But,

Tom, it wasn't about the money, but about the power that whoever owns that formula will have. We could rule the fucking world with a fountain of youth in our possession."

"I don't want to rule the world, John. Like I told you, I just want to start over with enough money to be able to travel and enjoy life and not have anything to worry about."

Ashby got a faraway look in his eyes. "I don't know if I can do that, Tom. I've been fighting and scrambling for so long, it's become a way of life for me. I just don't know whether I can sit back and just enjoy life without the excitement of living on the edge."

Alexander picked up his glass and stood up. "I'm having another, want one?"

Ashby nodded.

"Well, no one says you have to sit around and watch soap operas on TV, John. All your life you've been in the oil and gas business, which I think it is fair to say you've conquered. However, there are plenty of other worlds out there—communications, electronics, media, even sports teams. With nine billion and change, and being younger and smarter, it'll be the perfect opportunity for you to find something else to go and conquer."

Ashby nodded, his eyes far away, "You're right, Tom," he said faintly, "it is the perfect opportunity . . ."

"And besides, to tell the truth, John, I don't give a damn who owns the formula, as long as you keep your word and make sure no harm comes to my nephew."

"I am a lot of things, Tom, but no one has ever accused me of being a liar to my friends, especially not one as close to me as you are. I say again, nothing bad will happen to Kevin at my hands."

"Good. Now we'll have another drink, and then we'll go back into your bedroom and play out our little subterfuge about you going up to your summer cabin in Maine."

CHAPTER 39

Nick Fowler slammed the lid of his laptop shut. "What a fucking waste of time," he said to himself as he got up and began to pace around his living room. It had only a threadbare couch and one lopsided recliner in it since his wife had left and cleaned him out.

He'd watched several hours of Ashby video recordings and all he'd learned was that Ashby and his doctor, Tom Alexander, were evidently going to take a vacation up to his cabin in bugfuck Maine or some such place.

There had been no mention of the scientists or their possible location, and now that meant that Fowler was going to have to spend some of his meager savings on a trip to Maine to follow Ashby and Alexander. And, even worse, there was no way he was going to be able to get Ashby's house up there bugged, since he'd closed the active case file on Ashby.

He was on his fourth circuit of the tiny living room when his cell phone rang.

"Yeah, Fowler," he growled.

"Wow, someone's in a foul mood this morning," Sam Coburn answered cheerfully.

"Oh, hi, Sam. Sorry, just having the usual shit-ass problems with surveillance shortfalls."

"I got that, pal, but maybe this'll help cheer you up."

"What'cha got?"

"I don't know whether this is your boy, but we got a hit on a possible player coming into Houston last week. A mercenary slash smuggler slash private dick flew in in his private plane to the FBO out at Houston International."

"Sounds promising," Fowler said, getting out his notebook in which to take notes.

"Just what is this swinging dick's name?"

"Jackson Dillard. His plane is a twin-engine Cessna 425," he added, giving Fowler the tail number.

Fowler wrote it all down. "You got anything on this guy?"

"Nothing recent. Some old stuff, but he knew how to straddle the line between suspicious and outright illegal, so we were never able to bust him for anything. However, reading between the lines of our file on him, he is one tough cookie, so I'd be careful, Nick, and if you have to brace him, bring plenty of backup."

"Got it, Sam. Any idea on location?"

"Nah, he hasn't checked in to any hotels or motels that we can find, and he hasn't rented any vehicles under his name, but that don't mean anything with this guy. He's probably got a pocketful of false IDs he can use."

"Okay, thanks, Sam. I'll let you know if I turn up anything on him that you might be able to use."

"Roger, Nick. Like I said, pal, take care."

As soon as Nick hung up the phone, he got on his computer and logged in remotely to his desk at the FBI headquarters in downtown Houston. Once in, he searched the federal database for any information about Jackson Dillard. About the only thing helpful was a link to Dillard's website, where he got a look at a picture of the man.

"Huh, he doesn't look so tough," Fowler mumbled to

himself, but even as he said it, he knew he was whistling in the wind, because the son of a bitch looked tougher than nails.

Well, he figured, about the only thing he could do now was to stake out the man's plane and see what happened next. Hell, maybe they'd all show up there and he could do something to gain access to the formula that was going to make him rich.

Even though the new safe house on Memorial Drive had four bedrooms, Kat and Kevin continued to share a bed—though there was still a no-sex agreement in place. Of course, that didn't mean there wasn't some nice cuddling going on.

Kat awoke to find Kevin pressed up against her back, his right arm thrown over her and his right hand clasping her left breast.

She decided not to move just yet, for she found she quite enjoyed the feel of him holding her.

Suddenly, Angus, who was sleeping at the foot of the mattress, sat up, his nose making sniffing noises, and then he barked, jumped down, nosed the bedroom door open, and disappeared.

"I think the professor must be cooking bacon again," Kevin mumbled against her neck.

She jerked around. "How long have you been awake?" she asked indignantly, glancing down at his hand firmly grasping her breast.

He grinned sleepily. "Oh, for a while now. Just lying here enjoying the company."

She quickly removed his hand from her breast, though she couldn't remain angry with him. "Oh, so you are, are you?"

"Yes, and it was quite nice while it lasted."

She turned over and quickly got out of bed. "Well, it's

my turn to shower first today, so go have your coffee with the professor until I'm done."

"You want me to bring you a cup into the bathroom?" he asked hopefully.

She started to say yes, and then she saw the wicked grin on his face and shook her head. "And just in case, I'm locking the bathroom door."

Disappointed, he climbed out of bed and shuffled into the kitchen, where the professor was, in fact, cooking several massive skillets of bacon and eggs and home-style fries.

"God, that smells good," Kevin said as he prepared himself a cup of coffee at the machine on the end of the cabinet.

"Angus thinks so, too," Stone said, taking a piece of bacon that was cooling on a platter and throwing a small piece of it to Angus, who leapt up and snatched it out of the air in his jaws.

"Good catch, boy," Kevin mumbled as he added sugar to his cup.

Angus gravely nodded his thanks at the compliment.

After Kevin was seated at the kitchen table, Stone looked over at him with a sly smile and asked, "Did you sleep well, Kevin, my lad?"

Kevin glared at him over the rim of his cup. "You know darn well I didn't, Jordan."

Stone smiled and turned back to his cooking. "So, Miss Kat is still insisting on the no-sex clause to your sleeping agreement?"

"Yeah, and it's driving me crazy to be so close . . ."

"And yet so far?" Stone finished for him.

"Yeah."

"Perhaps a suggestion from an old soldier might be in order?"

"Suggest away, Professor."

"Perhaps Miss Kat is enjoying your proximity as much as you are, Kevin. To find out, maybe you should suggest, in a mild way, of course, that you are thinking of moving to the extra bedroom to join Mr. Dillard, as the current sleeping arrangements are causing you a loss of sleep."

"But what if she says okay?"

"That is a chance you must take, my boy. Remember, nothing ventured, nothing gained."

Burton and Sheila both entered the kitchen then, before Kevin could respond. While Sheila poured out two glasses of orange juice, Burton prepared them both cups of coffee.

"I must say, Jordan, even though I love the breakfasts you prepare, I think it only right that some of us also help in the cooking chores," Sheila said, putting the glasses on the table.

"Nonsense, Dr. Sheila," Jordan replied, turning off the stove and moving the skillets off the heat. "I love to cook, and it has been many, many moons since I have had the chance. Please let me continue to do this for you all, since you have done so much more for me."

She held up both hands. "Okay, Jordan, but if it ever becomes a burden, don't hesitate to ask for some help."

"Will do," he said, scooping the contents of the skillets out onto several plates and passing them out just as Kat came running into the room, her wet hair up in a towel.

"Am I too late?"

"No, on the contrary," Stone said, "You're just in time."

Angus, sitting in front of his bowl in the corner, barked loudly.

"Patience, big boy," Stone said, "I'll get to you in just a moment."

A sleepy-eyed Jackson Dillard shuffled into the kitchen, his mouth opened wide in a yawn.

"Good morning, Mr. Dillard," Stone said. "You are right on schedule for a nice breakfast."

"Not until I've had my coffee," he groaned. "Remember, I am up most of the night while you guys sleep, making sure no one has found us."

"Here, Jack," Kat said, jumping to her feet. "Take my seat and I'll get your coffee."

"Thanks, lass. Don't mind if I do."

"And I'll get your eggs and bacon," Kevin said, moving to the counter where the food was laid out on platters.

Once they were all seated around the breakfast table and had begun to dig into the feast before them, Stone said, "I have some good news."

"Good news is always welcome," Sheila said around a mouthful of home-style fries.

"In collaboration with Burton and Kat, who have finally consented to share the main ingredients of their portions of the Phoenix Formula with me, I believe we have found a way to separate the diverse facets of the formula into a more singularly acting medication. We've finally been able to devise different dosages of each of the parts of the formula so that, when combined in specific ways, the formula can be made to treat renal failure, or neurological deficits, or even a combination of both without causing undue age regression or unmanageable intelligence gains."

Stone held up his hands. "At least, not so they're major effects. There will always be some slight age regression and intelligence increase, but these can be improvements easily explained away as being due to the general increased healthiness of the individual from the treatment."

"That's great!" Kevin said. "That means the formula will be able to do what we always wanted it to do in the first place, help thousands of sick and injured people get better."

Burton shook his head. "Not so fast, cowboy. These changes are right now just theoretical and work out on paper, but as we've found out, that doesn't always translate to working or rats or people."

When Kevin looked puzzled, Kat added, "Burton just means that we think we've solved the problem, but we're still looking at months and months of experiments to nail down the exact doses of each individual ingredient to make the serum work as we hope it will."

"But I thought we'd all agreed we are going to take the serum and regress so we can disappear and be safe from Ashby. Now you're talking about months and months of more experimentation, when who knows whether we'll be allowed to stay alive long enough to complete the tests?"

"Yeah," Dillard added. "I know I signed on to keep you guys safe and off the grid, but I don't know how long I can reliably do that without someone like Ashby finding us."

Kat saw the disappointment in Kevin's eyes and knew it was because he had been counting on being with her after the regression. She reached over and put her hand over his. "Hold on, dear," she said softly. "You haven't heard the best part."

Burton said, "Our plans are still to take the formula and regress and go on to our own separate new lives . . . or on to our own together new lives," he amended, glancing at Sheila with a smile. "Professor Stone—Jordan—has graciously consented to form a new group of scientists to carry on our research under his now expert guidance."

"And with my share of a hundred million dollars, I should be able to afford to do it in style."

Kat added, "And believe it or not, Burton and I have also agreed to kick in twenty-five million dollars of our shares to help him along."

"Well, you're not going to donate a quarter of your shares unless I can do the same!" Sheila stated forcefully.

"And mine, too!" Kevin said with the same vehemence.

"Oh hell," Dillard said. "I can kick in a quarter of my fee, too, if it will help."

Suddenly, without thinking about it, each of the six reached out and grabbed the hand of the person on each side of them so that they were all holding hands around the table. Stone laughed and said in a mock-serious voice, "One for all!"

The others all echoed, "And all for one!"

Angus barked, jumped up on Stone's lap, put his paws on their outstretched arms, and barked loudly, to show he was one of them, too.

Later, after the breakfast dishes had all been done, the group retired to the patio furniture around the backyard pool and were sitting and talking when Kevin's phone rang.

He answered it and talked in a low voice for a few minutes, nodding his head occasionally before he hung up.

When the group looked at him expectantly, he said, "That was my uncle Tom. He and Ashby are flying to Ashby's Maine cottage tonight and want us to arrange to get the formula to them there as soon as possible, before the FBI can trace their movements and set up surveillance on them there."

"What do you think?" Dillard asked. "Are we ready?"

Kevin nodded. "I was just about to tell you that the accounts are all set up and ready to go. I've got the paperwork for each of you in my room. As it is set up, I can give Ashby one account number in the Cayman Islands into which he can deposit any combination of cash, jewels, precious metals, stock, or just about anything else of value as long as it adds up to five hundred million dollars. Once that is done, we can ship him the formula by overnight FedEx."

"Tell me again what happens to the money Ashby deposits," Dillard said. "A man like Ashby will have extensive international contacts, and I want to make sure that he won't be able to use them to trace your new assets."

Kevin explained, "The bank manager has instructions to split the money into five equal parts and immediately divert it to five different accounts, some in the Antilles, some in Lichtenstein, and some in the Canary Islands. Each of those account managers have the same orders to ship to different accounts, and so on. This will go on for about three or four transfers, at which time each of you will have the final account information so that when your money hits your final account, you can have it transferred to as many other accounts as you wish, as long as you leave enough money in your main debit card account to cover the expenses of the anonymizer bank account."

"Wow, that's complicated," Burton said.

"Actually, it is, but not to us. The anonymizer bank account does all of the work without knowing any of our names, only the numbers on our debit cards, at least until it hits the last account. All we have to do is make one phone call to make the final transfer and we're done. And I've given each of you a list of banks across the world that do not under any circumstances divulge account holders' information to anyone, including to the U.S. of A."

Kat flopped back in her chair. "That is a great relief, Kevin. So, as soon as we have our money and have shipped the formula to Ashby, we can take our shots and disappear forever?"

He spread his arms and smiled. "You got it, Kat. And then there will be nothing stopping us from starting our own new lives and new adventures."

Stone laughed at the relief on everyone's faces. "I almost envy you all," he said.

"Not too late to get someone else to work on refining the formula and starting a new life of your own without any responsibilities," Kat said.

He shook his head. "I said *almost*, dear Miss Kat. I am looking forward to doing something that would make my wife and daughters proud of their old man."

"How about you, Jack?" Kat asked, looking fondly at her uncle. "After all you've done for us, you deserve a shot at youth again, too."

He shook his head. "No, Kat, I think not. Besides, I believe I'll hang around with the Professor here and make sure he doesn't get into any trouble while he's fixing the formula. He'll need someone he can trust to watch his back until we're certain Ashby hasn't tracked him down."

CHAPTER 40

Ashby's plane landed at the Portland International Airport, it being the closest to his cabin that could handle a jet the size of his.

A fully equipped ambulance was waiting near the private jet terminal, and as soon as the jet stopped moving it pulled right up to the landing stairs.

Four tough-looking men, part of Ashby's huge security team, assisted Alexander in moving his stretcher down the steps and into the ambulance. Alexander made sure the IV fluids and the oxygen tube didn't get disconnected in the move.

Once Ashby and Alexander were in the ambulance, a black Suburban pulled up, and the security team all climbed inside. The SUV pulled out and the ambulance followed closely behind.

The drive to Ashby's cabin in North Waterford, Maine, took a little over an hour, even though it was only thirty-seven miles away. The Maine roads were not known for their speed of transport.

Finally, the SUV and the ambulance pulled off a small road onto a dirt road leading to the cabin. One of the security men was let out and stationed himself at the beginning of the dirt road, which ran for almost two hundred yards winding through a dense hardwood and pine forest.

Finally, at the end of the road sat a beautiful log cabin perched just thirty yards from a picturesque lake surrounded by rolling hills and dense forest. Ashby's house was the only one on the lake, since he owned all of the land for several hundred acres around it.

Four more men came out of the house and surrounded the ambulance, automatic machine pistols in their hands as they watched for anyone unknown in the vicinity.

Matt Dodson, Ashby's head of security, stepped over to the rear of the ambulance and was waiting when Alexander and the ambulance attendants wheeled him out on his stretcher.

Dodson dipped his head, "Good evening, Mr. Ashby. We've secured the cabin and the surrounding property as you requested, and as Dr. Alexander requested, I've arranged your bed to be in the living room, where you can look out the wall of windows at the lake and the surrounding forest."

Alexander put his hand on Ashby's shoulder. "I figured since we are up here in such a beautiful setting, it would be a waste if you couldn't enjoy the view."

Ashby put his good hand over Alexander's. "Thank you, Tom. That was very thoughtful."

"Speaking of the view," Dodson said, "there is a family of loons nesting on the shore of the lake, and they are great fun to watch, with the chicks following the mom and dad everywhere they go."

Ashby laughed. "I didn't know you were a bird-watcher, Matt."

The large, tough-looking man shrugged and blushed slightly. "When I have the time, which isn't often," he said.

A couple of hours later, the move-in was complete. Ashby was situated in his bed looking out of the windows while Dodson's men patrolled the property on a regular basis.

"Do we get cell service out here?" Alexander asked, pulling out his burner phone.

"Not ordinarily, but I had a cell-signal enhancer installed, so now we get pretty good service," Ashby answered.

"I'm thinking of checking with Kevin to see whether the money is in the account he provided yet."

Ashby wagged his head. "I doubt it, Tom. The accountant said to do it properly and not raise any flags with the government, it would take at least a couple of days. The transfer should be complete by tomorrow."

"That means we should be getting our serum by the day after tomorrow," Alexander said.

"If your nephew keeps his word."

"Kevin will keep his word, John. Of that I am completely confident." He stared hard at Ashby. "And now I can only hope you keep yours."

Ashby chuckled. "Don't tell me you don't trust your old friend, Tom."

Alexander gave a sigh. "I wonder how many men are in the cemetery who made the mistake of trusting you, John."

Now Ashby laughed out loud. "More than a few, Tom, more than a few."

"That's what I was afraid of."

"Oh, don't worry, Tom. I told you Kevin would be safe."

"From your lips to God's ears," Alexander replied and moved to sit and stare out at the loons out by the lake.

As the group met as usual around the breakfast table, Kevin said, "Well, the money is starting to flow into our main account, so I think it is time for us to all take our own injections and get the process moving."

"You don't want to wait until it is all there?" Kat asked.

Kevin shook his head. "No, because if it continues at this pace, it'll take at least another day, possibly two. By then, we will all be well on our way through the process, and when we send the formula to Ashby, we can then take off on our new journeys to our new lives and never look back."

"I think Kevin is right," Dillard said. "The sooner you all have changed your appearance and gotten your new IDs completed, the better I will feel about the entire process."

Sheila and Burton looked at each other, smiled, and took each other's hands. Then Sheila looked over at Stone. "Jordan, are you sure you can handle being nursemaid to all of us at one time?"

He nodded. "As you know, Dr. Sheila, I have studied up on all of the medical procedures that I might be required to undertake, from advanced CPR to IV fluids to medications for high temperatures, so I do believe I am as ready as I will ever be."

"And he'll have me to help him, Sheila. I've had extensive field experience with battlefield injuries and most forms of medical recuperation, so we should be okay," Dillard added.

"Then let's do it," Kat said, taking Kevin's hand and getting up from the table.

For convenience, they'd moved two beds into one of the bedrooms so the couples could both be watched at the same time as they went through the regression.

When they lay down on the bed, Angus jumped up, situated himself between Kevin and Kat, and looked from one to the other with his large brown eyes showing his concern for their welfare.

They each put a hand on his flank to reassure him, then they clasped hands as Stone gave them their IV injection of the Phoenix Formula.

Minutes later, he did the same to Sheila and Burton.

Kevin raised his head, looked over at the other bed, and gave a mock salute. "See ya on the other side, guys."

They both grinned and said, "See ya soon, Kev."

* * *

Fowler was getting disgusted that the BOLO he'd put out on Jackson Dillard had produced no results. It was if the man had gone to ground and not come up. No one reported having seen him, and the rental car companies had all said no one of his description had rented any cars in Houston in the past two weeks.

The only thing left for him to do was to go to the FBO at the George Bush International Airport, seek out Dillard's plane, and search it to see if there was any clue on board that would point to where he was or where the scientists he was helping were staying.

At the main desk of the fixed base operation terminal, he showed his credentials and said, "I'd like to see the hangar where Jackson Dillard has his plane stored."

The man looked over his half glasses and asked, "You have a warrant?"

"I'm not going to search the plane, I just want to see it," Fowler said irritably.

The man shrugged. "Don't matter, Mr. Fowler. I can't give you any information at all about our clients without you showing me a warrant."

"It's *Special Agent* Fowler, you dolt!" Fowler snapped.

The man grinned as if he was enjoying getting under Fowler's skin. "Sorry, *Special Agent*, no warrant, no lookie."

Fowler turned on his heel and stormed out of the office, wishing this was an active investigation so he could run the asshole in for obstruction of justice.

He stood on the curb outside the FBO office and glanced around. There were only four hangars nearby, and he fixed their locations in his mind. He'd come back later when the asshole was off work and just go straight to the hangars and search until he found Dillard's plane—and then he'd do whatever the hell he wanted with it.

Fowler went home to his apartment and took a nap until midnight, when he got up and dressed in dark gray pants and a long-sleeved dark gray shirt. The FBI had once done research on what colors best concealed an agent working in the dark or at night. Surprisingly, gray was much less visible than dark black, especially if the agent was on the move.

It only took Fowler two tries to find the hangar that held Dillard's plane. He checked the tail number against the one he'd written in his notebook. Yep, there it was.

He glanced around and saw no one lurking in the hangar, so he went right up to the stairs and tried the door to the plane. Locked. Well, somehow he knew it wasn't going to be that easy—he wasn't that lucky.

Pulling out his lock pick set, he quickly picked the lock on the door and entered the plane.

After an hour spent searching, he'd found nothing to be of any help to him, except one thing: At the rear of the plane was a small closet, just big enough for one man to hide in. If he could just figure out some way to get advance notice of when Dillard was going to be taking off, he could secret himself in the closet and jump out once they were airborne— Dillard wouldn't be able to resist since he'd be piloting the aircraft.

He sat in one of the passenger seats and thought about it for ten minutes. Finally, he realized that the plane would have to be fueled and serviced prior to taking off. If he could find the man in charge of fueling the airplanes in the FBO, he could flash his FBI creds and cross his palm with some money to see if he would give Fowler a call when he was ordered to fuel this plane. If worse came to worst, he could always claim Dillard was working for some terrorists and play upon the man's patriotism to get him to cooperate.

Early the next morning, Fowler snuck onto the FBO tarmac and made his way to the garage area. Luckily there was only one man working there. It didn't take long for Fowler to enlist his help in a forewarning of when Dillard was going to take off.

As Fowler drove back into Houston on the freeway from

the airport, he counted himself lucky that the garage man was a patriot—he'd only charged Fowler twenty bucks once he'd heard the plane might be transporting terrorists.

While Kevin and the others were undergoing their transformation, Dillard kept a close watch on the overseas bank account by using the computer.

Kevin had been slightly off on his prediction that it would take a little over two days for the money to be all transferred; in fact, it took three full days before the bank balance reached five hundred million dollars.

As per Kevin's previous instructions to the anonymizer account manager, the minute the account balance hit five hundred million dollars, the money disappeared.

At first, Dillard was frightened that Ashby had changed his mind and removed the money himself, but then he remembered Kevin stating that the money would be moved several times before coming to rest in separate accounts for each member of the group.

On the morning of the third day after the injection, Stone appeared in Dillard's bedroom doorway. "Jackson, you must come immediately," he said.

Dillard bounded out of bed and rushed after Stone, not bothering to change out of his pajamas. He was amazed when he entered the patients' bedroom to find each one of them sitting propped up in bed devouring huge helpings of bacon, eggs, home-style fries, and even a couple of plate-sized pancakes each.

"Hello, Jackson," a young lady said, a tentative smile on her face.

"Kat?" he said, disbelief in his voice. The young woman in the bed appeared to be no more than twenty years old at the most.

"Howdy, Jack," said the young man in the bed next to

Kat. Kevin looked to be seventeen or eighteen years old—almost like a younger Ryan Gosling.

"Well, what do you think, Jackson, old man?" said Burton from the far bed. He looked about twenty-five, as did his wife, Sheila, sitting next to him.

"Holy smoke!" Jackson declared, hurrying in to shake Kevin's hand, give Kat and Sheila a hug, and then to shake Burton's hand. "I guess I knew intellectually this was going to happen, but I swear I never really thought about the impact of seeing if for myself with my own eyes. It's a bloody miracle!"

"So," Kat said impishly, "you think we'll be able to fool Ashby and whomever he sends looking for us?"

"Heck-fire, Kat, I do believe you could fool your own mother."

He moved closer to the bed and stared at her. "If I look closely, I can see the old Kat in your eyes and some of your expressions, but that's 'cause I know it's you. No one else would ever recognize any of you in a million years."

He moved to the other bed, where a now slim and athletic-looking Burton was packing the last of his pancakes away. "And, Burton, you must have lost twenty or thirty pounds."

Burton smiled. "I guess Sheila will just have to get used to there being less of me to love."

"Uh, Jordan," Sheila said, pushing her empty plate to the side. "I do believe our increased metabolic rate has caused all of us to sweat profusely in our sleep, therefore showers are a must for all of us if we are to be in polite company. If the others don't mind, I'll go first, and then I can help you and Jackson cook up some more food while the others wash off the stink."

Stone just shook his head and laughed. "I'm afraid Mr. Jackson is going to have to make a food run. You gluttons have about cleaned out the pantry."

CHAPTER 41

Kevin couldn't believe how light and spry he felt as he followed Dillard into the living room. Jeez, he thought, it's not like I was a member of the over-the-hill gang or anything before the rejuvenation, but now I almost feel like I could fly.

Dillard stopped at the coffee table in the living room, picked up Kevin's burner phone, and handed it to him.

"Your uncle Tom has called several times and left increasingly hostile messages. He says the money has been in the account for almost twelve hours and they haven't heard from you. Ashby is getting quite paranoid that you are going to cheat him."

Kevin nodded and immediately dialed his uncle's number. When Alexander answered, Kevin said, "Hello, Uncle Tom. Sorry I haven't gotten back to—"

"Wait a minute," Alexander interrupted. "This isn't my nephew Kevin!"

Kevin suddenly realized his voice was half an octave higher since his transformation. He quickly cleared his throat and made an effort to lower his tone. "Uh, sorry, Uncle Tom. I think I'm coming down with a cold."

"Is that why you haven't returned any of my calls?"

"Yes, I took a cold medicine, and I've been sleeping almost all day trying to get over it."

"Well, what is going on with the formula?"

"It is all packaged up and being sent overnight as we speak. According to FedEx, it should arrive before ten a.m. tomorrow at the cabin's address you gave us in North Waterford, Maine."

Alexander's voice softened. "Are there any specific instructions for its use?"

"No, just don't let the air hit it. According to our studies, a moderately healthy individual will take from forty-eight to seventy-two hours to completely regenerate. The less healthy the individual, the longer it will take for the process to complete, but our first subject was on death's door and it only took him the full seventy-two hours. You will experience high fevers, shaking with muscle aches similar to the flu, and a vastly increased metabolic rate. Your hair will fall out and be replaced within hours by a new growth. There will also be some weight loss, so if Ashby is already thin, prepare to feed him a high caloric diet and plenty of it for about a week following the transformation."

"Anything else?"

"Nope, just enjoy your second chance, Uncle Tom, and thank you for all you've done for me over the years."

Alexander's voice became husky. "So, I guess this is it. We'll probably never see each other again."

"Right, if all goes well. So, good luck in your new life, Uncle Tom. Take care."

"You, too, son."

When the FedEx truck pulled up the next day, Ashby was ready for it. A bed had been placed directly next to his for Alexander's use.

Matt Dodson, Ashby's chief of security, followed Alexander as he brought the FedEx box into the living room where Ashby anxiously awaited him. He set the box on the bed, opened it, and found two syringes filled with a color-less fluid in a padded package within the box. He held the syringes up, smiling. "These contain our new lives, John. Are you ready?"

"Are the syringes marked with our names, or are they both the same?"

Alexander examined the syringes and found no external markings on them. "Both are the same as far as I can see."

"Good. Mr. Dodson, please shut the door and bring the syringes over to me."

Matt Dodson closed and locked the living room door, stepped over to Alexander, and held out his hand.

Alexander stared at Ashby for a moment, then he handed Dodson the syringes. "So, this is to be a classic double-cross?"

"I am afraid so, Tom. I just cannot take the chance that your nephew is bluffing when he said he booby-trapped the formulas. So, I am going to take mine, and if it works, I will do my best to have the other syringe's contents analyzed so that I might have control of the Phoenix Formula. Unfortu-nately, that means there won't be any formula left for you to use."

"So, what about me? Am I supposed to just go on as if nothing has happened?"

"Not exactly." Ashby shrugged his one good shoulder. "I am truly sorry about this, Tom. You have been a good friend to me, but I didn't accumulate ten billion dollars by being soft and sentimental. I am afraid there will be no place for you in my new life. I have no choice. I'll just have Mr. Dod-son shoot you in the heart and bury you in the woods."

"So, to keep the secret of your regeneration to a younger, smarter person, you are going to have me killed . . . by Matt here?"

"Sad, but true, Tom. I just cannot have anyone else know

about my transformation, it would be much too dangerous."
He sighed. "And I'm afraid that goes for your nephew and
his friends, too. I plan to spend whatever it takes to track
them down and do away with them, too."

Alexander shook his head. "Do you see what I meant,
Matt?"

Dodson nodded. "Yes, sir, Dr. Alexander. I am afraid
you were right on the money."

"What . . . what's going on here?" Ashby asked, alarm in
his voice as he looked back and forth between the doctor and
his hired man.

Alexander went over to the bedside table and picked up
two of Ashby's Montecristo Supreme Cuban cigars. After
first turning off Ashby's oxygen tank, he exchanged one of
the cigars with Dodson for the syringes. He lit Dodson's
cigar and then his own with a gold lighter. Finally, he sat on
the bed next to Ashby's, leaned back, and crossed his legs as
he got the cigar going to his satisfaction.

"I have learned a great deal from you over the years,
John," he said while watching his cigar smoke rise to the
ceiling. "For instance, the other day when you said you did
not get where you are today by trusting anyone, and how
there were a number of people in the cemetery who had
made the mistake of trusting you, well, let's just say it got
me to thinking. Why should I ever believe you would keep
your word to me?"

Ashby saw where this was going, and he almost yelled,
"Oh, come on, Tom. I was just kidding. I wouldn't do anything to hurt you."

"Please, John, let me finish. Anyway, I finally came to
the conclusion that there was simply nothing to gain for you
to let me live, and a great deal to lose, and you have always
been about the gain, John. Therefore, I knew you were going
to double-cross me—it was inevitable."

"But, Tom—"

Alexander held up his hand to silence him. "So, once I

figured that out, what was I to do? Last night, I decided to have a talk with Matt here, because, you see, he is in the same situation as me. As soon as you have made your transformation and he sees your new identity, he will become a loose end that you cannot allow to survive, either. We both know what you do with loose ends, John."

Ashby turned his attention to Dodson. "Mr. Dodson, I'll give you anything you want if you come in with me now against this crazy man."

Dodson pursed his lips as if thinking for a moment, and then he shook his head. "I don't think so, Mr. Ashby. I like my chances with the doctor much better."

"Here is what is going to happen, John. I have told Matt that I have no desire for vast riches. All I want is to start over with enough money to last me while I travel and enjoy the world that I missed while earning my medical degree and going through my many years of training. Matt, on the other hand, feels he has been sorely underpaid for the past fifteen years he has worked for you."

Alexander paused to take a puff of the cigar and blow out several smoke rings. "So, Matt and I will assist each other in transforming using the Phoenix Formula. Matt has wisely forbidden any of his men from entering the cabin—they are to patrol outside only. Once we are transformed, Matt will procure a body from a nearby cemetery and there will be a fire in the cabin. Unfortunately, you and I will not survive, John."

"Oh, please, please, Tom. Do not do this," Ashby begged. "Give me another chance."

"Don't interrupt, John. I am just coming to the best part. Once the inquest is over and you and I are declared dead, the now much younger and smarter Matt Dodson will assume the identity you have so brilliantly prepared, which will inherit your fortune. The Matt Dodson who was your chief of security will disappear, leaving the authorities to suspect he might have had something to do with the fire, but he will never be found and so no case will be able to be made."

Suddenly Ashby jerked the Enforcer pistol from beneath his blanket and pointed it at Alexander. "You won't get away with this, Tom, 'cause I'm gonna blow you to hell first"—and he pulled the trigger.

Alexander smiled and shook his head as the hammer fell on an empty chamber. The loud *click* was like a knife piercing John Palmer Ashby's heart.

Alexander reached over and took the pistol from Ashby's limp hand. "One of your problems is that you continually underestimate your opponents, John. But the good news is that this is probably the last time you'll ever do that."

CHAPTER 42

Dillard called the FBO and told them to gas up the Cessna and complete the other services to make it ready to depart. He then called the control tower and filed a flight plan for the Grand Cayman Islands. He figured they'd spend a couple of days there relaxing, then make their way down to Belize, and from there, it would be everyone for themselves.

As the group began to pack up their belongings, Dillard said, "Listen up, guys and gals, the Cessna only has a payload maximum takeoff weight of thirty-six hundred pounds above its empty weight, and when you figure fuel and passenger weight, we need to keep our luggage to a minimum. Only take a couple of days' worth of clothes. There are plenty of shops where we're going so no need to get crazy . . . besides, most of your old clothes no longer fit anyway."

"That's for sure," Burton said, pulling his waistband out to show he'd lost at least ten inches off his belly.

"Still, we don't want to leave them for anyone looking for us to find, so just pack what you don't need in a couple of large trash bags and we'll dump them on the way to the airport."

Once everyone was ready and in their safe cars, Dillard

walked around the house, spraying his bleach on just about every surface they might have touched. When he was finished, he hooked a canister of the bleach mix up to the airconditioning unit so it would circulate and erase any traces of the group that had been left in the house. Extreme measures that were probably not necessary, but Dillard figured being too careful beat being not careful enough every time.

An hour and a half later, after they'd left their safe cars parked in the long-term parking lot at the airport, they were loading the plane's cargo hold with their duffel bags and what small amounts of personal goods Dillard would allow them to carry.

The plane was designed to carry one pilot and seven passengers, so there was an extra seat at the back of the plane, where they placed Angus's bed.

As he was taxiing for takeoff, Dillard spoke on the intercom to the passengers in the back of the plane. "It's approximately eleven hundred and seventy miles to the Caymans from Houston, and the Cessna has a range of fifteen hundred and forty miles, so unless we hit extreme headwinds we should be okay."

"How long of a flight is it, Jackson?" Kat asked.

"Although this baby can hit three hundred and nine miles per hour, she gets maximum fuel efficiency at about two hundred and fifty miles an hour, so the flight should take about four and a half to five hours, depending on the winds at our altitude, which will be twenty-five thousand feet."

The takeoff went without incident, and soon they were cruising out over the Gulf of Mexico toward the islands five hours away.

Angus was sitting in Kat's lap, looking out of the window like he'd flown dozens of times before. She had her arms wrapped around him and her head resting on Kevin's shoulder as he sat next to her.

He would occasionally take a deep whiff of her lovely scent and then kiss the top of her head gently. He couldn't believe how much he loved her, and he was so glad they'd saved having sex together until after their transformations.

Burton and Sheila were in seats a row ahead and were busy discussing to which medical schools they might want to apply. Their college records would be no problem, because Dillard had already set them up with his forger, who, he said, could show them graduating from any schools they wanted with any grades they wanted.

They were already planning to set up practice together once they'd graduated, and since money or income would be no problem, they were talking about possibly working for Doctors Without Borders, or the Peace Corps, whichever would let them work together.

Burton took her hand in his, kissed it, and said, "The important thing is not where or for whom we work, but that we'll be together for the rest of our lives."

Kevin and Kat were now young enough that they had a few years before they'd even have to decide whether to attend college or just go straight into medical and graduate schools. Though they had enough money that they never needed to work again, both felt that life would be empty and unhealthy without a purpose to keep their interests engaged.

A half hour into the flight, there was a loud bump from the rear of the plane, and the closet door banged open. A rather obese, sweating man emerged holding a Beretta nine-millimeter semiautomatic pistol in his hand.

"Okay, people, hands up!" he shouted.

When Dillard heard the shout he quickly put the autopilot on and eased back into the rear cabin, his own .380 pistol in his hand.

Fowler immediately stepped over behind Kat and stuck the pistol against the back of her head, causing Angus to bare his teeth and give a low warning growl.

"Put the pistol down, Dillard, or I'll blow her brains all over the cabin."

"You can't fire that weapon in here," Dillard said urgently. "If you perforate a window, we'll decompress and all be killed."

"I'm not stupid, Dillard. When I knew I was going to confront you on an airplane, I loaded the gun with hollow points. They'll mushroom, but unless they hit a window directly, they won't perforate the plane's fuselage. They will, however, perforate a human body quite nicely."

"You must be special agent in charge Fowler," Dillard said, scorn in his voice.

"Oh, so you know about me, huh?"

"I know you're a traitor to your job and to your country and that you've gone rogue trying to get rich, like any of the two-bit criminals you used to put away."

Fowler's face turned red and blotchy, and sweat poured off his forehead. "A little bit more than a two-bit criminal, Dillard. Your formula is going to make me a billionaire."

Sheila said, "I don't think you're going to live to spend it, Mr. Fowler. It looks to me like you are about to have a medical crisis of some sort right now. Are you feeling okay?"

He looked startled by her question and suddenly got a funny look on his face and put his hand to his chest. "Uh . . . my chest and left arm hurt . . ."

Right at that moment, Angus put both paws on the back of Kat's seat and leapt over it right at Fowler. He flew through the air, hit the man square in the midsection, and immediately clamped his jaws on the wrist of the hand holding the pistol.

Fowler screamed in fright and pain and dropped the pistol, staggering back from the impact of Angus's hit.

Angus let go of his wrist and stood over the pistol, growling and baring his teeth in a terrifying display.

Fowler looked at the dog for a moment, trying to decide whether he should go for the gun, and then he looked surprised, grabbed his chest again, and keeled over onto his face.

Sheila and Kat raced to his side, flipped him over, and

both felt for a pulse—one on the wrist, the other on the carotid artery.

They looked at each other grimly. "Fluttering like a bird in flight," Sheila said. "I'm afraid he's going into ventricular fibrillation."

She glanced over her shoulder at Dillard, who was picking up Fowler's pistol. "Do you have a defibrillator on board?" she asked.

He shook his head. "Just the minimal first aid kit, but I do have an oxygen canister."

She shook her head. "Please get it, but I'm afraid he's not going to make it unless we can get him to a hospital very quickly."

Dillard shook his head as he pulled a small green oxygen tank with attached face mask from an overhead bin. "We're still several hours out from landing, and there's nothing between us and the islands ahead."

Kat suddenly jumped to her feet and ran to the rear of the plane, where she dug into one of the duffel bags. She came out a few moments later with a syringe and held it up so the others could see.

"What do you think?" she asked Sheila.

Sheila shrugged, "It might be too late, but it is the only chance he has."

Kat glanced at Kevin and Burton and Stone, who all nodded their assent.

She knelt next to Sheila, who made a tourniquet with her hands, which caused a vein to pop out on Fowler's arm.

Kat quickly inserted the needle and injected the Phoenix Formula into Fowler's antecubital vein.

Dillard turned the knob on the oxygen canister and handed the small mask to Sheila, who placed it over Fowler's nose and mouth.

The FBI agent continued to sweat and pant for several minutes, but then slowly his color returned to normal and he quieted down.

Dillard handed Kat a blanket and she placed it over him but kept him lying down in the aisle.

"I've got to get back to flying the plane. Is everything under control back here?" Dillard asked.

Both doctors nodded, and so he stepped back into the cockpit, stuffing Fowler's gun into his waistband.

Kat put her arms around Angus and squeezed him tight. "My little superhero," she said, while he grinned with pride over her shoulder at the others. "You flew through the air like Superman!"

Kevin reached over and patted Angus's head. "I think we should rename the big guy Superdog."

On their final approach to Grand Cayman Airport four hours later, Dillard radioed in that they had a medical emergency and had an ambulance waiting for their landing.

After Fowler was loaded and transported to the local hospital, the group gathered around the plane. "What the heck are we going to do now?" Kat asked. "When Fowler goes into his hypermetabolic state, it's going to scare the hell out of the doctors taking care of him."

"Not to worry," Dillard said, calm as always. "When planning the trip, I rented us a large four-bedroom condo on the beach about a mile from the town. I also reserved us a large SUV to get around the island in. Let's give the docs a couple of hours to get Fowler stabilized, and then we'll go rescue him from them and take him to our place."

"What makes you think they'll just let us take him out of the hospital?" Sheila asked.

Dillard grinned and pulled a wad of hundred-dollar bills from his pocket. "Human nature," he answered. "Now, get those passports out that my man sent to you, 'cause we have to go through Customs."

He held up Fowler's wallet. "I took this from Fowler. I'll show it to Customs and explain that he's on the way to a hospital. Shouldn't be a problem. The Caymans have so many tourists they don't check too closely."

Kat took her passport out, but before handing it to Dillard she took another peek at it. "I still can't get used to this picture you took of me for the passport. I look so young!"

The group took turns watching Fowler throughout the night, bathing him with tepid water when his temperature raged, covering him with blankets when he shook like he was freezing to death.

By the next morning, all of his hair had fallen out, and he had a fine black stubble growing in its place.

Dillard had gone to the nearest supermarket and stocked up on plenty of eggs, bacon, sausage, hamburger, potatoes, and steaks. He knew from experience that Fowler would be starving when he awoke the next morning, as would the rest of the group, whose metabolisms still hadn't quite gotten back to normal yet.

By nine o'clock the next day, Stone had fixed the largest breakfast he'd ever seen, and the whole group, including Fowler, was making it disappear like ice on a noonday sidewalk in Houston in July.

He laughed when he went into the dining room and saw all of them still in their pajamas with heads down concentrating on putting as much food away as they could as fast as they could.

"If I didn't know better, I'd think you people were hungry," he joked.

Kevin glanced up. "Are there any more pancakes, Jordan?"

He shook his head. "Nope, Fowler just ate the last three, and he's not even out of bed yet."

* * *

By the next day, Fowler joined them for breakfast in the dining room. When he entered the room and everyone looked up at him, he held out his arms and said, "What the hell happened, and why did you do this to me?"

"You had a cardiac event on the airplane," Sheila said. "You were moments away from dying, and the only way we knew to treat you was to give you a dose of our formula."

"And it saved your life," Dillard added.

Fowler glanced down at his new, slimmer body. He looked at least twenty years younger and much healthier, with a complexion free of the red, blotchy spots that had covered it a few days before. His paunch was gone, and he'd lost at least thirty pounds.

"How are you feeling?" Sheila asked, getting up and motioning him to take her seat at the table.

"Why . . . why, I feel wonderful," he said, amazement in his voice.

Stone brought him a plate with a couple of pancakes and some scrambled eggs and sausage and placed it before him.

He looked at the food and then up at the group. "I'm starving."

"That's part of the process," Sheila explained. "Your basal metabolism is vastly speeded up. That's why you've burned off all of your excess weight."

He picked up the silverware and dug into his breakfast, eating like he'd been starved for days.

Burton, a sour expression on his face, asked, "Just why did you go rogue, Fowler, and try to come after us?"

Fowler set the silverware down for a moment and had the grace to look embarrassed. "A lot of things, I guess. I'd been passed over for a promotion, I was about to be mandatorily retired from the only job I've ever loved, and my wife just left me." He looked over at Burton, pain in his eyes. "She called me a loser when she left." He sighed. "I guess part of it was that I just wanted to prove to her that I could do something . . . important."

"And get rich in the process?" Dillard added, though not unkindly.

Fowler shrugged. "That was part of it, of course, but I think mainly I just wanted to be a 'big' man, both to my wife and to my coworkers at the Bureau."

"What are you going to do now?" Kevin asked.

"I . . . I don't really know. All I've ever been was an investigator. The Bureau was my life."

Dillard sighed and leaned back in his chair, studying Fowler for a moment. "Well, you certainly can't go back to your old life, Fowler, not looking like this. It would raise far too many questions."

Fowler nodded and went back to picking at his food. "That's for sure."

"I'll tell you what. I've got a small business that could maybe use some help. One of my contacts could get you a new identity, and we'll even get you a private investigator's license. If I can't keep you busy, I have some friends in the business who can throw some work your way. What do you say?"

He looked up. "You'd do that for me, after what I tried to do to you?"

Dillard shrugged. "It's not charity, Fowler. I know the FBI, and a man doesn't rise to the level of special agent in charge without having some serious chops. Don't worry, you'll more than earn whatever I pay you."

"So, what now?"

"Now I'll take some pictures of you and get them sent to the man who creates identities for me, and he'll also get you a new passport and driver's license and a couple of credit cards. Then, when we get those, you can go back to Houston and start work, if you think you're up to it."

Fowler got a determined look on his face. "Just try me."

He suddenly got up from the table and looked a little embarrassed. "I think I've sweat so much I must smell like a goat. Is it all right if I go take a shower and change my clothes?"

"Sure, some of my new ones will fit you," Burton said. "Go start the shower and I'll bring you some clothes in a few minutes."

After he'd left, Kat put her hand on Dillard's. "That was very nice of you, Jack."

He grinned. "What else could I do with him sitting there looking like a lost puppy?"

When he heard the word *puppy*, Angus barked and stood up on his hind legs.

Stone tossed him a small piece of bacon, and he settled back into his bed, munching happily. "Some much-deserved pork for Superdog!"

"Now, on a more serious note," Dillard said, "we need to sit down and plan our next moves. It'll only be a couple of days before Ashby is on the mend from his use of your formula, and I expect he'll start to move heaven and earth to find us, so we need to be dug in somewhere where he won't think to look."

"You're still sure he'll come after us?" Kat asked.

Dillard shrugged. "He's got to. We're the only ones who know that the old J.P. Ashby is not dead and that whoever inherits his fortune has got to be the new Ashby, no matter what name he is going by. He cannot afford to let us live."

"By now our money should be settled into our own personal accounts," Kevin said. "Each of us needs to decide where to send it from there. We can look over the list of countries with friendly anonymous banks and talk about which of them has the best policies for us to make use of."

He glanced over at Dillard. "Jack, you need to be in on this, too, so you can decide where you want us to send your fees."

"As soon as I get Fowler's pictures taken and get his info sent off to my forger, we'll sit down and you can go over my choices with me. At first blush, I think the Caymans would be good, 'cause I can make it down here in my plane in one jump if I need to move some funds around without anyone knowing it, but we'll discuss it more fully later."

Two hours later, Dillard had finished his business with Fowler and the man was taking a nap, still somewhat exhausted from his transformation.

The group gathered around the dining room table, and Kevin went over the various international banks that would be suitable for them to use to park their huge fortunes.

Kat and Kevin decided on a bank in Lichtenstein, having decided that they would spend a year traveling throughout Europe before deciding what to do with the rest of their lives.

Watching them, Stone smiled at the way they continually held hands, as if they couldn't get enough of touching each other.

Burton and Sheila picked the island of Grenada, mainly because it was remote enough from the States so they'd be hard to find, and because it had a medical school that taught in English and was accredited by the United States in case they ever wanted to return there to practice.

Dillard decided on the Caymans, even though their banks weren't quite as secure from the United States government oversight as some of the other countries. He didn't plan to raise any flags to give Uncle Sam a reason to target his accounts.

Stone picked a bank in the Antilles Islands, because Kevin said there would be no problem with him getting wire transfers through the Caymans and then back into America to fund his upcoming research projects.

They decided it would probably be safe to spend a couple of days lying around the beautiful Cayman beaches and enjoying each other's company in the various nightspots before they all went their separate ways, never to be together again.

Fowler, once he had fully recovered from his transformation, proved to be a nice man whose company they all enjoyed. He even regaled them with some funny stories from his many years with the FBI, and he and Dillard found they had very compatible personalities. Dillard was actually looking forward to working with his new hire.

On the third day of what they'd begun to call their "final vacation," they were watching CNN on TV while sitting around drinking Red Stripe beer, an island favorite, when a report came on about a suspicious death in Maine. The serious-faced announcer stated that a remote cabin in southern Maine had burned to the ground, and the two victims were the notorious oil magnate, John Palmer Ashby, and his personal physician, Dr. Thomas Alexander, a heart doctor from Houston, Texas, who was reportedly on vacation with the oilman.

Dillard shook his head. "That is just too good to be true, guys. I think this must be a scheme Ashby cooked up to disappear and come back as someone else."

Fowler got up from the table. "I'll call the Houston office and see if I can find out what the heck is going on. They don't know that I'm gonna be gone for good yet, so I'll find out who is in charge of the investigation up in Maine and reach out using my FBI credentials. It won't be too suspicious since until recently we had an open investigation into Ashby."

He came back into the room twenty minutes later. "I have what I think is really good news for you guys."

"What?" Dillard asked, sitting on the edge of his chair.

"They are absolutely sure one of the victims is John Ashby. They've got a positive DNA match on the remains, and his chief of security stated that Ashby's doctor, this Alexander person, had warned him several times about not smoking his cigars while he had his oxygen tank going, but he said Ashby never listened. They are fairly sure the oxygen tank blew up, causing a fire that killed both men."

"What about the other body?" Kevin asked, his voice hoarse.

"They assume it is Dr. Alexander, based on the testimony of a Matt Dodson, the chief of security, who said the two men were together when the fire broke out, but they can't be sure 'cause the second body was burned too badly to even get a DNA match."

Kevin sat back and blew out the breath he'd been holding, relief evident on his face. He now knew his uncle was safe. He was much too smart to sit there while Ashby smoked a cigar with his oxygen going.

Dillard looked around at the group. "That is super news, guys. Now I think we can safely go about our business without having to constantly be looking back over our shoulders."

Kevin stood up and held up his bottle of beer. "In that case, I propose a toast."

When the others all held up their beers, he added, "To the Phoenix Group, survivors all."

The others repeated, "To the Phoenix Group, survivors all."

"I further propose that once a year, on the anniversary of this day of our freedom from worry, we meet back here on the Grand Cayman Islands and have a reunion."

"Hear, hear!" the group chanted, and all drank to the toast while Angus barked excitedly.